# A West Texas Cl

## Dedic

*For my three granddaughters, Madison Stella Román, Mackenzie Reese Saller, and Presley Davis Saller, I dedicate these three Christmas books to you with all my love.*

# A West Texas Christmas Trilogy

## Table of Contents

# A Hard Candy Christmas

By

## Hebby Roman

West Texas Christmas Trilogy Book 1

☆Estrella Publishing☆

# Hard Candy Christmas

## Chapter One

*Del Rio, Texas 1895*

Clint Graham folded his arms across his chest and rocked back on his heels. From beneath the wide brim of his Stetson, his gaze scanned the crowd, trying to assess its mood. What he saw, he didn't like. The crowd, composed mostly of ranchers like him, appeared edgy and restless. They'd listened to their fellow ranchers complain about the proposed rate hikes and how the new rates would ruin them. Now it was time for a representative of the Southern Pacific Railroad to speak. But the crowd didn't appear to be in a listening mood.

The railroad representative, a slight, balding man, formally attired in a suit, strode to the edge of the depot's platform. Lifting his hands above his head, he gestured for quiet. The ranchers glanced at him, shuffling their feet and clearing their throats. The representative began his speech, talking about the new laws Congress had mandated for the railroads, droning on about the cost to replace existing equipment with new safety devices.

The crowd shifted and muttered. The muttering grew louder, punctuated by boos and cat-calls. The ranchers, their fists raised in the air, weren't listening. They shouted curses, drowning out the railroad official's words.

A six-shooter roared, and the bullet whined overhead. The balding representative ducked and scurried to the back of the platform. An uneasy quiet descended on the crowd. The county sheriff, Lyle Cunningham, leapt onto the platform, demanding to know who had fired the shot. His answer was a second shot, which knocked the hat from his head.

Clint glimpsed the glint of sun on metal and reacted without thinking. Grabbing the shooter's forearm, he stopped the man from shooting again. They stood, locked together with Clint's hand

1

# Hard Candy Christmas

gripping the man's arm. The air sizzled with unspoken animosity. Clint stared him down.

The shooter, Pete Baker, a rancher with a penchant for picking fights, finally lowered his eyes. Clint took the gun from his hand and pushed him toward the platform. Sheriff Cunningham intercepted them and cuffed the shooter.

"That will cost you a night in jail for disturbing the peace, Baker," Cunningham said.

Then Cunningham did something unexpected. He ripped the badge from his shirt. "Taking Baker into custody is my final official act." Holding the badge up, he added, "Who wants it? I don't. I see trouble coming. You ranchers ain't willing to listen to reason. And I didn't sign on as a moving target."

More cat-calls ensued and shouts of "coward" filled the air. Cunningham shrugged and tossed the badge onto the platform before leading Baker away. The crowd watched them go, muttering and shaking their heads.

The mayor strode to the edge of the platform and declared they needed a new sheriff. He also said they didn't have time for a special election. And he urged the crowd to select a likely candidate.

"How about Graham?" A voice shouted from the back of the unruly mob. "He was quick enough to catch Baker. And he was a bounty hunter before he took to ranching."

At the suggestion, Clint lifted his head and glanced over his shoulder, wondering who thought he was sheriff material. He'd hated bounty hunting, but he'd done it because he had few options and it paid good money. He'd dreamed of settling on a ranch and living out his life in peace. Like most ranchers in the area, he'd lost half of his stock to bluetongue this year. And there wasn't any money to rebuild.

The sheriff's job paid good money.

Having made his decision, he swept the Stetson from his head and picked up the discarded badge. He nodded to the mayor and turned to face the crowd. "I accept your offer to be your new sheriff."

# Hard Candy Christmas

Abigail Kerr Sanford set the tray on the floor beside the heavy oak door and raised her hand to knock. Hesitating, she mentally reviewed her list of chores. The laundry was done, the empty room had been cleaned and the linens changed, the final meal of the day had been prepared and served, the larder stocked, and the menu for tomorrow planned.

Her father expected the boardinghouse to run with precision and a profit. He supervised the operation from the privacy of his suite of rooms, seldom mingling with the boarders. It was Abigail's job to carry out his instructions.

She knocked and waited.

"Come in, Daughter."

She turned the knob and pushed the door open a few inches. She bent to pick up the tray. With the tray occupying her hands, she widened the opening with her foot and entered the room.

Her father, William Kerr, sat in his favorite chair before a table in the curve of a large bow window. He raised his head from his newspaper and removed the spectacles from his long, thin nose. With his usual meticulous care to detail, he placed the spectacles on the table and folded the newspaper, putting it beside his glasses.

Abigail stood at attention, holding the tray and waiting for instruction.

He waved one hand. "I'm ready to be served, Daughter. You may put the tray down."

She set the tray on the table. Her father nodded, and she stepped back. He uncovered the tray, inspected its contents, settled the napkin on his lap, and re-arranged the silverware. Taking up his fork, he speared a piece of pot roast and chewed it slowly. Obviously finding the food to his satisfaction, he nodded again and inclined his head toward a chair.

Having passed the first test, Abigail exhaled and seated herself on the edge of the chair. She folded her hands in her lap and

# Hard Candy Christmas

composed her features. She waited for her father to begin their evening discussion.

"Good evening, Abigail."

The formal greeting was the only time he used her given name. Other than that he called her "daughter" to remind her that she was his possession, nothing more. And something less than a person.

"Good evening, Father."

"All is well with the boardinghouse?"

His opening words never varied, and he didn't like surprises. The ensuing list of questions might be long or short, but she limited herself to brief answers, rarely venturing

"Yes, Father."

"Did Juan post the 'Room for Rent' sign?"

Juan García was responsible for the heavier tasks at the boardinghouse. Elisa, his wife, shared the household and cooking chores with Abigail.

"Yes, Father, he put the sign out this afternoon."

William Kerr nodded for the third time and ate in silence for several minutes. Abigail waited patiently, knowing she couldn't rush him.

"That's good. With the shortage of housing we should have a new boarder within the week. Don't you think so, Daughter?"

"Yes, Father."

"Is the empty room cleaned and aired?"

"Yes, Father."

"And the shopping and laundry?"

"Both are done."

"Did you check my schedule?"

"Yes, Father. I stopped by the roundhouse this afternoon. You are to report at three o'clock tomorrow." Her father expected her to know his railroad schedule so she could plan meals and household chores with his convenience in mind.

"Good. That means my scheduled run hasn't altered. I checked the board when I returned from my last trip. They'll send a runner if it changes." He sliced a boiled potato. "And the menu for tomorrow night?"

"Liver with garden vegetables and cream pie."

"You remember well, Daughter." There was an uncommon note of approval in his voice. "I dislike liver, but it's an economical choice to serve our boarders." He put his fork and knife to one side and patted his flat abdomen. "And you know I don't eat cream pie. Too fattening. A competent railroad engineer must remain fit to properly execute his job."

Abigail said nothing, knowing he didn't expect a response. She'd never understood his avoidance of certain foods, especially rich desserts. His spare, wiry frame didn't possess an ounce of extra flesh. Viewed without his coat jacket, he appeared almost gaunt, silent testimony to his austere existence.

William Kerr raised his head and his gaze met hers. His eyes were gray-cold, reminding her of the snow-leaden skies of her former home in St. Louis.

She shivered and trembled, meeting his gaze. Knotting her hands, she willed the tremor to pass. Her father never looked at her directly unless he was angry or on very rare occasions, pleased.

She held her breath, afraid to avoid his penetrating gaze. She cast about in her mind for something she'd done or neglected to do that might have displeased him.

He wiped his mouth with the napkin and lowered his head. Rising from his seat, he signaled his finish. He moved to the large, curved window and pushed the heavy drapes aside. "It's a pleasant evening." Pulling his railroad pocket watch from his vest, he said, "I'll be leaving shortly for my deacon's meeting."

Abigail rose, too, and then almost collapsed backward, limp with relief. She'd been anxious for no reason. Her father wasn't displeased, he was thinking about his meeting. His one passion, besides the railroad and making money, was his allegiance to the Presbyterian Church. He'd served as a deacon for twenty years. She moved to the table and started stacking dishes on the tray.

# Hard Candy Christmas

"You've done well this month, Daughter. The boardinghouse is running with the precision of a railroad—as it should. I'm pleased."

Taking courage from his rare praise, she broached a subject that had been on her mind. "Father, I heard there was trouble today. Elisa said someone shot at Sheriff Cunningham, and the mayor selected a new sheriff. Do you know what happened?"

She saw his back straighten and his shoulders tense. Seeing his reaction, she wanted to snatch her words back.

"It's none of your concern, Daughter. The ranchers are bitter over the railroad raising their rates. The shooting was an accident. Sheriff Cunningham is a coward, and the new sheriff will have his hands full." He turned to face her, his features drawn in a stern line. "Your concern is the boardinghouse, not the town and its politics."

"Yes, Father. But if there is danger, I need to know for Kevin's sake."

At the mention of his eight-year-old grandson, William Kerr's features softened. "You're right, Daughter. I wasn't thinking. We can't be too careful where my grandson is concerned." He smiled—another rare gesture. "Have Juan walk him to and from school and keep Kevin close to home."

She nodded, agreeing with her father's precautions, while realizing how hard it would be to enforce restrictions on her active son. She lifted the tray and turned to go, waiting for her father's customary dismissal.

"Good night, Daughter."

\* \* \*

Clint Graham stood before the gabled, three-story Victorian house. It was a handsome place with two large bow windows in front and deep porches surrounding three sides. The setting sun glinted off floor-to-ceiling windows, reminding Clint of the lateness of the hour.

# Hard Candy Christmas

He'd intended to find a room to rent before nightfall, but he'd been delayed when Jezebel, his sorrel mare, had thrown a shoe. Not wanting to risk laming her, he'd walked the remaining miles, leading the mare.

When he took the job as sheriff, he'd realized he would have to move to town. If he was honest with himself, moving away from the ranch was almost as attractive as the salary he would draw. In the beginning, his small spread on the Devil's River had been a welcome refuge.

But that had been before the tragedy. Now the shimmering river was a daily reminder of his inadequacy and inconsolable grief. It had been a relief to leave his ranch in the capable hands of his foreman.

He would have preferred to live at the sheriff's office. But Del Rio's jailhouse was pathetically inadequate, consisting of one tiny room, half of the space taken up by an open cell for prisoners.

After giving it careful thought, he'd decided to live at Kerr House, a local boardinghouse. The place was known for its tasty food and cleanliness. The huge house fronted Main Street and was a scant block from the railroad yard.

Encouraged by the sign offering a room for rent, he tied Jezebel to the white picket fence. When he reached the ornately carved, multi-paned front door, he wiped his boots and removed his Stetson. Then he rang the doorbell.

A dark-haired Mexican woman, who was almost as broad as she was tall, answered the door.

Tipping his head, he announced himself, "I'm Clint Graham, ma'am, and I want to rent the room you have."

The woman bobbed her head. "I'm Elisa García, the housekeeper. You will need to speak with Mrs. Sanford. I will bring her."

"May I come inside to wait?"

"*Sí, señor.*" She opened the door wider. "*Por favor,* come inside. It is suppertime and we're busy serving, but I will bring Mrs. Sanford to you."

# Hard Candy Christmas

"If you're busy, I could come back at a better time."

"No, no, *señor*, it is no trouble." Urging him in front of her like a farm wife shooing chickens, she pointed to a large room off the front corridor. "*Por favor*, wait in the parlor. Only one moment, *señor*."

"Thank you."

She hurried off in a rustle of petticoats, and Clint entered the parlor. Glancing around, he was intrigued by what he saw. The fireplace boasted fine Italian marble. The wooden wainscoting was fashioned from rich mahogany. The cornices appeared to have been carved by a master and the bow window was magnificent. But the rug was a cheap imitation and threadbare. The draperies were old and stained. And the furniture consisted of ladder-back chairs, one worn rocker, and a moth-eaten settee.

The room was a curious study in contrasts. It looked as if it had been crafted for a millionaire, only to be inhabited by a pauper.

Hearing the light tread of someone approaching, he turned. His mind envisioned Mrs. Sanford before she appeared. She would be a no-nonsense, middle-aged woman with a dozen keys dangling from her ample waist. Contrary to his expectations, his gaze found a slender young woman of medium height who wore a stained apron.

She entered the room but hovered silently on the threshold. He thought her behavior odd but decided to take the initiative. He closed the distance between them and offered his hand. "I'm Clint Graham. Are you Mrs. Sanford?"

Staring at his outstretched hand, she made no move to take it. "Yes, I'm Mrs. Sanford."

Uneasy at her rejection, he dropped his hand. He thought he recognized her, but each time he'd glimpsed her in town, she'd had her bonnet pulled close and tight, hiding her features. He couldn't understand why she would hide her face.

Her features were attractive, especially her wide-set, green eyes and generous mouth. Even her hair, which was pulled into a severe bun, was comely. Her hair was thick and glossy, a deep chestnut color that glowed with hidden depths of fire. Mrs. Sanford wasn't what he'd expected, but he could easily adjust to such a pleasant surprise.

When she lowered her head, he glimpsed the faintest tint of rose coloring her cheeks. Realizing his scrutiny had embarrassed her, he chided himself for openly studying a married woman.

He cleared his throat. "I would like to take the room you have."

Lifting her head, she stared at a point above his shoulder and recited an obviously prepared speech. "The room rents for five dollars a week including board. The meals consist of breakfast and supper as well as a cold box lunch. Pets and members of the opposite sex aren't allowed in the rooms. I'll need two weeks' rent in advance, and your rent is due each Saturday."

"I don't have a pet, but I do have a hungry mare outside," he replied. "Do you stable boarders' horses?"

His question appeared to catch her by surprise. Her gaze slid over his face before she averted her eyes. "We don't usually get requests for stabling horses, but there is a barn out back and Juan could care for your mount. It would cost extra, and I would need to consult my father."

"Can you ask him? I had hoped to rent a room for tonight."

"He's not here. My father is William Kerr, and he's a railroad engineer. He's out on a run tonight. You can leave your horse at the livery stable for now. Is that satisfactory?"

Her answer cleared up one of the questions circling in his head. He knew William Kerr owned the boardinghouse but when the housekeeper had said Mrs. Sanford would see him, he'd assumed she was the landlady. It seemed all of his assumptions about Mrs. Sanford had been wrong. She wasn't a hired hand, and she certainly wasn't middle-aged and frumpy.

If she was the daughter of the owner, he wondered where her husband was and what he did for a living. Clint didn't get to town much, but Del Rio was a small place. He couldn't remember any Sanfords living in the area.

# Hard Candy Christmas

Glancing at her rigid, almost defensive stance, he realized she probably wouldn't be eager to answer his questions, especially personal ones. Besides, all he wanted was a decent room and a place to put his horse.

"Of course, I can leave my mount at the livery stable for tonight." Actually, it wasn't such a bad idea. It would give the blacksmith time to replace Jezebel's shoe.

Even though it was a solution to his problem, he was surprised Mrs. Sanford didn't have the authority to stable his horse for one night without her father's permission. And where was her husband? Couldn't he step forward to handle the situation?

He was starting to think he was obsessed with this woman's husband. Why was that? Because he found Mrs. Sanford attractive? The thought struck him like an open-handed slap, bringing him to his senses.

He'd never paid much attention to the ladies, especially married ones. Not that he didn't like women—in their proper place. But there was something about this one. Something that went beyond her emerald eyes and ripe mouth, a vulnerability that reached out to him, rousing his protective instincts.

But his reaction to her was plumb loco to his way of thinking. She had a father and a husband. She certainly didn't need an old saddle bum to protect her.

There was one question he might ask. It had bothered him, but he'd been busy thinking about his mare. He'd inquired around town, wanting to find the going rate for room and board, wondering how much of his salary he would be able to save. He'd been told the usual rate was six to eight dollars a week. Considering Kerr House's reputation, why was the rate only five dollars?

Thinking it foolish to raise the subject but curious to know, he said, "Your rent is lower than the other boardinghouses in town. I'm surprised you have a vacant room."

She tilted her head, and her eyebrows drew together. "Our boarders feel it's only fair they receive a lower rate because they

# Hard Candy Christmas

don't eat at the house every day. Most railroad men appreciate our flexibility, knowing they'll have expenses on the road."

"Railroad men?" He tugged on his earlobe. He wasn't a railroad man. And what was she saying about not eating every day?

"I thought you said the rent included breakfast and supper and a cold box lunch?"

"Yes, Mr. Graham, that's precisely what I said." Her gaze darted to his face, and her voice took on the note of an adult explaining to a child. "You must be new to railroad life. Perhaps you just hired on. I don't remember your face. You probably haven't considered you'll be away from Del Rio when you're on a run. During that time, you'll need to pay for your meals."

That she didn't remember his face when he'd recognized her from around town shouldn't have bothered him. But it did. He shook off the momentary twinge of displeasure.

Now he understood why their interview had been so bewildering. No one had mentioned Kerr House catered to railroad men and their peculiar lifestyle. But he didn't work for the railroad, and he wouldn't be traveling. He needed to know the rate for a full-time boarder. If it was double the railroad rate, he might have to rethink taking a room here.

"I need to know what you charge for a full-time boarder, Mrs. Sanford. You see, I'm not a railroad man. I own a sheep ranch on the Devil's River. Yesterday, I was asked to be sheriff."

Her eyes widened and she covered her cheeks with her hands. "Not a railroad man. A sheep rancher!" She shook her head and dropped her hands, twining her fingers together.

"Mr. Graham, you cannot board here."

# Hard Candy Christmas

## Chapter Two

"Mrs. Sanford, are you telling me I'm forbidden to rent a room because I don't work for the railroad?"

How could she explain that was precisely what she meant? Abigail had never encountered this situation before. Everyone knew Kerr House catered to railroad workers. To make matters worse, this man was a sheep rancher. Why on earth would he want to live in town?

Before she could fashion a reply, he said, "As I said, I've been appointed the new sheriff of the county. That's why I'm moving to town."

Abigail recoiled at this bit of information. Having the new sheriff, who was also a sheep rancher, living in Kerr House with railroaders was certain to cause friction. And she didn't want trouble.

Sliding a glance at him, she could understand why he'd been appointed the new sheriff. He was big man, tall and imposing, with broad shoulders and muscular forearms. And there was an innate air of self-confidence about him, too, as if he knew he was capable of taking care of himself, no matter the situation.

Even the features of his face underscored his powerful presence. He reminded her of a hawk, possessing an alert and watchful wariness.

Not that his features were unattractive. High cheekbones set off his clear blue eyes. His brown hair was cut short, fitting his head like a cap. The bold slash of his mouth might be considered generous if he would smile rather than frown. And the sharp line of his jaw and chin gave his face an air of authority.

His clothing was modest, faded Levi's and a denim shirt with the sleeves rolled above his elbows. Even though his clothes weren't fancy, they were neat and functional, fitting his muscular frame like a glove.

12

# Hard Candy Christmas

Despite her initial misgivings, she found her attitude subtly shifting. A lawman might prove to be an asset for the boardinghouse, especially in these troubled times. But her opinion wasn't important. Her father was out, and she had no idea how he would react.

And what about the other boarders? She couldn't envision them welcoming him with open arms. He *was* the new sheriff. His job should command respect, even from the railroad men. But it was a decision she didn't feel comfortable making, and she wanted him to understand her position.

"Mr. Graham, you must be aware of the, ah, the ill-will between railroaders and ranchers in this town. As you're a rancher yourself, I would think you've a difficult road ahead, convincing both sides you're not biased. Living among railroaders will make your job more—"

"I disagree." He shook his head and crossed his arms. "Granted, until I talked to you, I didn't know Kerr House catered to railroad workers. I chose your house because of its reputation for cleanliness and tasty food."

At his off-handed remark about the house, though it only obliquely referred to her efforts, a warm sensation spread through her body like the welcoming heat of a fire on a cold winter night. She wasn't accustomed to receiving compliments...any kind of compliments.

"Now that you've brought the subject up," he continued, "I think it would benefit my cause to live among railroaders."

"You can't be serious. Wouldn't you be more comfortable in another house?"

"Is it my comfort or yours we're talking about, Mrs. Sanford?"

She chose to ignore his provocative remark. "I fail to see why you would want to—"

"Confront this feud?" He cut her off again. "I think I can help settle it peacefully, Mrs. Sanford. I have a few ideas. But as you pointed out, some people will think I'm playing favorites because I

# Hard Candy Christmas

own a ranch. What better way to inspire confidence than to live among the railroaders?"

His argument made sense. And there was something about him, his air of self-confidence, she guessed, that made her want to have him around. But it wasn't her decision to make.

"Don't worry, Mrs. Sanford. I can take care of myself. And I won't take offense at anything your other boarders might say. After a time, I hope we'll become good friends." His gaze caught hers, and there was an expectant light in his blue eyes. "Could I see the room, please?"

"Mr. Graham, I understand your position. If it were my decision to make, I would…" She stopped herself, not comfortable with placing the blame on her father. Even though it might be true, she felt cowardly and disloyal, saying the words out loud.

"Is there someone else I can speak with?"

"Not tonight, I'm afraid. My father is out on the railroad," she repeated.

"Then I'll speak with your father as soon as he returns. I'm certain I can convince him."

"What will you do tonight?"

*Where had that come from?*

His welfare was none of her concern. She clutched her mother's cameo at her throat and twisted the ribbon around her index finger.

His features softened. He allowed himself a small smile, a lop-sided smile. She hadn't noticed before, but he had a scar at the right-hand corner of his mouth that pulled his lower lip down when he smiled. But even with just half a smile mellowing his features, he was a handsome man.

Then she recognized what his smile meant. It was a knowing smile, as if he was amused by her unexpected concern. Speculating on what he might be thinking, her face grew warm. Night had fallen since they'd started talking. She hadn't lit a lamp in the parlor. Lucky for her the room was shadowed.

# Hard Candy Christmas

"I'll take a room at the hotel for tonight, Mrs. Sanford. Thank you for your time." He started to extend his hand, checked himself and gave her a small bow instead. "I'll see myself out."

"Here, let me show you to the door," she offered.

Turning back, he threw out, almost as an afterthought, "What about your husband, Mrs. Sanford?"

The question took her by surprise. What did he mean? Had he noticed her blush and read more into it than he should?

As if he understood her startled reaction, he added, "What I meant to ask, is your husband around? Could I talk to him about the room?"

A sigh of relief escaped her. She hadn't realized she'd been holding her breath. He didn't know her circumstances. And she'd introduced herself as Mrs. Sanford. He would expect her to have a husband, but she didn't.

It was on the tip of her tongue to tell him that she was a widow. That would be the easy way out. But it was a falsehood, and she didn't like to lie. "My husband doesn't live here, Mr. Graham. He hasn't lived here for several years."

This time, it was his turn to look surprised. His gaze slid away, and he lowered his head. It was obvious he'd embarrassed himself.

"I'm sorry I asked. Please, accept—"

"That's quite all right," she interrupted brusquely. She crossed the parlor and went into the foyer. She opened the front door and nodded to him.

At the door, he replaced his Stetson and tugged the brim down with one finger. "Goodnight, ma'am."

"Goodnight," she replied, closing the door firmly.

\* \* \*

Sunlight spilled through the long windows, pooling like melted butter on the brown crust of the hardwood floors. The faintest promise of autumn tinged the air. It was Abigail's favorite time of year in Del Rio, when the sky was such a deep blue, it hurt

# Hard Candy Christmas

your eyes and the mild winter to come offered a welcome relief from the relentless heat.

The few hours spent in Elisa's sewing room were precious to Abigail, surpassed only by the time she spent with her son. With the morning's chores over, Kevin in school, and her father out on the railroad, she'd stolen the time for herself. She enjoyed learning to sew and the earthy pleasure of Elisa's never-ending stream of gossip. Sometimes, though, Abigail wished she could have shared these special moments with her mother.

Jean Kerr had been a gentle woman, completely devoted to her husband and family. Abigail, the youngest of five, had lost her mother to consumption when she needed her the most—the awkward time between childhood and the onset of womanhood.

As the baby of the family, her brothers and sisters did their best to protect her against the loss. They'd convinced their father to allow Abigail to finish her studies. Her father had grudgingly agreed, though he'd forced his other children to leave school early and work.

Her brothers and sisters had even encouraged her frivolous hobbies. When she was younger, she'd spent her spare time drawing with pastel chalks and composing poetry to accompany the pictures.

Now she possessed precious little time to spare, and she couldn't afford to spend it drawing pictures and writing poetry. Elisa taught her a more suitable pursuit, sewing beautiful bridal ensembles and trousseaus. Unlike ordinary seamstress work, the level of craft was exacting, with an obsessive attention to detail and fine seams. It also paid more than ordinary sewing. And she hoped it would provide her the means to leave Del Rio.

Like her brothers and sisters before her, she would be fleeing her father's unbending, miserly grasp. He had forced her mother and siblings to live in poverty, despite having a well-paid job on the railroad, so he could amass money. Money which he never spent. Money which he invested to make more money.

With one exception—this house.

# Hard Candy Christmas

After the death of his wife, her father had learned the Southern Pacific Railroad, which stretched from New Orleans to San Francisco, needed firemen in Del Rio, a remote frontier town on the Mexican border. He'd volunteered and been promoted from brakeman to fireman and then five years later, to the crowning glory of engineer.

Foreseeing opportunity in the ragged border town, he'd purchased town lots cheaply and built the commodious Victorian structure to keep his children at hand and working for him. But over time, they'd all escaped, leaving only Abigail behind.

Abigail had turned twenty-seven in July, and Kevin was growing up fast. She needed to begin a life of her own. She could live with one of her brothers or sisters, but she didn't want to be dependent. She had been too long dependent on her father. She wanted to stand on her own two feet and in order to be independent she needed a skill to earn a living.

With that thought in mind, she turned her attention to the satin fabric and its intricate swirls of seed pearls. Clutching the needle tighter, she passed it through the tiny hole in one side of a pearl and tugged the thread taut.

"You are unusually quiet today, *hijita mía*. Where have your thoughts flown?" Elisa managed to ask with her mouth full of straight pins while she pinned double rows of lace to the bodice of a wedding gown.

"I was wondering how much money I'll need to open my bridal shop."

"Have you decided where you will go?"

"Probably San Antonio or El Paso."

"Go to El Paso. You have a sister there."

Elisa and Juan had no children of their own. It was Elisa's biggest disappointment. She believed family was the most important thing in life. She mothered Abigail and treated Kevin as if he were her grandson.

"I want to be on my own, Elisa. I need to take care of myself and my son."

17

# Hard Candy Christmas

Elisa removed the last pin from her mouth and clucked her tongue. "You are a single woman with no man to protect you. It is better to go to El Paso where your sister lives with her husband."

"No man has protected me, Elisa. Quite the opposite."

Elisa didn't know everything about her past, but she knew Abigail felt used and mistreated by her father. "You shouldn't talk like that, *mi hija*. Your father has trouble expressing his feelings, but he does love the boy."

"Yes, he loves Kevin."

"Family is all we can depend upon. *Por favor*, think about going to El Paso rather than San Antonio."

Abigail sighed. "I know Leanna and her husband would welcome us, but this is something I have to prove to myself. San Antonio is closer, only a few hours away on the train. You and Juan could visit me."

"Even though you will be closer, you will be a woman alone in San Antonio. I will worry about you."

"You needn't start worrying yet. It will be a long time before I sew enough gowns to save the money I need."

"How much do you have?" Elisa asked with her customary bluntness.

"About two hundred dollars."

Elisa held her needle to the light and threaded it. She had her head cocked to one side, considering. "You're right. You will need double that amount for a shop. And you will need additional money to set up housekeeping if you don't live with your sister," she pointed out.

Sighing again, Abigail said, "Maybe you're right."

She really wanted to be independent, but Elisa did have a point. Why make things harder? Starting over in a city where she didn't know a single soul frightened her more than she cared to admit.

But that was the problem, wasn't it? She'd lived too long in fear, hiding in the shadow of her powerful and grasping father. And then there had been Lucas who had…

# Hard Candy Christmas

She swallowed hard and willed herself not to think of him.

But if she didn't face her fears and overcome them, she would never make a life for herself. Would she?

She dropped the sewing and raised her hands to rub her temples. Whenever she considered leaving home, her thoughts turned in circles, going over the same ground, like a dog circling a rug, trying to find a comfortable place.

"*Bueno*," Elisa said. "I hope you will go to live with your sister." She smiled. "Then I will be able to sleep nights."

"Oh, Elisa, sometimes I wonder who is the bigger worrywart, you or me? And I don't have nearly enough money saved so there is plenty of time to worry…and plan." She retrieved her sewing and concentrated on the seed pearls.

"When the time comes, I will help you any way I can, *mi hija*. And Juan will help you too." Elisa patted her shoulder.

Abigail leaned forward and put her arms around her friend's ample waist, murmuring, "Thank you, Elisa. I don't know what I would do without you."

Elisa returned the hug. Tears burned at the back of Abigail's throat. Gulping her tears, she realized she'd been especially sensitive lately, crying at the silliest things. She couldn't remember crying this much since she'd given birth to Kevin and her husband had deserted her.

Thinking of Lucas again, reminded her of talking with the new sheriff last night. Elisa, who knew most of the town's gossip, might be able to answer some of the questions she'd been wondering about.

Bending her head over the sewing, she said, "I met the new sheriff last night. He was the man you let in while we were serving dinner. Remember? Do you know him?"

"No, I didn't know who he is."

"His name is Mr. Graham, and he wants to board with us. Did you know he's a sheep rancher?" She didn't wait for an answer. "I can't understand why the mayor would appoint a sheep rancher

# Hard Candy Christmas

when there is a feud between the ranchers and railroaders. It's not exactly an unbiased choice."

"No, I didn't know he was a rancher," Elisa replied. "I heard the mayor was desperate when *Señor* Cunningham quit his job so quickly."

"What do you mean by quickly?"

"I told you someone shot at Sheriff Cunningham, didn't I?"

"Yes, but you didn't explain why, except to mention the feud."

"There was a meeting and one of the ranchers got angry. Sheriff Cunningham asked for order, but the angry rancher shot the hat off his head. Then the sheriff quit his job, saying he didn't want to be part of the feud. The mayor appointed the new man because he was a bounty hunter before he was a rancher. And everyone says he is very brave, this *Señor* Graham." She paused and bit the thread in two. "I would like for him to live here. A brave man is always welcome."

Not knowing the circumstances, Abigail had come to the same conclusion when she'd met him. There was something about him that inspired confidence and made her feel safe.

*But an ex-bounty hunter?*

# Hard Candy Christmas

## Chapter Three

Abigail pushed open the swinging door between the kitchen and the dining room, carrying a platter of fried chicken. She placed the heavy platter in the middle of the long dining table. The boarders were already seated, eagerly awaiting their evening meal.

Her eyes swept the table, making certain she hadn't forgotten the butter or gravy or some other essential item from the kitchen. When her gaze reached the bottom of the table, she caught her breath. In the chair that had been vacant for the past week sat Sheriff Graham.

Her father must have agreed to rent to him. Gazing at the sheriff, her heart lifted. Instinctively, she felt he was a good man. What had he said that first night? That he had some ideas to settle the feud peaceably. She liked his positive attitude.

Sheriff Graham snagged her gaze and smiled his lop-sided smile.

Glimpsing his off-center smile, her heart thumped against her chest. She wiped her hands on her apron and pushed an errant strand of hair behind her ear.

The boarders, all six men, rose from their seats and stood beside their chairs. Two seats were vacant; those lodgers were out on the railroad.

"Please." She waved them down. "Be seated, gentleman." Inclining her head toward the sheriff, she asked, "Have you gentlemen met our new boarder, Sheriff Graham?"

Mr. Palmer, a portly widower, who usually served as the spokesman for the group, replied, "We've not been formally introduced, Mrs. Sanford. But we all know Sheriff Graham by reputation."

Abigail touched the cameo at her throat. She was hesitant and uncertain of how to proceed. Usually when a new boarder arrived, the others knew him from the railroad yards.

21

# Hard Candy Christmas

But Mr. Palmer was polite enough to offer, "I'm Henry Palmer. To my left is Paul Farr, to my right is Matt Anderson, across from me is Zachariah Mooney, and next to Zach is Tom Weaver."

The railroaders followed Mr. Palmer's lead, offering to shake hands with the newcomer, except Tom Weaver. He'd lost a hand in a switching accident. Weaver might have a legitimate excuse to not shake the sheriff's hand, but the hate and anger blazing from his eyes told another story.

For a moment, Abigail wondered if it was a mistake to have Sheriff Graham stay. But her father had made the decision. It wasn't her concern. And four of the five men present were ready to accept him so that was a start.

"May I ask your given name, Sheriff?" Mr. Palmer requested.

"Of course, it's Clint, and I'm pleased to meet y'all."

The men nodded and mumbled among themselves, taking their seats. They passed the platters and bowls around the table. Abigail heaved a sigh of relief, glad to see things returning to normal. Except for Tom Weaver, who sat stiffly in his chair, refusing food and staring openly at the sheriff.

"What do you men want to drink?" Abigail asked. "Milk, buttermilk or coffee?"

Making a mental note of their choices, she returned to the kitchen to fetch the beverages. Entering the hot kitchen, she went to Elisa, who was pulling an apple pie from the oven. "I didn't know my father gave his consent for the sheriff to live here."

Elisa turned toward her. "I thought I told you." She straightened with the pie cradled in pot holders and then put it on a cooling rack. Shaking her head, she said, "No, you are right, *mi hija*. I forgot to tell you. I think the sheriff saw your father in town yesterday. *Señor* Graham moved in today while you were at the general store."

"Did he find the room to his liking?"

# Hard Candy Christmas

"*Sí*, he said the room was neat and clean." Wiping her hands on her apron, she tilted her head to one side. "I believe he said it was too good 'for the likes of him.'"

Abigail laughed, surprising herself. "That sounds like him."

Elisa narrowed her eyes, and she gazed at Abigail. "I thought you didn't know the man."

"I don't really know him, but I talked with him the other night." She decided to change the subject and said, "Elisa, please pour the coffee, three cups. I'll get the milk. The boarders are waiting. Oh, and do you have Father's tray ready? I'll take it to him while you serve the pie."

"*Sí*, your father's tray is ready. I will take the men their pie."

"Thank you. I'll be back to help clear and do the dishes."

Working together, they filled a tray with coffee and milk. Abigail backed through the swinging door into the dining room and served the men. Retreating to the end of the table, she watched as her boarders ate; satisfied they had everything they needed.

Only Tom Weaver bothered her. As far as she could tell, he hadn't touched a morsel of food. He sat, sipping his coffee; his gaze fixed on the sheriff. It gave her the shudders, but there was nothing she could do about it. Both Sheriff Graham and Tom were boarders, whether Tom liked it or not.

When she reached across the table to remove an empty bowl, the sheriff touched her arm. Glancing up, she found herself staring into his clear blue eyes. "Did your father tell you he agreed to rent to me?"

His touch on her arm, as light as it was, felt like a firebrand, burning through the thin cotton of her sleeve. Her gaze riveted on his brown hand. He must have sensed her discomfort because he let his hand drop. She straightened with the empty bowl.

"No, my father didn't mention it. And I haven't spoken with him today. But it's not important, Mr. Graham, whether he told me. I'm glad we can accommodate you. If you need anything, please let me know."

"Do you eat dinner with your father?"

# Hard Candy Christmas

What right did he have, asking such a question? It was much too personal. And why did he care?

"No, I don't eat with my father, but I take him his dinner. We usually talk then."

She refused to admit she ate in the kitchen with Kevin, Elisa, and Juan. She knew how it would seem to an outsider, to someone who didn't know her father and his peculiar ways.

"As a matter of fact," she purposely cut the conversation short. "I need to take his tray to him." With the bowl in hand, she returned to the kitchen, placing it in the sink and grabbing her father's tray.

\* \* \*

Clint leisurely sipped his coffee at the empty dining table. The other lodgers had retired to their rooms or to the porch for an after-dinner smoke. He'd purposely waited at the table, not wanting to thrust himself upon them too soon. Better to let them grow accustomed to him being around.

Tom Weaver was another story. That one would bear watching. Weaver fairly oozed hostility. Not that Clint could blame him. It must be difficult to make your way in the world with one hand.

After he'd drained the last of his coffee, he reared back in the chair and stretched, yawning. It was about time he turned in. Until he found someone to deputize, he'd taken it upon himself to walk the town after midnight for a couple of hours. Then he tried to get some sleep before beginning the day.

Hearing footsteps on the other side of the door, he brought his front chair legs down. It was probably Abigail, returning to clear the table. He found himself waiting for her, expectant.

Not caring to examine his feelings too closely, he watched as she came through the swinging door. Her gaze found him, and he glimpsed the surprise in her green eyes. She recovered quickly and nodded. He stifled a chuckle. It was obvious she wished him gone from the table but was too polite to say it out loud.

# Hard Candy Christmas

She gathered dirty plates, bowls and platters, stacking them in her arms. Even in her drab brown gown and voluminous apron, Clint couldn't help but notice the beguiling lines of her body. Her breasts were high and full, straining the threadbare material of her bodice. She possessed a slender waist, and its small span emphasized the womanly shape of her hips.

And when she bent to pick up a discarded napkin, the worn-thin material of the skirt hugged her shapely bottom, making perspiration pop on his forehead.

He didn't have much experience with women, at least, not respectable women. His background and choice of profession had precluded meeting women like Mrs. Sanford. But there certainly was nothing wrong with her build. Any saloon girl would be tickled pink to be put together like Mrs. Sanford.

"Mr. Graham, there's one cup of coffee left. Would you care for it?"

Her unexpected offer interrupted his wayward thoughts, making him wonder where he'd been headed. After all, she was a married woman. A married woman without a husband, but married, nonetheless.

Or was she a "grass widow?" There were a lot of grass widows in the West. Things didn't work out and the man moved on. Few bothered to formalize their permanent separation with legal papers.

"Yes, thank you, if it's no trouble," he said.

"No trouble, let me take these things to the kitchen, and I'll get the coffee pot. I won't be a minute."

Watching her balance the pile of dirty dishes and push through the swinging door, he had the strongest urge to help her. But he kept his seat, guessing his help would probably be frowned upon. She was a self-contained woman. He wondered if all respectable women were like that. If maybe that was what made them respectable in the first place.

# Hard Candy Christmas

He wouldn't know. His mother had been gregarious and fun loving and definitely not respectable. His sister had been talkative as a magpie and given to outbursts of affection.

The swinging door whispered open, and he looked up to find Mrs. Sanford had returned with a tin coffeepot.

He raised his empty cup. She took the cup without touching his hand. While she refilled it, he noticed her hair wasn't pinned up tonight. Her hair fell in long, burnished waves to the middle of her back. Its chestnut color shone in the soft lamplight, a tapestry of many hues, rich browns with threads of russet and gold. He wondered if her hair felt as silky as it looked.

He found it hard to believe she was a married woman with a son. With her hair loose and tumbling down her back, she looked very young. On the other hand, she acted far older than her age. Surrounded by men boarders, she remained aloof, avoiding contact.

Where was her husband? Why wasn't he here? If she'd been his wife, he wouldn't have left her alone.

Placing the refilled cup on the table, she asked, "Is there anything else I can get you?"

"No, no, thank you." He dropped two lumps of sugar into his coffee and stirred it. "After this cup, I'll be off to bed."

"So soon? It's early yet."

"Yes, but I get up at midnight and make the rounds of the town. Then I come back and try to sleep for a couple of hours."

"Oh, I didn't know. That must be difficult."

"Comes with the job."

"Would you like a piece of pie for later? We have some left."

Clint smiled and rubbed his stomach. "That sounds great. If I wasn't so full of your delicious dinner, I'd be tempted to have a second piece now."

She didn't return his smile, merely nodded and pushed through the door to the kitchen. Clint gulped down his coffee and stood, determined to get to bed, despite three cups of coffee. But it had been good coffee.

# Hard Candy Christmas

Mrs. Sanford returned with a slice of pie, wrapped in a napkin. He reached for it, meaning to take the pie from her hands, but she ignored him. Instead, she placed the pie on the table.

"I hope there's no trouble tonight," she said.

Before he could reply, she disappeared into the kitchen again. He stared after her. Her actions went beyond avoiding men. He remembered how she'd refused to shake his hand, and how she'd reacted when he touched her arm. Twice tonight, she'd pointedly avoided brushing her hand against his.

He shook his head. He didn't know much about respectable women. But he knew enough to realize Mrs. Sanford's behavior went beyond odd. If he had to put a name to it, he would say she was frightened to death of men.

*Where was her husband? And what had the man done to her?*

\* \* \*

"Kevin, Kevin, where are you?" Abigail called from the side porch.

Her son should have finished raking the leaves. In the arid climate of Del Rio, there were precious few trees. Her father had chosen this lot because it possessed a stand of pin oaks. And it was Kevin's job to rake the leaves.

But it was also his job to keep the wood box filled—his most important chore. Preparations for tonight's supper were underway, and they needed wood for the cook stove. The leaves could wait, supper couldn't.

*Where was the boy?*

Striding to the end of the porch, Abigail rounded the corner and stepped onto the front porch. Delighted squeals drifted to her from the other side of the house. She recognized her son's voice and wondered what he was doing.

She turned onto the third side of the wrap-around porch and glimpsed Kevin, poised to jump into a pile of leaves. Her son screamed at the top of his lungs, took a running leap, and landed

# Hard Candy Christmas

with a loud crunch, scattering leaves to the four winds. She could scarcely believe her eyes. Kevin was usually such a responsible boy.

But her son wasn't alone in his mischief. To her surprise, the sheriff stood beside the mound of leaves with a rake in his hand, laughing and urging Kevin on. They were an incongruous pair to say the least, her solemn son and the flinty-eyed lawman.

She opened her mouth to call to Kevin, to remind him of his responsibilities. But she couldn't do it. It had been a long time since she'd seen her son frolicking. She remembered her longings as a young girl when she'd watched other children play in the leaves. But there had been no leaves for her to play in. Her family had lived in a tenement apartment to save money.

A part of her wanted to stay and watch him, but she knew she couldn't spare the time. Her father expected the lodgers to be served their supper at six o'clock sharp. She didn't dare linger.

Tearing herself away from the happy scene, she decided to fill the wood box herself. She hurried to the back of the house where the woodpile was and gathered an armload of logs, taking them to the kitchen. When she returned for a second load, she heard Kevin and the sheriff approaching.

It was obvious, even to her casual glance; they'd been playing in the leaves. Both of them sported tousled hair interlaced with bits of leaves and sticks. And their clothes were a sight, too, dusty and strewn with stray leaves. They seemed completely oblivious to their appearance, as only men could be, laughing and joking. The sheriff's hand rested lightly on her son's head. They looked good together.

"Your son remembered he hadn't filled the wood box," the sheriff offered by way of greeting. He looked at her arms loaded with logs and added, "I guess you beat us to it."

"I didn't know you had met my son," she replied stiffly.

She didn't know what had made her say that. She hadn't expected the sheriff to take an interest in Kevin. His interest saddened her somehow, seeing them together. And at the same time, it made her angry, realizing what Kevin was missing.

28

# Hard Candy Christmas

"Well," the sheriff drawled in his low-key way. "I can't say we've been formally introduced. When I came up, I saw him raking leaves and one thing led to another…"

"Ma, don't be mad at him," Kevin said. "I'm sorry about the wood box. I plumb forgot. The sheriff was showing me how to—"

"Frolic in the leaves and forget your chores," Abigail finished for him.

"Aw, Ma, I promise to do better. You'll see." Then his face lit up. "The sheriff has a horse, and he's gonna brang—"

"*Bring*, dear, *bring* the horse here," she corrected.

"Uh, yeah, that's what I said. He's gonna *bring* the horse to stay in the barn out back. Grandpa said he could. And the sheriff is gonna show me how to ride and shoot his Colt pistol. Just like a real lawman." He turned to Sheriff Graham and excitement animated his brown eyes. "Aren't you, Sheriff?"

"I, ah, that is," the sheriff hemmed and hawed, looking sheepish. He glanced at her from the corner of his eyes. "Uh, Kevin, I don't know about riding and shooting. Your mother would have to agree to—"

"And I don't agree," she broke in, her voice firm.

Kevin's face fell. The light shining in her son's face disappeared as quickly as a storm cloud swallows the sun. Seeing his reaction, Abigail's heart squeezed.

"I don't mind you learning to ride if the horse is gentle enough," she said, softening the blow. "But I don't want you to touch the sheriff's gun. Not under any circumstances. Do you hear me?" The thought of Kevin handling a Colt pistol gave her the shudders. It reminded her of her husband, Lucas, and his unholy obsession with firearms.

"Aw, Ma," Kevin whined, thrusting his hands in his pockets and kicking at a dirt clod.

"No complaining, Kevin, you must listen to your mother," the sheriff said. "She knows what's best for you."

Abigail glanced at him, her throat suddenly tight. She'd never had anyone, let alone a man, back her up with regard to

# Hard Candy Christmas

Kevin's upbringing. His open support gave her a good feeling, a feeling of rightness.

"I'm sorry," Kevin said. "And I won't disobey, Ma." He looked to the sheriff for approval and stopped kicking the ground. Almost as an afterthought, he hugged her and said, "Thanks for saying I can learn to ride. I'll be extra careful, you'll see."

She returned the hug. "You're welcome, Son. We'll talk about riding later. And I don't mind filling the wood box occasionally but let's not make a habit of it."

"I won't. I promise."

"Let me take the wood for you." The sheriff stepped forward and opened his arms. She acquiesced, giving him the logs. Turning to Kevin, he directed, "Get another load for your mother. We'll have the wood box filled in no time."

"Kevin has never jumped in the leaves before," she said. "Did you give him the idea?"

He nodded, admitting, "Guilty as accused."

"You must have been raised where there are more trees. There aren't many in this area."

"I didn't get around trees much when I was a young'un," he said, "just dusty streets. But my ranch house is surrounded by trees. There are huge live oaks and pecans, drawing their life from the river."

But when he said the word "river," his face contorted and he turned away. She glimpsed a muscle jumping in his jaw.

Suddenly, he seemed in a rush to leave her. She watched him climb the back steps and take the load of wood into the kitchen. She wondered at his odd reaction. It was as if the word "river" had dredged up some awful memory.

The backdoor slammed and Kevin trotted into the yard again. "One more load to go," her son said before he went to the woodpile and filled his arms.

The door opened and closed again. The sheriff took the back steps, two at a time. Seeing Kevin with his arms full, he said, "That should do it. Good job, Kevin."

# Hard Candy Christmas

Hearing his words of praise, Abigail felt a prick of guilt. She didn't praise her son often enough. It was a bad habit she'd picked up from her father, taking the boy for granted. Making a mental note, she vowed she would do better in the future.

She watched her son climb the steps carefully, his arms filled with logs. When she glanced up, she found the sheriff there, standing so close she could touch him. She could feel the heat from his body and smell the pungent, honest male scent of him. The sensations unnerved her.

She retreated a few steps, thinking she needed to be inside, helping with supper.

He glanced around the back yard. "What did you plan on doing with the leaves?" As if answering his own question, he said, "I see you have a garden. Packed down and left to rot for two or three years, leaves make good fertilizer."

"So I've been told," she found herself responding when she should be rushing inside. "Unfortunately, the garden is Juan's domain. And he prefers…" She paused and wrinkled her nose, uncertain of how to broach the delicate subject.

"Animal droppings," he supplied.

"Yes, that's it," she agreed, grateful for his discretion. "I'm certain your mare will do her part."

He laughed and she found herself joining in, enjoying the warm timbre of his male laughter as it washed over her. The shared pleasure felt strange, and she realized it had been years since she'd laughed with a man.

Sheriff Graham was different from any man she'd met before. No other man had gone out of their way to take an interest in her son. She was glad her father had allowed him to stay.

"What happens to the leaves after Kevin rakes them? I like to see a job through to the finish."

"Juan usually burns them. But it's not your concern, Clint." Realizing what she'd said, her hand flew to her mouth and her neck warmed.

*She'd used his given name. It was unspeakably forward of her.*

31

# Hard Candy Christmas

"It's all right," he said. "I want you to call me Clint." He hesitated before asking, "May I call you by your given name?" Reaching up, he pulled her hand away from her face. His fingers lingered before he released her.

She heard his question as if from far away. Her immediate attention was riveted on his hand and where he'd touched her. Her flesh felt tender and sensitized. Wondrous and unfamiliar longings coursed through her body.

After years of avoiding a man's touch, she hungered for contact, was greedy for the feel of skin against skin. She grew warmer, heat flooding her face and cheeks. And she wanted to run away and hide.

# Hard Candy Christmas

## Chapter Four

"What is your given name, Mrs. Sanford?" He touched her arm.

His light touch, no more substantial than a whisper, drew her to the ground and suddenly, she wished he was holding her and touching her.

*My goodness, what was wrong with her?*

Her tongue felt thick in her mouth, but she managed, "My given name is Abigail."

"Abigail…Abigail," he tested her name, as if he were savoring the taste of it on his tongue. "It's a beautiful name but too formal. I shall call you Abby—that's it—Abby."

She shook her head, not knowing if she were agreeing or disagreeing. "My mother called me Abby," she said. Her heart twisted, thinking of her gentle mother. Swallowing, she ventured, "You may call me Abby but only in private Mr. Graham—Clint. Not in front of anyone else, even my son."

"I understand, Abby." The backdoor slammed and Clint looked up. "Here comes your son with a surprise."

She made an effort to compose her features, knowing Kevin would sense any lingering embarrassment. She watched his slow progress down the back steps, this time, hampered by a large, orange pumpkin.

"Kevin, where did you get that?" she asked.

When he reached the ground, he put the pumpkin down and ran to her, his eyes glowing with pleasure. "Ain't it wonderful, Ma? The sheriff brung it for me."

"*Brought* it for you, Kevin," she corrected again. Glancing at Clint, she found him grinning.

He held up his right hand as if taking a vow. "Guilty again."

Her gaze slid from Clint to Kevin and back again. Why was Clint taking such an interest in her son, bringing him gifts? And

# Hard Candy Christmas

wanting to call her by her given name? Did he have designs on her? Was he using Kevin to get close to her?

But she was a married woman. A married woman who had admitted her husband hadn't lived with her for years. Thinking about it, she cursed her honesty.

And her engrained wariness took over. She stepped back again, far enough so he couldn't touch her and sway her better judgment. She wished she hadn't called him by his given name because it encouraged a degree of familiarity. And with that familiarity, came a subtle shift in their relationship. A change she wasn't prepared to handle.

"Can I keep it, Ma? The sheriff promised to show me how to carve it." Kevin interrupted her troubled thoughts.

"Carve it?" She asked, not understanding.

"I saw it at the farmer's market on the way home," Clint explained. "It's almost All Hallows Eve, and I couldn't resist. I used to carve pumpkins when I was a boy. You've seen jack o' lanterns, haven't you? You don't mind if I show Kevin, do you?"

Abigail gazed at her son's expectant face. Excitement illuminated his features. She couldn't bring herself to deprive her son of such a rare treat. She would deal with Clint in her own way.

"Yes, I've seen jack o' lanterns when I was growing up in St. Louis. I know what they are." She moved to her son's side and stroked his hair, silently reminding Clint that, no matter how many surprises he might bring, Kevin was *her* son.

"Of course, you may keep the pumpkin. I have stubs of candles that should do nicely to light him. Have you thanked the sheriff?"

"Thank you, Sheriff," Kevin obediently said.

"And thank you, Mrs. Sanford, for giving your consent."

She nodded, gratified to hear him use her surname as she'd requested.

"I better get inside and help Elisa with supper," she said.

"When can we carve the pumpkin, Ma?"

# Hard Candy Christmas

"Not tonight, Son. It's too late. Maybe tomorrow afternoon, if that's agreeable with the sheriff." She glanced at Clint.

"Tomorrow will be fine," he agreed.

Abigail nodded again and hurried off.

Clint watched the provocative sway of her hips as she climbed the steps to the kitchen. He'd almost breached the wall she used to protect herself—almost. But for no reason he could fathom, she'd withdrawn again, as clearly as if she had shut a door in his face.

"Where should I put the pumpkin to keep it safe for tomorrow?" The sound of Kevin's voice brought him back.

He had forgotten the boy remained. He'd been naturally drawn to Abby's son. Timothy had been about Kevin's age when he... Stopping himself, he realized he couldn't think about his nephew. The pain was too fresh, and the guilt was like a living thing, gnawing at his guts.

He squatted so his eyes were level with Kevin's. "If it was my pumpkin and I wanted it to be safe, I'd keep it in my room."

"You don't think Ma would mind, do you?"

"Nah, I don't think she'll mind." Clint rose to his feet. "Now, scoot! Supper will be ready soon, and you'll need to settle the pumpkin and wash up." Turning his own hands over, he inspected his palms, smudged with dirt from raking leaves. "I think we both need a wash."

\* \* \*

On this particular All Hallows Eve, Abigail could almost believe in ghosts and things that "go bump in the night." It was as if evil spirits had invaded Kerr House, wreaking their own form of mischief.

From finding her wash basin cracked in the morning to the burnt pork chops at supper, everything had gone wrong. And when her father discovered he didn't have a clean pair of overalls to wear on his run, her spate of bad luck had culminated in a nasty scene.

# Hard Candy Christmas

Her laundry schedule had fallen behind while she dealt with several near-disasters in the kitchen and Kevin being sent home from school, scraped and bruised from falling out of a tree at recess.

The only lucky thing, if one could call it a perverse kind of luck, was Kevin's injuries weren't serious. With some iodine and bandaging, he was as good as new and thoroughly excited about tonight. So excited, he couldn't sit still.

Abigail grinned to herself, remembering what her mother would have said. Jean Kerr would have said her grandson had "ants in his pants."

Exhausted but determined for Kevin to enjoy the holiday, she joined her son on the front porch to light the jack o' lantern. Kevin spent half an hour positioning the carved pumpkin on the front porch for maximum effect. He sprinted into the street and strolled by the house, play-acting at being a passerby to view it.

Abigail watched him from the relative peace of the porch with her tired feet propped on a stool. Despite her fatigue, her son's animated antics revived her spirits. And she hoped, with the setting of the sun her jinxed day would end.

Clint hadn't come to supper tonight. It was the first meal he'd missed since moving to the boardinghouse. Unlike the railroad men, who spent their free nights at the local saloons and other "unmentionable" establishments, the sheriff spent his evenings at the house, usually retiring early.

Since the afternoon when Clint gave Kevin the pumpkin, he'd kept his distance, respecting her wishes. He'd shown Kevin how to carve the pumpkin and had given him riding lessons on his mare, but he didn't approach Abigail or call her by her given name.

At first, she'd been relieved, but with the passage of time, she found she missed talking to him, missed his lop-sided smile and deep laugh.

She wondered again why he hadn't been at supper.

When Kevin was ready, Abigail retrieved the candle stubs and sulfur matches from the kitchen. Experimenting together, she learned with Kevin how to place a candle in a pool of its own

# Hard Candy Christmas

melted wax, toward the front of the jack o' lantern, so the face glowed eerily in the dark.

Gazing at the effect they'd created, she exclaimed, "He's wonderful, Son! You did a great job."

"The sheriff helped," her son admitted modestly.

"I know," she replied. "I wonder why he hasn't come home yet."

"He'll be here," Kevin declared. "I know he wants to see our jack o' lantern." In an uncharacteristic gesture for his age, he grabbed her hand and drew her toward the chairs on the porch. "Come on, Ma, let's sit down and wait for him."

Nodding, she followed his lead, grateful for the opportunity to rest her feet again. Her son perched on a wicker chair beside her, his feet dangling. She glanced at him, noting his barely contained excitement and smiled. If she were a betting woman, she'd wager Kevin would beg to stay up late with his jack o' lantern for company.

"Ma, do you know any ghost stories? If you do, could you tell me some?"

Under the cover of darkness, she found herself smiling again. He was enjoying this impromptu holiday and so was she. It had been weeks since they'd shared special time together. And she was happy for him. This was what childhood was about. And all because Clint had been thoughtful enough to bring home a pumpkin.

"Let me see if I can remember. It's been a long time, Kevin."

He reminded her of her childhood, before her mother had died, and the thought brought a lump to her throat. She'd been fascinated by spooky stories, loving the delicious feeling of being both safe and protected by her large family, while frightened to death at the same time.

Gathering her thoughts, she happened to look up and glimpse someone approaching the house. Straining her eyes against the darkness, she made out the familiar shape of Clint's Stetson.

# Hard Candy Christmas

Kevin must have seen him coming, too, because he let out a whoop and jumped up, rushing to the street and pointing proudly at the glowing jack o' lantern.

They came up the steps of the porch together, Clint casually resting his hand on her son's shoulder and praising the boy for putting the grinning pumpkin in just the right place.

"Evening, Mrs. Sanford." Clint doffed his dun-colored Stetson. "I see you and Kevin are celebrating All Hallows Eve."

"Yes, good evening, Sheriff." Not wanting to appear curious but unable to stop herself from making reference to his tardiness, she commented, "It must have been a long day for you."

"Yes, it was a long day. I meant to send word I wouldn't be here for supper, but I was busy with meetings. My apologies."

"It was kind of you to think of us, but it's not a problem. Leftovers in this house seldom go to waste." Rising from her chair, she asked, "Are you hungry? I'm certain I can find something for you."

"No, no thank you, Mrs. Sanford. We held the last meeting over supper at the hotel."

"I see," she said.

He smiled his lop-sided grin, an unspoken apology for profaning himself by eating the hotel's inferior food. "May I sit with you and Kevin for a while, Mrs. Sanford?"

"Certainly, make yourself comfortable." She took her seat again. "Kevin asked me to tell him a ghost story. Do you know any?"

"Do I know any," he repeated dramatically, thumping his chest with his fist. "I'm the best ghost-story teller this side of the Pecos."

"Is that so?" Abigail shot back.

Kevin bounced up and down on the edge of his chair. His voice rose an octave when he pleaded, "Please, Sheriff, tell us, tell us."

# Hard Candy Christmas

Clint glanced at Abigail for approval. She nodded. She couldn't help but smile again. The last thing she'd expected was for Clint to brag about his story-telling prowess.

Settling himself in a chair, Clint crossed one long leg over the other. Adopting the hushed tone of a teller of spooky stories, he wove a tale about a dead Apache chief who had lost his family and returned from the grave, on nights when the moon was dark, to seek his revenge with a razor-sharp tomahawk.

Kevin listened, rapt, his head cocked to one side. Occasionally, he would stop the sheriff and ask a question, clearing up some point. Abigail felt a thrill of pride, listening to her son's intelligent and intuitive questions. This was a side of Kevin she rarely saw.

The story was plenty scary with enough blood and gore to delight an eight-year-old boy. Abigail enjoyed the story but was thankful when Clint ended it on a positive note. After much suffering, the Apache chief found a portal to the other world and went to join his family in the afterlife, no longer bringing terror to this world.

At that moment the candle in the jack o' lantern gutted out, as if a fitting ending to the story. Kevin jumped up and replaced the candle, babbling about the tale, and how he would have defended his family against the revenge-seeking ghost.

Abigail happened to glance up and find Clint looking at her. He inclined his head toward her son. As one adult to another, they exchanged glances over the top of his head. It was a strange feeling, Abigail realized, sharing her son with this man.

"It's your turn, Mrs. Sanford," Clint prompted.

"Yeah, Ma." Kevin plopped into his chair. "It's your turn. And the scarier the better."

She took a deep breath and decided to relate Washington Irving's classic tale of the headless horseman. And her son loved it. Clint applauded at the end, and Kevin joined him.

Then they alternated, dredging up ghost stories from their childhood. After spending two hours trying to best each other's

# Hard Candy Christmas

efforts, they realized the candle stubs had burnt out and Kevin was fast asleep.

Abigail reached over and smoothed her son's hair from his forehead. He looked so peaceful, curled in the wicker chair, despite the gory stories he'd heard. She'd thoroughly enjoyed the evening and knew it would be a night her son would remember for a long time.

Gazing at her son tenderly, she realized how vulnerable he looked while sleeping. A stab of guilt shot through her. Belatedly, she wondered if she and Clint shouldn't have exercised more restraint, rather than getting caught up in a friendly rivalry.

*What if Kevin had nightmares?*

"Thinking about letting him sleep with you tonight?" Clint asked.

Amazed he'd accurately gauged her thoughts, she replied, "How did you know?"

"I had a younger sister and a…" He stopped himself and shook his head. He shrugged. "I know how these things go."

She felt a sudden chill when he said *had* and then stopped. What did he mean by *had?* She remembered the day when he'd mentioned the river at his ranch. He'd reacted the same way, as if he didn't want to think about some awful memory.

What tragedies had he suffered and endured? Not that it was any of her business. If he wanted her to know, he would tell her.

As if restless, he rose and dusted his Stetson against his leg. Leaning over the rail of the porch, he said, "It's a beautiful night. The stars are out and the hunter's moon is bright as day."

She found herself rising, too, to stand beside him. Glancing up, she agreed, "Yes, it's a beautiful night. Thanks for keeping us company and telling Kevin stories."

"My pleasure, ma'am," he drawled. Turning abruptly, he faced her. "You didn't ask what the meetings were about that kept me from one of your delicious suppers. Aren't you curious?"

"Yes, ah, no," she sputtered, caught off guard by his unexpected question. "It's really none of my business, Sheriff

# Hard Candy Christmas

Graham." But even as she denied her interest, she felt gratified he wanted to tell her.

He hitched his shoulder toward Kevin. "He's sleeping, Abby, please call me Clint."

"All right, Clint." She laced her fingers together.

"I was late because the word came down from the Southern Pacific today. It's official. The railroad decided to raise its rates, just before the fall shipment of wool." He glanced at her, as if trying to assess her reaction. "Is your father out on a run?"

"Yes."

"He probably doesn't know yet. Not that it matters."

A strange prickly sensation ran down her spine, almost a presentiment of trouble to come. Her first loyalty was to the railroad, but she wished the Southern Pacific hadn't picked this time or place to raise its rates.

"Did the railroad give a reason?" she asked.

"Yes, and we ranchers knew it was coming. The new Interstate Commerce Commission has mandated the use of safety equipment for the railroad, such as mechanical brakes. And I know the safety equipment is necessary. But to pay for the equipment, the railroad is raising their freight rates across the board."

"My eldest brother is a brakeman in St. Louis. He lost three fingers working with manual brakes. And Mr. Weaver—"

"Mr. Weaver, who has one hand," Clint interjected.

"Yes, he lost his hand, using the manual coupler."

"So you know about the innovations?"

"Know of them?" She retorted. "We've been praying for them for years."

"I can't say I blame you. I'm sorry for your brother."

"Thank you," she replied stiffly. "You know, my father is a legend among railroaders," she added. "He started in the switching yards, over twenty-five years ago, and worked his way up to brakeman, then fireman, and finally, engineer. And he's never been seriously injured."

# Hard Candy Christmas

She shook her head. "But my father is the exception. Most men are maimed or killed if they work for the railroad long enough."

"What you say is true, Abby. I won't argue with you. The new equipment is necessary, but it's only one side of the story."

"What do you mean?" Was he finally going to show his true colors and side with the ranchers? After all, the rate increase would hurt him financially.

"The railroads could safeguard their employees and take a smaller operating profit. Financiers and investors have become millionaires overnight from the profits they make on the railroads."

"I didn't know that," she admitted, relieved he wasn't blaming the railroad men.

What he was saying was the railroad owners were abusing their power with both their employees and customers. She shouldn't be surprised; she was well acquainted with greed and the tactics that went with it.

"And it couldn't come at a worse time." He put one foot on the bottom railing of the porch and leaned over the top railing, staring into the night. "A year ago, the government lifted protective tariffs on our wool, making us compete with wool from Australia and South America. None of us ranchers made a profit last year due to foreign competition. Then this year, I lost half of my sheep to bluetongue, as did most of the other ranchers. I don't know how much longer some of us can hang on." He lifted his head and gazed at the stars again. "It's one of the reasons I took this job, to make money for my ranch."

She wanted to ask him what the other reasons were, to find out if they had anything to do with his sister or the river or whatever it was that was bothering him. It wasn't her place, though, so she remained silent. But she couldn't help leaning into him, instinctively moving closer, as if her presence might give him comfort.

"It doesn't sound good. What will you do?"

# Hard Candy Christmas

"I've some ideas. That's why the meetings tonight." He turned his head and looked at her. "Things will work out, you'll see."

"I hope so."

*  *  *

The headless horseman galloped through her dreams, his mount's hooves pounding in her head...pounding...pounding...

Groggy with sleep, Abigail rose to a sitting position. The pounding wasn't in her dreams. Someone was pounding on her door. Glancing at the window, it was still dark out, not even the whisper of dawn. Why would anyone want to rouse her now?

Half asleep, she groped for Kevin's unfamiliar form in her bed. Touching him, she found her son lying quietly on his side, deep in sleep. The pounding hadn't awakened him.

Pitching her voice to a stage whisper, she called out, "I'm coming. Just a minute."

Whoever was at her door must have heard because the pounding stopped.

She grabbed her wrapper from the bottom of the bed and pushed back the covers, swinging her legs over the side. Rising, she threw on the wrapper and belted it tightly at the waist.

In the dark, she fumbled to unlock the door and when she opened it, she found Clint standing there, holding an oil lamp. In the half-shadow from the lamp, his features looked drawn and deep hollows underscored his eyes, frightening her with his grave intensity.

She wrapped her arms around her waist and shivered. "What are you doing?" she asked. "It's not even dawn yet. What's wrong?"

"I hope I didn't wake Kevin." He'd ignored her questions. "No, he's fine. What's wrong, Clint?"

He ran one long-fingered hand through his tousled hair. "There's no easy way to say this, Abby. Brace yourself."

# Hard Candy Christmas

Fear shot through her, a shaft of pure ice, piercing her heart. But Kevin was fine, sleeping peacefully in her bed. Then it could only be…

*And she'd bragged tonight about what a legend her father was.*

"It's your father. He was killed in a train wreck. They think the old manual braking system and some twisted rails are to blame. The engine jumped the tracks."

The world started to spin, slowly at first and then with increasing speed. Clint's face, his voice, everything receded into the background. She felt so cold, so very cold and there was a roaring in her ears, like the rushing of the wind. Her body was heavy and her limbs were like blocks of granite.

Slowly, she slumped down, feeling herself crumpling but unable to stop herself from falling. Then two strong arms came around her, cradling her like a baby, holding her close.

# Hard Candy Christmas

## Chapter Five

Abigail sat at the long mahogany dining room table. Sniffing and fighting back fresh tears, she blew her nose into her sodden handkerchief. Father had been hard and exacting, but she'd loved him despite his mean ways. And without his protection, she was suddenly adrift in a big and frightening world.

At least, for the first time in years, she was surrounded by family. All four of her brothers and sisters and their spouses had come for Father's funeral. And then there was Mr. Samuels, the only attorney in town, who'd joined them after the funeral to read her father's will.

The boarders had been dispatched to the kitchen with Kevin, Elisa, and Juan.

The past week had passed in a blur of telegrams, funeral arrangements, and then each of her siblings arriving with their wife or husband.

At the end of the long table sat Will Junior, her eldest brother and his wife, all the way from St. Louis, riding on his railroad pass to Del Rio. To his left and across the table was her eldest sister, Viola and her traveling salesman husband, come from Dallas. Her younger brother, Paul with his tiny, child-like bride, Sarah, sat next to Viola. They'd come from Arkansas where Paul worked in a lumber mill.

To Kevin's disappointment, none of her siblings had brought their children, preferring to leave the young'uns at home during this time of sorrow.

Sitting next to Abigail was her youngest sister, Leanna, and her husband, Jim, who owned a mercantile in El Paso. Leanna didn't have children, but they still hoped. She and her husband had taken the Southern Pacific east from El Paso to arrive in time for the funeral.

In fact, all her siblings had taken the train to be here in time.

# Hard Candy Christmas

Trains were marvelous things, crossing hundreds of miles in a matter of days. But it had been a train that had killed her father and his crew. No passengers had died because her father's train had been carrying boxcars filled with freight.

Abigail twisted the wet handkerchief in her hands and tried to concentrate on the sonorous voice of the lawyer as he went down a list of modest cash bequests, along with some personal items, such as her father's pocket watch, to various members of her family.

There was a pause as Mr. Samuels turned a page and took a sip from his cup of tea. The room was hushed and tense. All of her sibling's eyes were fixed on the portly Mr. Samuels with his mutton chop whiskers. Abigail averted her gaze and looked down at her lap, twisting her hankie until it was shredded.

Mr. Samuels started again. "I do bequeath and assign to Abigail Kerr Sanford, deed and fee title for the boardinghouse located at 108 Main Street in Del Rio, Texas, along with the sum of five hundred dollars in cash for the upbringing and education of my grandson, Kevin Luke Sanford."

The attorney cleared his throat and finished. "And finally, the remainder and bulk of my estate, in cash and bonds, held in deposit at the Del Rio National Bank, are to be donated to the Texas Presbyterian Diocese in memory of my faith and service to the church. Executed this day, August the…"

A loud buzzing in Abigail's ears drowned the attorney's final words. She was stunned by her father's bequest. She hadn't expected anything from him. He'd never loved her and soon grew to despise her when she'd married poorly and then her husband had stolen his money and deserted her.

Kevin…the bequest must be for father's favorite grandson. She was merely the caretaker of Kevin, and as such, Father had left her the means to raise him. Her eyes filled with tears again at her father's unusual generosity.

With a rattle of papers, Mr. Samuels' looked up and asked, "Any questions?"

# Hard Candy Christmas

Abigail raised her head and glimpsed her eldest brother's face. He scowled and worked his jaw back and forth. Viola was frowning, too, and biting her lip. Paul thrust out his lower lip and cast his gaze upward, as if there was a bug crawling across the ceiling.

The tension in the room was a palpable thing, almost like a living creature, crouched in the corner of the room, waiting to pounce.

Will leapt to his feet and pounded the table, shouting, "Questions, no, Mr. Samuels, I have no questions. I shouldn't have expected more from the old miser! Leaving almost everything to the blessed church when I've a family of five to feed. Leaving me next to nothing after I slaved and sweated for the old skinflint from the time I was eight years old until I was twenty." He shook his head and lowered his voice, "No, I should have known better than to—"

"Mr. Kerr, you forget yourself," the attorney cut in, "speaking of your dead Father in such—"

"And you forget yourself, Mr. Samuels," Viola interjected, pointing her finger at the attorney. "You shouldn't castigate my brother, not knowing what he suffered at our dead father's hands." She rose and fisted her hands on her hips. "This is a family matter, and you're done here. I'm certain Father already paid your fee. You may leave now."

The attorney got to his feet and looked around the table. "I'm sorry to have distressed you in your time of grief." He grabbed his bowler hat and put it on. "I'll leave the document for you and bid you good evening."

Abigail sucked in her breath and got to her feet, feeling awful for Mr. Samuels and wanting to apologize. After all, he was a guest.

Viola rounded the table and thrust her face into Abigail's. "And you, you ungrateful baggage. After all we did for you as a child—for you to turn Father against us and make the most of his passing. Especially after your criminal husband stole thousands of dollars from Father and deserted you."

# Hard Candy Christmas

Abigail gasped and her chin trembled. How could her eldest sister say such a thing? She'd done nothing but slave for her father since her wicked husband had run away with his money. She'd tried to repay her father, making certain the boardinghouse ran smoothly and turned a profit each month. Viola couldn't know what she'd suffered these last six years.

She slumped and a wave of bile rose in her throat. Clutching her stomach, she needed to get away before she threw up on the pristine linen tablecloth she'd laundered and ironed.

Leanna touched her arm and pushed Viola back. "How can you say such to our little sister? You know she had nothing to do with her husband's thievery. And she suffered at his hands, too, she..." Leanna bit her lip.

When Lucas had beaten her and run with the money, Leanna had come home to take care of her. Of all her siblings, only her youngest sister knew what a nightmare her married life had been. And she'd wanted it that way, swearing Leanna to secrecy.

She glanced at Leanna and managed, "Thank you."

With her arms crossed over her roiling stomach, she faced the remainder of her siblings. Their lips were pursed and their eyes hooded and sullen. And they refused to meet her gaze. Avarice and jealousy shone on their faces.

She nodded and fled from the room through the swinging door to the kitchen. The boarders and Kevin were sitting down to supper with Juan and Elisa. They had a huge spread of food to choose from. Everyone in Del Rio and particularly all the Presbyterian ladies had outdone themselves, bringing covered dishes for the grieving family.

*The grieving family—more like the grasping family—except Leanna.*

Not that she could blame them. Living under her father's dominion hadn't been easy. She could understand their rage and frustration. But didn't they realize she was a woman alone with no husband to help raise Kevin? Even her father, miser that he was, had understood how dependent she was.

# Hard Candy Christmas

Elisa stood over the table, dishing out food to the men and her son. As Abigail stormed into the kitchen, all eyes turned to her.

She gritted her teeth and nodded again. "Good evening to y'all." Joining Elisa at the stove, she said, "Please, offer my family supper, too." She touched Elisa's arm. "I would help, but I just need a minute."

Elisa hugged her and said, "*Yo entiendo*, I understand. My sister, Rosa, could come over and help for a few days—if you can afford—"

"Yes, get Rosa, please. I can afford the extra help now." And she could, thanks to her father's bequest. But after her siblings were gone, she'd take up her duties and pay the money back.

*The cash bequest was for Kevin's future, not hers.*

From the corner of her eye, she saw Clint. He'd gotten to his feet when she came into the room, like the other men, but he hadn't sat down again. His gaze was fixed on her.

But she couldn't face him. Didn't want to face him. All she wanted was a little peace and some air.

She grabbed a kerosene lantern and opened the back door, stepping onto the porch. Glancing back, she realized the kitchen lamp light spilled outside, lighting her in silhouette. She hurried down the steps and went to the barn. She needed privacy.

The barn smelled of mustiness and horse and hay and…fresh manure. She went to Clint's mare, Jezebel, and held out her hand.

The mare hung her head over the stall door and nosed her open hand, searching for a carrot or a bite of apple. But she had nothing for the horse. Jezebel snuffled and tossed her head.

Abigail cradled the horse's velvety nose and laid her head against Jezebel's thick neck. And then the tears came again, scalding and boiling from her. Not for her father this time—but for her family—or what was left of her family.

\* \* \*

# Hard Candy Christmas

Clint wanted to go to Abby, needed to go to her. But when he looked at Elisa, the sturdy housekeeper shook her head.

He understood and reluctantly sank into his chair. He'd stayed in the background during the week, after breaking the news to Abby. He'd done what he could and tried to keep Kevin entertained when his duties allowed. But it wasn't enough.

Since All Hallows Eve when she'd collapsed in his arms, he couldn't forget the feel of her body cuddled against him. Couldn't get rid of the smell of vanilla in her hair—the plain and honest scent of her baking. He'd wanted to comfort her then and needed to comfort her now.

He picked at his food and sipped his coffee until the other men finished. This time, he followed them to the front porch and idly listened to the latest gossip. Gossip he'd have to investigate or he'd have an all-out war on his hands.

Tom Weaver wasn't there, and the other men were friendly enough, accepting him because he was the sheriff. They talked openly around him, muttering about sheep ranchers near Langtry, where the train derailment had happened, saying the ranchers had torn up the track in retaliation for the railroad raising its rates.

He'd heard the rumors in town, too, and thought they were a lot of nonsense. But he'd need to take action because the gossip wasn't dying down. If anything, it was getting more virulent with each passing day.

But tonight he wanted to find Abby and take her into his arms again.

The men said good night, and one after the other, they drifted away, either to sleep or down to the Prickly Pear Saloon.

*Was she still outside? Would she want him to comfort her?*

He had to find out. He rounded the three corners of the porch and stared into the night. The lamp shone in the kitchen window, and the back yard was empty. That only left the barn. She liked Jezebel and had let Kevin take riding lessons on his mare. Maybe she was in the barn.

# Hard Candy Christmas

He opened the double doors and slipped inside and saw her, curled in a pile of straw in front of Jezebel's stall. The kerosene lantern she'd taken was sputtering and almost out.

Was she awake? He didn't know, but he didn't want to startle her. Cautious, he cleared his throat.

She lifted her head and stared at him. In the flickering light, he could see the silvery track of her tears. His heart went out to her. He knew how grief could consume you, destroy your days, and make you wonder if your life was worth living.

He prayed she didn't feel that way—she still had Kevin…and him.

She wiped her face with a shredded handkerchief. "Clint, you shouldn't be here. I'm… I'm not myself."

He held up one hand. "I understand. Grief is tough, only time, a lot of time, helps." He wished he could take his own advice, but he wondered if there would ever be enough time to get over losing Jenny and Timothy.

"I don't know what you're saying. Are you grieving too?"

Maybe if he told her his sad tale, it would help. He wasn't good at this, and he'd never talked about his losses with another human being. But he remembered something Jenny had told him long ago—talking about your feelings helped—at least that was what his sister had said.

He cleared his throat again, hoping Jenny was right. He could try. He guessed there was a first time for everything.

"Yes, I've known my share of grief. Am still grieving. It's one of the reasons I took the sheriff's job."

She sat up and ran her fingers through her hair, pulling out bits of straw. He had her attention, and she hadn't asked him to leave again. Maybe his sister had been right.

He pulled a bale of hay over and sat down. Jezebel nickered, probably wanting his attention. But he was afraid to move closer to Abby. He knew how easily she spooked.

She wiped her eyes again. "Tell me about it."

51

# Hard Candy Christmas

He smoothed his hand over the stubble on his chin. "It's not pretty, my past. But if I don't tell you all of it, you won't understand."

She nodded.

"My mother was a…'lady of the night.' We moved from town to town in the West, mostly following the boom times, mining strikes, lumber camps. That sort of thing."

"'A lady of the night'—what does that mean?"

Good Lord, for a married lady, she *was* an innocent. He flushed, praying for the right words to explain. But there weren't any *right* words. The plain, unvarnished truth would have to do.

"My mother was a whore."

She gasped and then covered her mouth with her hand. She shook her head. "I'm sorry, Clint. Sorry for you."

"That I'm a bastard who never knew his father?"

"No, I make no judgments. It wasn't your fault. You can't help who your parents…or your family are."

He gulped and grit filled his eyes. Most people weren't so accepting. But he'd known from the first day Abby was different. Maybe that was what had attracted him or the gut-deep feeling that she needed his protection. All he knew was his arms ached, wanting to hold her and feel her snuggled tight against his chest.

"Thank you for your kindness. Most people…" He hesitated, not wanting to talk about what he'd suffered as the child of a whore. "My mother had another child, a little girl, Jenny, my half-sister. When we were young, we were inseparable. When Jenny turned eight and I was thirteen, I begged my mother to send her away to school, away from the saloons and…"

She dropped her handkerchief and wrapped her arms around her midriff. "That was very noble of you, but how did your mother find the money to—"

"That was the bargain I struck with my mother. I'd quit school…" He paused again, wondering how it would sound, spoken out loud. "We moved around a lot and my schooling was sketchy at best. But I was already a big guy, and I didn't need much sleep.

# Hard Candy Christmas

Found out I could work two jobs and get by and have plenty of money for Jenny's boarding school. My mother, she had a kind heart, but she was frivolous…" He shook his head. "Not much 'horse sense,' you know. Once she saw I could provide for Jenny, she sent her East to school."

"Did Jenny come back? What happened to your mother?"

"My mother died two years later of consumption. Jenny finished her schooling and met one of her roommates' brothers and married well. He was a doctor."

"*Was?* Isn't Jenny and her husband…"

He shook his head.

"Oh, no, I…I'm so sorry for *your* loss." She looked down. "How did it happen?"

"Train wreck, passenger train."

Her head jerked up and she shook it back and forth, slowly. "Oh, no, no, not another train wreck." She met his gaze. "How terrible for you. You loved your sister and sacrificed for her and then…" She clutched the cameo at her throat and twisted the ribbon around her index finger. "I'm sorry, Clint, so very sorry."

He rose and moved closer to her, a few steps away, hoping against hope she'd let him hold her and kiss her and…

*He'd never felt this way about another woman. Why was Abby different?*

"It gets worse, you might as well know all of it. My sister and her husband had a baby, and he survived the train wreck. My sister's husband had no family to speak of. I tracked the baby, Timothy, down." He lifted his shoulders and let them drop. "The poor mite had no one, just me. I'd become a bounty hunter because the money was good. I didn't spend much—saved most of my bounties. With the money I bought a sheep ranch on the Devil's River and settled down. Settled down to give Timothy a home."

"Where's Timothy? I'm surprised you didn't bring him to town. Kevin would love to have…"

Her eyes widened and she stared at him.

He shook his head again. "I lost Timothy two years ago on the river." He removed his Stetson and dusted it on his leg. He

# Hard Candy Christmas

trained his gaze on the hay-covered floor. "Most times, Devil's River is little better than a stream with a few deep pools. And Timothy grew up wading and swimming there. But two years ago, when I was out with the *vaqueros* in the north pasture, rounding up strays, Timothy decided to go swimming. And Leticia, my housekeeper, let him."

He sank back onto the bale of hay and hunched his shoulders. He clenched his jaw and ground his teeth. "That's when it happened. There was a thunderstorm in the hills and the river filled up faster than you could..." He paused and his eyes filled with tears. "We found Timothy, three days later, five miles downstream... He would have been eight years old the next week. He was all I lived for. I wanted him to inherit my ranch and—"

"Don't! Don't say it." She covered her ears with her hands. "I can't stand it." She rose and stood before him, tears trailing down her cheeks. "Too much sorrow, too much grief. There aren't enough words, there isn't enough...anything."

He rose and put his arms around her waist. And she didn't pull away. Instead, she slumped against him and buried her face in his chest.

Talking about what had happened made the grief fresh again, like a knife cutting out his guts. But at the same time, he felt a breath of relief, as if he'd cauterized a gaping wound, and stopped the bleeding.

*Jenny had always been wise for her years.*

He rested his chin on the top of Abby's head and sighed. Her hair was soft and silky. And holding her in his arms helped— just touching her. He hoped she felt the same way.

She lifted her head and gazed at him. "Kevin reminds you of Timothy?"

He nodded. "Yes, being with your son is the only thing that's helped. I took the sheriff's job to make money and restock my ranch. But the real reason was to get away from the river. I couldn't stand to look at it—to be reminded of what happened."

# Hard Candy Christmas

He trailed his fingertips along her cheek and down her throat. "I know I'm a crazy man, Abby. But being around you and Kevin makes me less crazy." He snagged her gaze. "That should be a good thing, right?"

"Yes, Clint, a good thing." She ran her pink tongue over her ruby-red lips.

And God help him, he bent his head and touched his lips to hers.

At first, she started to pull away, but he made himself go slow. He brushed her lips lightly, gently. She sighed and leaned into his embrace. He caressed her lips with his, angling his head this way and then that, but careful not to seek entrance to her mouth.

She might be the mother of an eight-year-old boy, but she acted like a virgin.

He cradled her and she snuggled closer, offering her mouth to him.

He groaned.

*Would he ever get enough of her?*

Clint's groan startled her, bringing her back to the moment, making her realize she was a married woman, allowing another man to kiss her.

*Lucas' kisses had been sweet at first—sweet and tender. But once they'd married, he'd shown his true side, his twisted desires. He'd forced her to do unnatural things with her mouth and tongue to arouse him. And if he couldn't...wasn't able...then he'd taunt her and say terrible things. Tell her she wasn't a real woman.*

And now, another man was touching her, kissing her. She jerked her head back and pushed at Clint's chest. "I can't." She shook her head. "I can't."

He stepped back. "I understand. It's too soon after your father's death." He took her hand and interlaced his fingers with hers. "I apologize, but I've never told anyone else what I told you and..."

"But I'm a married woman, Clint."

# Hard Candy Christmas

"How long since you saw your husband?"

She shook her head. "Six years, but it doesn't matter. In the eyes of God, I'm still married."

He exhaled. "I know, I know. Please accept my apology."

Tentatively, she reached out and touched the right-hand corner of his mouth, letting her fingers trace the scar that tugged at his full lips. "How did it happen?"

He covered her hand with his. "Oh, that's from when I was a boy."

"And?"

"Got in a fight with a bigger boy. He pulled a knife."

She gasped. "What were you fighting over? It must have been awfully important."

He shrugged. "Thought it was at the time. I was fighting over my mother's honor. I learned not to...after that and...after the school master explained to me."

She shuddered and crossed her arms. Between her father and Lucas, her life hadn't been a bed of roses. But she couldn't begin to imagine what Clint had gone through with his mother and her profession.

# Hard Candy Christmas

## Chapter Six

Abigail turned away and went back to Jezebel's stall. She reached up and grasped the mare's halter, stroking the horse's nose. "You've been so honest with me, Clint." She slanted a look at him. "So honest, I can do no less for you." She faced him and tilted her chin up. "It's not just about my marriage and my father's passing."

Shaking her head, she said, "I'll tell you the real reason I was hiding in the barn. Not because of my grief but because my family, or at least, my oldest brother and sister attacked me because Father left me the boardinghouse and the rest of his fortune to the Presbyterian Church."

He sucked in his breath and squeezed his eyes shut.

She shook her head again. "That was Father, he never cared about people's feelings—only his money. He left me the house so I could raise Kevin." She paused and licked her lips. "But my father didn't protect me from my husband...he could have. But he didn't care enough."

He reached out his hand. "Oh, Abby, I didn't know." His eyes widened and he let his hand drop. "Protect you, what do you mean?"

Her neck and face heated, and she looked away. "I can't, can't say anymore. Not right now. Maybe one day."

*How could she tell this good man what her husband had done? Why she feared a man's touch and kisses? But at the same time, a tiny part of her craved to be close to Clint.*

"To be fair to my brothers and sisters, they were victims of my father, too. He made them quit school and work for him, turning over their wages, from the time they were Kevin's age. Even the girls took in sewing." She shook her head. "Except for me. I'm the youngest and when Mama died, my brothers and sisters, like you helped Jenny, begged my father to let me finish my schooling. He agreed because they fought for me. I'm the only one who had a childhood. The rest were my father's slaves."

# Hard Candy Christmas

She faced him again. "So, you see, I can't fault them for being disappointed and taking it out on me."

"But you didn't make your father leave his fortune to the church or ask for the boardinghouse, did you?"

"No, but it doesn't matter, does it?" She twisted her hands together. Spying her dropped handkerchief, she bent and picked it up, stuffing the shredded cloth into her apron pocket.

She straightened. "The damage is done. I'm the scapegoat. They know Father didn't care, didn't care enough to leave them anything." She dropped her head and hunched her shoulders.

She'd already cried a river. Her mouth and throat felt like a desert. She hadn't known her body held so many tears. She sniffed and wiped her eyes with a corner of her apron.

"Abby, you can't—"

"I know, I know. I can't change anything. At least, not about what Father did." She touched her mother's cameo, her talisman, the only thing that remained of Jean Kerr. "Maybe I can make it up to my brothers and sisters. I could sell the boardinghouse and split the proceeds with them. Then, at least, I would have done the fair thing."

"But they're all married, and you're alone in the world. As you said, your father wanted you to take care of Kevin."

"I've saved some money. Elisa taught me how to sew bridal trousseaus. With what I've saved and my share of the house, I'd have enough to open a shop." She hesitated, considering. "Leanna, my youngest sister, and I are close. She defended me when Will and Viola... She and her husband don't have children. Kevin and I could live with them in El Paso while I get my shop going. And her husband owns a mercantile. He could refer me business."

He rubbed his chin. "I know you want to be fair with your brothers and sisters, but please think it over before—"

The barn door squeaked, startling them both. Clint grabbed the butt of his holstered Colt pistol and spun around.

# Hard Candy Christmas

Henry Palmer stuck his head inside. "Sheriff Graham." He exhaled and his gaze skimmed her. His eyes narrowed and then he looked back at Clint.

"Whew, am I glad I found you, Sheriff. Been looking all over." He hitched his thumb over his shoulder. "Big brawl down at the Prickly Pear. We need you *now*."

Clint nodded and let go of his Colt. "I'll be right there, Henry."

Facing Abby again and for the benefit of nosy Mr. Palmer, he said, "Thank you, Mrs. Sanford for checking on Jezebel and getting her to eat some carrots. She's been off her feed, and I was worried. Seems like she's perked up now."

"My pleasure, Sheriff Graham. Kevin has enjoyed learning to ride your mare. I wanted to help."

He replaced his Stetson and tipped the brim. "I'll wish you good evening, Mrs. Sanford."

\* \* \*

Clint drew his Colt pistol and fired it in the air.

The heaving, brawling mass of men jumped apart, sputtering and shaking their heads. Eyes wide and filled with fright, they looked around and their gazes settled on him.

From the looks of things, the vicious gossip had done its work. Tables and chairs were overturned and broken. Mugs of beer lay on their sides, their smelly brew soaking into the sawdust-strewn floorboards.

*And the familiar lines were drawn.*

Sheep ranchers on one side and railroaders on the other. Despite having only one hand to fight with, Tom Weaver was in the thick of it.

Clint shook his head. Some people never learned.

Tom Weaver clenched his jaw and lurched forward. "We don't need you, Sheriff." He spat on the floor. "Just a friendly tussle. That's all."

# Hard Candy Christmas

"Oh, but I think you do need me, Mr. Weaver. Unless you want me to pull you in for disturbing the peace." He glanced down at the tin star pinned to his shirt. "I'm the law here and whether you like it or not, I'll decide what's a friendly tussle."

He straightened his spine and let his gaze sweep the room. "What's the problem here?" He wanted to ask who'd started the fight but knew better. No one was going to tell him that.

Pete Baker, the man who'd taken a pot shot at Sheriff Cunningham and scared him off, stepped up. "These damned railroaders think we ranchers pulled up track and caused Mr. Kerr's train to wreck." He fisted his hands and raised them, ready to go at it again. "The lying sons of bitches."

"Pete, how'd you like to spend another night in jail. Wasn't one night in that hell hole enough for you?" Clint asked.

Slowly, hesitantly, Baker lowered his fisted hands, his chin in the air and his stance guarded, as if he expected to be jumped at any moment.

"Okay, I've had enough of this gossip about the train wreck," Clint said, raising his voice over the muttering men. "Since everyone is so doggone interested in the wreck and can't wait until the railroad investigates—"

"We ain't trusting no railroad investigation." Autry Lamb spoke up. Autry was a neighbor of his, his spread lay west of Clint's ranch, along the river.

Clint nodded. "I thought that might be the case." He unknotted the bandana at his neck and wiped his face. "I've been thinking on it, and I believe I have a fair solution. We're going to convene our own investigation. I'll need six men, three railroaders and three ranchers. I'll head up the team, but everyone will have a say-so. What do y'all think?"

The ranchers and railroaders each bunched together, discussing and gesticulating. He shook his head again. If he didn't take the initiative, they could argue all night.

"Weaver and Baker," he barked.

# Hard Candy Christmas

The men fell silent. Both Weaver and Baker straightened and looked at him.

"Each of you pick two men. You're my official deputies for the investigation. Pick your men and meet me in front of the Sheriff's office at sunup tomorrow. Be sure you have a sound mount, rations, and a bedroll. We'll be riding to Langtry and be out for a couple of nights. We'll take a look at the damage and decide on what we find. Then we'll compare what we uncover with the railroad's results."

Weaver and Baker stood with their feet wide apart and their mouths open, gaping at him.

"Weaver, will your railroaders be able to take the time off?"

Weaver shut his mouth and nodded.

"Good, we need to get this done before shearing time. I'm assuming you ranchers won't have a problem being out for a few days."

"Nah, no problem, Sheriff," Baker said.

"Okay, that's settled." He turned to Fred, the barkeep. "Who owes what for the broken chairs and spilled beer?"

Fred wiped his hands on his apron. "Well, now, let me take a look." He moved from behind the long, wooden bar and glanced over the damage.

"Bout three dollars should do it, Sheriff, but I couldn't tell who started—"

"Here's your three dollars, Fred." He flipped three silver dollars to the barkeep and Fred caught them in his right hand. He nodded. "Much obliged, Sheriff."

Clint brushed the brim of his Stetson with one finger. "Tomorrow morning, gentlemen. And don't make me come and get you."

\* \* \*

Abby pushed open the swinging door to the dining room. Supper was over, her boarders served by Elisa and Rosa. Her brothers and sisters had gone home, back to their children and jobs.

61

# Hard Candy Christmas

Leanna and her husband had lingered the longest until Leanna's husband had insisted he needed to get back to his store. Reluctantly, she'd seen them off that afternoon.

Clint sat at his usual place, sipping a mug of coffee. She stopped and took a deep breath, startled by his sudden appearance. He hadn't been there for dinner. And she hadn't seen him since the night in the barn.

Her gaze swept him, lingering on his full lips and muscular forearms. He'd held her and kissed her. She shook her head, not quite believing it. And she'd missed him, missed him more than she cared to admit.

"Mrs. Sanford, I just got back from Langtry. Elisa was kind enough to give me a cup of coffee."

"Supper is over, but I know we have some ham and potatoes left—"

"That's kind of you, but I ate at the hotel again." He smiled his lop-sided grin and there was a twinkle in his eye. "Not half as good as the food here, but I needed to meet with the townsfolk as soon as I got back."

She found herself smiling for the first time since she'd learned of her father's accident. "I guess we'll forgive you again, Sheriff Graham, since it was in the line of duty."

He nodded and lowered his voice. "Is there a quiet place we can talk?"

His question took her by surprise. He wanted to talk with her privately? She had a lot of questions for him, too, and she wanted to tell him how much Kevin had missed him. But should they meet privately? Would he kiss her again? Did she want him to kiss her again?

*And what if someone, like nosy Mr. Palmer, broke in on them?*

She should tell him no, but she couldn't do it, couldn't turn him down.

"We can talk in my late father's study. With the door open for propriety's sake. Will that do?"

# Hard Candy Christmas

"Yes, that will do." He rose and grabbed his Stetson from a peg on the wall.

"This way." She led him to the other side of the house and opened a door. The smell of her father's pipe tobacco and bay rum washed over her. She sagged against the doorknob.

Clint clasped her elbow. "Steady now. Are you certain you're ready for this? Maybe the parlor would be—"

"No, no, I've got to face it sometime. All the boardinghouse ledgers and books are here. And I need to balance the books for October. I've let it go long enough."

"Okay, if you're certain." He guided her to a chair in front of the roll-top desk, careful to leave the room's door ajar. Then he took the seat across from her.

"Kevin missed you," she said. "He kept asking and wondering when you would get back. I didn't know what to tell him. Just the gossip going around."

He swiped his chin with his hand. "I'm sorry I didn't have time to tell you—"

"That's what I thought, and it wasn't really any of my business but—"

"Did you miss me, Abby?"

She glanced at the half-open door and then looked down, twisting her hands in her lap.

*Should she tell him the truth? Wouldn't it send him the wrong message? But he'd been brutally honest with her that night in the barn. He deserved the truth.*

"Yes, I missed you." She lifted her head and gazed into his blue eyes. "Rumor has it you went to Langtry to investigate the...my father's, uh, wreck."

"Yes, but the train had already been cleared by the railroad. I had to try and find out *why* the wreck happened." He shook his head. "I had to move fast to avoid an all-out war. So, I took three ranchers and three railroaders."

"Including Tom Weaver?"

# Hard Candy Christmas

He nodded. "I had to be unbiased. It was the only way to calm both sides."

"That was clever of you, Clint."

"Why, thank you, ma'am," he drawled. "I'll take that as a compliment."

He reached for her hands, but she glanced over her shoulder at the open door. He dropped his hands and clutched the chair arms.

"We looked over the rails. Your father's train derailed on a side track, according to the railroaders, to let the passenger train go by and stay on time."

"Did you find anything?"

"Yep, rotten boards, missing spikes and twisted rails, most likely from a flashflood that swept through the cut in the hills…a lot like what caught my nephew…and…"

She exhaled, not realizing she'd been holding her breath. "Oh, Clint, I'm sorry it had to remind you of Timothy." She shook her head. "But I'm glad you learned the truth. That no one damaged the rails and caused the wreck. That it was weather and…neglect." She wanted to reach out to him but was concerned someone would pass by and think the wrong thing.

"And it's terrible to hear the railroad didn't maintain the tracks as they should. That…their negligence…helped to kill my father." She clasped her hands together. "What you said about the railroad owners is probably true—everything for profit, nothing for their employees."

He rose and patted her shoulder. "I wanted you to know the truth, even though it wasn't the best of news. And at the hotel, we told half the town what we'd found." He sat down again. "Then I stayed to organize the ranchers into a cooperative."

"What's a cooperative?"

"A cooperative is where a group of shippers, who have the same kind of freight, group together and bargain with the railroad. In this case, we sheep ranchers will ship our wool together. And

# Hard Candy Christmas

when we bargain with the railroad as a group, we should get lower rates, based on volume."

"What a marvelous idea. Did you read about this, too?"

He grinned and wiped his forehead with his hand. "Whew! Was that another compliment?" He winked at her. "Keep this up, and I could get used to it."

She smiled. He was smart and kind and good. Why hadn't she met Clint Graham instead of Lucas Sanford? But then she wouldn't have Kevin.

He took his seat again. "Have you decided what you're going to do, Abby? I didn't see any of your brothers and sisters around. Have they left?"

"Yes, they're all gone. And no, I haven't decided what to do. I offered to sell the boardinghouse, but no one really wanted that. They were angry with our father for cheating them." She sighed. "Just as I thought. They apologized and Leanna and her husband stayed until today. I told her about my idea for a bridal store, but she said I should wait at least a year to make a decision." She lifted one shoulder in a half-shrug. "For now, that's what I'm doing."

"Your sister sounds very wise, like my sister, Jenny."

He leaned forward and took her hands. This time she let him. And she didn't care who saw them. Twining her fingers with his calloused ones felt good and...right. She drew strength from him, thinking maybe things would get better now. Maybe the worst was behind her.

"I think you need some time to yourself, Abby. You and Kevin. And I have to leave again for my ranch. It's fall shearing time. I still have half of my sheep left, and I need the money from the shearing."

"I thought ranchers only sheared in the spring when winter was over."

He nodded. "We shear in late spring. And some shear only once a year, but a few of us have found you get a better grade of wool and less prepping if you shear twice a year." He squeezed her

# Hard Candy Christmas

hands. "The climate in south Texas allows us to shear twice. Most winters are mild and there's seldom a problem."

"Oh, I see." She nodded. "Kevin will be disappointed. Are you leaving again soon?"

"I need to go in the next couple of days after I get the wool cooperative organized." His fingers stroked the palms of her hands, sending tingling sensations through her and raising goose bumps on her arms.

His voice was low and husky when he said, "I want you and Kevin to come with me. Visit my ranch. Between the shearing we can picnic and Kevin can practice his riding. I'll even teach him a little about ranching. Who knows, maybe it will come in handy."

He gazed at her, and the look in his eyes was silently pleading.

"What about school? Kevin will miss school."

"It will only be for a little over a week." He shook his head. "My herd is depleted and shearers move fast. You'll see. And besides, a lot of the ranchers' kids will miss school. And Kevin's a smart boy. He can make up the work."

"I know he'd love a holiday. Christmas seems so far away when you're eight years old, though it's just around the corner."

"Say yes, Abby. Elisa has help now, right? And you could use the time away. It will be good for you and Kevin…after what you've been through." He looked down at their intertwined hands. "And you and your son being there with me…it would help me to face the ranch and the river again. Say yes, please."

How could she refuse him? She wanted time away from the boardinghouse and the grieving she couldn't quite put away. And Kevin would love staying on a real ranch and riding the range. Clint needed them…needed her. She could hear it in his voice.

She looked up and met his gaze. A smile tipped her lips. "Thank you for the invitation. How can I say no? Kevin will be pleased."

# Hard Candy Christmas

## Chapter Seven

A soft breeze lifted the hair from her neck and caressed her cheeks. Late November in southwest Texas was a special time. The weather was mild but sunny, not too hot or not too cold, just right.

*Like somebody's porridge in her son's favorite fairy tale of "Goldilocks and The Three Bears."*

She cantered alongside Clint, allowing the wind to play havoc with her hair. He'd asked her to leave her bonnet off, and she'd done so, knowing the bright sunshine would be mild…and there would be no gossips to remark on her appearance. Not on Clint's ranch.

Kevin, riding a dappled roan mare called Esther, who was several hands smaller than Jezebel, roamed far ahead, crossing the pasture and urging his mount to the top of a hill.

Her son reined the mare around and waved, calling at the top of his lungs, "Look at me!"

She and Clint reined in and waved back, grinning.

"He loves it here," she said.

"I'm glad, Abby, really glad. I've enjoyed having y'all here."

Abby's mare, a gleaming chestnut named Rachel, sidled next to Jezebel and whickered, throwing her head over Jezebel's neck. Abby pulled her mare's head up and patted her neck, "Why are all your horses mares, Clint? And why are they all named for women in the Bible?"

Clint's grin widened. "Because I like female horses. They make the best mounts. Geldings are too surly, and stallions too rambunctious. Mares are the best." He paused and stroked Jezebel's mane, sifting the long brown hair through his fingers. "And I like the old Bible names. Makes my mares seem even sweeter."

Abigail snorted. "Not the name Jezebel. She was a bad woman in the Bible, a heathen, through and through."

Clint laughed and swung his gaze to her. "Kinda like my mother?"

# Hard Candy Christmas

A wave of heat crept up her neck "Oh, Clint, I didn't mean that…I didn't think, I, ah—"

"No matter. I'm just joshing you."

She relaxed and said, "You must have had a reason for calling her Jezebel."

"Yep. That I did." He nodded. "When I went to break her, she was a bitch to…" He wiped his hand over his face. "Uh, that is, she was awful hard to break to halter and saddle." His face turned an unhealthy shade of red that matched the bright bandana he kept knotted at his neck.

It was her turn to laugh, knowing he'd embarrassed himself.

She lifted her head and gazed into his blue-as-the-sky eyes. Their gazes caught, snagged, and held. She felt his gaze touch her mouth and linger on her neck, trailing down to rest on her bosom.

And she knew exactly what he was thinking…without him saying one word. Her body responded, too, tightening and leaping to life. Her breasts flushed, and her nipples pebbled, pushing against her camisole. Lower, the core of her body felt molten, liquid with heat. She wanted to rub herself against the saddle, she ached so down there.

She'd never felt like this before. Not with Lucas, her husband. Not before him or after. For the first time in her life, she was acutely aware of her body and all the secret sensations a simple look could arouse.

She shook her head, trying to shrug off the way she felt. "We should start back." Looking up, she made a show of squinting at the sun. "Isn't it getting late? Won't Leticia expect us for supper?"

He nodded and put two fingers in his mouth, whistling and then calling out, "Kevin, time to go back to the ranch house. Come on."

Kevin spurred his mare. And Esther scrabbled down the hill, her front legs straight in front of her and her hooves grabbing for the dirt. Kevin whooped at the top of his lungs and circled them, galloping off toward the ranch house. "Race ya'll there. Can't beat me and Esther."

# Hard Candy Christmas

They shook their heads together and glanced at each other, exchanging a grownup look. Urging their mounts forward, they cantered after her son.

"Kevin has become quite the rider, hasn't he?" she said.

Clint nodded. "Yes, ma'am, your son is a natural."

"Hmmm, I think you're prejudiced, Sheriff Graham."

"I think you're right, Mrs. Sanford."

They giggled.

Her son had disappeared through a copse of live oaks that grew in a draw, leading down to the river. So far, Clint had shown them everything on his ranch, except the land fronting the Devil's River.

They rode under the trees and Clint reined in, stopping short.

Abigail stopped beside him, suddenly alert to possible danger. Had Clint seen a rattlesnake or was there something else?

"What's the matter?" she asked.

He glanced up at the rough-bark branch of a live oak tree overhanging the winding path. From the branch hung a light-green, twigged plant with white berries.

"Mistletoe." He pointed over her head. "You know what mistletoe is good for, don't you?"

She knew, but she didn't want to make it easy for him. "No, what's mistletoe good for?"

His mouth gaped and his eyes widened. "For kissing, of course, everyone knows that."

She nudged Rachel forward, laughing. "Only at Christmas. Not quite Christmas yet, Clint."

He snorted and thundered after her. And she could hear him muttering, "Close enough, it's close enough to Christmas."

* * *

Abigail stretched out her arms and flopped over in the big, soft bed. Outside her open window, a mockingbird whistled and cawed, mimicking another bird.

# Hard Candy Christmas

She'd slept like a baby again. Clint's ranch was restful, and her room was far from the clatter of the kitchen. And Leticia was an excellent housekeeper. At first, Abigail had been surprised to find Leticia at the ranch, especially after what had happened to Timothy.

But Clint was a good and fair man; and he must have known Leticia hadn't meant Timothy harm. She shook her head. Most people wouldn't have been as forgiving.

She couldn't fault his judgment, though. Leticia had welcomed her warmly. Over her protestations, Abigail had helped out in the kitchen, especially at dinner. But for the most part, Leticia took care of them. And Abigail had learned it was good to be pampered and sleep late for a change. Something she hadn't done since she was a child.

Their visit to Clint's ranch had been pure heaven. But this was their last day. Clint had proudly shown them his one hundred and sixty acres. And he'd worked with Kevin on Esther, helping her son to become an accomplished rider. They'd wandered and picnicked during the day and played checkers and shelled pecans in front of the fireplace at night.

Clint had included her and Kevin in the shearing, a dusty and brutal-appearing business, to her way of thinking, with the docking of new lambs' tails and the dousing of them for worms. Clint had even taught her son how to shear, which was a lot harder to do than it looked.

She shook her head, knowing it would be hard for her son to return home to his books and classroom.

*And how would it be for her—to return home—to a place that held such unhappy memories?*

She didn't like thinking about it. Clint would be there, too, of course, and that would help, but still... Sinking her hands into the soft feather mattress, she levered herself up and swung her legs over the side of the bed. She needed to make her way to the outhouse, but first she'd dress and brush her hair.

# Hard Candy Christmas

For their last day Clint had promised them a special treat, a picnic beside the river. He'd surprised her with his offering. The shearing crew had left the day before, and she'd thought Clint would take them back to town without going near the river.

She liked to think Clint's offer meant their visit had helped…helped him to heal. At least, she hoped so.

* * *

Clint raised his arms and helped Abby dismount. He held her tightly, and she slid down the length of his body. He stifled a groan. Just feeling her against him, he grew and lengthened, hard as a fence post.

And Abby must have felt his body's response, too, because her eyes widened and she licked her lips. And oh, how he'd love to kiss her, right here and right now. But not in front of her son. Not yet, not until there was an understanding between them.

*An understanding…when had he decided to marry her? Because that was where he was headed, wasn't it?*

She threw him a sidelong glance and backed up a step.

He moved to Jezebel and undid a knot holding the quilt bunched behind his saddle and handed it to Abby. She took the quilt from him and wandered toward the river, stopping on a knoll overlooking the rushing, tumbling water.

He closed his eyes and said a silent prayer for strength.

*Why had he suggested this? They were leaving tomorrow. Was it some kind of test he'd given himself? And if it was—would he get through it?*

Chewing the soft inside of his mouth, he managed to swallow, fighting down the bile in his throat. He grabbed the picnic basket Leticia had packed. His housekeeper had filled it to the brim with biscuit sandwiches stuffed with slabs of ham and chunks of Cheddar cheese, along with deviled eggs, homemade pickles, and a peach cobbler.

Abby had returned and proudly pointed at Kevin, ranging over the pasture on Esther. "I can't get over how easily he's learned to ride."

# Hard Candy Christmas

"I told you the boy was a natural." He stroked his jaw. "I should give him Esther, don't you think?" He unknotted two canteens with sweet tea and slung them over his shoulder.

Abby covered her mouth with one hand. "Oh, Clint, I don't know... A horse is such a big responsibility. And I would have to feed her. I don't know..."

"Make Kevin responsible for her keep. You have another stall in the barn. He'd only need to make a little money to keep her in hay and oats."

She turned on him, her green eyes flashing and her hands fisted at her waist. "I don't want him to work—not like my brothers and sisters. I don't want that for his childhood."

He understood her position, given what her family had been through. But he disagreed. If children worked or did chores and learned to be responsible for things *they* wanted, it was different than what her father had done.

He followed her to the quilt and set the basket and canteens down. "Why don't you ask Kevin what he wants, to have Esther and work odd jobs or not have a horse?"

She lifted her chin and looked at him. He could almost see the wheels turning in her head. She nodded. "You're right. It's only fair to give Kevin the choice. I think I see the difference from what my father did... It might be a good way to teach him responsibility."

He touched her arm. "I'm glad you understand what I meant."

She leaned into him, and he ached to take her into his arms and kiss her until she begged for air. But her son wasn't far away, and she'd avoided him in the live oak copse under the mistletoe.

*What did she want from him? A friendship? He didn't know if he could leave it at that—he'd never wanted a woman like this before. Never felt as if he was destined to share his life with a woman.*

Not long after the food was spread out, Kevin had wolfed down his lunch in a matter of moments. And then he'd headed

# Hard Candy Christmas

straight for the river. For a young boy, the river held an irresistible pull. Thinking about it, made Clint's heart ache.

He had managed to choke down a few bites of Leticia's cooking with the help of generous swallows of sweet tea. He'd stayed on the quilt with Abby while Kevin ranged up and down the river, tossing stones into the water. Kevin had even shucked off his boots and gone wading for a few minutes, but luckily, this time of the year, the water was too cold and he'd come back fast enough.

But the whole time Kevin was at the river, Clint couldn't take his eyes off him, couldn't relax. He was wound as tight as the old grandfather clock in his ranch house's parlor.

Abby, God bless her, had rested her hand on his thigh as they sat with their legs stretched out on the quilt, letting the touch of her hand reassure him that nothing terrible would happen.

A flock of his sheep came into view and they filed by, one-by-one, down to the river to drink.

Clint plucked a blade of grass and nibbled on it, watching his sheep. "Carlos, my foreman, thinks I should replace some of the sheep with goats. A lot of ranchers are doing it. Goats forage on weeds and brush the sheep won't eat. It would be a better use of the land. And mohair is fashionable in Europe right now." He spit out the blade of grass. "I want to do a little research when we get back to town, but I'm seriously considering it."

"Is that what they call goats' coats—mohair? I never knew. If you cross to México, there are a lot of blankets and serapes made from mohair. Elisa has a goat-hair serape she wears when it rains, and she says it sheds water."

"Yeah, the Mexicans have been raising goats on this land for a couple of centuries. And the goats give rich milk for cheese, too."

"Sounds like a good idea, Clint."

He nodded and looked up to see Kevin coming back from the river. Clint hoped they could wrap this up and return to the safety of the ranch house.

But the boy had a shit-eating grin on his face and was hiding something behind his back. He skidded to a halt at the edge of the

# Hard Candy Christmas

quilt and held out his hands, showing what he'd been hiding, an old cane fishing pole and a dented tin can, overflowing with dirt.

"Look what I got, Ma and Clint. Miguel gave me the pole, and Leticia let me dig for worms in her vegetable garden." He angled his gaze at Clint. "I've never been fishing, Sheriff, would you teach me how to fish, please."

Clint sucked in his breath, not knowing how to respond, not wanting to appear a coward in the boy's eyes. But he couldn't tell Kevin about Timothy. It just wouldn't be right to call up the specter of his nephew and dampen Kevin's enthusiasm.

He shut his eyes for a moment. He wasn't surprised by Miguel's gift before the shearing crew had moved on. Miguel was their foreman, and he'd asked to fish the river while the crew had been camped here. Clint had readily agreed.

But Leticia. He shook his head. He couldn't believe she'd been complicit in this…not after what had happened and him forgiving her.

*Maybe she felt it was time for him to move on. But it wasn't her place to push him.*

Kevin must have seen him shake his head because the boy's face fell and his shoulders drooped. The cane pole fell to the ground, forgotten.

Abby rose to her feet and went to her son. "The Sheriff isn't feeling well right now. What if I showed you how to fish? I used to fish when I was young girl. I think I know how to thread a worm on a hook."

"Aw, Ma, I'd rather the Sheriff and me—"

"Sheriff Graham has a touch of indigestion." She glanced sharply at her son.

"Oh, all right then." He hunched his shoulders and kicked at a dirt clod.

Clint gulped. It was kind of Abby to understand what he was going through and try to rescue him. But he couldn't let her

# Hard Candy Christmas

face his demons for him, and he didn't want to disappoint Kevin either. It was obvious the boy wanted a man to teach him to fish.

*But could he face the river...for Kevin's sake? It was harder than facing down a drunk, vicious killer during his bounty hunter days.*

He shook himself. It had to be done, especially if he was thinking about marrying Abby and making Kevin part of his family.

He got to his feet. "Your Mama's being kind, but I'm feeling better now." He leaned down and picked up the tin can and poked at the dirt inside. "Hmmm, looks like a bunch of good worms."

Kevin's face lit up like a Christmas candle. "What kinda fish do you think we'll get? Miguel said the fishing is awful good here."

"Yep, Devil's River has some nice fishing. I'd say we'll get some perch and small-mouth bass. Maybe even a catfish or two. All good eating fried up in corn meal."

Kevin tugged on his arm. "What are we waiting for?"

Clint managed a grin. "Let's go then." He threw his arm around Kevin's shoulders but stopped long enough to turn and look back at Abby. "You want to come with us?"

She stood at the edge of the quilt, gazing at them, as if rooted to the spot. Her green eyes were watery and she was fingering the cameo she always wore.

She shook her head. "No, you two go ahead. I'll stay here and repack the picnic basket and enjoy the sunshine. But don't take all afternoon. Time enough for another day."

His heart wrenched in his chest, she was so kind and understanding and...wise. Like his sister Jenny had been. Love poured through him, chilling his skin for a second with the intensity of the feeling.

He nodded. "We won't be long. The fishing here is pretty easy. Bunch of hungry fish, especially for juicy worms." He winked at her. "Holler if you need us."

# Hard Candy Christmas

## Chapter Eight

Abby sat across from Clint in front of the crackling fireplace. The night had turned cool and the fireplace's warmth was welcome. Soon Christmas would be upon them. She slanted a glance at Clint and knew exactly what to give him for Christmas.

But first, they'd need to get back to town, and in some ways, she dreaded it. The ranch had been peaceful for her and a much-needed holiday for her son.

Clint had faced his fears and taken her son fishing. They'd brought back a string of bass and catfish in no time. Leticia had fried them up for dinner with corn meal hush puppies and string beans from her garden.

Kevin had been exhausted from the long day and elated when Clint offered him Esther for keeps. Her son had whooped and hollered and jumped up and down, thanking them both over and over. With his chest puffed out, he'd trooped off to bed early, eager to get home and show off his new horse to his classmates.

For the first time, Clint had brought out liquor and poured them each a glass of whiskey, neat. She seldom imbibed, so she took tiny sips, but her head was light and her thoughts warm and fuzzy. They sat in companionable silence, staring at the fire.

Since she'd been a little girl, fires had fascinated her. She loved to gaze at the deep red heart and dancing blue flames. The fire mesmerized her with its changing shapes and flickering light.

She closed her eyes and settled her head against the back of the horsehair settee. She could almost imagine herself living here, in peace and contentment with Clint...almost.

She heard a rustle and opened her eyes to find Clint had risen from his chair and crossed to her, going down on his knees before her. He took her hand in his.

Her heart fluttered and rose to her throat. She looked at him and saw the naked yearning in his eyes. She knew that look,

# Hard Candy Christmas

understood his longing. For she'd learned about yearning from him, and it was all she could do to keep her feelings in check.

He pulled her forward and she let him. Going into his arms felt natural, natural and right. Not like what she'd lived through before...not like Lucas. But she wouldn't think about Lucas now, couldn't think about him or she'd flee and hide.

And she wanted Clint to kiss her...and touch her. To teach her the gentle side of loving.

His arms tightened around her waist and he lowered his head, capturing her mouth. Like the whisper of a moth's wings, his lips gently brushed hers. His mouth was warm and moist, and soft, too, so soft for such a big, rough man. She kissed him back, savoring the taste of him.

And her body responded again, just as it had before. Her nipples hardened and peaked into tender buds. Between her thighs, she ached and grew wet. All of her skin was one sensitive organ that felt tight, like a too ripe plum. She needed him closer, wanted to rub against him like a purring cat. Wanted to feel his rock-hard chest crush her breasts and his calloused hands stroke her...all over.

*Could she? Did she dare? Could she be as strong as Clint had been and face down her demons?*

His kisses grew more heated, more passionate. She sighed and opened her mouth. Lucas had taught her how to kiss with an open mouth. But with her husband, it had seemed an obscene act. With Clint, all she wanted was to be closer to him, to savor the strength of his arms and relish the white-hot tingle of lightning that sparked between them.

Tentatively, he touched his tongue to hers and she responded, sliding her tongue inside his mouth and exploring there. He smelled of whiskey and leather and all man. She couldn't get enough of him.

He plundered her mouth and then reined himself back, retreating to kiss the corners of her mouth, nibbling on her bottom

# Hard Candy Christmas

lip and running his tongue over the outline of her lips. She clung to him, letting him taste her, letting him love her as no other man had.

*Love her?*

His fingers were busy, too, parting the neck-high buttons on her calico dress. Enthralled by his touch and his tongue sliding down her neck, she let him unbutton her dress.

He pulled back and rested his hands on her shoulders. The heat from the fireplace warmed her neck and chest. The lace of her camisole peeked from beneath the open wedge of her dress. His gaze drank her in, and for once, she felt feminine and desirable, eliciting his desire without trying. So unlike Lucas.

*She wouldn't think of Lucas, wouldn't allow the awful memories to ruin the moment.*

He lifted his gaze and she read his silent question there. And God help her, she nodded.

He smiled and smoothed his hands down her arms, stroking gently. Then his clever fingers strayed underneath her arms and he stroked the fullness of the sides of her breasts. Her breath caught and she puddled beneath his tender touch, her insides turned to a mess of porridge.

His hands moved up and cupped her breasts, and his thumbs flicked over her too-sensitive nipples. She gasped and threw back her head, offering herself, pushing against his hands. Feeling the pulsing need, like an unbreakable cord, running from her breasts to between her legs.

He kissed her again and then trailed his lips down her throat. At the hollow of her throat, he licked and then blew on her heated flesh. She melted and leaned into him, craving his hands on her breasts and his mouth on hers.

His lips trailed down and he parted her dress wider with his hands. Now only the camisole covered her achy, flushed breasts. He lowered his head and drew one breast into his mouth, along with her silky camisole. And then like a baby, he suckled her.

# Hard Candy Christmas

She arched into him. He kissed and suckled her, and his hand strayed down and he cupped her woman's mound through the covering of her dress. Her body responded and she pressed herself against his hand.

His tongue flicked over her breast, and his clever fingers rubbed her between her thighs in her secret woman's place. Her woman's passage contracted and throbbed. She wanted to scream, to throw herself at him, to do something. She'd never felt like this before, never known what it meant when a woman…

And then the crest of pleasure spilled over her, carrying her along on wave after wave of ecstasy. She splintered and broke, like a fine crystal vase shattering. The pleasure was so pure as to almost border on pain. Now she understood why Lucas had forced her to do the things he had to make him…feel like this. For if this was the way she felt, how much more pleasurable must it be for a man when he spilled his seed?

She slumped against Clint and leaned forward, touching her forehead with his. Their breaths intermingled. The experience had been so intense tears stung the backs of her eyelids.

"I never knew how it could be for a woman…how it could feel."

He kissed the top of her head. "I'm happy to show you this…and more. Much more." He grasped her hand and placed it on the bulge in his jeans. The length of his shaft was as hard as an anvil.

She gasped. He was ready for her, so unlike her husband.

*Was she ready?*

Clint got to his feet and pulled her into his arms. He leaned down and caught her beneath her knees, lifting her. He carried her through a long hallway on the opposite side of the house from her bedroom and Kevin's. He opened a door and then they were in another bedroom—Clint's bedroom. He kicked the door shut behind them.

She gazed at the big bed and then the awful images started.

# Hard Candy Christmas

*Lucas and his obscene demands. Lucas and his ugly, hideous words thrown at her like angry bullets, stripping away her humanity. Making her nothing better than an animal, doing anything to make him happy, anything to stay safe. She couldn't do this. She'd thought she could, but she couldn't.*

She pushed against Clint's chest with the flat of her hands. "Please, please, put me down."

"All right." He put her down and nuzzled her neck.

But she pulled away. Taking his hands in hers, she said, "Clint, I can't do this. I thought I could." She looked down at the hardwood floors, covered with brightly-colored rag rugs. "I know it isn't fair, not after...not after..."

He went down again, kneeling on an orange-and-yellow oval rug. "I apologize, Abby, but when you...responded, when I was able to—"

"Give me *pleasure?*" She wanted to choke on the word.

How terrible she was. She'd taken his gift, learning she could feel the pleasure of a woman. But because she couldn't face her own demons, she was refusing him that same gratification.

"I got carried away. I should have known better." He lowered his head. "I know you're a God-fearing woman." He raised her hands to his lips and kissed her knuckles. "Abby, I want to marry you. I'm asking you to marry me...if you'll have me. I know I'm not—"

"Oh, Clint, don't, don't." She shook her head and pulled her hands free. "You're so smart and kind and... It's not you, Clint. It's me. I'm already married. I can't marry you."

"But your husband has deserted you. He's been gone for six years. Kevin doesn't even remember him." He lifted his head and locked his gaze with hers, and the look in his eyes pleaded. "You're a grass widow already. After five years, you're technically free."

She opened her mouth to tell him she couldn't marry like that—not being free of Lucas in the eyes of God.

But he held up one hand as if to stop her from arguing.

# Hard Candy Christmas

"I understand that's not enough for you, Abby. But Mr. Samuels can put your case before the circuit judge when he comes to Del Rio, and you'll be divorced." He snapped his fingers. "Free to marry me."

*Divorced…a grass widow. What would her father have thought? He would have condemned her. In his eyes she'd be an adulterous, fallen woman.*

Her father's opinion didn't matter anymore. What mattered was how she felt, and how she was feeling would be difficult to explain to Clint. No matter how much she wanted him. And wanted to believe he'd be good to her and Kevin after the honeymoon was over.

But she'd been down that road before. Could she trust Clint? Could she trust herself? Her judgment? She'd been so wrong before and now it wasn't just about her. She had Kevin to think of. What if she made another mistake?

She turned her head and gazed at Clint's bed.

"I can't, Clint. I'm not a normal woman. I don't know how to explain, but you will tire of me soon. I won't…I'm incapable of making you happy in the…the bedroom." She hung her head. "I'm sorry, but it's for the best."

He scrambled to his feet and took her into his arms. "What are you saying? You're more than…more than anything I might expect. You're responsive and willing and so sweet." He leaned in and whispered into her hair. "And I love you, Abby." He moved back and held her at arm's length. "Don't you care for me?"

Lucas had said he'd loved her. She remembered their sweet spooning on her father's porch. He'd been so good and tender…until they'd married.

"Oh, Clint, don't you understand? My husband told me the same sweet lies—that he loved me. That he would always love me. But all he wanted was my father's money. And when Father made him work hard for every penny; he grew to hate me."

"But I'm not like your husband. I don't need or want your father's money. I have my own ranch and a good job."

# Hard Candy Christmas

She turned away from him. "I know, I know, everything is different. I'm older and I have Kevin now, but that's even more reason for me not to tie myself to another man."

"Tie yourself to another man—is that how you see it? I've told you I love you and want to marry you. But you don't want me; that's easy to see."

"I can't, Clint. I can't make the same mistake twice." She shook her head again and crossed her arms over her waist. "I won't be able to share the marriage bed with you."

"What…what are you saying?"

*Could she tell him? Could she bare her soul to this man? Did she have a choice? He wasn't taking "no" for an answer.*

"All right. I can see you won't believe me unless I tell you the ugly truth." She tugged at her cameo, knotting and kinking the ribbon around her index finger. "After the first few times, my husband said I didn't…I didn't please him in the bedroom." She let go of the cameo and covered her face with her hands. "I had to do things with my mouth and hands to make him…to make him…ready."

# Hard Candy Christmas

## Chapter Nine

Clint gently removed her hands from her face. "There's nothing wrong with you. You felt how aroused I was. How you always arouse me." He fisted his hands at his sides. "The problem isn't yours. It was your husband's. Something was wrong with him. Believe me, I know about—"

"About how women and men act because you grew up in a whorehouse?"

His face flushed, and he exhaled, his breath hissing. "That's a low blow. And not what I expected from you." He shook his head. "It wasn't what I was going to say either."

She'd made him angry. Maybe that was good. Lucas had never been angry before they'd married. But after...when her father made him work like a slave, he'd been plenty angry. And he'd taken his anger out on her. Maybe, if she made Clint angry enough, he would show her his other side...his animal side, as Lucas had.

"What were you going to say?" she asked.

He brought one fisted hand down and slapped his other hand with it. "Forget it, Abby. I don't know how to reach you. To make you understand not all men are like your husband."

"Or mean and miserly like my father?" Her voice was a sob now, and her eyelids stung. But she wouldn't cry. She'd shed so many tears when her father had died. And for what? Because he'd left her a boardinghouse to take care of her son?

Crying had never helped. Lucas had gloried in her crying, taunting her and making her do horrible things to make him hard enough to have married relations. After what Lucas and her father had done, how could she trust any man?

He reached out to her again, and she could see he'd gotten control of himself. His voice was low and gentle, "How can I make you realize not all men are like your husband and father?"

She pushed past him, grabbing the doorknob. "You can't change what has happened to me." She shook her head and lowered

# Hard Candy Christmas

her eyes. "How I wish I was seventeen again and starting my life. But I'm not. I'm twenty-seven and I have a child to worry about. I can't make silly mistakes."

"Abby—"

"Don't call me that! Only my mother called me Abby," she said. "And all Lucas wanted was my father's money, not me. He couldn't stand the sight of me, once we'd married, unless I was naked and groveling on my hands and knees and...and..."

She drew herself up. "When he got tired of that and Kevin kept him awake, crying at night, like babies do, he took the safe's key from my father's desk and stole thousands of dollars. I caught him at it and would have told my father, but he beat me senseless to stop me. It was the first and only time he beat me, but once was enough. Then he ran off with the money, leaving me and his son."

He gasped and lowered his head, shaking it back and forth. "Any man who touches a woman is a coward and a bully and should be horse whipped. I was glad when I got big enough to protect my mother from that kind of treatment. There are men who enjoy, who enjoy..." He lifted his head. "I shouldn't be telling you these things. I'm sorry."

"No, you shouldn't. It frightens me. And makes me realize how vulnerable and weak I am." She titled her chin up. "I never want to feel that way again. Never want to be dependent on a man."

"And the humiliation and degradation didn't stop there." She shook her head. "That was just the beginning," she said, grasping the doorknob until her knuckles turned white. "When he left me behind to face my father, I had to make reparations. I had to pay back my father for the theft. After all, Lucas had been my husband."

She choked on a sob, and tears streamed down her face. And she hated her weakness. Hated the tears that wouldn't stop.

"I paid with six long years of servitude and groveling with no hope in sight. I can't marry you, Clint." She raised her hot and flushed face to him. "Don't you see, I can't marry any man."

He reached out his hand to her and his eyes were watery.

# Hard Candy Christmas

She ignored his outstretched hand and opened the door, fleeing to the sanctuary of her room.

* * *

Leticia woke her and Kevin at sunrise. It was a day-long trip back to Del Rio, and they'd be lucky to get to town before sunset, as this was the time of the year when the days were shortest.

Kevin rode Esther alongside the wagon piled high with bales of wool from the autumn shearing, and Clint rode Jezebel. Abigail directed the mules for Clint, as they'd agreed to earlier. Carlos had gone ahead with the other wagon filled with wool and another *vaquero* a day or two before. The two *vaqueros* would wait in town and then drive the empty wagons back to the ranch.

At midday, Clint called a halt beside a small stream that fed into the Rio Grande, and they ate the leftovers from yesterday's picnic. This time, though, there was precious little conversation and her son didn't bolt down his food.

She glanced at Kevin and realized he looked tired. More than tired. His eyes were bloodshot with purple smudges under them. She hoped he wasn't coming down with something.

Clint cleared his throat. "Kevin, let's give Esther a rest, okay? I think you should ride in the wagon with your mother and tie Esther behind."

Her son looked up and nodded.

She was surprised he'd agreed. She knew how proud he was to have his own horse, and she'd expected him to argue, wanting to ride Esther into town to show her off. Either he was very tired or ill.

"Kevin, come over here." She lifted her hand and motioned to her son.

"Aw, Ma, what now?"

"Kevin, do as your mother asks," Clint said.

Kevin huffed but scooted over. She reached up, feeling his forehead. He felt a little warm to her touch but not hot. If he was taking ill, he didn't have a fever...yet.

# Hard Candy Christmas

"Okay, young man, tie Esther up and get in the wagon beside me," she said.

He nodded and unsaddled his mare, wedging the saddle in between the bales of hay. Then he tied Esther to the back of the wagon and climbed in beside her.

She patted her son's arm and flapped the reins. "Get up, mules."

Glancing over her shoulder at the saddle, she realized not only did her son owe Clint for the horse, but he'd provided a serviceable saddle as well. She sighed. She should at least pay Clint for the saddle. It was enough he'd gifted her son with a horse.

Thinking about how kind Clint had been, she felt a twinge of conscience for the way she'd treated him last night.

*What if he wasn't like other men? What if he was different?*

She shook her head. It didn't matter. She couldn't share a bed with him, not with him or any other man. Last night had taught her that. She'd live her life alone, except for her son. And when Kevin was grown, she'd be completely alone.

They bumped along the rutted trail for several more hours, not talking. Kevin sat beside her, but he was strangely listless. He must be getting sick. She prayed it wasn't anything serious, like the typhoid fever that had taken her mother.

When the sun was sinking slowly in the west and the lights of Del Rio hadn't come into view, she broke the tense silence by asking, "How far before we make town?"

Clint raised his head and squinted at the horizon. "Another couple of hours at least."

"What about that thundercloud?" She pointed to the southeast.

He shrugged. "Looks like it might catch us before we make town. Is Kevin all right?"

She touched her son's forehead, and she thought he felt a little warmer than at midday. "I'm not certain. He might have a fever."

# Hard Candy Christmas

Clint cursed under his breath; something she'd never heard him do before. He brought Jezebel beside the wagon and leaned down, pulling open a box under her feet. The lid lifted and he said, "Here are some oil slickers. If it starts raining, wrap up Kevin and put the other one on."

"What about you?"

"I'll be fine. You just wrap yourself and the boy."

"Thank you," she mouthed to his back as he spurred Jezebel ahead.

Two miles outside of Del Rio, the downpour started. Abigail pulled the oil slickers out and wrapped one around Kevin. And then she covered herself. By the time she pulled her son close, he was shivering and his teeth chattering.

She touched his forehead and found his skin was hot.

Clint circled back and joined them. She flapped the reins over the mules' backs, urging them to a trot. They lurched forward for a few yards and then settled back into a slow, grudging walk.

"Kevin is burning up with fever," she yelled over the downpour.

Clint heard her and nodded. He dipped his head and curtains of water fell from the brim of his Stetson. Taking the lead mule by the halter, he urged them forward at a trot.

The muddy outskirts of Del Rio loomed into view. Shanties, outhouses, cabins, and then the substantial homes on Main Street flew by. Clint brought the mules to a halt in front of the boardinghouse.

Abigail slid from the wagon, trying to hold Kevin up. Despite the sheets of rain, he was like a live coal in her arms, burning with fever.

Clint dismounted and gently pushed her to one side. "Let me get him." He grabbed Kevin by the shoulders and beneath his knees, swinging the boy into his arms.

Elisa opened the door, and they fell inside, muddy and soaking.

"I'll take him upstairs to his room," Clint said.

# Hard Candy Christmas

"Please. Thank you." Abigail turned to Elisa. "Kevin has a fever. Get some cool compresses and send for Doc Rodgers."

\* \* \*

For Abigail, the next few days passed in a haze of worry and fatigue. Kevin's fever was up and down. Some days he was almost a normal eight-year-old boy, cranky and bored, and wanting to be let out of bed.

Abigail played checkers and cards with him. Clint helped, too, telling the boy stories and teaching him the more complicated game of chess.

Then there were the days when her son's fever raged, and he was miserable and agitated. Doc Rodgers came and examined him the night they got back from the ranch, saying Kevin didn't have typhoid or any other life-threatening ailment. It was his opinion her son had caught a chill in the downpour and was suffering from the flu. Abby knew Kevin had been sick before they were caught in the thunderstorm, but she held her peace and was glad the doctor didn't find evidence of a more serious illness.

After the first night, Doc Rodgers visited every other day and left a noxious-smelling medicine that Abigail suspected contained too much grain alcohol and little in the way of medicinal content.

Instead, she sent to Elisa's *curandera* across the border for willow bark and hot ginger teas to bring down her son's fever, along with suffusions of elderflower to make Kevin sweat.

She alternated between trying to lower Kevin's fever with the teas and by sending Juan to bring back cool, clear water from San Felipe springs for the compresses. Other times, when the compresses and tea didn't work, she mounded blankets on Kevin, started a roaring fire in the fireplace, and gave him the elderflower suffusion to sweat out the fever.

And when she could get him to eat, she urged beef broth and soft foods on her son.

# Hard Candy Christmas

In between, she grabbed snatches of sleep and a few bites of food for herself.

When his sheriff duties allowed, Clint came and helped. His strong arms were especially useful when she needed to shift Kevin's feverish body and apply the compresses.

At the end of a week, Abigail was cautiously optimistic. For the past forty-eight hours, her son's fever had been low grade. She hoped and prayed the worst was over.

It was late evening, past supper and Kevin was sleeping fitfully, tossing and turning, but his forehead was barely warm to the touch. She'd eaten a few bites of beef steak and mashed potatoes from the dinner tray Elisa had sent up. But mostly, she needed sleep, at least a short nap.

She sat down in the rocker by the hearth and her head sank forward on her chest. A moment later, someone touched her shoulder and she jerked awake. She gazed up at Clint's blue eyes.

"I didn't knock because I didn't want to wake Kevin," he whispered.

She nodded. Her tongue lay thick and heavy in her mouth, and she was so tired it was an effort to speak.

"How's our patient?" he asked.

She wondered at his use of the pronoun *our*, but her mind was too fuzzy to latch onto the significance of what he'd said.

"I think he's better. His fever has been low for the past two days. If he can get through tonight without a high fever, maybe he will turn the corner." She touched her mother's cameo, as if for luck.

Clint nodded and sank to the floor beside her rocker. He took her hand in his. Their fingers tangled together and despite her exhaustion, his mere touch made her feel flushed and set her nerves to jangling.

"Is the cameo your mother's?" he asked.

She opened her eyes and said, "How did you know?"

"A good guess." He laid his head on her knee. "What was your mother like?"

# Hard Candy Christmas

She gulped, not wanting to cry. Every time she thought of her mother, she cried. "She was good and kind and loved her children more than anything." Her free hand stroked his short brown hair. She closed her eyes again, savoring his soft hair, loving that he allowed her to be tender with him, despite her rejection of him at the ranch.

He lifted his head and gazed at her. "Then you're a lot like your mother."

*Her face flushed at the implied compliment. What had she done to deserve him? Or instead, should she ask herself what had she done to deserve Lucas as a husband?*

Surely, being young and foolish wasn't a crime. For that was why she'd married Lucas in the first place. But life had taught her there were always second chances. If you were brave enough to embrace them.

That night at Clint's ranch, the ugliness of her past had overwhelmed her. But since then, Clint's unselfish concern for her sick son had broken down her reserve and made her question her fears and doubts. Every night he was here, willing t help with Kevin and ready to comfort her. He was her rock. And his kindness and caring had made her come to terms with her feelings.

*She was in love with him. Despite her fears and despite what had happened to her in the past. She couldn't help herself. She loved the man. She should tell him, but something stopped her. When Kevin was well, she'd tell him, but not now.*

"Thank you, Clint. That's kind of you to say. My mother was…is…an angel."

He nodded and laid his head on her knee again, while keeping her hand tangled with his.

"I'm glad Kevin is doing better," he murmured. "If I fall asleep and you or Kevin needs me, wake me up."

"I will." She squeezed his hand.

\* \* \*

# Hard Candy Christmas

Abigail woke with a start. The last log in the fireplace snapped and fell with a thud. She looked up, blinking and rubbing her tired eyes with her fists. It was dark except for the dying embers in the fireplace and must be the middle of the night. After comforting her, Clint had gone to bed hours before. She glanced at Kevin and saw he was tossing and turning and had kicked off his covers.

He half-raised himself and called, "Mama, Mama."

She jumped to her feet. Her son hadn't called her "Mama" since he was three years old. She rushed to his side and took him in her arms. And almost screamed when she touched him.

*He felt as if he was on fire!*

He curled into her and whispered, "Mama, I'm so hot. Can I have a drink of water?"

Panic sluiced through her, squeezing her heart and knotting her stomach. With a shaking hand, she grabbed the jug of water on the bedside table and poured a glass. Holding the glass to his mouth, Kevin gulped down the water.

She eased him down and pulled the covers to his chin. "Kevin, let me get some cool compresses. Try to rest and I'll be back in a minute."

He groaned and sank into the bed.

She pulled open the door and started toward the servants' back stairs for Elisa and Juan's room, which was situated off the kitchen. But with her hand wrapped around the newel post, she hesitated.

Clint had told her to call on him if she needed help, and he was great at lifting and turning Kevin, allowing her to apply the compresses to her son's feverish body. On the other hand, someone needed to send Juan to the springs for fresh water. She dithered for a moment, fear for her son muddling her thoughts and making it difficult to come to a decision.

*She needed Clint—he would know what to do.*

# Hard Candy Christmas

She sprinted up the stairs to the third level and knocked on his door.

"Who's there?" he called out, making her wonder if he ever slept or maybe he'd just returned from his late night rounds.

"It's me, Clint. Kevin is worse. His fever is spiking," she raised her voice, not caring if she woke the other boarders. "Can you help me?"

She heard the sound of his feet hitting the floor and then he flung open the door. He combed his hand through his tousled hair. His shirt gaped open, revealing his well-muscled chest.

"You say he's worse. When did this happen?"

"Just a few minutes ago, I think. Should I send Juan to the springs?"

"No, I have a better idea. I've been reading some medical journals at the library." He pulled his shirt together and started buttoning it. "I'm going to help Juan haul the hip-bath to Kevin's room. I want you and Elisa to bring up buckets of lukewarm water, not cool, but lukewarm."

She grabbed his arm. "Not cool and immerse him in a bath? Oh, Clint, are you sure?"

"It's the latest treatment prescribed by John Hopkins."

"Who or what is John Hopkins?"

"It's the best new hospital in Baltimore. Their doctors are the smartest on the East Coast and I read an article that said—"

"You've convinced me." She pulled on his arm. "Let's go. There's no time to waste."

An hour later Kevin sank against the back of the tub and closed his eyes with a sigh.

Abigail brushed the hair from his forehead. He was cool to the touch. She sobbed and crumpled beside the hip bath.

Clint grabbed a towel and moved to the other side of the bathtub. "Here, son, let's get you dry and back in bed." He helped Kevin to his feet and dried off the upper part of the boy's body. Then he lifted Kevin out and finished drying his legs.

"Does he have a fresh nightshirt?"

# Hard Candy Christmas

"What, what?" Abigail lifted her head and dashed at her eyes with a corner of her apron. It was the first time she'd allowed herself to cry in front of Kevin. He was sick enough without witnessing his mother's fears.

But this time, she hadn't been able to control her feelings. His high fever had been terrifying and gut wrenching. At first...at first...she'd been afraid she would lose him.

*Clint had come to her rescue again.*

She sniffled. "Yes, in the chest of drawers." She pushed to her feet. "I'll get it."

Together they pulled the clean nightshirt over Kevin's head, gave him another glass of water and tucked him into bed.

Dawn was breaking outside her son's window, a gray December dawn. Arm in arm, she and Clint staggered to the window and looked out.

"Thank you, Clint," she murmured. "He might have...might have...if you hadn't read about the bath." She turned her face into his chest. "I don't know what I would have done without you."

"Shhh, it's all right now. Everything's all right." He stroked her hair. "You need some rest, too, Abby...Abigail. I can stay with Kevin while you sleep for a few hours."

"Please, call me Abby. I shouldn't have...shouldn't have..." The words wouldn't come; she was too tired to talk.

He lifted her into his arms. "I'm taking you to your room and putting you to bed...Abby."

She nodded and snuggled against him, comforted by the familiar masculine scent of him, horseflesh and leather.

# Hard Candy Christmas

## Chapter Ten

*"Joy to the world! The Lord is come*
*Let earth receive her King!*
*Let every heart prepare Him room*
*And heaven and nature sing*
*And heaven and nature sing*
*And heaven, and heaven and nature sing*
*Joy to the world! the Savior reigns*
*Let men their songs employ*
*While fields and floods*
*Rocks, hills and plains*
*Repeat the sounding joy*
*Repeat the sounding joy*
*Repeat, repeat the sounding joy."*

The warbled notes of the Christmas carol sounded beneath Kevin's window. Abigail turned and looked. Kevin was slumped against his pillow, listening to her read the serialized edition of *"Treasure Island"* by Robert Louis Stevenson that Clint had brought from the library. But when he heard the singing, her son perked up and he threw back the covers.

Abigail reached out to touch his forehead, but her son dodged and said, "Aw, Ma, I'm fine. I haven't had a fever in three days." He pointed at the window. "And they're singing outside. Can I go and see?"

She picked up his robe and threw it over his shoulders. "Okay, put this on before you go to the window in your nightshirt."

With her hand on his shoulder, they both went to the window and looked below. Standing in the front yard of the boardinghouse was an assortment of adults mixed with children, holding hymnals and candles, and singing in a variety of voices, some on key and some slightly off.

94

# Hard Candy Christmas

"What are they doing, Ma?"

"They're caroling. But it's the first time I've seen it in Del Rio. Carolers used to go around in St. Louis where I grew up."

Kevin tugged on her sleeve. "But what's caroling?"

"Uh, it's where some people, usually from church, gather together before Christmas and go around to their neighbors' homes, singing Christmas hymns."

"Oh, looks like fun, 'specially getting to go around at night with candles. Not as good as my jack o' lantern but still... I wish I could go caroling." He tugged again and she glanced down. "And you promised I could go back to school tomorrow and visit Esther."

She smoothed his unruly hair from his forehead, and this time, he didn't duck away. "Yes, you're going back to school tomorrow. And you'll have to work hard to catch up, as much school as you've missed and with Christmas coming."

Kevin's brown eyes lit up. "How many days until Christmas, Ma?"

"About ten days."

"And this Christmas will be different, right? You promised me while I was sick. Remember?"

"Yes, I promised you and I meant it. We'll go to church like we always do, but we'll have a big feast with lots of sweets. And after dinner, we'll light the Christmas tree's candles and open the gifts under the tree."

Kevin clapped his hands and skipped across the room. "Aw, Ma, I can't wait."

She smiled and said, "I know, Kevin, I can barely wait either." But she was concerned, too, knowing she'd need to get busy to give Kevin the kind of Christmas she'd dreamed about but had never experienced.

Living under her father's stern and miserly rule, Christmas had always consisted of church-going, a nice meal with the customary one dessert, and maybe a stocking filled with a few pieces of hard candy.

# Hard Candy Christmas

*A hard candy Christmas—it was all she'd ever known.*

She wanted more for her son, wanted Christmas to be a special time for him to remember. But she'd better get busy, if she wanted to pull it off.

Luckily, when Kevin had fallen ill and demanded all of her time, she'd had extra help. Elisa's widowed sister, Rosa, had stayed on. And the boardinghouse had run smoothly and still turned a profit even though she'd had no time to help.

She'd hired Rosa permanently the day before. Abigail would continue to supervise the running of the house, ordering supplies, paying bills and balancing the ledgers. But the day-to-day cooking, carrying, scrubbing, and laundry would be done by Elisa, Rosa, and Juan.

When Kevin had turned the corner, she'd taken the past couple of nights to balance the boardinghouse books, and she'd been surprised to learn her father had paid his personal expenses through the house, while contributing nothing of his salary. His salary had been scrupulously put into the Del Rio National Bank each payday and the Presbyterian Church had been the beneficiary.

She refused to be bitter—the past was the past. Knowing and learning to love Clint, after all she'd been through she had to believe in second chances.

The carolers had finished *"Joy to the World"* and *"Silent Night"* beneath Kevin's window. With calls of "Merry Christmas" and lots of goodbye waves, they moved down the street, starting another carol, *"O, Little Town of Bethlehem."*

Abigail waved back and called down to her neighbors. Kevin stood on tiptoe, looking over the windowsill and waving, too.

The door opened behind them, and they turned. Clint stood on the threshold, a new bright-blue bandana tied at his throat, making the blue in his eyes appear even brighter. "Sheriff!" Kevin shouted and ran to him.

Clint scooped her son up and gave him a hug. He glanced at her and smiled his lop-sided smile. "When is your Mama going to let you out of jail? Do I need to spring you?"

# Hard Candy Christmas

"She says tomorrow I can go to school and visit Esther."

He set Kevin down on his feet. "That's good." He grinned at the boy. "I was beginning to think you were in for a life sentence."

"Nah, Ma would never do that." Kevin grinned back.

"And what are you going do as soon as you're back in school and on your feet?"

Kevin stared down at his feet and then his face brightened. "Ask around town for odd jobs so's I can take care of Esther."

"That's my boy." Clint squatted down and poked Kevin in the chest. "And what did you think of the carolers?"

"You sent them?"

"Yep, needed to get you out of your sick bed and into the Christmas spirit." He rose and exchanged a grownup look with Abigail over Kevin's head. "Time's a'wasting and Christmas is almost here."

"I've never seen carolers in Del Rio before," she said.

"They came over from the Methodist Church. Told them we had a convalescing boy who needed some Christmas cheer."

"That was kind of you." She pursed her lips. "Maybe we'll go to the Methodist Church for Christmas services." She looked up and caught Clint's eye. "I've not much cared for the Presbyterians."

Clint nodded. "We'll all go, come Christmas morning." He scrubbed a hand over his jaw. "I've always been partial to the Methodists. They helped me and my Mama some times when we got into scrapes."

"What else are we gonna do for Christmas, Sheriff?" Kevin asked. "Ma said we could get a tree. I've never had a Christmas tree before."

"Yep, we need a tree. We'll ride out on Saturday and get us one," Clint said.

"Yippee!" Kevin whooped. "And I'm coming with you on Esther?"

"You bet." Clint tousled Kevin's hair. "I wouldn't think of picking a tree without you. You're my chief tree picker." He

# Hard Candy Christmas

grinned. "Now scoot back to bed. You need to rest up for tomorrow."

"Yes, sir, Sheriff." Her son drew himself up and saluted.

Clint chuckled and followed her son to bed where he tucked him in and turned down the wick on the gas lamp.

Clint turned and faced her. And the look in his eyes was filled with yearning and a kind of hunger, too.

She lowered her head, not certain how to respond, especially in front of her half-asleep son. She knitted her fingers together. "Where will y'all find a Christmas tree in west Texas?" she asked, thinking of the lush-branched pine and fir trees she'd seen in pictures.

"You know those fat *piñon* trees in the hills. We'll get one of those."

Abigail clapped her hands. "I hadn't thought of a *piñon* tree. They're so short and squat."

"Yeah, but they decorate pretty. Plenty of your neighbors get them for Christmas."

Sadness swept her, thinking about what he'd said…and what she'd missed. Before, she'd been closed up in this house with no neighbors or friends to speak of and no one to share special times with. Clint had brought the carolers and now he and Kevin would get a tree to decorate.

Thinking of it, her heart lifted and she was excited. Like a little girl, she didn't want to wait another day for Christmas. But the grownup part of her cautioned there was much to be done: baking, making ornaments for the tree, and buying gifts. She knew exactly what she wanted to give Clint and Kevin for Christmas. And for once, she had the money to pay for her purchases.

*It was an exhilarating feeling.*

Clint closed the gap between them and took her hand. "Can you figure out some decorations for the tree?"

She smiled. "I think I can come up with something."

\* \* \*

98

# Hard Candy Christmas

Abigail stood on the threshold to the boardinghouse's parlor and gazed in wonder. It was Christmas Eve and this would be a holiday to remember.

Clint, with the help of her son, had outdone himself, finding a huge, round, six-foot tall *piñon* tree. Elisa and Rosa had helped, too, cutting and gathering fragrant cypress branches and armloads of the native chaparral plant with its bright red berries and light-green leaves.

The mantel and all the window frames were festooned with the evergreen branches and crimson berries. Fat, yellow-wax candles nestled among the branches overlaid on the mantel, dancing and twinkling in her mother's best brass candelabra, rescued from the attic and polished to a golden glow.

She glanced over her head. Trust Clint to not have forgotten the most important item—a big branch of white-berried mistletoe, suspended from the doorway overhead.

Last night, the few remaining boarders had been banished from the parlor, and she, along with her son, Clint, Elisa, and Juan had made merry into the wee hours of the night, decorating the Christmas tree.

They'd popped corn in the fireplace and strung it on thread and circled the tree with it. She and Elisa had spent afternoons sewing sparkling ornaments of sequins and bright-colored braid. Kevin had colored countless strips of paper and glued them into loops, stringing them together as another chain, circling the *piñon* tree.

Along with her mother's candelabra from the attic, Abigail had found small toys that had belonged to her family: a stuffed bear and some other stuffed animals, a few dolls and tin soldiers, some tops and yo-yos and hoops, old agate-eye marbles she'd pierced and strung on yarn, and even a pair of silver bells Leanna had fastened on her ice skates in St. Louis. All of these reminders of her childhood got some spit and polish and were hung from the tree branches.

# Hard Candy Christmas

Then they'd attached small candles cupped in tin foil to the ends of the biggest branches and tomorrow, before they opened their presents, she'd light each one of the candles and they would enjoy the magical glow of their first real Christmas tree.

Clint, with his usual dash, had added the final adornment—the only store-bought ornament—an enormous and glittering silver-painted star, to represent the Christ Child's Star of Bethlehem.

Looking at the tree, Abigail couldn't quite take it in. The wonder and awe of it, the festive and glorious sight. She sighed.

*How good was life? How good and sweet it could be.*

And tonight after they went caroling, they'd return to their rooms to wrap their Christmas gifts for one another. And she couldn't wait to see everyone's faces tomorrow when they opened her gifts.

She'd gotten Elisa a bolt of shimmering blue crepe for a dress and a new sombrero for Juan. For her son, she'd bought him a new bridle and bit for Esther. And for Clint, she'd noticed, the first time she'd cleaned his room, how threadbare his toiletry kit was. She'd purchased him a new comb and brush, along with a silver-handled razor.

*How good it was to give gifts—to know the joy of giving. For her, that was the essence of Christmas—remembering the Christ Child by giving with an open heart.*

And wouldn't her son be surprised by Clint's gift? Clint had wanted to give Kevin a new rifle. She shuddered, not wanting to remember Lucas' fascination with firearms.

She'd told Clint the second-hand saddle for Esther was more than enough. But with his usual generosity, Clint had deferred to her wishes about the rifle, but he couldn't resist having a gift for Kevin to open. He'd sent away for a baseball mitt and ball. He wanted to teach her son the sport, saying it would hone Kevin's reflexes...whatever that meant.

# Hard Candy Christmas

Hugging her midriff, she couldn't help but wonder what Clint had gotten her. Excitement, like a troop of butterflies, rioted in her stomach.

She heard the scrape of boots and the jingle of spurs against the hardwood hallway floor and knew Clint was coming.

Glancing up, she saw his broad shoulders filling the doorway. Underneath his right arm, he had a paper-wrapped package. Was the gift for Kevin or for her? Or for someone else?

*She loved wondering and guessing about their gifts for one another, along with all the decorations, making Christmas such a joy.*

"Happy Christmas Eve," she said.

He tipped the brim of his Stetson. "Merry Christmas to you too."

He put his package and hat on a side table in the foyer and took her elbow. Swinging her around as if she weighed no more than a rag doll, he drew her into his arms. His gaze raked her form, taking in her new red velvet gown, trimmed with white lace.

"You're looking good enough to eat—like a Christmas cake with icing."

She smiled and dipped into a curtesy. "I will take that as a compliment, kind sir."

He pointed over her head. "See that?"

"You mean the mistletoe?"

"Yep, *now* it's Christmas."

"Yes, it is."

He lowered his head and captured her mouth. His lips were warm and soft and tasted like heaven. Why, oh why, had she ever refused him?

Fitting her mouth to his, she wrapped her arms around his waist. And then the heat began, slow and simmering. Her blood warmed and curled through her veins, slow and sweet as honey. Her breasts peaked and ached. And lower, lower, she wanted him, wanted him in that most complete sense between a man and a woman…forever more.

# Hard Candy Christmas

He lifted his head, breaking their kiss and gazing into her eyes. "Marry me, Abby." He nuzzled her neck. "Marry me, please."

"Clint, I have to tell you something. I should have told you before, while Kevin was ill, but it wasn't the right time." She drew herself up and looked into his eyes. "I love you, Clint. I had to tell you because I didn't know if I could ever love again." She lowered her eyes. "But I do, Clint. I love you," she repeated.

"That's good enough for me, Abby." He grabbed her around the waist and spun her around. He threw back his head and laughed. Then he calmed and set her on her own feet. He swiped his face with his hand. "How soon can we marry?"

"Oh, Clint, are you certain you want me? I carry a heavy load from before—"

"I don't care. I've my own demons to wrestle with." He brushed her lips. "We'll wrestle them together and—"

"Ma?" Kevin's falsetto voice called to her. She heard footsteps and pulled away.

"Oh, Ma, I didn't know you and the Sheriff were spooning." He covered his mouth and giggled. "There's someone here to see you." Kevin hitched a thumb over his shoulder.

Who could it be on Christmas Eve? Most of the boarders had gone to spend Christmas with family or friends.

"Not spooning, Kevin, we were just—"

"Well, if that ain't special now," the mocking voice carried from the kitchen doorway.

*Lucas! She would have known his voice anywhere.*

Her long-absent husband elbowed his way past Kevin and stood in the foyer. He looked the same, except deeper lines bracketed his mouth, his straggly hair looked greasier than ever, and his eyes appeared unfocused, as if he'd been drinking.

"I don't know who you are, Mister, but I'd appreciate it if you'd unhand my wife." Lucas demanded with a sneer.

Clint backed up a step but kept his hand on her elbow. "I'm Sheriff Graham, and I assume you're Lucas Sanford."

"Yep, I'm *Mister* Sanford to you."

# Hard Candy Christmas

"Lucas, what are you doing here?" Abigail asked. "It's been six—"

"Don't matter how long it's been, you're still my wife." His gaze skittered over Kevin, and she *knew* he'd been drinking. "And I suppose this brat is mine, though he don't look nothing like me."

Kevin's head jerked up as if he'd been slapped. He turned to her with a question in his brown eyes. "Ma?"

Clint placed his hand on the butt of his pistol. "Well, now, *Mister* Sanford, it was nice of you to stop by—"

"Shut up, Sheriff."

Abigail felt Clint tense. He drew himself up, and she could see he was ready to spring.

Clint turned and faced down Sanford. Abigail had gone still and her eyes were wide in her face. Kevin stood between them, his mouth gaping open.

"You're a thief, Sanford. I have a circular on you. You stole several thousand dollars from Mr. Kerr when you lived here."

"Well, ain't you the smart-ass lawman," Lucas snarled and moved quickly to grab Kevin around his neck. "And I'd come for a friendly Christmas visit, for a little reunion with my family." He snorted. "'Cept you had to mess that up, Sheriff, calling me a thief and all that."

"Lucas, let go of Kevin," Abby said, her voice rising. "Why have you come?"

Lucas ignored her question and pulled Kevin tighter, almost strangling him. Kevin squirmed and struggled, obviously desperate to get away. Lucas cuffed him and tightened his hold until the boy's eyes bulged.

"Sheriff, if'n you don't want nothing to happen to the boy, you best take your hand off your pistol and unbuckle your holster. Let it drop real slow like and kick it and your gun over here." Lucas pulled his pistol and put the muzzle against Kevin's temple.

"Lucas, don't, please don't hurt him. He's your son." Abby's voice bordered on hysteria and she twisted her hands.

"Ma, I don't—"

# Hard Candy Christmas

"Shut up, kid." Lucas dug his fingers into Kevin's windpipe and cocked his pistol. "Sheriff, your gun."

Slowly and with his mind churning for an opening, he unbuckled his holster, dropped the belt with the gun still in its scabbard, and kicked the holster toward Sanford.

Sanford, in turn, kicked the holster to the other side of the hallway. Too far away for Clint to make a grab for it. He cursed himself under his breath for not being better prepared. For not drawing his gun the minute the low-life, thieving bastard had shown up.

"That's better, Sheriff. Now we can have a little talk without any interference." He looked at Abby. "And don't think Juan or Elisa will come to help you. I made certain to tie them up before coming in. They weren't too happy to see me, and I didn't want to see them neither." He spat on the floor.

"All right, Lucas, what do you want?" Abby had lowered her voice and except for her hand plucking at the cameo at her throat, Clint could see she was struggling to keep a tight rein on her fears.

"What do you think I want, now your dear Pa is dead? The money he left you. I want my share." He snorted. "Hell, I want my share and yours, too. Everything you've got. And I know where the safe is."

"Father didn't leave me any money, just the house so I could raise Kevin. He left his money to the Presbyterian Church."

Sanford's head jerked back. "Don't tell me no lies. I know you've got money. Your Pa had bundles of it."

"Hey, Sanford, I was here when the will was read. What Abby is telling you is true. Her father left his money to the church. Her brothers and sisters were plenty mad about it."

"Why don't you horn out, Sheriff, this ain't your party." He leered at Abby and winked at him. "Tell you what, Sheriff, she weren't much use to me in the biblical way, so's you can have her. I just want the money."

Clint fisted his hands, wishing he could bury them in Sanford's sneering face. Wishing he could wipe the knowing smirk

# Hard Candy Christmas

from the man's mouth, once and for all. If only Sanford would loosen his hold on Kevin.

"And if Abby doesn't have any money to give you, what will you do, shoot your own son?" Clint asked.

Sanford stared at him and looked down at the boy. "Nah, I wouldn't shot my own kin, if'n he *is* mine. I'd just take him with me. Teach him how to be a man."

Abby lunged forward, her arms outstretched. "Nooo, you can't take him. You can't."

Sanford tightened his grip on Kevin's neck again and lifted his pistol, aiming it straight at Abby's heart. "Get back, woman. If'n he's my kid, I have a right to him. Ain't that right, Sheriff."

"Not if you're locked up in prison for stealing," Clint replied.

"Yeah, well that ain't gonna happen." He waved the pistol and his brown eyes glittered.

Clint would wager he was more than half drunk. It was a small chink in Sanford's armor, but it was something. At least his reflexes might be slower.

"I know you've got money in the safe. I'll just take what ya got and go. Whatever you have." He pulled his lips back in the semblance of a smile. "That's my Christmas present to you, woman."

"And you'll let Kevin go."

He shook his head. "Not right away. Maybe later, somewhere outside of town. He's my guarantee the Sheriff won't be coming after me anytime soon." He stared at Clint with his unfocused glare. "Not if'n y'all don't want the kid hurt."

"But Lucas, you can't take him. It's cold and he's been sick and—"

"Shut up! Quit your whining! You'll do as I say. Now let's get to the study and open the safe and see what you've got for me." He loosened his hold on Kevin's neck and nudged him. "Get going, kid."

# Hard Candy Christmas

"I'm not going with you, Mister, and you're not my Pa!" Kevin turned on Sanford and dug his elbow into Sanford's side.

Clint knew there wouldn't be a better time. He made a flying lunge for his gun holster.

Sanford cursed, straightened, and backhanded Kevin. The boy shrieked and went skidding across the floor, cupping his jaw.

Abby rushed to her son's side.

Clint came up with his gun and pointed it at Sanford.

Sanford's gun went off and Clint felt the searing, white-hot pain tear into him. He fired at Sanford, and the man dropped his gun, grabbing his gut and groaning.

"Stay back." Clint gritted his teeth and clamped his jaw. "Abby and Kevin, keep back until I see if he's still alive."

"But Clint, you're hit," Abby said.

"It's just my shoulder. I'll be fine." With an effort of will, he kept his pistol trained on Sanford. He stumbled to his feet and crossed to the man. Slowly and carefully, with his pistol leveled at the downed man, Clint leaned over and felt for a pulse in Sanford's neck.

He exhaled and lifted his head. "He's dead."

Abby flew to his side and started tearing her apron into strips. "Kevin, get Doc Rodgers. Tell him the Sheriff took a bullet. Hurry!"

Kevin nodded and took off running, slamming the front door behind him.

"Ah, Abby, I wish, I wish—"

"What do you wish?" She cradled his wounded arm, appalled at the blood seeping from his wound.

"I wish your husband hadn't come and ruined Christmas."

"Oh, Clint," she half sobbed. "My poor Clint, I need to bind your shoulder until the doctor gets here."

"Kiss me first, Abby. Just so I know the nightmare is over."

# Hard Candy Christmas

## Epilogue

*Four Months Later*

Abigail clasped her bouquet of crimson Indian paintbrush, white primroses, and her favorite Texas wildflower, bluebonnets. She stood at the top of the aisle of the Methodist Church and let her gaze wander over the church.

Leanna was to the left of the altar, serving as her matron of honor. Across from her was Clint, her bridegroom, and Jim, acting as his best man. Paul and his wife, Sarah, sat in the front pew. Will Junior and Viola hadn't been able to come. Elisa and Juan, along with Rosa, sat behind Paul and his wife. All her boarders were here, along with a sprinkling of Clint's rancher friends and new acquaintances from the Methodist Church. Everyone who mattered was here.

She inhaled and swished her long, off-white skirt. She and Elisa had outdone themselves, sewing a beautiful satin wedding gown, liberally overlaid with delicate white lace. She fingered the single strand of pearls at her neck, Clint's Christmas gift to her.

Her gaze rested on her intended. His shoulder had healed and he stood tall and handsome in his new gray, broadcloth suit with a string tie. He smiled at her, his sweet, lop-sided smile.

*And the look of awe and pure love in his eyes took her breath away.*

It had been so hard, after that terrible Christmas Eve, to not marry Clint right away. But she'd wanted to give Kevin time…time to understand what had happened. Her son had needed to work through his fear and hurt and come to terms with who his father had been. And then move past the sorrow and pain…to a new beginning.

Because in all the most important ways, Clint was Kevin's father, not her late husband.

She held out her arm and said, "Kevin, are you ready?"

# Hard Candy Christmas

"Yes, Ma, I'm ready." Her son, attired in a miniature version of Clint's suit she and Elena had sewn, stood beside her. He straightened his spine, lifted his chin, and took her arm.

*The other handsome man in her life…her son.*

Music from the pipe organ swelled, announcing her as the bride and cueing her to start marching down the aisle. The wedding guests stood.

"What are we waiting for, Son?" She curled one hand around Kevin's hand on her arm. "Give your Mama away to Clint…my bridegroom."

Kevin glanced at her and then at Clint. He grinned. "You bet, Ma!"

# Hard Candy Christmas

## Copyright

# Let It Be Christmas

By

## Hebby Roman

West Texas Christmas Trilogy Book 2

☆Estrella Publishing☆

# Let it Be Christmas

## Author's Note

As a girl growing up in Del Rio, Texas, I was raised on the notion of Judge Roy Bean being a local hero, as Langtry, Texas is around forty miles from Del Rio. I'd never read a western romance set in Langtry and when I decided to write this book, I researched Judge Bean, as a secondary character, and was surprised by what I found. Although, in some ways, he brought law and order to a lawless corner of Texas, I learned he also used his position to swindle customers and administer his own form of eccentric justice. As Wikipedia puts it: "Langtry did not have a jail, so all cases were settled by fines. Bean refused to send the state any part of the fines, but instead kept all the money. In most cases, the fines were made for the exact amount on the accused's person." For any of you who are Judge Roy Bean fans, I hope you will understand my portrayal of Judge Bean is based on historical facts, not my personal feelings.

# Let it Be Christmas

## Prologue

*Del Rio, Texas June, 1896*

Abigail Kerr Sanford, now Abigail Graham, put her teacup down and said, "I wish you could stay longer than one night. I was so excited when I got your telegram."

Lindsay MacKillian gazed at her childhood friend. She took a sip of tea to wet her dry throat. "I wish I could stay more than a night, but I shouldn't."

"If you stay a few more days, my husband and son will be back from spring shearing and you can meet them."

Lindsay wished she could stay, too. Make this a happy reunion, but she'd already alerted her brother she'd be on tomorrow's passenger train when it stopped in Langtry. Besides, the sooner her brother knew why she'd returned home, the better. But first, she *needed* to tell someone else. And Abby, a woman, and her only friend this side of the Mississippi, was the obvious choice.

"I'd love to stay, Abby, and I promise to come for a visit and meet your new husband and son. But I telegraphed my brother I'd be home tomorrow, and I'm certain he will ride in from the ranch to meet me."

"Oh, I'm sure he will. He must have missed you."

Lindsay wasn't so certain about that. Most likely, he'd look upon her as an additional responsibility. At least, he'd acted that way when she'd come home four years ago for their father's funeral. Then, Chadbourne, or Chad, as she called him, had been more than happy to send her back to their aunt, Minerva O'Rourke, in Boston.

And she was certain her Aunt Minnie would eventually telegraph Chad. She hadn't exactly spelled out the reason for returning home to Texas in the note she'd left, but her aunt was sharp enough to put two-and-two together. The most she could hope for was Aunt Minerva would honor the veiled plea in her note and let her tell Chad in her own way and time.

# Let it Be Christmas

She wanted to make pleasant conversation with Abby, but her shameful condition preyed on her mind, night and day. She *needed* to tell Abby first. Not only to unburden her soul but to gauge how bad the reaction might be.

Thinking about what faced her, she let her gaze drop to the large bump in Abby's lap. "You got remarried this past spring? You and your husband didn't waste any time."

Abby's face flushed, and she lowered her gaze. "Given the circumstances, Clint and I *anticipated* the event... a bit. After Clint... uh, after Lucas... ahhh." Abby lifted her head and squared her shoulders. "Clint brought home a bottle of champagne for the New Year. I should have been in mourning, but—"

"You don't have to explain to me." But if it was going to be this hard for a married woman to admit she'd *anticipated* her nuptial vows, what would it be like for her?

"No, I guess not." Abby took a sip of tea. "You got my letters?"

"Yes, I got them." Lindsay patted the carpetbag she'd brought into the parlor. "Kept them all, too."

Her family had been the Kerr's first boarders when her father had come west to look for land to ranch. Even though they'd only been fourteen, she and Abby had formed a lasting friendship, keeping in touch for more than ten years through letters.

She set her teacup on the sagging coffee table, wondering why the magnificently-constructed parlor had such poor furniture, actually, the same furniture when she and her family had lived here.

But it wasn't her place to disparage Abby's boardinghouse, she remembered how miserly her friend's father had been and guessed Abby hadn't had time to replace the shabby furniture.

She lifted her teacup and took another sip. "I hate to speak ill of the dead, but I was very happy to learn Lucas Sanford is no more. That man was hideous, a grotesque monster."

Her friend gazed out the huge bow window. "I'd forgotten how I poured out my heart to you when Lucas first left me." She bowed her head again. "Yes, he was a monster. Money was

113

everything to him. He was willing to sacrifice his own son for... for..."

Abby caught her breath, and her eyes looked watery.

The last thing Lindsay wanted was her friend to go down memory lane and be reminded of the past few years before she'd met her new husband.

She lifted her handkerchief and dabbed at her mouth. "I'm sorry. I shouldn't have brought Lucas up. Actually, I'm glad I never met him. I might have been tempted to hurt him."

Her friend exhaled, and she grabbed a handkerchief, too, dabbing at her eyes. "I wouldn't have wanted you to meet him. He wasn't, wasn't... normal. I know you're brave, but I can't answer for what he might have done."

Abby had always been the demure one. Lindsay, on the other hand, had been a tomboy growing up. And she'd possessed no compunctions about mixing it up with her older brother, Chad.

"No, I probably wouldn't have known what to do. But I'm surprised your father..." She let her voice trail off. Another painful topic, Abby's cold and skinflint father. If she kept bringing up painful topics, she'd never get to the real reason she'd stopped in Del Rio on her way home.

A long, low whine broke the tense silence.

She leaned over and said, "Hush, Minnie. I'll see to you in a minute. You just have to be patient."

Abby's face brightened, and she stared at the crate beside Lindsay's feet. "What kind of dog is it?" She shook her head. "He's so tiny and furry." She glanced at her friend. "And you say he's 'house-broken' and stays in your room? I've never seen such a dog."

"Minnie is a she, not a he, and she's what we call a 'lap dog' back East, meaning the dog stays inside, even sitting on your lap. But they must be house-broken." She lowered her voice. "You know what I mean—the dog must be trained not to leave any, uh, unwanted reminders in the house."

She unlatched the crate and reached inside. "At least that's the theory, though, sometimes, accidents happen."

114

# Let it Be Christmas

"And you want to keep her in the bedroom with you tonight?"

"That's my preference, though I can understand how you might be concerned about your boardinghouse floors. But I promise to keep her in the crate." She lifted Minnie out and said, "Would you like to hold her?" Minnie wriggled around and managed to lick her chin. "She's a Maltese, a breed of dogs that have been around for thousands of years. And she loves people."

"Oh, how sweet she is!" Abby put her teacup down and held out her arms. "So white and fluffy. And she has such cute button-black eyes and a pink tongue, too." Her friend took the squirming dog and hugged her. Minnie promptly licked Abby's face.

"If Kevin sees her, he'll want a dog just like her. How did you ever find her?"

"Aunt Minerva has had Maltese dogs for a long time. She has two now, older ones, a male and female. Minnie, named for my aunt, was one of their pups. Aunt Minerva gave her to me after I lost my father. Minnie was quite a comfort, and I enjoyed training her."

"Training her?"

"Yes, you have to teach them to be house-broken. And she knows how to sit, lie down, shake hands, roll over, and beg. I taught her all those 'tricks' with some bacon slices and a lot of work."

"Really? How wonderful!"

"Do you want to see what she can do? Though, I probably should take her out first to, ah, to relieve herself."

"Oh, please do." Abby turned the little dog around and placed a kiss on her fluffy topknot. "I wouldn't want her to be uncomfortable, and of course, you must keep her in your room. I don't mind. She's such a sweet little thing."

"Thank you, Abby. That's kind of you." She rose and snapped her fingers.

Minnie looked up and panted.

"Come, Minnie, heel."

# Let it Be Christmas

The little dog followed her, and Abby clapped her hands. Lindsay had a tether for Minnie when necessary, but usually, the Maltese tagged after her.

A few minutes later, they returned to the parlor. Lindsay put the dog through her repertory of tricks, and her friend clapped after each one. Then Lindsay tucked her dog back into the crate.

*No more distractions.* She'd already delayed telling Abby long enough, and it was a wonder they hadn't been interrupted.

She dusted her hands and held out her teacup. "Could I please have another cup of tea?"

"Of course." Abby took her teacup and poured from the teapot. "Two lumps of sugar, right?"

"Yes, please."

Her friend held out a plate, which had materialized while she'd taken Minnie to do her duty. "How about a sandwich or piece of cake? Elisa put these together for us. And you don't need to eat with the other boarders—they're a bunch of rough railroaders. You'll eat with us in the kitchen."

"I'd like that." Actually, she hadn't thought past the moment—about how hard it would be to face people, once she'd voiced, even in private, her shame.

She took a slice of yellow cake with chocolate frosting and another napkin. She didn't see any silverware. Abby was as informal as she remembered, expecting her to eat the cake with her fingers, which suited her.

She wished she'd had time to visit with her friend four years ago when she'd come home for her father's funeral. Then they wouldn't have so much to catch up on. But that had been a bad time, both for her and her friend. And she probably would have said something to upset Abby's father if she had visited.

*Now was the time.*

"Abby, I'm going to have a baby."

Abby's mouth gaped open, and she dropped the piece of cake she'd been holding onto the faded, reproduction Turkish rug beneath her feet. She gazed at Lindsay with her mouth hanging open.

"You're, you're—?"

"Yes, you heard me correctly." She fingered her mother's gold wedding band she wore around her neck on a ribbon. That ring should be on her finger. She flushed, thinking about it.

"I'm carrying a child. Just like you. Only I'm not as far along as you, of course." She spread her hands over her lap. "I'm only a couple of months gone, but I'm certain."

"But how, how…" Her friend finally closed her mouth and stared hard at Lindsay's left hand. "You're not married. Are you?"

She shook her head.

"What happened to your fiancé? I meant to ask before, but there's so much to talk about and—"

"Seamus is the father."

"Oh, so, you and he *anticipated*, like Clint and I did. But then why are you here—"

"I won't be marrying Seamus." She gazed at the crumbled cake at her friend's feet. "I probably won't be marrying anyone." She raised her head and crossed herself, looking directly at Abby. "If I have my way, I'll have the baby, return to Boston, give the child up for adoption, and enter a convent. It's the only right thing to do." Tilting her chin up, she said, "I've sinned, and I must pay the price."

"Oh!" Abby got to her feet and reached across the coffee table, holding out her arms. "Please, please, don't say that! You're *not* sinful. We all make mistakes. Look at my first marriage."

Lindsay rose and leaned into her best friend's arms. They hugged each other for a long time, and Abby patted her back.

"Does your fiancé know?" Her friend pulled apart and gazed at her. "Does your aunt know? Does your brother?"

She let go of Abby and stifled a sob. She would *not* cry. She had to be strong. "No one knows, except you… now."

"But why didn't you tell Seamus and marry—"

# Let it Be Christmas

"Because my aunt had him investigated and unmasked him as a money-grubbing fraud. And even though…" She paused and swallowed past the boulder lodged in her throat. "Even though we'd *anticipated* the carnal side of our marriage, as soon as my aunt told Seamus she was giving my inheritance to the Church, he disappeared."

"No!" Abby cupped her cheeks in her hands.

"Yes, and then I missed my cycle and I knew."

"Has anyone confirmed your condition?"

"I got off the train in Chicago for one night and saw a specialist." She nodded as if to emphasize the point. "I'm with child. Not too far along, but—"

"*Señora* Abby," someone called from the hallway. "*Señora* Abby, I wanted to ask if you're ready for me and Rosa to serve supper. It's almost six o'clock."

Lindsay looked up to see Elisa hovering in the doorway.

Abby laced her fingers together and cleared her throat. "Yes, please, go ahead and serve." She glanced at Lindsay. "We'll be along in a minute, but my friend will eat with us in the kitchen."

"Yes, *Señora* Abby."

"I don't know what I would do without Elisa. There were times when Father was still alive and… and… she was the only one who gave me hope." She turned back to Lindsay. "And you mustn't give up hope, either. And you'll *not* give up your child."

"I'm a ruined woman. I don't know what else I can—"

"Lindsay MacKillian, before I let you give away your baby to strangers, Clint and I will raise your child. We want a houseful of children, and yours would be like our own." She crumpled her handkerchief and lifted it to her eyes, quietly sobbing. "I won't let you give your baby up!"

She reached out and patted Abby's arm. "I know it's a shock. And for a Protestant, probably hard for you to follow my reasoning." She lowered her voice. "We'll talk more, after supper."

Abby leaned into her and laced her arm around her waist. "When are you due?"

# Let it Be Christmas

"Christmas."

"Let it be Christmas."

"Yes," Lindsay said and crossed herself. "Let it be Christmas."

# Let it Be Christmas

## Chapter One

*Langtry, Texas 1896*

"Chad!" Lindsay cried out when she caught sight of her brother through the railroad coach window.

The train ground to a stop with a jerk and a groan. She leapt to her feet and hurried to disembark. As she stepped onto the platform between the two cars, she called her brother's name again and flew down the steps.

"Welcome home, little sister!" Chad MacKillian opened his arms wide.

Hugging him, she hoped he would protect her during this difficult time.

Chad returned her hug before pulling away and holding Lindsay at arm's length. He cocked his head and slanted back the fawn-colored Stetson on his high forehead. He studied her from the crown of her ostrich-plumed hat to the last button of her high-top boots and emitted a low whistle. "My, my, you look even better than you did four years ago, Lindsay."

Given his reception, her aunt must have honored her request and not telegraphed him yet. But there was no telling how long her aunt would stay silent.

"Four years ago, I cried all the way here on the train. We'd just lost Father."

Her brother released her and stared down at the bleached-out caliche dirt beneath his cowboy boots. "Of course, you're right." He glanced up. "But I didn't expect to see you back here." He shook his head. "Half-expected a wedding invitation by now."

She gulped and knew she was turning red. But she couldn't tell him her shameful secret here, on the main street of town. She laced her arm through his and lowered her head. "The wedding was called off."

"But I thought—"

# Let it Be Christmas

"Chad, could we wait until we're home to discuss such a private matter?"

"Sure, sure, Sis."

Annoyed at caring what other people might think but unable to stop herself, she glanced over his shoulder to see who was watching their reunion.

The focal point of Langtry, the Jersey Lily saloon, squatted beside the railroad tracks like a misbegotten bird of prey. The saloon looked the same as when she'd last seen it, perhaps more weathered. The hand-lettered sign mounted above the saloon still proclaimed: *"Judge Roy Bean, Law West of the Pecos."*

And the usual hanger-on's clustered around the legendary judge, all of them gawking and hawking tobacco juice into the dirt.

Judge Bean hadn't changed much either. With his full, grizzled beard and large pot-belly, he looked exactly as the popular dime novels, which had established his reputation, portrayed him.

He always stood outside his saloon when the passenger train arrived, counting on his legendary status to lure railroad passengers into the Jersey Lily to refresh themselves by purchasing whiskey at inflated prices. He enjoyed fleecing gullible Easterners by refusing to make change when they paid and if they dared to protest, he'd fine them for disturbing the peace and keep the remainder of their money.

Chad grasped her elbow and squeezed it. "This being June already, the heat must be quite a shock after Boston."

"Yes, I had almost forgotten what it was like," she said.

Ignoring the rowdy crowd in front of the saloon, she let her gaze roam over the remainder of her small hometown. Langtry was merely a whistle-stop on the Southern Pacific Railroad. Perched precariously on the edge of the Chihuahua Desert, the small town baked three-quarters of the year under a relentless sun.

It was a frontier town, spawned by the building of the railroad only a scant fourteen years before. Haphazard wooden buildings sprouted among the indigenous adobe structures. Purple sage, creosote bushes and a variety of prickly cacti served as the

# Let it Be Christmas

town's stunted and thorny vegetation. Only the stately yuccas with their waxy, yellow blooms and the spindly ocotillos, rising like outstretched fingers with red plumes on their tips, grew tall enough to interrupt an endless view of the horizon.

Chad propelled Lindsay toward the buckboard wagon. "You wait here, and I'll fetch your trunks."

She nodded, and her brother boosted her onto the high seat of the wagon. She touched her brother's arm and said, "Please, be careful with the crate. I think you'll be surprised by its contents."

She smiled, eager to see his reaction to Minnie. Around here and on the ranch, no one had heard of a lap dog. There were working dogs to herd the sheep, or hounds for hunting, but no one kept a dog inside.

He patted her hand. "I'll be extra careful. It's good to have you home." He headed toward the tiny depot.

She arranged her skirts on the rough plank board. The fashionable bustle of her serge traveling suit wasn't designed for such an unyielding surface. It bunched behind her in an uncomfortable lump. Sweat beaded her brow, and she realized her stylish headgear was also ill-designed for West Texas. She wished she'd included a parasol as part of her ensemble, but in Boston, it had seemed like an affectation.

She pulled a lace-edged handkerchief from her reticule and mopped her forehead. Her gaze wandered back to the shaded porch of the Jersey Lily.

On the edge of the porch, a stranger broke away from the mob of milling men and propped his right foot against the porch rail. Even at this distance, there was something about him that drew her attention.

The charcoal-gray broadcloth of his suit strained at his shoulders and clung to the muscular contours of his thighs. He removed his dark Stetson and wiped his brow. His black hair was a deeper shade of night against the twilight shadows of the saloon porch. Too far away to discern his features, she imagined he would be handsome with piercing eyes and full, sensual lips.

# Let it Be Christmas

She shook herself and lowered her head, purposely looking away. *What on earth was she thinking?* Daydreaming about some stranger on a saloon porch. Wasn't her sin with Seamus enough of a stain on her conscience? Must she be drawn to the first attractive man she'd seen?

Was she truly a bad woman, beyond redemption?

If her Aunt Minerva had taught her anything about being a lady, it was to keep herself occupied and not give in to sinful thoughts. Her aunt had also championed charitable works of every kind as a proper calling for a lady.

Until she got too big with child, she must find some charity work to fill her days and thoughts. She crossed herself. After all, what more fertile ground could there be for works of charity than Langtry, Texas?

\* \* \*

Bartholomew Houghton squinted against the lowering sun, watching Chad MacKillian's buckboard until it bumped over the first hill northwest of Langtry.

The ill-timed arrival of Chad's sister had interrupted their business negotiations. Chad and he were preparing to finalize their deal when Chad's sister telegraphed she would be coming home. Suspending their negotiations until he could talk with his sister, he'd admitted she owned half of the ranch but was quick to point out he'd failed to mention the joint ownership because he'd expected her to marry and remain in Boston.

Bart snorted, remembering his initial chagrin at feeling he was being "suckered" by the fresh-faced Chad. He'd almost walked away from the deal. But upon further reflection, he'd decided to see what would happen. Most women followed their menfolk's advice in matters of business. If Chad knew how to handle his sister properly, she shouldn't prove to be an obstacle.

Despite his confidence in male superiority over the weaker sex, Chad's sister as part owner of the ranch would definitely alter the financial arrangements of the original deal. He hoped he could

# Let it Be Christmas

come to an equitable arrangement with Chad because Langtry and the MacKillian's ranch suited him.

He was tired of roaming. With the United States filling up, civilization encroached farther west each year. The free-wheeling days were over. Believing it was time to settle down and build his future, he chose West Texas because of its sparse population and frontier atmosphere. And the border of Old México stood only a few hundred yards to the south of Langtry.

The MacKillian's sheep ranch was a tempting investment. Chad's father had bought large tracts of acreage as well as stocking it with prime wool-bearing sheep.

But his first glimpse of Chad's sister had set off warning bells in his head. He couldn't help but notice her graceful carriage and shapely bosom. The sun gilded her palomino-colored hair, making it shine like the seven golden cities of Cibolo.

A woman like Chad's sister shouldn't be living in a place like this. It was a waste... and a temptation.

\* \* \*

Lindsay thrust the broom beneath the pump sink. Searching the darkest recesses of that uncharted territory, she brushed the back wall and then drew the broom toward her, inch by inch. Whatever she was fishing for smelled like a dead buzzard with a full gullet. Just the horrible stench made her more than apprehensive of what she might find.

As her trophy came into view, Lindsay's eyes widened and she gagged. Whatever it was, it looked as if it might still be alive. The shape provided no clue, but the green fur covering it was more than disturbing—it was revolting.

She muttered a string of French words--naughty French words. Words she'd learned at her finishing school in Boston. Cursing wasn't ladylike, but it certainly was satisfying, especially if no one understood your slip from proper decorum.

She retreated a few steps and retrieved the dust pan. Tying a dish towel over her mouth and nose, she squared her shoulders and

# Let it Be Christmas

advanced upon—the *thing*. Gingerly, she swept her discovery into the dust pan, praying the hideous blob would remain unmoving until she could toss it on the rubbish heap outside.

A small, black nose appeared over the edge of the dust pan, sniffing. Startled, she almost dropped the pan but managed to retain her grip and wave the brush.

"Minnie, bad girl! Get away! It's not something to eat."

Minnie cocked her head and blinked her black, gum-drop eyes. She lowered her head and tail and slunk off, crawling under the kitchen table.

Lindsay lost no time disposing of the green muck outside. Returning to the kitchen, she sank into one of the ladder-back chairs ringing the oak dining table.

Sighing, she untied the dish cloth and made an attempt at wiping the perspiration from her face. But as soon as she wiped, the moisture returned—and it was only June. August would be even hotter—so hot the very air would feel scorched and heavy to breathe.

In her rush to return home and hide her shame, she'd overlooked many of the more disagreeable details of life in West Texas. The oppressive heat, the insects invading every corner of the house, the layer of alkaline dust settling on each piece of furniture, and the dangerous animals—ranging from poisonous snakes to an occasional marauding bear from México—made civilized life a daily challenge.

Faced with the hardships imposed upon her, she wondered if it wouldn't have been better to confess to her aunt and go directly to a convent. To retain a ladylike demeanor, especially as she grew larger with child, wouldn't be easy. Her dresses clung to her, drenched in perspiration, until she felt as if she was *drowning* in this arid wasteland.

And as her first good deed, she'd set herself the task of *redeeming* her brother's living arrangements before she attempted general reforms in Langtry. After all, family came first. But she hadn't known her bachelor brother lived like a pig.

125

# Let it Be Christmas

She sighed again and leaned down, scratching behind Minnie's ears. Looking over the kitchen, she could see how her efforts were making inroads; the entrenched grime had retreated in some areas. But even working diligently from dawn to dusk, it would take a long time to strip away four years of accumulated dirt and neglect.

She shifted in the chair and glanced at her mother's cherished oak dining table. When Lindsay had left the first time for Boston, shortly after her mother's passing, the table was in pristine condition. Now it bore splotched stains that resisted her best efforts, as well as nasty scars marring its once-beautiful surface.

Her mother's table had survived the railroad trip from Massachusetts, fourteen years before, without a scratch. Even after her mother's death, Mrs. Baker, a widow who acted as their housekeeper, kept the table in perfect condition. But when Lindsay's father was accidentally killed, everything changed.

Tears pooled in her eyes at the changes four years had wrought, but she knew it wasn't the ruined furniture and filth that upset her. The house had changed during her absence, and it no longer felt like home. Before, she could remember her parents in this house, which her father had built with his own hands.

*Her home was so different now.*

When she'd asked her brother why Mrs. Baker hadn't stayed, he'd told her Mrs. Baker had remarried and moved away. She'd demanded to know why he didn't retain another housekeeper. He'd replied housekeepers were difficult to find in West Texas. And he'd learned to get by with the wife of one of his Mexican shepherds, who was willing to cook for him and do some light housekeeping.

*Light, indeed.*

She'd confronted her brother's housekeeper, Serafina Gómez, and learned Serafina had eight children at home. With that bit of information, Lindsay understood the problem. Serafina needed the small housekeeper's allowance to supplement her

# Let it Be Christmas

husband's income. Unfortunately, with the demands at home, she possessed neither the time nor energy to keep the ranch house properly.

Relieving Serafina of her daily cooking duties, Lindsay took them upon herself, promising to continue her monthly salary if Serafina would help with the heavier chores. Serafina had agreed, but so far, she'd only called upon her twice this past week, preferring to tackle the cleanup chores herself.

Or wanting to keep so busy and exhausted she continued to delay telling her brother why she'd come home. And Chad, bless him, hadn't pressed her.

The grandfather clock chimed loudly in the adjacent parlor and startled her. The afternoon was advanced. She needed to start supper.

She'd asked Serafina to help today, but her youngest child was ailing. The responsibility for tonight's supper rested squarely on Lindsay's shoulders. And her brother had requested she prepare something special because he was bringing home a business associate for supper.

She was honest enough to admit her cooking skills were only passable. She'd not bothered to learn after her mother died because capable Mrs. Baker did their cooking. In Boston, Aunt Minnie employed kitchen help. At her aunt's insistence, she'd reluctantly learned some of the basic principles of the culinary arts.

But truth be known, she found cooking a boring chore, and she already regretted relieving Serafina of her daily duties, even though she knew it was a necessary step to have the woman's help with the house cleaning and laundry. Once she returned the house to a semblance of order, she hoped Serafina would have the time to do some of the cooking.

If Chad didn't prove too troublesome.

Already, in typical male fashion, he'd settled into the new routine of Lindsay's uneven attempts at preparing meals. He'd even possessed the effrontery to offer her a back-handed compliment by praising her for attempting variety at meal times.

# Let it Be Christmas

Serafina, on the other hand, exhibited a severely limited repertoire in the kitchen. Chad's 'housekeeper' served rice, *frijoles*, tortillas, and fried *cabrito* or salt pork for every meal—seven days a week.

To fulfill her brother's request for a special meal, she'd asked him to slaughter and dress a lamb. After all, they lived on a sheep ranch; they should learn to eat mutton. In Boston, mutton was in great demand and, when properly prepared, could be very tasty.

She rose from the chair and straightened her apron. The mutton, vegetables, and potatoes awaited. Raising her chin in determination, she felt certain she could provide an edible meal—if she could remember the proper heat level and cooking time for the lamb.

Three hours later, she poked at the haunch of lamb and found very little 'give' to her fork. But the potatoes, carrots, and turnips had already turned to mush. And there was precious little gravy to be had in the bottom of the roasting pan.

She dropped the fork and wiped her forehead with the back of her hand. It was too late to change anything. Chad and his business associate would be here any minute. She crossed herself and said a prayer.

Then she heard boots on the porch and went to the front window to peek out.

With Chad was the stranger—the man she'd glimpsed on the Jersey Lily's porch.

She couldn't restrain a small gasp as she clung to the front door for support. When she'd heard their approach, she'd rushed to the door to greet Chad and his guest. But she didn't expect—that man. She'd expected a stout, balding wool factor, but this man was neither stout nor balding—and she sincerely doubted he was a wool factor, either.

*He was as handsome as she had imagined him.*

Seamus had been a good-looking man, but beside this stranger, he would have looked like an ugly jug head. Gazing at her

128

# Let it Be Christmas

brother's business associate, her mouth refused to form the welcome she'd rehearsed. But she did manage to gulp and hold out her hand.

He clasped her fingers between his large, tanned hands. Warmth spread from his fingertips, coiling thickly through her blood and making her want to pant like Minnie when she was excited. Ashamed of her reaction, heat flooded her neck and face.

No words—just one touch of this man's strong hands had completely unnerved her. Was she desperate for a man's touch? Was that why she'd succumbed so easily to ruin? Was she, at heart, as wanton as a saloon girl?

She hoped not, especially if she intended to take the veil.

"This is Bartholomew Houghton, our guest for supper." Chad introduced him. Crossing the threshold, her brother stood beside her with his arm draped around her shoulder. Facing their guest, he finished the introductions, "Bart, this is my sister, Lindsay MacKillian."

Bartholomew Houghton bowed low. "My pleasure, Miss MacKillian."

The sound of his voice was a lazy southern drawl—it reminded her of butter spreading over warm biscuits. And she experienced the queerest sensation again--spreading through her body—just from the sound of his voice.

She shivered and stared at Bartholomew Houghton.

Chad cleared his throat and squeezed her shoulder.

Startling, she silently chided herself. *What was happening to her?* She felt warm and then cold all over. Was she coming down with a fever?

"So... ah, so... glad to meet you, Mr. Houghton. Won't you please come in?"

"Yes, thank you." He stepped through the door. "But you must call me Bart. My full name might be Bartholomew, but it's a mouthful." He smiled. "And I'm not long on formalities."

"Of course." Not only was he handsome, he smelled good, like he'd come straight from a barbershop. She could smell the

# Let it Be Christmas

tangy odor of his hair tonic. Most men in West Texas smelled distinctly foul.

Chad glanced at her and frowned. She realized her brother wanted her to return the favor and tell this 'Bart' he could use her given name. But she had no intention of doing so, and she hoped Chad understood. The stranger's mere presence was already affecting her in ways she'd never imagined possible. She didn't dare allow him liberties with her name.

She settled the men in the parlor with scotch whiskeys and excused herself to put the finishing touches on her meal. When she reached the relative sanctuary of the kitchen, she shut the door and leaned against it. Her heart pounded and her chest heaved.

Closing her eyes, she counted to ten and willed her mind to go blank, a technique her Aunt Minnie had taught her to deal with unladylike responses. Usually the ploy worked, but this time, her mind refused to cooperate.

The stranger's—Bart's handsome countenance—was indelibly etched on her mind. Thinking of him gave her the strangest feeling she was falling and couldn't stop herself.

She opened her eyes and cursed low in French. Willing her limbs to move, she approached the stove and checked the pots and pans. Everything smelled all right, the subtle vegetable flavors mixing with the piquant smell of lamb. But she didn't see the food; it blurred before her eyes. She stirred the contents, but couldn't seem to focus on the meal.

Praying again that everything was properly prepared, she blindly heaped meat, vegetables and potatoes into platters and bowls. With the food sending ribbons of steam into the already overheated kitchen, she opened the door and called, "Supper's ready."

She sat at the table and unfolded her napkin, spreading it on her lap. She thought if she was seated and her attention diverted by serving the meal, she might be able to avoid staring at Bart.

# Let it Be Christmas

She heard their boots again, this time, crossing the small hallway. She had her head down, but like a magnet tugging toward north, her head came up with a will of its own. Her gaze met Bart's.

He had the most unusual blue eyes she'd ever seen. Eyes of such a light and penetrating blue they reminded her of the summer sky in West Texas when the sun had scorched the blue from the horizon until the sky appeared almost white. His pupils were a dark violet color, near black, in sharp contrast with the luminous hue of his blue irises.

And his lips *were* full and sensual looking. Sculpted like the Greek gods she'd studied in school, his mouth both enhanced and softened the bold masculine planes of his face. A raven lock of hair curled over his forehead, lending an unexpected boyish appeal to his features.

"Lindsay, may we be seated?" Chad asked.

His question jolted her. She *had* been staring. Heaven help her, with her mouth hanging open. She closed her mouth with a snap and tried to make an eloquent gesture with her hand, indicating the other two place settings.

Wetting her dry lips with her tongue, she said, "Please, sit where you like."

She tried to cover her nervousness by focusing on the meal, and she started passing the bowls and platters before the two men were settled, urging them, "Please, help yourselves."

Chad shot her a look and sat down quickly, taking the proffered platter from her trembling hands before he pulled his chair under the table.

Silently, she thanked her brother. She couldn't help but steal a glance at Bart from the corner of her eye. But he appeared to be blissfully unaware of anything odd. He was taking his time, settling into his chair and unfolding his napkin.

In point of fact, he seemed completely unaware of her.

And for some strange reason—Bart's indifference hurt more than when Seamus had deserted her.

# Let it Be Christmas

## Chapter Two

Chad took a helping from the platter and passed it to Bart. "Lindsay talked me into slaughtering a lamb for tonight. She says we should learn to eat mutton because we grow our own." He shrugged. "Our sheep are wool producers, but I'll try anything once. I hope you like mutton. My sister prepared the meal from a recipe she learned in Boston."

With her brother's complimentary words ringing in her ears, she managed to recover some of her aplomb. Crossing herself, she said, "I've been remiss, gentlemen, before we eat, would you please say grace, Chad?" She bowed her head.

Chad lowered his head, mouthing a quick prayer, thanking God for the bounty he'd provided. Everyone said "amen" and raised their heads.

Lindsay watched as her brother tried to cut his meat. What if the mutton was scorched? She tended to overcook meat on the outside while leaving it raw on the inside. And why had she allowed Bart's presence to upset her so much she hadn't properly checked the meal?

*Again, it was too late.*

Bart was cutting into the meat, too. "It's been some time since I was in the East, but I remember dining on some excellent lamb. I'm looking forward to sampling your cooking, Miss MacKillian." He raised his head and glanced at Lindsay. His lips curled into a polite smile, making his handsome face even more appealing.

Lindsay's face felt frozen at the thought that this man—Bart—would be comparing her cooking with other mutton dishes he'd sampled back East. She squeezed out a tiny smile and waved her hand in dismissal.

She certainly hoped she wouldn't have to cook when she became a nun. She knew the sisters all had jobs to do in the Boston convent she'd attended for her theology classes, but with her

# Let it Be Christmas

finishing school education, she hoped they'd let her teach. Not cook.

"It's just simple food, Mr. Houghton. I can't hope to compare with fancy hotels or restaurants you might have—"

"Did I mention I'd dined on mutton in fancy hotels or restaurants, Miss MacKillian?" His question was softly spoken but carried an unmistakable challenge, and his blue eyes seemed to see right through her.

"No, but I assumed that..."

Chad cleared his throat and said, "Let's eat. I'm starving. We can continue our conversation while we eat."

Lindsay and Bart nodded in unison. And the three of them cut into their meat and took a taste of the vegetables, except Lindsay didn't really taste her meal. She was too afraid of what she'd find; instead, she sawed at the mutton and pushed the mushy potatoes and vegetables around her plate.

And if she was a proper hostess, she should be making brilliant forays at polite conversation, but her mind was like a lake of quicksand, ideas bubbled to the surface only to sink again. She had a million questions, but when directed at Bart, they seemed strangely intimate to ask.

"Pardon my reach." Bart stretched his hand toward the loaf of bread.

Lindsay nodded and smiled.

And she couldn't fail to notice his fingers as he helped himself to a slice of bread. They were long and tapered, the nails clean and rounded. The hands of a gentleman, but something more, too. She had experienced their tensile strength and rough surface when he'd held her hand. They were the hands of a *man*.

Chad cleared his throat again, startling Lindsay from her study of Bart's hands. She dropped her head and vowed to stop staring at him. She must carry off this supper for her brother's sake.

She searched for something innocuous to say but before she could open her mouth, Chad resuscitated the lagging conversation.

133

# Let it Be Christmas

"Bart is from the South. You might have noticed his accent, Lindsay."

She swallowed a bite of parsley steamed potatoes. "Yes, I noticed." She turned toward Bart, but was careful to stare at the pearl buttons of his vest.

If she could manage to avoid looking at his face, or any other part of him, she might be able to sustain an intelligent conversation.

"What part of the South are you from, Mr. Houghton?"

"Please call me Bart, Miss MacKillian."

"But you called me Miss MacKillian," she pointed out.

"Gentlemanly courtesy. Though, if you call me by my given name, I'll call you Lindsay."

She refused to rise to his challenge. "So, what part of the South are you from?"

"I'm from Alabama, born and bred."

"But he's traveled all over the West for many years," Chad said.

"How interesting. In what capacity have you undertaken your travels, Bartholomew?"

"Bart, not Bartholomew," he corrected. "Are you inquiring after my profession, Miss Lindsay?"

Chad rolled his eyes. She was surprised by her brother's reaction. After all, she was only trying to make conversation. What could be wrong with asking the man's profession?

"I am... was... a professional gambler," Bart said.

She gulped and gazed directly at Bart's face, despite her best intentions.

Having taken her first bite of the mutton, it was as she'd feared, raw on the inside and burned on the outside. Almost choking on her failed experiment, she was aghast to learn this unsettling man—this stranger—this Bart—was a professional gambler.

*She hated gamblers!*

# Let it Be Christmas

Gambling was a sin and a disease. Almost as bad as the sin she'd committed... or maybe, even worse.

Seamus' family had been wealthy, at one time, but her Aunt Minnie's investigator had learned he'd gambled the family fortune away—all before he'd turned thirty-five years old. If not for gambling, she might be married and settled in a big house in Boston, counting the months until she birthed a healthy son for her once-upon-a-time fiancé.

But after *knowing* her in the most intimate of ways, when Seamus' failed fortunes were uncovered, he'd fled. But if her aunt had known she was pregnant, she would have forced them to marry and given Seamus her inheritance.

After all, that was what he'd been after. And then like Abby's first disastrous marriage, she'd be shackled to a man who didn't love her, who only wanted her for money. She'd thought long and hard about her choices before returning home. And really, she'd had no other choice.

"Forgive my sister's startled reaction, Bart. She's been delicately reared by our widowed aunt in Boston," Chad explained.

Turning to Lindsay, her brother clarified, "Bart says he's a professional gambler. But he no longer pursues the profession. He's in Langtry to find an investment to suit his future plans."

"How commendable," she said, but she couldn't keep the note of sarcasm from her voice.

And her sarcasm wasn't lost on Bart. "I hope, Miss MacKillian, you will show me the error of my ways."

She gasped at his effrontery. "I won't apologize for my views, Mr. Houghton. I can't abide gambling in any form." She bobbed her head. "There. You've forced the truth from me."

"How commendable, Miss MacKillian," Bart echoed her.

"I brought Bart home because he wants to invest in our ranch and become a part owner."

Her mind spun in dazed amazement, and her fingers went numb. She couldn't believe it. This man—a stranger and professed gambler—a part owner of their ranch?

# Let it Be Christmas

*What was her brother thinking?*

Bart glanced at Lindsay, and he touched the linen napkin to his mouth. He leaned toward Chad, offering, "I think it would be wise if I excused myself so y'all can discuss my partnership in private."

But Bart wasn't just excusing himself from a sticky situation; Lindsay hadn't missed the pointed message in his light blue eyes. It was obvious he was surprised and dismayed with Chad, too. Bart must have thought her brother had already explained the purpose of his visit. It made her angry to think Chad hadn't told her. Why would he keep something so important to himself?

*Because he feared her reaction as much as she feared his when he learned his unwed sister was pregnant?*

And she'd been hopelessly naive. In her effort to appear ladylike, she'd focused her energies on the house, cooking, and laundry. She hadn't asked about the ranch and how it was prospering. A mistake she vowed not to repeat. After all, half of the ranch belonged to her.

"Let's not be hasty, Bart," Chad said, touching Bart's arm. "Please, finish your meal. My sister and I will talk later."

Glancing in Lindsay's direction again, Bart hesitated and then nodded. When he returned the napkin to his lap, he speared his first bite of meat.

Lindsay watched him as he slowly chewed the half-cooked lamb. She'd wanted to serve a perfect meal. But when Bart swallowed the mutton with difficulty, followed by a deep drink of water, she shuddered and was embarrassed.

They ate in silence for several minutes. Then, the peaceful interlude was broken by her brother's knife and fork clattering on the rose-patterned china plate. He'd eaten his potatoes and vegetables, but his unconsumed portion of mutton lay on his plate like a silent reproach.

Her brother gazed at her and lifted one eyebrow, disappointment etched on his features.

# Let it Be Christmas

Lindsay's momentary embarrassment evaporated when confronted by her brother's attitude. Resentment burned in the pit of her stomach at his injustice, and she felt as if he was using the poorly-prepared leg of lamb to bludgeon her into accepting Bart's partnership in the ranch.

Faced with difficult circumstances, she recalled her Aunt Minnie's advice as clearly as if she was standing there: *'Maintain your ladylike demeanor in the face of adversity and no man can vanquish you.'*

Remembering her aunt's words gave her courage, and she took several deep breaths, dispelling her anger. Returning her brother's gaze, she smiled prettily while he tried to stare her down. And she managed to finish her mutton, by cutting it into tiny pieces, smiling all the while, between bites.

Chad grunted and looked away.

One down and one to go, she thought smugly.

Wanting to know Bart's reaction, she slanted her gaze at him. And she was secretly relieved to find he'd finished his lamb and everything else on his plate.

Wiping his mouth with his napkin, Bart said, "Lovely meal, Miss MacKillian. I'm much obliged for your hospitality."

Despite her mixed feelings, a warm glow suffused her. She inclined her head and hoped she wasn't blushing.

Chad wiped his mouth, too, and half rose from his chair. "Bart, if you'd be kind enough to wait upon the porch with coffee or a drink, I would like to speak with my sister."

"My pleasure. I'll take a cup of coffee, if it's not too much trouble," he replied, placing his napkin on the table and scraping back his chair.

But before he could rise, there was a loud yelp.

*Minnie!*

Bart glanced down and cursed under his breath.

Lindsay looked under the table at the same time Bart reached down to find her dog's tail pinned between his chair leg and the table.

"Minnie!" Lindsay cried out and leapt to her feet.

# Let it Be Christmas

Chad jumped to his feet, too, and roared, "You promised to lock her up!"

"I thought I did, but sometimes, she worries the latch open with her nose."

"Well, use a damned padlock then!"

Lindsay shot Chad a venomous look. Her brother didn't like Minnie. It had been one of the many disappointments she'd faced when she returned home.

She held out her arms and leaned down, crooning softly to coax the tiny dog. Bart had already freed her Maltese's tail, thank heavens.

Chad frowned and took a step around the side of the oval table, looking as if he'd like to drown her dog in the horse trough.

Bart considered them both, advancing upon him, swinging his head back and forth, before he drawled, "Ambushed, and now I'm surrounded on both sides. I never realized how dangerous Langtry was."

Chad stopped abruptly and looked confused. It was obvious he couldn't decide whether Bart was joking or not. Lindsay ignored the two men and scooped up her dog, feeding her a tiny piece of mutton from the platter.

Bart smiled and patted Minnie's fluffy, white topknot.

But her brother wasn't so easily deflected. He lunged for the dog and bellowed, "By God, what are you doing? Feeding that animal at the table like he's a human?"

"Minnie is a she, named after our Aunt Minerva," she said.

"I don't care," Chad replied. "I want her out of the dining room and back in her crate."

Lindsay hugged her dog close and frowned at her brother. But Bart forestalled Chad by gently lifting the Maltese from her arms and settling her in his lap. He reached across his clean plate and plucked another bite of mutton from the platter, feeding it to Minnie.

"She's a sweet little pup," he said. "Where did you get her?"

# Let it Be Christmas

"Worthless bit of dog, not good for hunting or herding." Chad groused and sat back down.

Bart stroked Minnie's soft fur and chuckled.

The tension drained from Lindsay when she realized Bart, unlike her brother, liked her dog.

"My Aunt Minerva has had Maltese dogs for a long time. Her husband owned a shipping fleet. He brought them back from the island of Malta," she explained. "Their breed is ancient, going back thousands of years. Minnie is the last pup from the two dogs my aunt still has."

He nodded. "I've read about the breed. Like greyhounds, who the Egyptians bred, they *are* an ancient breed." He lifted Minnie in his hands and looked her over. "Interesting, indeed."

"Yeah, that dog might be the Queen of Siam, for all I care. But what's she good for?" Chad asked.

"For companionship and comfort," she said. "Our aunt gave her to me when I returned to Boston after Father died."

Chad lowered his head and grunted again, crossing his arms over his chest.

"What happened to your father, Lindsay?" Bart asked, cradling Minnie in his arms.

"He tried to ride a half-busted bronc." She shrugged, but inside, she was still grieving. "The bronc threw him, and he broke his neck."

"My condolences." He glanced at her and then Chad. "To you both."

"Thank you," she and her brother answered.

"You've been very gracious, Bart," Chad said. "I appreciate your forbearance with this—my sister's bizarre pet."

"Not so bizarre, lots of royalty and nobility have small dogs for companionship." He glanced at Lindsay. "Aren't they called 'lap dogs?'"

"Yes, that's correct," she said. Her initial animosity toward Bart was melting, like a flake of snow in a Langtry winter. He'd

# Let it Be Christmas

asked all the right questions about Minnie, hadn't been condescending or nasty, like her brother.

"Lap dogs. Useless things." Her brother snorted. "That's about all they're good for, to take up someone's lap."

She trembled at her brother's mean words. Why couldn't he be more understanding, like Bart? Was this a sample of the reaction she'd get when she told him about her shameful condition?

"Lindsay, could you please remove the *animal* and fetch Bart the coffee he requested," Chad said. "I want to talk with you in private."

Lindsay raised her chin a notch. "I'll take Minnie and get Bartholomew's coffee right away."

Leaning forward, she stretched her arms out.

Gently, Bart cupped the Maltese in his two big hands and lifted her into Lindsay's waiting ones. Their fingers touched briefly, and she experienced the same jolt of heated current pass between them again. This time, instead of the sensation alarming her, exhilaration fizzed in her veins like a fine champagne. Tendrils of heat spread through her, and she knew her face was turning a deep red.

With Minnie safely cradled in one arm, she turned away, not wanting the two men to see her blush. But before she'd taken more than a few steps to return Minnie to her crate, a thought occurred to her.

"Could you excuse us for a moment? I need to take Minnie out. She's house-broken, but she's been locked up too long."

"What in the Sam Hill does that mean?" Chad asked.

"That Minnie, if taken outside, will do her duty and not stain your carpets or foul her crate," Bart said, glancing at Lindsay. "Am I right?"

"Yes, thank you, that's correct." She turned to her brother and announced, "And tonight, she stays inside with me. Not in the barn."

Chad stared at her as if his eyes could have shot bullets.

140

# Let it Be Christmas

But Bart, gentleman that he was, sprang to his feet and bowed low, his Southern-accented voice dripping molasses and honey. "I'm happy to have been of assistance, even if it was a lucky guess on my part." His gaze met hers, and she read both an offer and a challenge there. "I've often depended upon my luck and seldom been disappointed."

Understanding his double meaning, she lowered her gaze. He was daring her to accept him on his own terms, his shady past as a gambler interwoven with his unusual tenderness toward her pet. He wanted her to see him as he really was—not as a sinner and man of ill-repute.

Lindsay didn't know how to respond. She wanted to accept him, but a part of her held back. A professional gambler must also be a good actor. What if his kindness was only a facade to win her acceptance? Having been fooled before, it was hard to trust.

She splayed one hand over her belly, as if protecting the child there.

# Let it Be Christmas

## Chapter Three

Bart balanced his coffee cup on one knee and lounged against the porch rail. He couldn't help but overhear the raised voices coming from the house. Chad and Lindsay were obviously having a heated discussion. Not that he was surprised. On the contrary, he had expected it.

Taking a sip of the strong, black coffee, Bart empathized with Lindsay. It had been damned foolish of Chad to have neglected to prepare her. Why hadn't he told his sister what they were planning before bringing Bart to meet her?

He prided himself on his diplomacy and skill with people. But if Chad intended for him to charm Lindsay so she'd accept him as a partner, he should have warned him. And she didn't strike him as a woman who was easily swayed. She struck him as very high-minded and principled, not easily influenced by charm.

Chad's idea, to purchase her interest over time, had convinced Bart to go through with the deal after he'd learned she owned half of the ranch. Chad intimated Lindsay would probably marry and return to Boston, using their buy-out as her dowry.

He set his empty coffee cup to one side and removed a Cuban cigar from his vest pocket. He lit and puffed on the cigar, but his thoughts kept returning to Chad's unmarried sister.

Men outnumbered women by at least three to one in West Texas. Despite Lindsay's limitations in the kitchen and her stiff and formal demeanor, she should have plenty of suitors, even if she didn't go back to Boston.

Yes, Lindsay was one handsome woman with a fine figure. She possessed wide, hazel eyes and glorious golden hair. Her nose was pert and her strawberry-red mouth ripe for kissing. And he didn't dare dwell on her lush body beneath the fashionable clothes. If he was the marrying kind, he'd almost be tempted. Lucky for him he'd never aspired to be a family man.

# Let it Be Christmas

Still, Lindsay MacKillian wouldn't be a bad way to spend the rest of his life.

He doubted she'd be with them for long, though. Men would probably flock from four counties to court her. But Chad needed her consent for their business arrangement, and he was dismayed to think Chad had already bungled the deal by mishandling her.

Drawing on his cigar, he watched as the evening stars appeared in the sky, one by one. If he strained his ears, he could hear the contented bleating of sheep bedding down for the night. The acrid tang of creosote bushes wafted to him on the twilight breeze. He breathed deeply of the fresh air, enjoying this wild and largely uninhabited place, where a man could see the unbroken horizon stretching away for hundreds of miles to the mountains deep in México.

He couldn't bear to think of settling anywhere else.

\* \* \*

"Why didn't you tell me about Mr. Houghton? I never dreamed you wanted a partner. When I went back to Boston, the ranch was making a tidy profit," Lindsay said.

"And when you left, there was tariff protection for domestic wool producers. Since last year, there's been no protection. Our wool has to compete with Australian and South American wool," Chad explained.

"Oh," his sister said. "I didn't know."

"And I didn't bother you with the details because I thought you'd marry and remain in Boston."

She looked down. Chad wasn't the only person keeping secrets. She'd had a whole week to tell him about her shameful state, but she'd said nothing. She glanced out the front window toward the porch. Telling him while Bart was only a few feet away wasn't her ideal way to bare her disgrace. Besides, she wanted to know more about the ranch, first.

"I need to know how bad the financial situation is, Chad."

143

# Let it Be Christmas

Her brother puffed out his cheeks, as if he was taking a deep breath before plunging over his head. "Without tariff protection, our wool didn't make a profit from the last two shears. Not after shipping and overhead. All of the money we'd saved, I've put back into the ranch. But it isn't enough if we're going to compete. We need to grow bigger so we can obtain preferred shipping rates on the railroad, and we need more Merino rams to upgrade our wool. And there are some major repairs that should be made, such as replacing the entire northern fence line."

He combed his fingers through his hair. "That's about it, Lindsay. Now you know."

"Yes, I'm beginning to understand. Have you thought of taking out a loan at a bank?" She asked.

"Of course, I have, but I would rather grow with a partner whose capital is committed to the ranch, than go into debt when the times are uncertain. And as the ranch grows, I'll need help. A partner seemed to be the perfect solution." His shoulders drooped. "I've given the matter a great deal of consideration. I don't want to mortgage the ranch and run the risk of losing it."

Lindsay patted his shoulder. "I didn't realize what you've been going through. You should have written me or at least told me when I came home. I want to help. I wish you would have explained before bringing Mr. Houghton to supper." She smoothed her skirts. "What are you going to do about my share?"

"Bart and I are going to buy you out, over time."

"And how much of the ranch are we giving Bart for his capital?"

"He will own one-third. In the meantime, you and I will own the other two-thirds, as equal partners. Just as father left it." He gazed at her. "But if you're going to marry, we need to buy you out now."

"Why?"

"Because once you marry, your husband will own your share, not you, Lindsay. It was one of the reasons I wondered why

144

# Let it Be Christmas

Father left you half of the ranch. I thought he would have set aside a dowry for you."

"I don't think it works that way in Texas. Aunt Minnie was very knowledgeable about business affairs. She explained that, in Massachusetts, anything I inherited becomes the property of my husband. But Texas' laws are based on old Spanish customs. They have a law called community property, which means anything I inherit is still mine, even though I'm married. Though half the income belongs to my husband."

"Is that so?"

"Yes, and I think it's one of the reasons Aunt Minnie is going to leave you half of her shipping business and warehouses in Boston. Because, as a man in Massachusetts, your half would stay in the family."

Chad grunted. "That's nice to know Aunt Minnie is including me, too."

"I think she and Father decided to do it this way, split both inheritances between the two of us, so we'd be certain to have a stake in each place, whether I decided to stay in Boston or come home." She sighed and lowered her head. "But now it doesn't really matter. I won't be needing my part of the ranch or Aunt Minnie's inheritance, either."

It was past time to tell him, with or without Bart around. Besides, *everyone* would know her secret soon enough. Chad had shared his situation with her, and he needed to know what she planned to do, so he could deal with Bart and move forward with the ranch.

She went on tip-toe and kissed his cheek. "I'll sign over my part of the ranch to you. That will make it easier for you and Bart."

His eyes widened, and his mouth went slack. "Why... why would you do that?"

She lowered her head again and gazed at her high-top boots. In her hurry to get supper started, she'd missed one of the holes to lace them up.

# Let it Be Christmas

He raised his eyebrows and pulled a crumpled piece of paper from his pocket. He thrust it at her. "This just came from our Aunt Minnie. I got it when I picked up Bart in town. I don't quite understand it, but I know you will."

Gazing at the crumpled telegram, her heart plummeted and a wave of nausea crawled up her throat. The half-cooked mutton lay like a pile of bricks at the bottom of her stomach. But she'd known it was coming—that Aunt Minnie would telegraph or write her brother.

She took the crumpled paper from her brother and smoothed it out, silently mouthing the words:

> "Hope Lindsay arrived in Langtry
> safe. STOP Please advise. STOP She
> left Boston in hurry. STOP She is
> welcome back. STOP No matter
> what Seamus did. STOP"

"I thought you were engaged to this Seamus. What is Aunt Minnie talking about? What did he do to you, and why did you rush home without explaining?"

"I'm going to have a baby."

He stared at her, his eyes bulging in his face. He took a deep breath and then another. He was panting, breathing hard, like when he wrestled a sheep to the ground. "You're what?"

"Please, don't make me repeat it." She glanced out the front window again.

He fisted his hands and brought them up in a fighter's stance. Good Lord, was he going to strike her? She'd never expected her beloved brother to lay a hand on her, no matter what she'd done.

"And this Seamus, your fiancé, he's the one who did it to you. Right?" His face had turned a mottled red, and he leaned closer, thrusting his face into hers.

She backed up a few paces and nodded.

# Let it Be Christmas

He cursed under his breath. "I'll kill him! I'll get on the first train to Boston and kill the man. I swear it."

She reached out and touched his arm. "He's gone, Chad. Aunt Minnie had him investigated and learned he'd gambled his family's money away. She let it be known I wouldn't be inheriting from her." She cleared her throat and felt the familiar creep of heat flooding her neck and face. "He fled Boston. I'm certain Aunt Minnie's investigator could find him, but she didn't want me to marry him. He was a fortune hunter."

His mouth gaped open, and he glanced at her stomach. "Then how did he—"

"Get me with child?" she whispered, keeping her head lowered. "It happened before Aunt Minnie found out he'd lost his fortune. I let him seduce me, let him *anticipate* our wedding night." She plucked at her brother's sleeve. "I'd waited so long to marry, and I thought Seamus…" She shook her head again. "I'm twenty-eight years old and—"

"And you came home to hide and have your baby?"

She nodded and then lifted her head, gazing directly into his eyes. "But I'm prepared to atone for my sin." She fingered her mother's wedding ring beneath the stiff layer of her bodice. "I'll have the baby, return to Boston and enter a convent. I'll spend my life as a nun, asking God's forgiveness." She crossed herself.

"What about the baby?"

"I had thought to take the child to an orphanage in Boston, but when I saw Abby—"

"Abby, who is Abby?"

"You probably don't remember her… or you remember her as Abigail Kerr."

"The girl your age at the boardinghouse in Del Rio?"

"Yes."

"What's she got to do with this?"

"We've stayed in contact over the years by writing letters. She's grown up, and she's been widowed and then remarried. She has an eight-year-old son with another on the way."

# Let it Be Christmas

He crossed his arms over his chest. "I still don't understand."

"I stopped in Del Rio and told Abby about my condition." She gazed at him, hoping he could see the pleading look in her eyes. "I needed to practice before telling you." She hesitated and laced her fingers together. "And then Abby said, rather than taking my baby to an orphanage and letting strangers raise my child, she and her new husband, Sheriff Graham, would raise the child as their own."

Thinking about Abby's offer, tears burned at the back of her throat. She sniffed, not wanting to cry, especially in front of her brother.

"Is that what you want, Lindsay?" he asked.

She twisted her fingers together, pulling at them until the joints hurt. "I guess it's better than an orphanage, isn't it?"

"And you want to be a nun?"

"Not really. I don't have a true vocation. But I'm a ruined woman. What else is there for me?" She turned aside, not wanting her brother to see the hot tears spilling over.

"There's another way. A way you can keep your baby and stay here. What if it's a boy?"

She lifted one shoulder. "What if it is?"

"Don't you see, he's family. You should want to raise your own child."

"What if my child is a girl?"

Chad hesitated, as if considering. Then he shook his head. "Same thing."

"But the child, what about the child? He or she would be stained as a bastard. I know Langtry is a wild kind of place, but there are people who would—"

"Bart will marry you and give the child a name. I'll make it part of our partnership agreement." He snapped his fingers. "It's the perfect solution." He gazed at her, his lips twitching, almost smiling. "I'd thought when y'all met that maybe, since you hadn't said anything about your engagement, you'd be attracted—"

148

# Let it Be Christmas

"Attracted? Attracted, indeed? What do you take me for?" Not a fair question, considering she was with child and unmarried. She closed her eyes and whispered, "Forget I said that, but why would he marry a ruined woman for a business partnership?"

"Because he owes me." Chad looked down and kicked at a worn spot in the parlor rug with the toe of his boot. "I saved his life at the Jersey Lily. Some of the boys thought he was cheating. He's so damned good at cards, it looks like cheating, but it isn't."

"And this is the kind of man you want me to marry? To partner with and raise my child? A professional gambler? I just told you what happened to my fiancé; he gambled his inheritance away."

"Bart's not like that. He comes from a good family. His father was a preacher or something. He learned early he was good at counting cards, it gave him an advantage, and let him drift around the West without having to work."

"Chad, that's what I mean, he's a gambler. A bad man, he's—"

"But he's done with gambling. He's seen the West and knows it's filling up and changing. He's tired of roaming, and there's nothing for him in Alabama. And he's saved his money. He wants to invest his money in our ranch."

She shuddered. "Blood money. Bad money."

"You shouldn't judge."

She sucked in her breath and leaned over, clutching her stomach. If he had struck her, he couldn't have hurt her more. Her stomach heaved, and she was afraid she'd be sick.

But he must have realized how she felt because he reached out and took her into his arms. "I shouldn't have said that, Lindsay. Shouldn't have judged you." He grasped her shoulders and held her at arm's length. "None of us should judge. Bart wants to start over. Is that so bad?"

"No, no, I can understand." She backed up a pace, as he released her. "But I don't want a husband." She shook her head from side to side. "I don't want a man to touch me again. Never!"

149

# Let it Be Christmas

"I understand, Sis. But the marriage could be in name only. After you have the baby, you could get a divorce or something. Then you'd be free to do as you please, but you'd still have your child and the child would have a name."

She hung her head. "I don't know, Chad. I don't know. It's all too much." She lifted her head and gazed at him. "Can I have time to think about it? And don't you need to get Bart's agreement, too?"

"Yes, I need to explain to Bart. But the sooner you get married, the better or—"

"Or tongues will wag and all of Langtry will be counting backwards on their fingers."

"Yes."

She shook her head. "I don't know. I need to think it over."

\* \* \*

"You want me to do what?" Bart asked.

"Marry my sister as part of our agreement," Chad said.

"Because she got herself in the family way, and her fiancé ran off?"

"That's about the extent of it."

"Does Lindsay want this? Want me?" Bart scrubbed his chin. "She didn't seem to take to my past profession."

"She's thinking it over, Bart." Chad snagged his gaze. "I won't lie to you. But the marriage could be in name only. Then you could divorce."

"And all three of us would live here on the ranch, not to mention her child?"

"She might return to Boston. Our aunt said she was welcome back, no matter what."

Bart paced to the edge of the front porch, thinking. A sham marriage to give Lindsay's child a name. His blessed mother would have said it was the Christian thing to do. And even though Chad hadn't mentioned it, he did owe Chad his life.

# Let it Be Christmas

But could he pull it off, marry Lindsay and keep his hands off her? Keep their relationship strictly business? She was a beautiful woman, and even though she seemed stiff and even judgmental, he couldn't help but be attracted to her. Underneath all that primness, he thought he'd glimpsed a giving heart and a generous nature.

There was a lot to like about Chad's sister. And even though he'd never envisioned himself as a family man, he might be willing to settle down, if they were suited to each other. And they'd have plenty of time to find out—until she gave birth.

He stroked his chin, considering. Would it bother him to raise another man's child? Not really. He'd often wished someone would have adopted him after his mother died. Then he wouldn't have been subjected to his father's mean-spirited and tyrannical rule. Children were innocent and deserved a loving start.

Having made his decision, he turned and crossed the porch. He clasped Chad's hand and shook it. "Partner, you have yourself a deal. I'd be honored to be part of your family… no matter the circumstances."

# Let it Be Christmas

## Chapter Four

Bart found Lindsay where Chad had said she'd be—coming from the one-room schoolhouse in Langtry, which also served as the town's church on Sunday. It had been two weeks since Bart had eaten supper with the MacKillians, and Chad had asked him to marry his pregnant sister to give her child a name.

At first, he'd been shocked by the proposal. But the more he thought about it and how much he liked Lindsay, along with feeling sorry for her situation, he knew he couldn't refuse. And besides, it was the decent and Christian thing to do.

But the sooner they got married, the better. Time was a' wasting.

Chad had told him Lindsay needed time to think it over. He shook his head. He would have thought she would have leapt at the chance to give her baby a name and cover her shame.

*Women! What man in his right mind could understand them?*

One of the reasons he was still single but not for much longer, at least on paper.

He watched as Lindsay approached with a basket dangling from her arm. Chad had told him she was trying to raise money to construct a separate building for a church in Langtry. According to her brother, it was her first objective in a long list of items she wanted to accomplish for the betterment of her hometown.

In theory, Bart admired Lindsay for her high ideals and willingness to help others. But in practice, he believed it was better to mind your own business.

Lindsay's chosen calling reminded him of his mother and her never-ending round of charities and volunteer committees. A preacher's wife was expected to take on those commitments, but Bart realized at an early age his mother was happiest when she was helping others.

*And it had been the death of her.*

# Let it Be Christmas

After his mother was gone, all the softness and warmth had disappeared from his home. His father was a self-righteous, tyrannical man of the cloth, long on discipline and short on love. Bart fled his unhappy home as soon as he was able to support himself.

Good at arithmetic, it had been easy to learn to count cards, and he'd drifted into playing cards for a living. And there was a side-benefit, too, it had scandalized his self-righteous, bigoted father.

He'd never enjoyed being a gambling man, only the advantages it afforded him to travel and see the West. He'd always known he'd settle down, so he'd saved his money to invest in a business and, after weighing all his options, he believed ranching suited him.

As he waited for Lindsay, he couldn't help but notice how the hot July sun reflected off her golden hair, creating a nimbus of light around her head. Almost like a halo. His angel, the thought came to him, unbidden. A fallen angel, perhaps, but still an angel.

She looked up and when she glimpsed him, her eyes widened. She wore a green cotton dress, and her hazel eyes reflected the color of the dress, a cool green that reminded him of the jade good-luck piece he'd won from a Chinaman in San Francisco.

Being married to Lindsay, even in name only, was going to prove even trickier than he'd initially thought. He couldn't help but be attracted to her. Unfortunately, her brother had made it clear she didn't want a man to touch her. And that might prove to be quite a challenge… not touching her.

Maybe, with enough time, he could change her mind.

He tipped his hat and greeted her with, "Good morning, Miss MacKillian."

"Good morning, Mr. Houghton, ah, Bartholomew. I'm surprised to find you here."

"Chad told me where you'd be. I was waiting for you." He held out his hand and offered, "Let me carry that basket for you."

"Thank you, but there's no need. It's empty." She stepped past him and continued down the dusty path.

# Let it Be Christmas

But he wasn't going to let her off that easy. Falling in beside her, he matched his stride with hers. She carried herself proudly, striding with purpose. And he savored how good she smelled, like lavender, if he was any judge—a subtle but beguiling perfume.

Hell, he was so busy admiring her, he'd almost forgotten why he'd intercepted her. Pulling himself back to the business at hand, he considered the situation. Should he just blurt out what he was thinking? He was usually a straight-forward kind of man, but maybe a little polite conversation might make a tricky situation easier.

"Chad tells me you're trying to raise money for a new church. What's wrong with using the schoolhouse? There's no school on Sundays."

Lindsay stopped and stared at him. He couldn't help but notice how her full, rounded bosom rose and fell provocatively beneath the thin cotton of her dress. He was certain she had discarded her corset since the last time he saw her. Privately, he approved of her courageous choice. It was far too hot in Langtry to be wearing a corset during July, no matter what fashion might dictate. And not to mention her figure would soon be expanding, and no amount of corseting would conceal it.

Her eyes narrowed, and the tone of her voice betrayed an attitude of self-righteousness he'd learned to despise. "I'm not surprised someone with your background, Mr. Houghton, would question the need for an edifice solely devoted to the worship of God."

He hadn't expected such a sharp retort. He felt a sinking sensation. He'd hoped they could get along and learn to like each other. But her priggish attitude was becoming more and more disappointing.

He clenched his teeth to keep from throwing her words back at her, pointing out she should be the last person to judge him.

"Just because I was a professional gambler, Miss MacKillian, doesn't mean I was birthed on a poker table and suckled on whiskey. I, like you, had a mother and she taught me about God and

# Let it Be Christmas

Jesus. And I've been known to darken the interior of a church on occasion."

Lindsay's face was a study. Her mouth pursed into a startled 'O,' and her amply-endowed chest heaved up and down. He had purposely chosen the image he wanted to convey, speaking openly of birthing and suckling, to strip away her prudish defenses.

She closed her mouth and took several deep breaths, but she wouldn't meet his gaze. "Forgive me, Bartholomew, I didn't think how I sounded. It was rude and un-Christian of me to suggest—"

"Forget it, Miss MacKillian. You were about to tell me the reasons Langtry needs a new church."

"Uh, yes, well, if you're interested." She took another deep breath and launched into what sounded suspiciously like her rehearsed pitch to raise money. "We need a separate building for the church because moving desks every Sunday to accommodate worshipers is inconvenient and because there are other occasions for a church during the week, such as for prayer meetings, bible studies, the ladies circle and..." She shrugged. "There are many reasons why Langtry needs a church."

"I think it's a commendable task you've set yourself. It should benefit everyone in Langtry." He hesitated, needing to take the plunge. "But I doubt it will be ready in time for us to marry."

"Oh... uh, yes. Uh, I mean, no. Or..." She threw up one hand and her face turned red.

She could blush at the drop of a handkerchief. He'd lost count of the times she'd blushed during their supper. But then again, what he'd proposed, no pun intended, considering the circumstances, was blush-worthy.

"Have you thought about what your brother is recommending?" he asked.

"Have I thought about it? Have I thought about it?" She shook her head. "It's all I think about. Night and day. Waking and sleeping."

"And have you reached a conclusion?"

155

# Let it Be Christmas

"No, I can't… I mean, I don't understand how this would work. Chad explained to you I wouldn't be a real wife. Didn't he?"

"Yes, he explained, and I understand. But I believe you should be thinking of your child. Don't you want your child?"

She spread her hand over her stomach. "Of course, I want my child. What do you take me for, Mr. Houghton?"

"I wanted to hear you say it."

She tossed her head. "I've said it. I *want* my child."

"Then, can you be ready tomorrow morning? Chad can bring you to the Jersey Lily and give you away."

She wrinkled her nose, as if something smelled bad. "Have that old reprobate join us in marriage? I despise Judge Roy Bean and his conniving ways. Besides, he lost the last election. He's not even the real Justice of the Peace anymore. He just keeps operating as if he is."

"Which makes him the perfect choice. Dissolving a marriage later should prove easy."

"I see. Does that mean you can't wait to be rid of me, after you do 'the right thing' to help my brother?"

"That's not what I meant." He wanted to grab her shoulders and shake some sense into her. "I thought it was what *you* wanted."

"Well, yes, you're right."

He took her elbow. "Let me escort you to your buckboard. That way, people will see us together."

She let him take her arm. "We won't be fooling most people, Mr. Houghton."

"I know, Miss MacKillian, but we must try to put a good face on it." He glanced at her. "I'll expect you tomorrow morning at ten o'clock, sharp."

She turned her face away. "Indeed. I'll tell Chad."

\* \* \*

"And do you, Bartholomew Houghton, take this woman, Lindsay MacKillian, to be your lawfully wedded wife? Do you

156

# Let it Be Christmas

promise to love, honor, cherish and protect her, forsaking all others?

"I do." Bart's lazy drawl brought Lindsay back to her senses.

Luckily, at ten o'clock in the morning, the Jersey Lily was deserted. The saloon smelled of sweat, stale beer and sawdust, but at least they were alone, except for the Judge.

She wondered if Bart had thought of that when he'd proposed the time and place. If he had, she silently thanked him from the bottom of her heart. Though how she would explain their hurried marriage, with Judge Bean officiating, to Parson Samuels and his wife, when she was working with them to build a new church, was something she didn't like to think about.

Possibly the difference in their religions? After all, she *was* a professed Catholic. And there was no priest nearby. No, for a Catholic priest, they would have to send to Del Rio. She hoped Parson Samuels would understand, or at least, act like he did.

The remainder of the wedding vows passed in a haze. She managed to croak "I do." And then the Judge asked, "Do ya have a ring, Bart?"

Bart sucked in his breath and replied, "No, I forgot." He gazed at Lindsay, and if she understood the look in his eyes, he wanted her to believe he really *was* sorry. "We were so caught up in the moment."

Judge Bean snorted.

Lindsay reached inside her light blue, second-best, organza dress and tugged hard on the ribbon around her neck. *Her mother's wedding ring.* She hadn't thought it would serve such a purpose. But her mother would have wanted her first grandchild to have a last name.

She handed the simple golden band to Bart. "Here."

"Thank you." He gazed at her, the look in his eyes asking her forgiveness.

"It was my mother's."

He kissed the ring and said, "Bless your mother's soul."

# Let it Be Christmas

"Yes." She held out her left hand with her ring finger extended.

He slipped the ring on her finger.

"Good," Judge Bean said. "I pronounce you man and wife." He looked at Bart. "You may kiss the bride."

But when Bart turned to kiss her, she wanted to bolt. They'd agreed it was a sham marriage, so why did she have to kiss him?

*To keep up appearances.*

She puckered up and closed her eyes, holding tightly to Bart's arm. His lips brushed hers, a light, quick touch. But just that touch left her lips burning, as if she'd bitten into a *jalapeño* pepper.

Not thinking what she was doing, she reached up and touched her lips with her fingertips. She wanted him to kiss her again. Heaven help her. She wanted him to kiss her long and deep.

*What was wrong with her? Was she really a wanton woman? What would happen when they dissolved the marriage? Would she chase everything in trousers?*

But kissing Seamus had never been like that. She'd thought she loved him, but maybe, she'd just been in love with getting married. She'd come late to her Aunt Minnie, mostly unschooled in the social graces. She'd had to learn everything about society and etiquette and then come out at the ripe old age of twenty-one-years old.

To make things tougher, the Boston Irish were considered *nouveau* rich by the Brahmin Bostonians of the social register. Wealthy Irish mixed with other wealthy and Catholic Irishmen, and there weren't many Irish socialites. Seamus Finnegan had been an answer to her prayers. He was part of her Aunt Minnie's social circle and a man of means, or so they'd thought. And he'd been interested in her.

Now she knew exactly why he'd been interested and so fervent in his wooing. Even then, he'd often been away on *business*, especially during the summer months when the horses were running at Saratoga.

# Let it Be Christmas

She'd been past twenty-five years old when she'd finally met Seamus. Was it any wonder, she'd been so eager to marry she'd *anticipated* the event. And now she was married, after a fashion, and yet, as the old saying went, 'she was as nervous as a long-tailed cat in a room full of rockers.'

"Would you care for luncheon?" Bart asked. "I've asked Mabel at the Vinegaroon Hotel to prepare us a special lunch." He glanced at Chad. "Your brother will join us, of course."

"Yes, that would be nice. Thank you." Anything to not have Bart accompany them back to the ranch. So far, he'd stayed at Mabel's hotel.

He fished a silver dollar from his pocket and handed it to the Judge. The Judge nodded and said, "Felicitations to you both." He glanced at her waist. "And many children, too." Then the Judge put one finger alongside his nose and quipped, "And don't let married life get ya soft, Bart. Y'ere always welcome at the Lily to start a friendly game."

"Friendly." Bart snorted. "Friendly almost got me killed the last time."

"Yeah, but them Boyd brothers haven't been around fer awhile. Y'ere plenty safe here. I run a tight ship, don't ya know."

"Sure, Judge." Bart slapped him on the back. "I won't be a stranger."

Then the Judge turned his gaze to her and said, "Don't I get a kiss from the blushing bride?"

Lindsay shuddered. The thought of touching the old rascal made her nauseous. And like most men from these parts, the overwhelming smell of stale perspiration wafted from him. But she couldn't refuse. She pulled away from Bart and went on tip-toe, giving the Judge a loud smack on his filthy, oily cheek.

"Wahl now, that wasn't what I expected, but—"

"It will need to do, Judge," Bart said. "I'm a very possessive man."

159

# Let it Be Christmas

She glanced at her new husband. *Did he really mean it?* Of course not, more window dressing. But somewhere, deep inside, she wished he had meant it.

An hour later, they left the Vinegaroon Hotel, and Bart helped her onto the buckboard. Chad climbed in back.

Will Handley, the youth who ran the telegraph office, ran up and offered a telegram to Bart, saying, "Mr. Houghton, this just came for you from Tucson."

Bart handed him a nickel and took the telegram, tearing open the envelope. Silently, he read the telegram. He looked up and caught her brother's gaze. "Chad, can I have a word with you in private?"

Lindsay huffed out her breath and settled on the hard wooden seat. Married a little over an hour and already, she was nothing more than yesterday's news—to be excluded from men's conversations. Not that she should be surprised. Before they'd married, the three of them had signed the partnership agreement, conveying a third of the ranch to her for-now husband. And then he'd followed through and married her.

Now, with the formalities out of the way, she was of no consequence. Or that's what the men thought. She still owned as much of the ranch as each of them.

* * *

Bart led Chad over to the other side of Langtry's main street and said, "I need to tell you what the telegram says. It involves you."

"Yes, what is it?"

"It's from Rose Gallagher in Tucson."

Chad narrowed his eyes and glanced back at his sister. "Who is Rose Gallagher, and what does she have to do with us? I know this marriage is in name only, but please, Bart, don't bring your 'fancy' woman to the ranch. My sister has—"

"It's not like that." Bart understood his partner's protective stance towards his sister, but this was serious. "Rose may be a 'fancy' woman, as you put it, but she's not *my* fancy woman. I knew

160

# Let it Be Christmas

her as a girl back in Alabama. Her stepfather beat and raped her. She was ruined, but unlike your sister, she had nowhere to go, so..."

Chad shook his head and thinned his lips.

Bart knew he shouldn't remind Chad about his sister's fall from grace, but he wanted his partner to understand the gravity of the situation.

"I hadn't seen Rose in years, but the first time I went to Tucson, I found she was running a 'house' there."

"Good God, Bart, I don't want to discuss this. What on earth—"

"Will you please listen?"

"All right, shoot."

"Rose and I were reacquainted." He gazed directly at Chad. "For a while we were intimate but not for long. We became friends. Unfortunately, that's also where I met the Boyd brothers—in Tucson at her house."

"And?"

"Couple of things. The money I need to pay you for my part of the ranch is in her keeping. Or to be more exact, her attorney's keeping. He has a double-enforced, steel safe." Bart shook his head. "I don't believe in banks. Seen too many of them robbed. But I was planning on sending to Rose for my money. Her attorney can wire one of those Western Union money orders to the bank in Del Rio, and you should be able to draw on it."

"All right. Since Langtry doesn't have a bank, that's where I keep my money anyway."

"I'd planned on getting your sister home and settled first and then come back to wire the money."

"That's fine with me, Bart. But no fancy women. All right?"

Bart shook his head. "Unfortunately, there's another part to Rose's telegram. And this is where you come in." He inhaled and stood up straighter. "Festus Boyd died of blood poisoning, after a long illness."

Chad clenched his hands into fists. "That scum I shot in the thigh last February?"

161

# Let it Be Christmas

"That's him."

"And the Boyd brothers followed you here from Tucson?"

Bart shook his head. "I don't think so. I believe they came for the prize fight, like everyone else. But I'd won a bunch of money off them in Tucson. They knew better than to take me on at Rose's place. But here..." He shrugged. "Probably looked like easy pickings for them."

"And I saved your hide and shot one of them."

"Yes, and the Boyd brothers' don't forget a slight, especially the eldest brother, Red. Even though, he wasn't in Langtry that night."

"But you think they'll be gunning for us now?"

"I'm sure of it. That's the way they operate. And Red gets back twice what is done to him and his kin. He's meaner than a rattlesnake."

Chad looked down. "Then we'll need to be especially careful when we come into town." He raised his head. "Actually, I think when one of us needs to come to town, we should come together."

"Not a bad idea. And we need to let our shepherds know. So they can be on the lookout."

"All right."

Bart gripped Chad's shoulder. "I'm sorry for bringing this down on you, partner. Never thought someone as mean as Festus Boyd would die from a flesh wound to his leg."

"Me neither. I only know I did what I had to do when you were facing two men at once."

"And I owe you my life for it. I haven't forgotten." He patted Chad on the back.

* * *

Lindsay pulled her handkerchief out and mopped her brow... again. She needed to order a parasol if she was going live through Langtry's summer. And if they didn't come back soon, she'd begin to smell, too.

# Let it Be Christmas

She glanced at the men, huddled across the street. What on earth could they be talking about—and why did she have to be excluded.

After what seemed like an hour but must have been less than ten minutes, Bart patted her brother on the back, and they broke apart.

Bart tipped his hat to her, and her brother climbed into the back of the wagon without a word. But the set of his face was grim. She wondered, for the hundredth time, what that telegram had said.

*Looked like no one was willing to share.*

Frustrated, she crossed her arms over her chest when Bart climbed in beside her and took up the reins. Northwest of Langtry, they reached the rutted road to the ranch and clattered along, the wagon bucking and heaving beneath them. She uncrossed her arms and grabbed the flat-brimmed straw hat on her head with one hand, while she braced herself against the teeth-rattling wagon with the other.

She glanced back to see Bart's sleek leather suitcase in the flatbed of the buckboard. He'd moved out of Mabel's hotel, lock-stock-and-barrel. Of course, it would have looked strange for Bart, a newly-married man, to remain at the hotel while she went home with her brother.

Her childhood home had three bedrooms. Her father had built it that way, so both his children would have their own room—an unheard of luxury at the time. There was a room for Bart, and he would probably expect her to cook and clean and do his laundry, too, just like her brother.

How would they get along, huddled in the same house? Married but not married. She still didn't approve of his past profession, and as much as he attracted her, she firmly believed he appealed to her baser nature. And that baser nature was the reason she was in this mess in the first place.

She cupped her stomach. But she wouldn't wish her child away. Now she was married and had given her baby a name, she was excited to be pregnant. She didn't particularly look forward to being

# Let it Be Christmas

with Bart, day-in-and-day-out, when she got huge with child. Unfortunately, there was no help for it.

She sighed and gripped the side rail of the wagon tighter.

"You've been raising funds for a new church. Going around to the businesses and married ladies in town and asking for donations. Right?" Bart asked.

He clucked at the horses and they broke into a shambling trot, jerking her from side to side. "Yes, I have. Why? Would you care to contribute?"

He smiled. "Maybe. It's a worthy cause."

"Yes, it is."

"I'll contribute, if you'll do your brother and me a favor."

"What do you want me to do?"

"Ask the ladies of the town and neighboring ranches to bring food for a cabin raising. Kind of like a barn raising, but a little more complicated. And they'll need to bring their husbands, sweethearts, brothers, and fathers to do the actual work." He fisted the reins in one hand. "I'd like to install indoor plumbing, if possible. I know how to rig it. But I'll need about a month to get all the materials together."

"You want me to go around town and ask people to come to a cabin raising for you, Bart? Why not just take out an ad in the Del Rio paper, announcing we're not really married?"

And when she mentioned Del Rio, she thought of Abby, and wished her best friend could have been at her wedding. But there had been no time, she'd dithered too long and Bart had forced her hand. She had written Abby a letter and posted it before the wedding, though.

Bart chuckled. "Nope, we're going to tell everyone the cabin is for Chad. He doesn't want to intrude on the newly-weds. But when it's finished, I'll be the one living in the cabin, not your brother."

"Won't people figure it out?"

# Let it Be Christmas

"Not if we don't have guests to the ranch," Chad interjected. "And our shepherds won't talk about it, at least not if we tell them not to."

She empathized with their shepherds, ten families that depended on the ranch for their livelihood. And then there were all the other poor people in Langtry. Her aunt had taught her to have Christian mercy on the poor. She hoped, especially after her baby was born, to help the poor people in and around Langtry. To make their futures brighter.

She'd been pondering what she could do. For now, and in honor of her coming baby and Christmas, she wanted to give the poor children Christmas gifts, particularly a decent set of clothes. Most of them went around almost naked or in rags.

"What do you think, Lindsay? Can you help us with some vittles and organizing a dance for after the cabin raising?" Bart asked.

"Of course, give me a date, but you realize August is our hottest month here. Building a cabin will be like—"

"Like visiting hell," Bart interrupted. "I know, but it's also one of the slowest times for sheep ranchers."

"If you have your own cabin, who will cook and clean and do your laundry?" She asked.

"I'm a pretty fair cook. When I get settled, I'll invite you over." He winked at her.

She cringed, sinking lower in the wagon and wishing the wooden slats would open and swallow her. Remembering the one sample he'd had of her cooking, she could imagine he'd rather cook for himself.

*Well, let him, then. And welcome to it.*

"As for cleaning and laundry, I thought your Serafina might know of one of the other shepherd's wives who would like to make a little extra money."

She nodded. "I think Serafina has a younger sister, who's married to one of our shepherds. Let me ask."

He patted her hand. "Thank you, Lindsay. I appreciate it."

# Let it Be Christmas

At his kindness, a warm feeling flooded her. Bart was treating her like a lady, despite knowing her shame. She appreciated his thoughtfulness.

*Maybe being tied to him in a sham marriage wouldn't be so bad.*

# Let it Be Christmas

## Chapter Five

Lindsay leaned over the pump sink to get a better view from the kitchen window. Bart and her brother toiled outside in the home pens, docking and marking the new crop of spring lambs before shearing began in September.

Docking consisted of cropping a lamb's tail to about two or three inches for sanitary reasons. Marking meant cutting a pattern of notches into a lamb's ear to serve as an identifying mark of ownership. Docking and marking had to be two of the bloodiest and most odious chores on a sheep ranch. And the smell of sheep dung, mixed with blood, was almost enough to deter her from keeping her kitchen window open.

But she didn't dare close the window. Then she'd have no breeze at all.

Wiping the perspiration off her brow with a corner of her apron, she couldn't help but admit Bart was a big help for her brother, beyond bringing new capital to the ranch. He learned quickly, possessed strength and agility, and never complained.

She was finding it increasingly difficult to cling to her initial negative reaction. In fact, she found it difficult to cling to a single shred of normal decency while he worked, outside her kitchen window, without a shirt covering his chest.

*She couldn't keep her eyes off him.*

The way his perspiration-sleek muscles bunched beneath his tanned skin as he bent to a task made her heart accelerate. The breadth and strength of his shoulders awakened flutters in her stomach. And the rich sable mat of his chest hair, plunging into a V just above the waistband of his trousers, left her breathless.

Lindsay had never been so acutely aware of another human being's body, or the raw response it could elicit from her. Not even that one fumbling time she'd been with Seamus. Unfamiliar feelings and subtle urgings coursed through her whenever she looked at Bart. It was disturbing to say the least.

# Let it Be Christmas

Trembling, she turned from the window. Bart hadn't started on his cabin yet, and with him helping her brother every day, she felt obliged to feed him. Usually he accepted her invitation with quiet thanks, but some evenings he ate supper in town.

She crossed the kitchen to the back porch where the milk was stored, intent upon fetching some buttermilk to make biscuits for their mid-day meal. She didn't like to admit it, but Bart's presence had improved her cooking. Even though she still found the process of cooking a tedious chore, she managed to pay enough attention to ensure the food was properly prepared. Both her brother and Bart had been lavish in their praise.

Retrieving the buttermilk, she thought of Minnie, locked in her crate on the other side of the porch. Lindsay had penned Minnie so she wouldn't get in the way while Serafina did the weekly laundry.

Serafina had already emptied the washbasin and hung out the wash to dry before going home. Minnie would be ready to go out, and then she could keep Lindsay company while she prepared the mid-day meal. With that thought in mind, she approached her dog's crate, surprised Minnie had been so quiet all morning.

Usually when she was locked up, her puppy had a disconcerting habit of whining and barking. She rounded the corner of the porch. At first, she couldn't believe her eyes. Her heart leapt into her throat. She blinked twice but nothing changed. The crate door was open.

*Minnie was gone!*

Lindsay dropped the pail, not caring when buttermilk splattered over the porch floor. Dazed, her eyes darted to each shadowed corner of the room, searching for her dog. How long had Minnie been loose? Where could she have gone?

With a sinking feeling, she knew Minnie must have escaped when Serafina went outside to hang the laundry. Otherwise, her dog would have come to the kitchen, looking for her. But the lure of the outdoors must have proven too tempting.

Panic skittered along her nerves, making her tremble. She had purposely limited her pet's outside excursions to the ranch yard.

# Let it Be Christmas

It was too dangerous to do otherwise. The wild country surrounding the ranch was filled with predators, both the four-legged variety as well as the two-legged kind.

Pressing her suddenly throbbing temples between her hands, she willed herself to think. What should she do? Where should she start? Opening the back door, she trotted to the barn, wanting to saddle a horse and circle the ranch until she found some trace of her dog. She thought about calling or whistling for Minnie, but she wasn't certain if she wanted to alert the men yet, especially her brother, knowing they'd probably get into a heated argument.

But before she reached the barn, a boy came riding into the yard. She recognized his carrot-top head; he was Bill Sanderson's boy, Mark. The Sanderson's owned the ranch west of them.

The boy's head swung between the house and the pens where the men were working, as if he couldn't make up his mind. Praying he'd brought news of Minnie, Lindsay called out, "Good morning, Mark. What brings you to our ranch?"

The boy squinted against the bright sun at her back. "Judge Bean sent me to fetch you, ma'am, if'n you're the one that owns that—"

"Small white dog," Lindsay said.

"Yes, ma'am."

She breathed a sigh of relief. Her Maltese had been found—presumably safe and sound.

"You said Judge Bean sent you. Is that where Minnie is, in Langtry?"

Mark bobbed his head. "Your dog has taken quite a shine to the Judge's bear, Bruno."

"What!" She shrieked.

Mark looked down. He shook his head and tugged on his mount's reins, obviously feeling the need to flee in the face of a hysterical female. But his conscience must have gotten the better of him because he said, "Yer dog is safe and at the Jersey Lily, ma'am. Much obliged."

# Let it Be Christmas

And then he was gone, before Lindsay could admit she was the one who was obliged to him, no matter how upsetting his news was.

*Bruno, the bear!* Her thoughts tumbled. That old horrible, beer-guzzling bear the judge kept chained to a post in front of his saloon to lure curious train passengers. With one swat of his mighty paw, Bruno could make Maltese mincemeat of Minnie!

She had to get to town fast before the bear hurt her puppy.

Chad and Bart appeared, obviously drawn by her panicked outburst. Chad looked annoyed, beating his dusty Stetson against his equally filthy pants and demanding, "Lindsay, what happened? We heard you scream."

"It's Minnie. She got out and went to Langtry. She's at Judge Bean's saloon with his bear!"

"Is that all," Chad remarked.

Lindsay shot a poisonous look at her brother. "It's enough. I've got to get to town fast. I know Minnie is nothing more than a nuisance to you, but I love her and—"

"Don't worry, Lindsay," Bart interrupted, "it's only two miles to Langtry. I'll saddle your horse, and we'll be there in no time." Blood-streaked and filthy from the docking and marking, he turned to Chad and a look passed between them. "You'd better come, too. Tell the shepherds to keep the sheep penned for us."

*Why must Chad come as well? More secrets?*

"Sure, I'll tell the men. We'll both go. Lindsay shouldn't be near the saloon without an escort, anyway."

Bart nodded and strode quickly toward the barn, stopping only to retrieve his shirt from one of the corral posts. Lindsay watched his retreating back, gratitude and relief surging through her, warming her heart and dispelling the worst of her fears.

But while she waited for him to return, renewed worry nagged at her. She hopped from one foot to the other and twisted the gold band on her ring finger. She was grateful for her in-name-only husband's help, but his assistance was no guarantee they would safely retrieve Minnie. After all, he wasn't a miracle worker.

170

# Let it Be Christmas

And Minnie... her poor Minnie... could anyone rescue her beloved pet before it was too late?

\* \* \*

Lindsay knew what the crowd beside the Jersey Lily signified before she pulled her bay mare, Gypsy, to a sliding halt. They were watching Minnie. Her beloved Maltese had become the latest sideshow to entertain the rough crowd hanging around the saloon.

Judge Bean, in his customary fashion, was making the most of the unexpected windfall. His barkeep, Joseph, circulated among the gawkers, selling beer and shots of whiskey.

The crowd roared, and a fresh wave of panic washed over her. Unable to catch a glimpse of her pet through the dense mob, she had no idea what the crowd was shouting at, but she feared Bruno was mauling Minnie and the mob was cheering on the bear with their drunken approval.

Vaulting from the mare's back, she forgot about Bart in her frenzy to reach her dog. With tears clouding her vision, she rushed forward, cursing in French and slapping at the mass of men. She pushed to the front of the mob and stared... and smelled. The scent of rotting vegetation filled her nostrils, wafting from the moth-eaten brown bear, Bruno.

Bruno squatted on his haunches with his huge paws dangling in front of him. His pig-like snout drooped forward onto his massive chest, snuffling the air. Minnie ran circles around the bear, yelping at him. Bruno, half-drunk on beer, just watched the little dog with glazed eyes, shaking his head to clear away the buzz of flies.

Lindsay's stomach roiled and bile filled her throat. Her initial terror melted away, to be replaced by embarrassment and dismay. Her dog didn't appear to be in any immediate danger, but she certainly was making a spectacle of herself. She could imagine what her brother would say when he saw her pet's antics.

Lulled by the bear's passivity, she broke away from the crowd, intent upon retrieving her pet.

# Let it Be Christmas

*But her sudden movement was a mistake.*

Bruno came to life, roaring like a lion and rearing up. He swatted at her, his broken and dirty claws slicing through the air. She cringed against the inevitable impact and then she was grabbed from behind and rolled to the ground, knocking the breath from her. The onlookers jeered, making ribald suggestions.

The bear advanced, snapping the end of his chain taut. Minnie, unperturbed, sat back on her haunches and postured with her best begging stance.

Dirt scrapped Lindsay's back as she was hauled away from the bear's reach. Dazed, she looked up to see Bart's face, covered in perspiration, looming over her. Mortified, she pushed at his chest with the palms of her hands and struggled to rise, amidst more suggestive taunts from the crowd about newly-weds.

"Don't struggle. Don't give them a show." His strong arms pinned her to the ground. "Are you all right, Lindsay?" He whispered and shook his head. "I mean the babe and all? If there had been any other way…"

She could only nod. It was a moment suspended in time. The nasty mob faded. Her senses centered on Bart. Their hearts pounded as one, curiously synchronized, and their breaths mingled, lightly caressing. The tensile strength of his arms, and the warmth of his embrace enfolded her.

She melted against him, pliant to his touch, blood surging through her veins. Her nipples, crushed against his shirt, peaked into hard points.

"Minnie's fine, but we'll need the Judge to get her away from Bruno. Do you understand?" he asked.

She heard his words as if from far away, they tumbled through her mind but failed to make an impression. Her body's reaction to him filled her senses.

Bart's light-blue eyes drilled into hers. He shook her and repeated, "Lindsay, do you understand me?"

The urgency in his voice finally penetrated. The low murmur of the mob swelled into a roar. Turning her head from Bart's

# Let it Be Christmas

disturbing gaze, the world above her took on a razor-sharp clarity. She nodded.

He exhaled. "Good."

He released her and rolled to one side and then got to his feet. The hot July air felt suddenly cold on her skin without Bart's body covering her.

Leaning down, he grabbed her hands and pulled her to her feet, announcing, "Show's over, folks. Where's Judge Bean?"

The forest of men surrounding them shifted and grumbled, making a path through their midst. Curving his arm protectively around her, Bart led her to the outside of the ring, and they came face to face with Judge Roy Bean again.

"Judge, we need your help," Bart said.

"And what might that be, newly-weds? I was a'likin' the show."

"Yes, but the puppy there," Bart inclined his head. "That's my wife's dog she brought all the way from Boston."

The Judge stroked his fingers through his grizzled beard and asked, "How much do ya want for 'er?"

Lindsay took a step back. "I beg your pardon. I love Minnie, she's my pet. I don't want to sell her."

Judge Bean narrowed his close-set eyes. "That's too bad. She'd be a useful distraction."

"You mean a sideshow," Lindsay retorted.

Bart squeezed her shoulder. She knew what he was trying to say without words. She needed to calm down and deal tactfully with the Judge.

Judge Bean hawked and spat a muddy stream of tobacco juice at the ground, narrowly missing her foot. "To put a fine point on it, Mrs. Houghton. That's exactly what I want your pet fer. What's yer price?"

"No price, Judge. I plan to keep Minnie."

The Judge turned to Bart, obviously expecting him to overrule his headstrong wife.

# Let it Be Christmas

But Bart disappointed the Judge by asking, "Can we get Minnie back?"

The Judge snorted and spat again, this time, hitting the toe of Bart's cowboy boot. Shrugging, he said, "You're free to take yer dog. I won't interfere."

"And you won't call Bruno off?" Bart asked.

"Nope. Do what ya have to do but don't 'arm my bear." The Judge walked back to his saloon.

Rage boiled inside Lindsay. She twisted in Bart's grasp, wanting to break free. Wanting to scratch the Judge's eyes out.

Bart held her tightly and tried to reason with her. "It won't do any good. If you attack him, he'll just fine you. And he won't help. It's not worth it, Lindsay."

"He can't get away with this," she huffed. "How can he be so—"

"Callous," he finished. "That's the way he is, anything for a dollar. He's living on borrowed glory, and it's a thin line. But provoking him won't help. He's been ousted in elections and investigated by the authorities from Del Rio, but he always manages to hang on. We'll have to get Minnie without his help."

"How?"

"Have you tried calling Minnie? You said she was trained."

She shook her head. "I—I wasn't thinking."

"Try."

She leaned down and snapped her fingers, calling, "Here, Minnie. Here, girl. That's a good girl."

Her Maltese looked her way and whined, wagging her tail. But she didn't come, she just started circling the bear again and sniffing.

"All right," Bart said. "Let's try it another way." He turned to her. "Can you be patient and wait with your brother?"

"Of course, but—"

"No buts—no arguments. Just be patient." He traced his index finger along her jaw, his light touch evoking fluttery feelings in the pit of her stomach.

# Let it Be Christmas

She raised her head high, purposely avoiding Bart's unsettling touch. And then she squared her shoulders and walked to her brother's side at the back of the mob.

Waiting, she watched the shifting crowd. The sun was at its zenith. Part of the mob broke away, in twos and threes, to seek the relative sanctuary of the Jersey Lily's deep porch. Peering through the broken circle, she glimpsed Bruno and Minnie lying side-by-side in the dirt, surrendering to the heat.

She relaxed a little but kept her eye on the slumbering animals and waited for Bart. She saw him approach with a paper-wrapped package in his hands from the only dining establishment in town, the hotel.

He put the bundle on the ground and winked at her. Then he began unsaddling his dun gelding. Wrapping his arms in the dun's saddle blanket, he picked up the package and walked into the vacant ring of ground surrounding the sleeping animals.

Lindsay tracked his every move, wanting to understand his plan. But when he approached the bear, a cry rose to her throat. She crossed herself and prayed he'd be careful. And she bit her lip to stop from screaming and awakening the bear.

He approached the dozing Bruno. When he was within a few feet, he opened the package and tossed a huge beefsteak on the ground in front of him. Snorting, Bruno awakened, scenting the meat and rising up on his haunches. Still drowsy from his nap, the bear groped blindly for the steak before snagging the hunk of meat and pulling it toward him.

Lindsay worried her dog would smell the meat, too, but the hike from the ranch and all the excitement must have exhausted Minnie. Heavens be praised, she stayed asleep.

Bart retreated a few steps with his blanketed arms held in front of him, a paltry form of protection against a sudden swipe of Bruno's deadly paws. Standing perfectly still, Bart's gaze was trained on Bruno, watching the animal's every move.

# Let it Be Christmas

The bear devoured the steak in the hot sunshine. After the last bite, he reared back, as if on the attack again, but his eyes drifted shut and he tumbled to the ground.

A loud snore rent the silence. Bruno had fallen asleep again. Bart stepped forward. Lindsay's heart stuttered to a stop. And the very breath in her lungs was suspended—waiting.

Bart scooped up Minnie from the ground. The sleepy Maltese lay curled in his arms. He crossed the distance in three long strides and halted beside Lindsay. "Here she is, safe and sound. Take her."

Tears stung the back of her eyelids, and she gulped down the lump in her throat. Opening her arms, she cradled her precious dog. "Thank you, Bart."

\* \* \*

Lindsay put the basket of food in the shade of a drooping willow. Bart had chosen a large bend in the creek to build his three room cabin with an attached horse shed. And he'd gotten Manuel Longoria, the only shepherd who knew some carpentry, to help him lay the pier and beam foundation.

Now he and Manuel were digging a trench beneath the wooden beams leading to a large pit, several hundred yards away, they'd also dug. Bart had explained this was for the indoor plumbing he was installing, using copper piping to carry the waste away.

She'd asked him why he didn't pipe the waste into the creek, and he'd replied it would foul their neighbor's water, downstream. She hadn't thought of that, but it was nice to know Bart was considerate of others.

Having lived in Boston, she knew about indoor plumbing, but most homes in West Texas made do with outhouses. She and Chad had an outhouse, and Abby's boardinghouse had one, too. She was surprised Bart was so fastidious about his personal hygiene.

Most of the remainder of the building materials had arrived and were stacked in the barn or under tarps in the yard. The cabin

# Let it Be Christmas

raising would take place Saturday next, just in time before the ranchers started to prepare for fall shearing.

And after what had happened with Bruno, the bear, she'd found everybody wanted to come, and all the women were pitching in and bringing food, too.

As a couple, their escapade with the Judge's bear had gained them a bit of local notoriety. And it had even helped her to win more donations for the new church.

Now, if she could find someone who was good with a needle, she could get started on her Christmas project, sewing clothes for the poor children of Langtry. She'd have to try harder to recruit ladies to help her with that particular charity, as it would take a prolonged effort of work and time, not a simple donation.

But the harder she worked, the better. It kept her from daydreaming about Bart or thrashing around in her lonely bed at night.

No matter how much she wanted to look away, she couldn't help but gaze at his muscular back as he bent over the trench. Just seeing him half-clothed made her heart go pitter-patter. And she remembered exactly what he'd felt like, stretched on top of her when he'd rescued her from Bruno.

*She was a wanton—that much was obvious.* Because she couldn't stop thinking how it would be for him to hold her again, with his big, rough hands exploring every inch of her.

And beyond her wicked desires, since the day he'd saved Minnie, she felt the slow, sweet seep of tenderness toward him. After all, he'd been nothing but kind to her. Sometimes, kinder than her own brother.

Feeling tender toward him, she'd not been able to do enough for him. That was why she'd made him and Manuel a picnic lunch of fried pork chops, turnip greens seasoned with bacon, and her special steamed parsley potatoes.

He straightened and put his hand to the middle of his back. He must have seen her, standing beside the willow because he

# Let it Be Christmas

smiled and waved. Then he thrust his shovel into the hard-baked caliche and pulled out a handkerchief, dusting his hands.

She returned his wave and smiled, too, calling out, "I've brought lunch. You should rest during the heat of the day."

He turned to Manuel and pointed to the trench, saying something in Spanish.

Manuel nodded and Bart trudged toward her, grabbing his shirt from the branch of a live oak tree and shrugging it on. Even so, in this heat, he didn't bother with the buttons and she glimpsed the springy, black hair on his chest. And his well-defined pectoral muscles, along with his washboard-flat stomach were a sight to behold.

She cupped her stomach, knowing she was starting to *show* and doubting anyone, much less a handsome man like Bart, would have wicked thoughts about her, given she was pregnant with another man's child.

He came and stood beside her. "Thank you for lunch. That was kind of you."

"Aren't you going to let poor Manuel eat?" She was teasing, of course. Bart was kind to the shepherds, too. "I brought enough for two."

He smiled again and winked. "What if I want it all to myself?"

She blushed, wondering if what he was saying was as innocent as it sounded. "You shouldn't be greedy."

He lifted a tendril of her hair that had escaped her bun and brushed her ear with the feathery tip.

She trembled and gooseflesh sprang up, covering her arms. She crossed her arms over her chest and tried to act nonchalant, but inside, all she wanted was for him to take her in his strong arms.

"I won't be too greedy." He winked again. "There's only a couple more feet to dig. I told Manuel we'd stop for today after he finished. Your timing couldn't have been better."

She curtsied and said, "Why, thank you, kind sir."

# Let it Be Christmas

He reached out and brushed her cheek with his fingertips. She turned her face into his hand, wanting to kiss his fingers. His gaze captured hers, locked and held. And he moved closer to her, half a pace.

Despite working in the heat, she savored the smell of him, this close up—real man mixed with the piquant scent of the hair tonic he used. She wanted nothing more than to have him kiss her.

*But would he kiss her? Here in front of Manuel and God and anyone who might be looking?*

And what if he did? They were married, after all. Only Chad knew the truth. No one else.

She closed her eyes and leaned toward him. She puckered her lips and waited.

Bart cupped her chin and then, he released her.

She almost fell in a puddle at his feet.

He touched her arm. "Thank you again, Lindsay. Would you like to share lunch with us? We can take our shoes and socks off and put our feet in the creek. It's some cooler there, under the willow."

Disappointed and frustrated, she felt as if the skin all over her body was too tight, as if she was going to burst at the seams. She'd thought he was going to kiss her. As a husband might kiss his wife.

*But what a little fool she was.* Their marriage was a sham. And no man would want her, anyway. Not after what she'd done.

She forced her mouth into the semblance of a smile. "Thank you, Bart, but I've already eaten. And I've got some cleaning to do. Please, bring the basket back. Will you?"

She didn't wait for an answer, turning away and climbing up the hill to the ranch house.

# Let it Be Christmas

## Chapter Six

"Thank you for coming to help build my brother's cabin," Lindsay announced. "The cabin looks neat and sturdy. We all appreciate your help."

Bart wondered if she was nervous. It was hard to reconcile this radiant creature, standing on the improvised dais they'd erected in the barn, with the everyday Lindsay who cooked and cleaned and didn't mind getting her hands dirty.

"Thank you again, folks." She lifted her arm and indicated the long table, piled high with bowls and platters overflowing with food. Just the smell from all the different dishes their neighbors had brought was making his mouth water.

"Please, help yourselves to all you can eat. We ladies are proud to serve you hard-working men." Then she turned to the improvised band of musicians standing behind her and clapped her hands three times, proclaiming, "Let the music begin. Dancing will be here in the barn."

Bart watched as Lindsay was assisted, by at least four men, from the nine-inch height of the dais. He understood their solicitude. Lindsay had never looked more beautiful.

She was dressed in a fitted gown of aqua satin. The dress must have come straight from Boston. It was, by far, the most fashionable of all the ladies' dresses. Bustled in back and edged with ivory lace at the throat and hem, its high neck made the gown, at first glance, appear demure. But the way it clung to every voluptuous curve of Lindsay's body, left little to the imagination.

Surrounded by ranchers' wives in calicos and simple cotton dresses, she stood out like a peacock among a flock of sparrows. And every man, from eight to eighty, was aware of it. The women's reactions, on the other hand, were harder to gauge. And he worried their envy might be her undoing, in the months to come. He hadn't thought she'd wear such a provocative dress just before her

# Let it Be Christmas

pregnancy started showing. The contrast would be hard to miss. He shook his head and wondered what she'd been thinking.

For him, the color of her gown was even more enticing than its stylish cut. The effect was subtle, but being accustomed to well-dressed ladies from New Orleans to San Francisco, he fully appreciated the result.

Aqua enhanced Lindsay's natural coloring, making her sparkle like a finely-crafted gemstone. Her palomino-colored hair took on an added luster, her peaches and cream complexion glowed, and her strawberry-red lips seemed brighter in contrast, as if she'd applied lip rouge.

But it was her hazel eyes the gown complimented best. Her changeable eye-color was reflected in the color of the dress, and they shone with the blue-green depths of the Caribbean Sea.

A queue of men formed around her, laughing and talking, competing for her favor. She chose a tall lieutenant, dressed in the uniform of the United States cavalry, as her first partner. The lieutenant's presence was an indication of how few social events there were in this remote area. He and several other officers had traveled at least seventy miles from Fort Clark to attend the cabin raising and dance.

Watching Lindsay whirl away in the young officer's arms, Bart turned aside. He should have helped her down, should have asked her to dance. After all, he was her lawful husband. But he had the distinct impression she'd dressed as she had to tweak his interest.

During the past week since that day by the creek, she'd been purposely distant. And he could guess why—he'd seen her pucker her lips—as if she'd expected him to kiss her. What made it worse, was he'd wanted to kiss her, badly. But if he'd stolen a kiss from his wife-in-name-only, where would that leave them?

He didn't know. Did he want Lindsay as his *real* wife? Enough to overlook her mistake and love her and another man's child as his own. He was sorely tempted, wanting her in the Biblical sense every time he looked at her.

# Let it Be Christmas

*He couldn't stay away from her—couldn't stop thinking of her.*

And it was too late to leave Langtry and the beguiling Lindsay behind. His capital was invested in the ranch. He and Chad had already purchased the wire and contracted for the posts for the northern fence line. During the winter, they were planning to travel to San Antonio to purchase Merino rams to upgrade their flocks. And he'd spent the remainder of his savings on materials for his cabin.

*There was no turning back.*

But where did that leave him and Lindsay? Once she had the baby, would she get a divorce and return to Boston? And if she did, could he forget her? He didn't know, and he dreaded the day.

Thinking about their future set him on edge. He quit the dance and wandered outside. He sat on the edge of the water trough and pulled a Cuban cigar from his vest pocket. Then he removed the full flask from his coat. He unscrewed the cap and turned it up, gulping the fiery whiskey. The pungent-smelling liquor hit his stomach like a bolt of lightning and curled its warmth through his body—just like Lindsay's touch.

Shaking his head, he took another long drink, seeking oblivion, swift and sure. He wasn't normally a drinking man, but some occasions called for it. He wiped his mouth with the back of his hand and set the liquor aside, scratching a match on his boot to light his cigar.

When the end glowed red, he lifted the flask again and drank. A welcome numbness followed, and he gazed up, studying the stars in the wide West Texas sky.

He felt alone in the universe. A tiny speck beneath the immense mantle of the night's firmament. It was a good feeling, relegating his petty concerns to their proper place. There was no reason he couldn't eradicate Lindsay from his mind.

He'd done many things in his life requiring a supreme effort of will. One time, he'd crossed the Sierra Nevada in winter to

# Let it Be Christmas

recoup a large gambling debt owed him by a gentleman in San Francisco. Forgetting Lindsay should be child's play in comparison.

*Maybe she was merely a passing fancy.*

But the contradictions of her nature intrigued him. Most women fit in one of two categories: wife and mother or… the other kind. But not Lindsay. Despite getting pregnant without the sanction of marriage, she was prudish in the extreme. But tonight she'd dressed in a gown crafted to make men lust after her—a gown worthy of a goddess.

He wanted the goddess. But he couldn't have her… unless… the thought of a *real* marriage no longer seemed foreign to him. Lindsay in his kitchen—Lindsay sitting beside his hearth—Lindsay in his bed. He couldn't help but imagine possessing her as his own.

He shook his head. She'd been desperate enough to marry him to give her child a name, but he was an ex-gambler, an unworthy reprobate in her eyes. She might want him to kiss her, but would she ever think of him as a real husband?

The scraping sound of boots penetrated his dismal thoughts. Raising his head, he strained his eyes against the darkness, partially illuminated by the bright lights of the barn dance. His guard went up, and he reached for his Colt. Keeping his hand on the butt of the revolver, he waited, until a figure emerged from the darkness.

He recognized Will, the telegraph operator from Langtry. Bart relaxed and released his hold on the Colt.

Will stopped and squinted in the darkness. "Is that you, Mr. Houghton?"

"Yes, it's me, Will. I have a flask. Would you care to join me?" Bart offered.

Shaking his head, he declined, "Can't, official business." He dug inside the waistband of his trousers. "I came looking for you because my shift was over, and you've a telegram. Another one, all the way from Tucson."

# Let it Be Christmas

Bart accepted the envelope and said, "If your shift is over and you've delivered the telegram, your duties are done. Join me in drink?"

The young man lowered his head. "I don't drink, Mr. Houghton. My Pa was a drunk and Ma made me promise—"

"I understand, Will, and I won't press you." He reached inside his vest pocket and produced a silver dollar. "Thanks for coming to find me."

Will accepted the money and tipped his hat. "Appreciate it, Mr. Houghton."

"Why don't you stay and have a bite to eat? There's more than plenty. And then there's the dance, you're welcome to stay."

"Naw, never learned how to dance, and I've already et. I wished I could have come and helped with the raising, but I was on duty today."

"Doesn't matter. You're still welcome."

Will looked longingly at the whirl of dancers but shook his head. "Reckon I'll head back to town."

"All right. Goodnight, Will."

"Goodnight, and I hope it's good news. I like to bring folks good news."

"Thank you, I'm sure it will be," he agreed, while knowing most telegrams held bad news.

After Will left, Bart finished his cigar and took a few more sips from his flask. He'd have a headache in the morning. He wasn't used to liquor. Drinking in his former profession was dangerous. The lilting strains of the music from the barn dance ceased. It was early; the band must be taking a break.

He replaced the flask in his coat pocket and stood up, unsteady at first, but regaining his balance after a few moments. If he wanted to read the telegram, he'd need to return to the light in the barn. Moving toward the brightly-lit structure, he stopped outside one of the doors. There was just enough light, spilling from the side door to see the telegram clearly.

# Let it Be Christmas

Despite his decision to remain outside, he couldn't keep from looking inside, searching for Lindsay's perfect profile and provocative figure.

He found her, among a herd of men, who were offering her refreshments. She accepted a cup of punch and drained it quickly. Her thirst must have overcome her too-perfect manners. Her face was flushed and tiny beads of perspiration clung to her upper lip. One of the men took away her empty cup. She declined further refreshment and opened her reticule. Withdrawing an ivory lace fan, she fanned herself briskly while talking and laughing with the men.

Bart dropped his eyes, not wanting to spy on her. He tore open the envelope and unfolded the telegram. The message read:

"Boyd brothers on way to Langtry. STOP I'll be there on train by end of month. STOP Boyd's are traveling on horseback. STOP Might be good time to go home to Alabama. STOP"

Bart folded the telegram and put it in his vest pocket. Rose Gallagher wanted him to run from the Boyd's, returning to Alabama. She'd probably need to stay overnight, and she was a very beautiful woman—Tucson's premier madam.

And he could guess Lindsay's reaction when Rose came to see him.

\* \* \*

Standing beside the punchbowl, fanning herself and drinking the sweet punch, Lindsay decided she didn't want to dance any more. The circle of men paid her lavish compliments and begged for the next dance, but she merely smiled at them. Their words didn't reach her ears. She'd looked forward to tonight, only to be disappointed.

She'd enjoyed her instant popularity, at first. But after innumerable dances with men who didn't possess one ounce of grace and frequently stomped on her toes, she'd changed her mind. The evening had grown long and tedious. It was hot and dusty in

185

# Let it Be Christmas

the barn, and the ivory lace on the hem of her favorite gown was ruined forever.

Not only had she spoiled her favorite dress, she shouldn't have worn it in the first place. In Boston, the form-fitting gown was the latest fashion, but in West Texas it was totally out of place. The animosity emanating from the plainly dressed womenfolk was palpable.

Not realizing she'd stick out like a sore thumb, she knew she'd made a serious blunder. Without the support of the local womenfolk, she would be hard pressed to find volunteers to sew clothes for the children.

And she didn't enjoy attracting men's attention, either. She'd worn the gown to attract one man's particular attention—her husband. Even heavily corseted, she knew after tonight, she wouldn't be able to squeeze into the dress again. But she'd wanted him to realize, for one last time, just how desirable she could be. To remind him, despite her one shameful mistake, she was a lady of quality. But she wasn't certain he'd even noticed her.

She'd caught a glimpse of him after her speech, and then he'd disappeared. His absence at the dance made her disappointment keener, leaving a bitter taste in her mouth, which no amount of too-sweet punch could wash away.

Sighing, she excused herself from the flock of remaining men with, "My fan isn't sufficient for the heat. If you'd be so kind to step aside, I'd like a breath of fresh air."

Several men offered to escort her, but she shook her head. "I'll only step a few feet from the barn. Thank you, but it isn't necessary." She exited through one of the barn's side doors.

Standing in the dark, she filled her lungs with the clean air and stared at the stars. Muted murmurs of conversation from inside drifted out, mixing with the metallic whirring of cicadas. She found the Big Dipper, riding low in the late summer sky. The solitude and stillness of the night soothed her.

The sound of a man clearing his throat interrupted her thoughts. Turning toward the noise, she peered into the shadows of

186

# Let it Be Christmas

the sloping barn roof. She smelled burning tobacco and the pinpoint glow of a lit cigar pierced the darkness. She discerned the figure of a man, slouched against the side of the barn.

She recognized him at once, she would have known the shape of Bart's body anywhere. The outline of his broad shoulders gave him away, even in the semi-darkness.

Glimpsing him, her heart accelerated, pounding so hard she was certain he could hear its rhythmic beating. Her skin grew hot and flushed, and her breathing became uneven, making her feel as if she was gasping for air.

Bart pushed away from the side of the barn, tossed his cigar aside and approached her. She experienced a momentary desire to flee, but fought the urge, not wanting him to know the effect he had on her.

She straightened her shoulders and nervously twisted her mother's wedding band. As was proper, she waited for him to greet her first.

Stopping within a few feet, Bart tipped his Stetson. His voice was different tonight, low and slower than usual, as if he chose his words with especial care. "Evening, Lindsay."

"Good evening, Bartholomew." If anyone overheard their stilted exchange, they'd know their marriage wasn't real. But so far, they were alone, on the far side of the barn.

"Enjoying the dance?" The unusual timbre of his voice piqued her interest. His words were more elongated than usual. A sudden realization came over her, the difference was that his words were slurred.

*He was drunk!*

She narrowed her eyes.

Without the prop of the barn, he swayed slightly on his feet. Moving closer, he repeated the question. "I asked if you were enjoying the dance?" He gazed at her from beneath eyelids at half-mast. "You seem to be the belle of the ball."

His whiskey-laden breath washed over her. She retreated a step. She knew most men took a few drinks at barn dances. But no

# Let it Be Christmas

self-respecting man would get blind drunk in front of the womenfolk. She wondered if his charade was over. If the *real* Bart, the professional gambler, whom she'd suspected of being disreputable in the beginning, was finally showing himself.

With a lightning swiftness that belied his inebriated state, he closed the distance between them and took her arm, clutching it. The sour smell of whiskey on his breath all but choked her as she struggled to free herself from his grasp.

"If you won't answer my questions, then at least you should dance with me, to keep appearances up. You are my wife, after all."

Twisting, she wrested her arm from his grip. "I don't dance with drunks, Mr. Houghton."

She gathered her skirts and ran toward the barn. But her legs, hindered by the tightness of her hemline, couldn't carry her fast enough to outdistance his ugly words.

"You're a hypocrite, Lindsay Houghton, through and through. You may style yourself an honest married woman, but we both know better."

* * *

Lindsay felt as if she'd been caught, unprotected, in the middle of a West Texas sandstorm. Her eyes stung and burned, and her flesh felt abraded, as if someone had run sandpaper over it.

Bart's ugly accusation echoed in her head. Tonight was a total disaster, in more ways than one, and all she wanted was to return to the ranch house and pull the bedcovers over her head. But she needed to tell her brother, so she drifted through the barn, fending off would-be suitors and searching for him. But as hard as she looked, he was nowhere to be found.

Fighting the urge to go outside and look for her brother among the knots of men talking and drinking, she decided not to make herself any more conspicuous than she already had. Instead, she'd wait. Chad usually didn't drink much. She was certain he would return as soon as the band started playing again.

# Let it Be Christmas

In the meantime, she wanted to hide in the barn's darkest recesses. Realizing such an action was both cowardly and impossible, she crossed the deserted dance floor, getting as far away as she could from the raised dais where the band had been playing and where a crowd of people had gathered. If she couldn't hide, she could at least find a secluded place to wait.

She sought out an empty stall at the far side of the barn and leaned against it, hoping the shadows would obscure her. When her breathing returned to normal and her heart slowed its pace, she closed her eyes and wished she could start this night over.

A rustling noise penetrated her unhappy thoughts. Startled, she opened her eyes and turned toward the sound, realizing she wasn't alone. A young woman emerged from the deeper shadows of the stall, her gait hesitant and her features registering surprise.

Overcoming her own surprise, Lindsay remembered her manners and stretched out her hand. "I'm sorry to have intruded. I didn't see you there. My name's Lindsay Mac, er, Houghton."

The woman lifted her eyes and met Lindsay's gaze. She took Lindsay's hand in her slender fingers and shook it. Her skin was clammy, and she detected a tremor in the woman's grasp. What was this young woman doing buried in the depths of a deserted stall in the midst of a barn dance?

"I know who you are, Mrs. Houghton." The young woman's voice was barely a whisper. "Everyone knows who you are, especially after your work to get money to build Langtry a church. I'm proud to meet you." Almost as an afterthought, she added, "My name's Virginia Brown, but most folks call me Ginny. That is, Ginny with a 'G' not a 'J' because it's short for Virginia."

She smiled at the young woman's explanation about the spelling of her name. Ginny looked young, in her early twenties. She wore a faded calico dress and a nondescript bonnet that didn't match her dress. Her slippers were scuffed and cracked. But her petite figure was slender and her feet were tiny. She had light brown hair, and a delicate oval face with a pointed chin. It was too dark in the stall to see the color of her eyes.

# Let it Be Christmas

Wanting to draw Ginny out, she said, "Nice to meet you. I hope you're enjoying yourself. It's been a marvelous dance. Don't you think? I wonder when the musicians are going to play again?"

A look of surprise flitted across Ginny's features, as if she was amazed Lindsay would start a conversation with her. "You don't have to be polite with me, Mrs. Houghton." She inclined her head toward the opposite end of the barn. "The band is returning now. All of your admirers will be waiting."

Ginny's words sounded genuine. Lindsay couldn't detect the faintest thread of sarcasm or mockery. Her heart squeezed at the young woman's unselfish and self-deprecatory offer. For the first time tonight, she was eager to make a new friend.

"Please, call me Lindsay, not Mrs. Houghton, and I'll call you Ginny. Agreed?"

Ginny smiled shyly and nodded.

"I don't want to return to the dance. I'd rather talk with you."

Ducking her head, Ginny giggled, but her laughter sounded strained, as if she was trying to disguise her nervousness. "Please, don't bother on my account… Lindsay."

"I'm not. I want to stay," she protested. "Believe me, I'm hiding out, too."

Ginny stared hard at her. Even in the shadowy stall, Lindsay could detect the gleam in her eyes and the faint smile curving her lips.

"You're hiding out? But you're the belle of the ball, every man wants to dance with you."

She shuddered when Ginny innocently used the same term Bart had. She didn't need to be reminded of their acrimonious encounter. And she hadn't meant to make reference to Ginny concealing herself.

"I didn't mean to sound as if I were saying—"

"That I'm hiding out?" Ginny finished. She lifted her pointed chin and asked, "Why should I lie about it? It's the truth."

"All right, then, why are you hiding?"

190

# Let it Be Christmas

Ginny shrugged. "I'm ashamed of my clothes, and I don't know how to dance."

She opened her mouth to contradict Ginny but when she looked in her new friend's face, she changed her mind. Ginny might be timid to start, but she obviously wasn't afraid of the truth, and she didn't simper and mouth platitudes like other members of Lindsay's sex.

"I can teach you to dance. As for your clothes, they aren't the latest fashion, but neither are most of the other women's dresses." Lindsay glanced down at her aqua gown. "My dress has caused more trouble than its worth. I should have never worn it."

"You can't mean that! I think it's the loveliest dress I've ever laid eyes on."

"Maybe so, but it gives the men the wrong ideas and makes the women jealous."

Ginny stared at Lindsay and then covered her mouth, turning to one side, her small body convulsed in laughter.

"You're laughing at me!"

Stifling her giggles, Ginny said, "Laughing with you, not at you. I think your attitude is so, so—"

"Amusing?"

"Not amusing—refreshing and honest."

"I've been living in Boston, and this is my best gown. I expected everyone to be dressed in their best tonight."

"But they are, Lindsay."

She sighed and closed her eyes. Of course, it went without saying the women would be wearing their best dresses. But not having had the benefit of living a pampered life in Boston, their best dresses were homemade and plain.

She felt a light touch on her arm and opened her eyes. "I understood what you meant," Ginny said. "You were just explaining. I'm like that, too. I try so hard to explain, and sometimes, the words come out sounding harsh. I don't mean it; it just happens."

# Let it Be Christmas

She couldn't help but smile. She liked Ginny Brown a great deal and wanted to know more about her.

"You're right, I didn't mean to sound arrogant or spoiled." She paused and then said, "As you must know, my husband and brother own this ranch. Where do you live? Is your father a rancher, too?"

"No, my father was a railroad brakeman. He was killed in a train accident about eight years ago."

Lindsay shook her head. "My condolences for losing your father." She gazed at her new friend. "My father was killed on our ranch four years ago. Horse threw him and broke his neck."

"I'm sorry for you, too, Lindsay. And your mother?"

She lowered her head. "She died shortly after we settled here of cholera."

Ginny patted her arm. "I understand. My younger brother died of the cholera, too. At least I have my mother, and we manage. We're both seamstresses. We live in Langtry down by the springs."

Lindsay looked up. She was surprised at the location of Ginny's residence and wondered if the young woman was putting a brave face on. The area surrounding the springs was inhabited by the poorest people in Langtry.

Ginny must have read the unspoken question on her face because she added, "My mother washes clothes, as well as mends them. The springs provide the water, and we employ several of the local Mexican women to help."

Lindsay crossed herself and offered a short prayer of thanksgiving. Her new friend was a seamstress! Her prayers had been answered. She was so excited, she grabbed Ginny's hand.

But before she could open her mouth, there were loud shouts from the other end of the barn. While she'd been talking with Ginny, the band had resumed playing, but they screeched to a halt in the middle of a square dance. And then she heard more shouts, mingled with screams.

Ginny and Lindsay exchanged looks of alarm and gathered their skirts in their hands, rushing toward the commotion.

# Let it Be Christmas

Someone clasped Lindsay's shoulder and when she turned to see who it was, she stared into her brother's face.

He pulled her to one side. "It's Bart. He's gotten into a fight. Three men jumped him. I've got to help, but I want you to be safe." He squeezed her shoulder. "Go inside the house and bolt the door."

# Let it Be Christmas

## Chapter Seven

Bart stowed the flask in his vest pocket and strode to the front of the barn. There was nothing for him here. He'd already personally thanked each one of the men for helping to build the cabin.

And he wanted to get as far away from Lindsay as possible. He wished Rose was already here. It would be nice to be around a woman who wasn't judgmental—and a hypocrite to boot. Pushing past three men clustered in front of the barn, he heard a snatch of conversation.

"Fits her like a second skin, it does," one man said.

"Never seen a dress like that—'cept on a whore," the second man added.

"You'd think her new husband would control her better." The third man snickered. "But then, him being a professional gambler, turned rancher, maybe he don't know no better."

Bart's ears burned. There was no doubt who the men were discussing. He'd said almost the same thing to Lindsay's face, only moments before.

The men snorted and guffawed. One of them observed, "I'd like to peel that there dress off'n her."

Bart's heart pounded, pumping molten fury through his veins. Lindsay didn't deserve their filthy comments. He wished she'd chosen her dress with more care, but her gown didn't give these men the right to besmirch her honor.

They snickered again and one of them said, "If'n I got her in a dark corner, I'd know how to make her ferget her husband."

Coiled and ready, Bart launched himself into their midst, delivering a wicked undercut to the jaw of the man who was speaking.

The man toppled like an axed tree. His cohorts shouted and swore. One of the two remaining men grabbed Bart from behind and pinned his arms. The other man punched Bart's face and gut.

# Let it Be Christmas

Swinging around, he dodged the punches and tried to shake off the man holding his arms. The man hung on. Bart kicked backwards, and the man screamed as Bart's cowboy boot connected with his shin. Bart took advantage and pulled free. He turned on the man and landed several jabs to his jaw.

The man swayed. Bart yanked back his fist, intent upon finishing him. Pain sliced through his side. Whirling around, he found the third man wielding a half-empty whiskey bottle like a club.

Bart lunged at his assailant, but the man stepped to one side. A crowd loomed before him, pairs of avid eyes watching the fight. Chad's distraught face swam into view.

Fireworks exploded in his head and agony stabbed his skull. He stopped short, suspended for a heartbeat, before the ground rushed at him.

* * *

Lindsay held Bart's head in her lap. Occasionally, he would groan and toss his bandaged head from side to side. The fight had broken up the dance, and her brother had thanked everyone and sent them home.

She and Chad had brought Bart into the ranch house and laid him in the bedroom he'd been staying in until his cabin was finished. She'd changed from her aqua gown and uncomfortable corset into a plain chemise and faded cotton dress. Since there was no doctor in Langtry, they'd managed to clean and bandage Bart's head wound, where the whiskey bottle had left an ugly gash in his scalp. The coppery scent of his spent blood intermingled with the tangy smell of his hair tonic, making her sad he'd been hurt at his own cabin raising.

In reality, instead of feeling sorry for him, she should be furious with him for getting drunk and ruining the dance by starting a fight. And she *was* angry, but he was hurt and it would be un-Christian to withhold what comfort she could give. And despite her

# Let it Be Christmas

aching shoulders and back, she was willing to hold him and bathe his forehead.

Stretched out helpless on the bed, with his left jaw swollen and bruised and a purple shiner ringing his right eye, he'd never looked more appealing. The stark white bandage contrasted against his deeply tanned skin, and the one unruly lock of his hair had escaped its bindings to lie across his brow, making him look younger than his years.

Her gaze roamed over his face and body with a desperate hunger. With Bart unconscious, she was free to look at and touch him as much as she wanted. They were alone together in the final hours of darkness before dawn. Chad had gone to bed to nurse the cuts and bruises he received while extricating Bart from the unequal fight.

Reaching for the washbasin, she wrung out the cloth and dipped it into the cool water. Gently, she stroked his temples and over the tender spots on his mangled face.

Growing bolder, she put the cloth to one side and unbuttoned his shirt to the waist of his trousers. The warm glow of the lantern gilded his chest golden, making him appear like a pagan god of antiquity. Even in repose, the sculpted swells of his chest muscles and the wash-board flatness of his abdomen drew her like a moth to a flame.

Tentatively, she discovered the poetry of his flesh, running her fingertips over his warm skin, tracing the masculine contours of sinew and muscle, so different from her own body. Dipping her fingers lower, she touched the springy male pelt covering his chest. She closed her eyes and threaded her fingers through its soft but wiry texture, marveling at the feel.

She ached for him, in places too intimate to even think about. *What was wrong with her?* Her thoughts were sinful, full of licentiousness. It must be the darkness surrounding her, dense and deep, and that most vulnerable of times, the hours before dawn.

She shook herself as if to banish her yearning. She retrieved the cloth and dipped it into the basin again, sponging his chest and

196

# Let it Be Christmas

intending to re-button his shirt when her index finger grazed the flat male pap of his nipple by mistake. To her surprise, it responded to her touch, the flesh puckering and tightening.

*It was magic—a magic of the flesh.*

Curious, she touched her own breast through the thin fabric of her cotton dress and got the same response. Her and Seamus' coming together had been hurried and unpleasant. But now she understood, with Bart, there was power in touching. A primeval power beyond conscious thought.

She traced her nipples until they felt like tight little acorns, swelling with need, sending shivers of pleasure through her body. When the sensation became too potent, too almost-painful to bear, she abandoned her breasts and their aching fullness.

"My angel, my Lindsay," he moaned. His eyes fluttered open.

She gazed into his eyes, their light blue color turned cobalt in the dark room. Awareness glittered in their depths. He must have been half-awake, and he knew what she'd been thinking—how she'd been feeling.

Hot humiliation flooded her. She drew back and tried to lift his head from her lap. But he rose on one elbow and curled his other hand around her neck. Pulling her face down to his, he whispered, "You are my angel, aren't you? And I want you, too, Lindsay. Like I've never wanted another woman." He touched his forehead to hers. "I care for you. Do you care for me—just a little?"

Then his mouth found hers, and his generously sculpted lips molded against hers. He kissed her hard and deep, just as she'd dreamed about on their wedding day. And like the flesh of his nipples, his lips were warm and responsive. They possessed her eagerly, fitting her mouth perfectly.

His lips moved over hers, gentle as a spring rain, and then hard and demanding as a thunderstorm. They tasted and teased, sucked and skimmed, plundered and played.

# Let it Be Christmas

And when she'd accustomed herself to his mouth, his tongue pushed at the seam of her lips, testing the corners and tracing the sensitive swelling of her bottom lip.

She raised her arms and circled his neck, pulling him closer, reveling in the heady sensation of their mouths joined together, clinging and exploring.

His tongue parted her lips, and her initiation began all over again. He explored the inner contours of her mouth, abrading yet gentle, tender yet compelling. She met his invasion, thrusting with her own tongue.

The sweet, sultry spiral of desire bore them along on its crest, their bodies clinging to each other. Lindsay strained against him. Her body was on fire. She felt the secret male part of him, heavy and hard, pressed against her thigh.

His lips lifted from hers, and he groaned into her neck. "Lindsay, angel of mine. Do you care for me?"

She couldn't look at him. She laid her head on his shoulder. "Yes, yes, Bart, I do."

"Enough to make this a real marriage… after your baby comes."

She pulled back and gazed into his eyes. "Do you mean that?"

"Yes, I think I do. It's all so new to me." He picked up a tendril of her hair and twined it around his finger. "You're so beautiful, and I think I like being married to you."

"But… but… you'd want another man's leavings… to raise another man's child?"

He stroked her cheek. "What will you do when you have the child?"

She shook her head. "I don't know. Go back to Boston. Pose as a widow." She lowered her head. "I can't think."

He tilted her chin up. "Then think about us, Lindsay. About staying here. About being my wife in truth."

"All right. I will." She nodded. "I'll think about it."

He smiled and then he kissed her again… long and deep.

# Let it Be Christmas

\* \* \*

Chad discovered them in the early morning light, completely clothed but curled together like two orphaned kittens who'd lost their mother. Looking upon them, he knew his initial instincts had been right. Lindsay and Bart belonged together and not just in a sham marriage.

He couldn't help experiencing the smallest twinge of envy. He was engaged to Vi Lea Baker, but he seldom got to see her. Didn't know when they would marry. She hadn't even come to the cabin raising and dance because her mother was ailing again. But he didn't know if he really cared for Vi Lea or the thought of joining their ranches was what had attracted him in the first place.

He was so uncertain of his feelings; he hadn't even told Lindsay about his engagement.

Lindsay must have sensed him because she stirred. Sitting up, she stretched and yawned. Rubbing her eyes, she noticed him and said, "Good morning. I guess I fell asleep."

He gestured for her to follow, whispering, "Let's go to the kitchen. I don't want to disturb Bart. I've got coffee going."

Lindsay dutifully followed him, glancing briefly at Bart.

Once inside the kitchen, Chad seated his sister in a chair. "You've been up half the night. Let me get your coffee. Just sit and rest."

Cradling the cup of coffee in her hands, Lindsay took small sips from it. "Bart woke up last night. I think he'll be fine. He's got quite a hard head, you know." And then she smiled.

"I'm glad. He'll probably be up and around by tomorrow."

"Yes, probably." She pursed her lips and seemed deep in thought. Then, she shook her head and said, "I know Bart was drinking last night. Is that why he started the fight?"

"It wasn't like that, Lindsay. But you're right. Bart had a few drinks, but I've never seen him drunk before."

"So, if he wasn't drunk, how did the fight start?"

"Over a matter of your honor."

# Let it Be Christmas

"My honor? What on earth do you mean?"

"I think you should put away your gowns from Boston. You need to buy some calico fabric and—"

"Make dresses like the other women." She set her coffee cup down.

"Yes."

"I realized that last night. It was awful, knowing the women envied my dress. And besides, I'll be showing soon. I only have a few dresses that will fit me when I get bigger."

He sighed, relieved his sister was so level-headed. He reached across the table and patted her hand. "My wise sister. I'm glad you understand."

"But what does my gown have to do with the brawl or my honor?"

He lowered his head and drank his coffee. Then he puffed out his cheeks. "Men talk, especially about beautiful women."

"What do you mean?"

"I don't know how to put this delicately—"

"Then, don't. Just tell me."

He expelled his breath. "Three men were standing outside the front of the barn. They were drinking and talking. Bart happened to pass by them and hear them speculate on your virtue because of the gown you were wearing.

"Bart took offense, and he jumped all three of them. And no one offered to help. The three of them managed to get in quite a few licks, including a whiskey bottle broken over his skull before I stopped the fight."

She stared out the kitchen window. "I'm surprised he bothered to fight for my honor, especially given the reason he married me." She lowered her head. "And last night, when I spoke with him earlier, it was obvious he didn't like my gown, either. In fact, he accused me of dressing like a... a... loose woman."

She lifted her head and gazed at her brother. "I don't understand."

# Let it Be Christmas

"Oh, Sis, if you thought about it hard enough, I think you'd understand. Jealousy does strange things to a man, even to a *sham* husband." He drained his coffee cup and rose, putting the cup in the sink. "Think about it."

\* \* \*

Lindsay followed the dusty track to Ginny's house by the springs. Half-naked urchins tumbled at her feet, like friendly puppies, clinging to her skirts and asking if she'd brought candy. Reaching into her pockets, she distributed hard candy to the children. They jumped up and down, squealing with delight and hugging her.

It took the better part of an hour to walk to the Browns' house from the ranch. The first day she'd called upon Ginny, she'd rode Gypsy, but she didn't ride to Ginny's any more. She preferred to walk among the children and bring candy.

Twice, she'd brought Minnie with her, and the children delighted in the small white dog. The boys chased Minnie and rolled on the ground with her. The little girls held her close to their chests, pretending she was their baby while they petted her.

Since the night of the barn dance, she hadn't missed a day, coming to Ginny's. She'd turned over the cleaning and laundry to Serafina. She came early in the morning and was home by mid-afternoon, in time to cook her brother's supper. Bart, true to his word, cooked his own dinners and had Delfina, Serafina's younger sister, take care of his new cabin.

She'd shared the news of her pregnancy with them, and they were working to sew her several dresses for when she got bigger. And they'd struck another bargain—Lindsay would help them sew for their customers for free. And in between their paid-for work, they'd all sew clothes for the ragged and poor children of the town. Lindsay would furnish the cloth, thread, and buttons.

After only a few days, she'd grown close to Ginny and her mother and enjoyed their company. The constant sewing and rounds of talking kept her mind occupied until the evenings. It was

# Let it Be Christmas

only at night, after seeing Bart at the ranch, she had time to think about what he'd offered and what her brother had said.

Over the past few days, perhaps two dozen, carefully chosen, perfectly polite words had passed between them. Their mutual attraction was still there. But it was as if they were suspended in time, waiting for her to make up her mind.

Bart had said he *cared* for her, but nothing about love. She knew, beyond a shadow of a doubt she desired him. But did she *love* him? She'd already made one mistake. She didn't want to make another.

Thankfully, Bart's bruises had faded to a garish yellow color, and the gash on his head had scabbed over. His strength had returned. He and Chad were busy rounding up the sheep for the autumn shearing.

She reached the adobe house the Browns called home and turned into the weed-strewn front yard. Going around to the back, she found Ginny, her mother, and the two Mexican women who were helping the Browns, hard at work.

The Browns' laundry was located in the back yard of their home. Since Langtry experienced few inclement days, having the laundry outside, next to the springs, was practical. Being enclosed in a building with a steaming laundry during the summers in Langtry would have been unbearable.

The Browns had also built an arbor of grape vines under which to sit and sew. The arbor provided shade while allowing the breeze to waft through.

Waving, Lindsay greeted them all with, "Good morning. I see y'all are plenty busy."

Ginny looked up from her sewing and waved back. Mrs. Brown, a stouter and older version of her daughter, straightened from stirring an astringent-smelling boiling pot and said, "Good morning. Glad to see you today, Lindsay."

The two Mexican women, Lucia and Isabella, bobbed their heads and chorused, *"¡Hola! Señora* Houghton."

# Let it Be Christmas

Lindsay returned their greeting and asked Mrs. Brown, "Where do you want me to start?"

"With Ginny, we have some delicate tatting to do. Womenfolk are already getting ready for the dances, following the autumn shearing."

That reminded her, she needed to feed the shearing crew, but she didn't know how ungainly she'd be by then. And another dance? She'd be too big to dance. Maybe Ginny could help her to feed the shearing crew and organize the dance, celebrating the shearing.

"Oh, but I'm not good with the fine work, is there anything else I can do?"

"Well, Ginny will teach you," Mrs. Brown said.

"All right, Mrs. Brown. I just hope Ginny doesn't have to pull apart all my work and start over."

"Naw, you're quick. You'll get the hang of it. I'm sure. And how many times must I tell ye, call me by my given name, Emma."

"All right, Emma. I'll do my best. Will there be any time to—"

"Don't worry, soon as I get these clothes boiled, Lucia and Isabella will take over, and I'll get back to work on the trousers for the boys."

"That's wonderful. We're making progress, don't you think?"

"Yep, should have plenty of clothes made for Christmas time."

And Lindsay had already set aside most of her spending money to buy sandals and a toy for each of the children. She'd made the rounds of Langtry and had counted forty to fifty children under the age of ten.

Lindsay sat down beside Ginny under the arbor.

"I'm glad we get to work side-by-side today," Ginny whispered. "We've been so busy lately we haven't had time to talk. How are things at the ranch?"

# Let it Be Christmas

"Going well. Chad and Bart are starting to bring the sheep in from the far pastures for shearing."

"And how's your handsome but injured husband?"

"He will be healed in no time, and he's working like he'd never been hurt."

"Well, y'all didn't lose any time. Getting in the family way, I mean. I didn't hear about your marrying until—"

"Ginny!"

Ginny held up one hand. "I won't ask any more questions. Maybe, later, when you're further along, you'll want to talk about it."

Lindsay shook her head, but she knew her new friend was right. One day she'd have to tell Ginny everything, but for now, she wasn't ready. And she was still confused, too. Was Bart waiting for her to take him up on his offer of a real marriage or was he embarrassed and sorry he'd said anything?

And why, when he didn't think she was looking, would he gaze down the road toward Langtry, as if he was waiting for someone?

"I will admit Bart has helped Chad a great deal around the ranch, despite his injuries. And thanks to him, we should turn a profit on our wool this time."

"That's wonderful!" Ginny exclaimed. "Most of the ranchers haven't turned a profit since the tariff was lifted. What did Bart do?"

"Had us join the Wool and Mohair Cooperative in Del Rio. They ship in bulk and get lower freight rates from the railroad. I never realized freight was such a significant cost of getting our wool to market, but it is. What we save on freight should give us a small profit this time. If all goes as planned."

"Good for Bart. You must be in heaven, having such a handsome husband." Ginny tossed her head. "Course your brother is easy on the eyes, too."

"Why, Ginny Brown!" She grasped her friend's arm. "If I didn't know you better, I'd say you were sweet on my brother."

# Let it Be Christmas

Ginny ducked her head. "What if I am? He'll never notice me. I'm poor and mousy."

Lindsay squealed and threw her arms around her friend. "What are you saying! You're not poor and mousy. He should be proud to have you. And just think, then we'd be sisters. And you and your mother could move to the ranch and..." She hesitated, wondering what would happen between her and Bart by then.

"Chad's not spoken for, is he?" Ginny asked.

"No, not that I know of. He didn't bring anyone to the cabin raising."

Ginny bit her lip. "Then there's hope."

"More than hope. I was wondering how I would take care of the shearing crew and then another dance. I'll be further along and though Serafina and Delfina can help, I'll still need your assistance."

"Oh, please, I want to help you, Lindsay. I'd love to, and I'm sure Mama will want to help, too." Ginny paused and added, "That is, if you want us."

"Want you! Are you teasing me?"

"I just needed to be sure."

"Do you think your mother would let you come and stay at the ranch house during the shearing. I could certainly use your help."

"I'm sure she will."

"Good, that's settled then." She hugged Ginny. "And we'll take in one of my dresses for you and do your hair and maybe a little rouge." Lindsay held her friend at arm's length. "We'll make certain Chad notices you, Ginny."

\* \* \*

Two weeks later, Lindsay trudged home in the heat of the day from the Browns. It had been a long day, and she was exhausted. She hadn't known her brother had taken Ginny out the day before and admitted he was engaged to Vi Lea Baker, a rancher's daughter Lindsay didn't care for. Why had her brother picnicked with Ginny if he was already engaged? His admission had

# Let it Be Christmas

devastated Ginny. And why hadn't Chad told Lindsay he'd been engaged since last Christmas?

She shook her head and wondered what Chad was doing? Comforting Ginny had been mentally exhausting, along with a long day spent sewing. She was so tired, she almost wished for her mare. But really, it was better she didn't ride anymore. This week, she'd felt her baby moving. He or she was alive and real, very real.

And once she held her baby in her arms, what then? Could she and Bart make a go of it? They came from such different backgrounds. But he was a hard worker and had already helped with the ranch. But what if, like her attraction to Seamus, their attraction wore thin. *What then?* She didn't know.

She glanced up to see Bart in the yard in front of the ranch house, helping down a woman from the buckboard. The woman was voluptuous-looking with bright red hair that appeared anything but natural. She had on a form-fitting, neck-plunging dress in a red silk that clashed with the color of her hair. She also sported one fine parasol made with the same black lace edging the neckline of her dress. And the smell of her rose-scented perfume was overwhelming, making Lindsay want to hold her nose.

And Bart, the scoundrel, was hugging the woman!

Knowing how bedraggled she must look after working in the heat all day, she advanced upon their happy scene.

Bart released the red-haired trollop long enough to fetch her trunk from the back of the wagon. *Fetch her trunk!* Was this woman staying? And where was her feckless brother when she needed him?

# Let it Be Christmas

## Chapter Eight

Chad came out of the barn, wiping his forehead with the shirt of his sleeve. He glanced up and plastered a smile on his face for Bart's sake. He inclined his head at the woman and said, "You must be Rose, Bart's friend." Then he glanced at Lindsay and motioned to her. "Hey, Sis, come on over. Let's meet Bart's friend."

Lindsay came and stood by his side. He wasn't certain of how Bart was going to act with Rose. And even though they'd talked about how to handle the situation, he couldn't see how this was going to end well.

"Lindsay and Chad, this is Rose Gallagher from Tucson." Bart made the introductions. "She's an old friend of mine. I told Chad she'd be stopping by. She's on her way home to Alabama. Her mother is ailing."

Chad glanced at his sister and could see she was appalled and upset. Her eyes were narrowed, her mouth was pursed, and she'd crossed her arms over chest.

"I believe my mother won't be with us for long," Rose stated. "And I wanted to tell Bart to be especially vigilant about the Boyd brothers showing up."

"Who are the Boyd brothers?" Lindsay asked.

Chad lowered his voice. "The men I saved Bart from before you came home."

"Does that mean they're—"

"Shhh, I'll explain more later."

"You bet you will." She glared at him. "And don't shush me."

Chad returned Lindsay's glare and turned back to Rose. He wanted to squash his sister's temper and welcome the woman for Bart's sake. "Ah, Mrs. Gallagher, good to meet you. You're more than welcome to stay the night. We have an extra bedroom."

Lindsay tugged on his sleeve and hissed, "I won't allow that woman in our home."

# Let it Be Christmas

"I heard that, Lindsay, no need to whisper," Bart said. "She can stay in my cabin for the night."

"But you and she would be unchaperoned," Lindsay interjected. "And you're married to *me*. It would look very awkward."

"I didn't know you'd gotten married, darlin'," Rose said, giving Bart a side glance. "You didn't mention it in your telegram."

"Why would he?" Lindsay said. "It's a 'fake' marriage anyway. He wanted to be a partner in our ranch and my brother, my brother…" She turned away.

"Sis, don't. Not here, not now." Chad put his hand on her shoulder. We don't want to be rude to our guest, and besides, wouldn't it be better if Rose stayed in the house with us?"

Lindsay pulled free of his grasp. "No, I don't want her in our parents' home. Don't you understand?" Tears rolled down her cheeks. "And get your own supper. I need time to think, so I'm going to saddle Gypsy and ride for a while. Don't wait up for me."

\* \* \*

Lindsay guided Gypsy into the barn well past dusk. She prayed she hadn't hurt her baby by riding, but she'd had to get away. She didn't want that woman in her home, and she refused to watch Bart show her to his cabin, either.

Maybe she should have ridden all the way to Del Rio. She'd gotten a letter, earlier in the week from Abby, telling her that her time was nigh and asking if Lindsay would come to see her new baby and meet the rest of her family. She'd been busy with the Browns and her Christmas charity and though she wanted to see Abby and her family, she didn't know if she had time to go.

But now, she couldn't wait to get away from Bart and his fancy woman. After thinking about it, she'd decided to leave first thing tomorrow. She'd need to tell the Browns she'd be gone for a few days, and she'd travel by train. She couldn't have ridden all the way to Del Rio on horseback, even if she wanted to.

# Let it Be Christmas

She dismounted and found a lantern and a tin of safety matches. She lit the lantern and then she saw him. Bart had been hiding in the shadows, waiting for her.

But she didn't want to talk to him. Maybe, if she ignored him, he would go away.

She grabbed Gypsy's reins and led her into a stall, making certain there was a bucket of water and oats. She loosened the mare's cinch, but before she could lift the saddle, Bart was behind her, lifting it for her.

"Fine," she said, tossing the mare's reins at him. "You do it, then. I'll go inside."

He dropped the saddle and grabbed her wrist, saying, "Not so fast. We need to talk. Please."

She pulled free and crossed her arms over her chest. "I have nothing to say to you. Except one thing, and one thing only—I cannot believe you brought that... that woman to our ranch."

"Why not, she *is* an old friend, and she's brought me news of the Boyd brothers."

"Who are they? Chad wouldn't tell me. Said he'd explain later."

"They're the ones who had me cornered after the Fitzsimmons prize fight last February. They knew me from Tucson where Rose's house is, and they wanted to win their money back. No holds barred. If you know what I mean."

She shook her head and pursed her mouth. "I was right! She does own a brothel. She is a madam, isn't she?"

"Yes, but before that, I grew up with her. And her profession wasn't *chosen*, Lindsay."

"What do you mean?"

"Rose didn't choose to be a madam or a 'fancy' woman. She was beaten and raped by her stepfather when he was drunk. Young, ruined, and with no money, what was she supposed to do? She chose to run away, and the only way she could support herself was to become... what you called her. She believed it was better than starving."

# Let it Be Christmas

Lindsay took a deep breath, sucking in the familiar odors of the barn, dusty hay mixed with pungent horse dung.

"I feel for her, as one woman to another," she admitted. "And that's terrible what happened. Worse than…" But she couldn't say it, wouldn't say it.

She'd made a mistake. One mistake with a man she'd been engaged to, but it wasn't like she'd embraced the life of a whore. Not like Rose.

But Bart finished her thought. "Worse than what happened to you?"

"Yes, worse than that. At least I was willing to atone for my sin, willing to go to a convent. Until you and Chad cooked up your half-baked marriage scheme."

"So, that's all this has been to you? A half-baked scheme." He thrust his face into hers. "And to think, I was beginning to *care* for you. Wanted us to be a real family."

She covered her ears with her hands. "And don't tell me, you've never slept with Rose, once she established her profession." She glared at him and uncovered her ears. "I saw the way you held her when you helped her from the buckboard. I might not be a woman of the world, but I have eyes in my head."

"And a tongue like a viper, you little hypocrite. How can you be so judgmental? You may have been ready to atone for your sin, but you still sinned. Didn't you?"

"You slept with her, didn't you?"

He gritted his teeth but his face had turned a deep, mottled red. "All right, what if I did? When I was young and wild and first found her in Tucson. She's an old friend. I'm a man. It's not the same—"

"Well, it should be the same. And now, you'll sleep with her again. Won't you? After all, it's pretty convenient with her staying in your cabin." She fisted her hands and planted them on her hips.

"Rose and I are just friends now, that's what would stop me. Get your mind out of the gutter, Mrs. Houghton. I saw the way you looked at me that night after the fight."

# Let it Be Christmas

"Because I was taking care of you that night, and I, I..." She threw her hands into the air. "Oh, what's the use. You're the one with *your* mind in the gutter."

"Really? I thought you liked it when I kissed you. Thought you believed me when I said I cared for you. But you didn't return the sentiment, did you?" He shook his head. "You may be attracted to me, might even want me in your bed." He grabbed her shoulders. "But deep down, you don't think I'm good enough for you. Isn't that right?"

She twisted from his grasp and backed up against the stall wall. "What if I do think that?" Not that she did—her feelings for Bart were more confused and involved than simple arrogance. "After all, it's your unsavory connections that have brought Rose here and those men, the Boyd brothers."

He crossed his arms over his chest. "Rose is going to home to her sick mother. I don't see how you can blame me for that." He shook his head again. "I was going to explain about the Boyd brothers, but you don't want to hear about that. Do you? Instead, you want to know all the intimate, dirty secrets between Rose and me."

"Enough about Rose. And I *do* want to know about the Boyd's. But I think I know the worst already. Chad kept them from killing you, didn't he?"

"Yes, if it hadn't been for your brother, I'd probably be dead now."

"And you admit they were looking to get their money back from you. Weren't they? Money you cheated from them, playing cards."

He ground his teeth again and hissed, "I never cheat, but I do know how to 'count' cards. It gives me an advantage."

"I don't know what counting cards means, but it sounds like one step away from cheating. And now these men, these Boyd brothers, are coming back for my brother and you. You and your slimy profession and the people you know have brought this down

# Let it Be Christmas

on my poor, honest brother's head." She stared at him. "Haven't you?"

"Yes, I guess, in a way, I have." He dropped his arms and fisted his hands. "I hadn't thought of it that way."

"Well, you think on it while you're holed up with your… your whore." She wanted to slap him, but he wasn't worth it. "I'll worry about my brother, praying he won't get shot down in the street, like a dog, by some thugs you cheated at cards."

He exhaled and reached for her again, but she twisted away. "I'm sorry, Lindsay, I never meant for Chad to be in danger. That's why I've been taking all the precautions and—"

"Don't speak to me. Don't touch me. Don't ever say another word to me." She gathered her skirts in one hand and ran to the front door of the barn. "I wish I never had to lay eyes on you again. And I'm getting a divorce the minute I have my baby."

* * *

Lindsay got her train ticket and went to stand on the platform. She'd argued with Chad this morning before she left the ranch. He hadn't wanted her to go alone to Del Rio because of the dangerous situation Bart had created. But he couldn't get away from the ranch, not with the sheep to bring in for shearing.

And she'd given him a tongue lashing about not telling her that he'd gotten engaged. Not to mention he'd led Ginny on, devastating her shy friend.

*Men! They could be so ornery!*

Even so, she'd had to beg her brother to take care of Minnie. She certainly couldn't ask Bart to take care of Minnie, not after last night. Chad still didn't like her dog, but she hoped he'd be good to Minnie while she was gone.

Besides, she couldn't stay another minute at the ranch. She needed time to think things through, and seeing Abby and her family would be a balm to her spirit.

She might have stayed with the Browns, but she wanted to get away from Langtry. She'd stopped by this morning and told

# Let it Be Christmas

Ginny she was going to see her friend in Del Rio, who was due to have her baby. She'd confided some of what had happened to Ginny. Her friend, who was still upset with Chad, had understood and wished her a safe trip.

When she had her baby, she'd get a divorce and return to Boston—get as far away as possible from Bart. She and her aunt had "made up" through a series of letters they'd exchanged. Her Aunt Minerva understood what had happened and had forgiven her, which was a miracle, in and of itself.

Her aunt was tough as an old shoe. She and her late husband, Uncle Sean, hadn't been able to have children, and as the captain of a ship, he'd often been away for months at a time. When he'd bought more ships and built warehouses, he still went to sea and left Aunt Minnie to run their expanding business.

Being thrust into a shipping business where women were scarcer than hen's teeth, had honed her aunt's instincts, making them razor sharp. She had to make decisions quickly and trust her gut feelings. Her aunt was quick to judge people and seldom backed down from her opinions.

Shaped by her aunt at an impressionable age, Lindsay had learned to formulate strict opinions, too, and judge people on their merits. Or so she'd thought, until Seamus. He'd managed to fool her with his ardent wooing. But he hadn't fooled her aunt—some instinct had warned Aunt Minnie to have him investigated.

Given her aunt's strictness and firm opinions, she was thankful to have won her aunt's forgiveness and to know Aunt Minnie wanted her and her child to return to Boston.

Her aunt must have grown to love her as a daughter. And knowing she was loved, no matter the mistake she'd made, gave her courage. She could forget Bart and start her life over, especially with her aunt's support.

She threw back her shoulders and straightened her spine. She checked the watch pinned to her shirtwaist and peered down the rail lines, wondering if the train would be on time.

# Let it Be Christmas

Then she saw Bart, escorting Rose to the platform. She hadn't realized the madam would be sharing the same train, going east. If she'd thought about it, Bart had said she was only going to stay the night. But it didn't matter; they didn't have to sit in the same railway car.

Just seeing them together and wondering if they'd slept in each other's arms last night, her stomach knotted and her heart executed a funny flip-flop in her chest. The last thing she wanted to do was greet them.

She moved back inside the depot, hoping Rose already had her ticket.

Glancing past Bart and Rose, she noticed two men jumping over the railing on the Jersey Lily's porch. She thought that was odd. Why were they in such a hurry?

The sharp bark of gunshots startled her.

Alarmed, she stepped back and glimpsed the bright sun glint off metal. Now, she understood why the men had moved so fast.

*They were gunning for Bart!*

She stuck her head out and screamed, "Behind you, Bart!"

He shoved Rose onto the platform behind some heaped crates and whirled around, dropping to the ground. He drew his gun from its holster.

More shots blasted. A veritable barrage of gunshots pelted the air like a swarm of angry bees. The acrid smell of gunpowder blanketed the air, making it hard to breathe.

Lindsay covered her ears with her hands and tried to draw breath into her lungs. She shook like a leaf, and her heart lodged in her throat. She couldn't believe her eyes. Watching Bart lying in the dust while the bullets pocked the ground all around him, she felt as if she'd descended into a hideous nightmare.

Crawling along the ground, Bart dodged and weaved, like a grotesque puppet pulled by invisible strings. Keeping low and constantly on the move, he proved to be a difficult target. But the bullets kicked up the dirt behind his feet.

# Let it Be Christmas

Lindsay bit her knuckle, stifling the scream building in her throat. She didn't dare make a sound because it might distract Bart from his death-defying course. It was obvious, despite his zig-zag path, he wanted to reach the cover of the crates. But to do that, he'd have to climb onto the platform, offering the two men shooting at him, a perfect target.

His two attackers emptied their four guns before they stopped to reload. In the open street and vulnerable, Bart got several shots off and one of the men dropped in his tracks.

When the other man saw his partner hit the ground, he grabbed the fallen man's guns. Yelling obscenities at the top of his lungs, the red-headed man ran toward Bart, firing again and again. Bart writhed and twisted. And then he sank into the dust.

*Bart was shot!*

The horrible realization tumbled over and over in Lindsay's head, but she couldn't believe it. Her benumbed mind refused to grasp the meaning of his crumpled form.

The man who'd shot him looked over his shoulder toward the Jersey Lily. He must have seen the Judge with a shotgun in his hands because the red-headed man jumped on the nearest horse and spurred it into a gallop, heading west, out of town.

Forcing her hollowed-out legs to move, she ran to where Bart lay in the dust and dropped beside him. Rose came out of hiding and joined her.

Lindsay tugged at Bart, crossed herself, and pleaded, "God, please God, don't let him die. Please, God."

With gentle hands, Rose nudged her to one side and said, "Mrs. Houghton, let me turn him over and see how bad he's hurt." She captured Lindsay's gaze. "I've seen a lot of gunshot wounds in my profession."

Numbly, Lindsay nodded. Tears poured from her eyes, and her ears rang from the shots. The awful shots still echoed in her head.

Rose touched her arm. "He'll be all right. They got him in the shoulder. But the bullet needs to come out. Is there a doctor in

215

# Let it Be Christmas

Langtry?" Rose squeezed her arm. "Mrs. Houghton, do you understand me?"

She nodded again, holding onto Rose's words that Bart would be all right, as if they were the only words in the universe. Repeating them over and over in her mind like a benediction.

She took a deep breath, willing her panic to subside. She must think calmly, must help Bart. She twisted the wedding band on her left hand.

"No, we don't have a doctor here. We'll need to get him to Del Rio. I was going there. I'll buy him a ticket and tell the clerk to send Will to let my brother know what happened."

Rose nodded and bent to lift her skirt and tear off a piece of petticoat. "We need to stop the bleeding. I'll stay with Bart."

Lindsay wet her bone-dry lips and croaked, "Yes, that's a good idea."

"How far on the train to Del Rio?"

"Not long, less than an hour."

"Good. Get the ticket and send word."

Lindsay went back inside to buy another ticket, hoping the train would be on time. Through the smeared and dirty window of the railroad depot, she saw Judge Bean organizing a posse to go after the red-headed man. For once, the Judge was good for something. She hoped they got the man and strung him up.

She went back outside and could see the smokestack of the approaching train. She thanked God for it being on time. Now if they could take on water and load the crates fast enough.

Rose had Bart's head in her lap. Seeing them, Lindsay couldn't help but feel bitter and jealous, though she realized Rose must know a great deal more about taking care of a man who'd been shot.

Bart's eyes fluttered open. "It was the Boyd brothers, Rose."

"Yes, I know."

"I think I got one of them."

"You got Phineas."

He winced and bit down on his lip. "Is he dead?"

216

# Let it Be Christmas

"Looks like it, but the Judge will make sure."

"Wish it had been Red. He's the meanest. And he'll be back again."

At his words, Lindsay's heart squeezed. *The nightmare was going to continue?*

"Judge Bean is getting together a posse," Lindsay said. "They'll do their best to catch him."

Bart sighed and turned his head away. "Lindsay, I didn't know you were here."

"I was going to Del Rio, to visit a friend. We'll get you to the doctor there."

She glanced down to see his blood had already soaked through Rose's petticoat. The metallic smell of it was overwhelming, making her want to retch. She reached down and tore off a large piece of her own petticoat. After folding it into a square-like-bandage, she handed it to Rose.

Bart groaned, and he gazed at her. "Rose will take care of me, Lindsay. You needn't bother."

# Let it Be Christmas

## Chapter Nine

Lindsay held Abby's baby son and paced in front of Bart's door. There had been a vacant room at the boardinghouse, and Abby had been kind enough to let Bart have the room to recuperate.

Doctor Rodgers had dug out the bullet and said Bart should recover if the wound didn't get infected. She'd wanted to help take care of him, but every time, she came to check on him, Rose had turned her away.

Rose had been polite enough about it, claiming he was eating or sleeping or in too much pain, but Lindsay knew excuses when she heard them. He didn't want to see her. She remembered how he'd spurned her when they were waiting for the train.

Little Timothy, named in honor of the beloved nephew Abby's husband had lost, started to fuss. He smelled so sweet, as only babies did, the subtle scent of milk clinging to him. She rocked him in her arms and tried singing a low lullaby. But the baby kept fussing, and she went downstairs where she had a cot in the kitchen.

She heard footsteps and the kitchen door swung open. Abby, in her nightgown and with a shawl wrapped around her shoulders smiled and crossed the room.

Gently, she took the baby from her arms, saying, "Thank you for walking with him, but I heard him crying. And it's about his feeding time anyway." She unbuttoned the front of her nightgown and sat on the edge of the cot, giving the baby her left breast to suckle. She arranged her shawl to cover Timothy's head and most of her breast.

Lindsay watched in awe. As the youngest child of her family and then being raised by her widowed aunt, she knew nothing about birthing and babies. Soon she'd need to know. Her unborn child gave her a kick as if in agreement, and she cupped her hand over her curved stomach.

# Let it Be Christmas

Abby had given birth only a couple of days before they'd turned up on her doorstep, and her friend had still been in bed when they'd arrived. Fortunately, Elisa, and her sister, Rosa, had helped get Bart settled in the vacant room and been very helpful, fetching and carrying for her wounded husband.

"Don't look so frightened, Lindsay, breast feeding is natural. You'll get the hang of it. I'm certain."

She gulped and swallowed. "I hope so."

"And I appreciate your help with Timothy so I could sleep a little longer. But you need to rest, too, especially for your child."

She nodded and reached out, stroking Tim's soft cheek with her fingertip. "Yes, I'm tired, but I can't sleep. I can't stop thinking about Bart and how he won't see me."

"He'll see you." Abby patted her hand. "I know he will."

"When? It's been a week now, and he only lets Rose take care of him." She shook her head. "He'll never forgive me."

"Forgive you?" Abby shifted the baby to her other breast and re-arranged her shawl, keeping her baby warm and snuggled. "What are you talking about? You told me your marriage was in name only."

"It started out that way to give my child a name. It was Chad's idea, when we took Bart on as a partner." Her baby gave another kick, and she couldn't help but smile and smooth her hand over her abdomen.

Abby returned her smile. "Your baby is restless tonight."

"Yes, restless and kicking like crazy." She leaned back on the cot. "But there's more to the story about Bart marrying me, and it's also the reason he was shot." She trembled, thinking about the shootout and knowing it wasn't over.

"Chad saved Bart's life, but in the process, the man Chad wounded died from the injury. That's why his brothers gunned down Bart. But one of the brothers got away. And now, Chad has telegrammed me that the posse didn't catch him."

Abby squeezed her shoulder. "You *do* need to sleep. I asked you about Bart forgiving you, and then you told me about the

# Let it Be Christmas

shooting. You're talking in circles, Lindsay. Do you want Clint to look into it?"

"No, you told me Clint turned in his badge when you had Timothy."

"He did. The county elected another sheriff. Clint promised to give up his badge when we had a child. But he can go to the new sheriff and have him put out a circular on the man who shot Bart and got away."

Lindsay nodded. "I'd appreciate that. It couldn't hurt. I doubt the Judge alerted the proper authorities." She touched her friend's arm. "You're so lucky. Clint is such a good man, and a great father for Kevin."

She'd met Abby's husband and son and been impressed by what a nice man Clint was and how polite and well-mannered Abby's son was.

"Yes, I love all three of my boys. But I miss the other two. Wish it wasn't shearing time at the ranch, but if wishes were horses…"

"I should be getting back to help my brother, too. I just wanted to see, with my own eyes, if Bart was on the mend. And ask his forgiveness."

"Forgiveness for what?"

"For being judgmental of him and his past profession. He was a gambler, and all these shootings are because of his past associations. And then I was jealous of Rose."

"Rose? But she's just his childhood friend, though, I can see with her profession, how you might think the worst." Timothy had fallen asleep at her breast. Abby kissed his chubby cheek and closed her nightgown.

"Yes, and our marriage had started to be something more. Bart is really a nice man and a hard worker. He said he cared for me, and maybe we should try for a real marriage."

"Oh, Lindsay, that's wonderful!" Abby covered her mouth with her free hand. "If that's what you want, of course."

# Let it Be Christmas

"I thought maybe it was, but I couldn't get past his unsavory connections and former profession."

Abby giggled. "Clint has Bart beat by a mile on that score."

She raised her head and gazed at her friend. "What do you mean?"

"Clint's mother was a 'lady of the night' and he doesn't know who his father was. He practically raised himself, his sister, and then his sister's son. But he's a good and upright man, nevertheless." She patted Lindsay's arm. "You need to forget about his past and give the man a chance. Sounds like he deserves it."

"Even if he brought this killing into our lives because of his gambling?"

Abby sighed. "Men do what they have to do. It doesn't make them all bad. But I'm sorry you're worried about your brother."

"And Bart, too. As soon as this Boyd brother learns Bart has survived, he'll come back. And according to Bart, he'll be gunning for my brother, too."

Abby shook her head. "That's too bad. But maybe this man won't return. Maybe the posse scared him off, or maybe, if he's so mean, he'll get in another gunfight and not survive." She shifted the sleeping baby in her arms. "None of us knows what the future will bring."

"Yes, but you asked Clint to give up being sheriff."

"I did. Being sheriff is like walking around with a target on your back. I doubt Chad and Bart will be doing that. Didn't you say they'd been taking precautions?" She kissed her baby's forehead. "And besides, between Clint's ranch, this boardinghouse, Kevin, and starting a family, we had our hands full."

"I wish I could be more like you, Abby." Her friend was wise beyond her years and took her responsibilities seriously. "I wish I didn't worry so much, and I could believe everything will work out for the best. Like you do."

Abby got up and said, "Little Tim and I are going back to bed. And you should try and get some sleep, too."

# Let it Be Christmas

Lindsay nodded and smiled, but she was silently chastising herself for forgetting what was important. How could she have allowed her jealousy to matter more than Bart's life? Why hadn't she accepted his explanations and believed him?

*Could he... would he... forgive her?*

\* \* \*

Lindsay was packed and ready to return home. She still hadn't seen Bart, but she knew he'd return when he was well enough. And Chad needed her because it was shearing time. She was definitely showing now, but she'd supervise the women to feed the shearing crew, while she remained in the background.

She stopped in the foyer and gave Abby a hug and Timothy a kiss. She would miss them.

"I'd like to see you more often," Abby said. "Maybe I'll bring Timothy to visit after your baby comes, and we can decide who has the prettier one."

"Hah! That will be a contest nobody wins."

"You're right. No baby could be prettier than my Tim." She smiled and patted Lindsay's shoulder. "I know you'll be all right, but if you need to, just send for me."

"I think I'll have plenty of help. Ginny's mother, Emma, has birthed some babies, and she knows an excellent mid-wife, Constanza Guadalupe. She births almost all the babies in Langtry."

"Good. And you think you're due around Christmas."

"I'm certain. It's easy to count when you only had relations, the one time."

"Well, the winter is our slow time, so when your baby is born, we'll all come and visit you." Abby paused, as if considering. "Do you have room?"

"Yes, I would like that, and we have plenty of room. We've three bedrooms in the main house, and Bart's cabin has two bedrooms. Not to mention an indoor privy."

"Really? How nice. I would love to see it and to use it, too." Abby chuckled.

# Let it Be Christmas

"Yes, they're nice. I got accustomed to them in Boston."

"Do you need anyone to walk with you to the station?"

"No, I'll be fine. It's only a couple of blocks. The train should be along in less than hour."

"If it's on time."

They kissed and hugged again.

But before she could open the front door, someone called to her from the top of the stairs. "Lindsay, wait. Do you have a minute before you go?"

Hesitant, but brimming with hope at the sound of Bart's voice, she dropped her carpetbag and ascended the stairs. He was leaning against the doorway, his left arm in a sling. He was thinner and his deep tan had faded. He looked as she had imagined he would, weak and pale.

Gazing at him, a lump rose in her throat, and her eyes stung with unshed tears. Not trusting herself to speak, she merely nodded and walked inside his room. He moved to one side to let her pass and then followed her.

The room was empty. Where was Rose? Out back, no doubt, soon to return.

She shook her head; she mustn't think that way.

She had to get past being judgmental. After all, everyone made mistakes. Why couldn't she, like Abby or Ginny, accept people for themselves, instead of labeling them as if she was identifying some rare specimen for a zoo—as if she had to apply a distinguishing sign like marking a sheep? Couldn't she just deal with each person as an individual?

She'd believed, when she did charitable works, she was helping people. But did she see those people as individuals with wishes and hopes and dreams like hers, or were they merely subjects upon whom she carried out experiments in social work to boost her own self-esteem or atone for her sins?

Had she learned too well the lessons from her Aunt Minerva, size people up and make a quick decision as to whether they were acceptable or not? But her aunt had also taught her about

# Let it Be Christmas

charitable works. How could she separate the two? Were only certain people deserving of her charity—and if that was so—was it really charity?

Love... love made the difference. Her aunt was rigorously strict to the point of severity. But she'd forgiven her sin, hadn't she? Why was that? Because her aunt loved her. And to be truly charitable, you had to have love in your heart or it was an empty gesture.

*She loved Bart and always would, no matter what happened, and that changed everything. Didn't it?*

Finally finding her voice, she asked, "Where's Rose?"

"Didn't Abby tell you?"

She shook her head.

"She left this morning on the eastbound train."

"I didn't know she was leaving."

Bart started to shrug, but he winced and stopped himself. "It was time for her to go. Her mother needs her. She only stayed to be sure I was all right." He paused and added, "As you can see, I'm getting around."

Lindsay felt a twinge of regret. She had dismissed Bart's story about Rose's stepfather when he told her, but she hadn't forgotten it. She'd hoped to make amends, not to Bart, but to Rose. If Lindsay didn't have her rich Aunt Minerva and half of the ranch to support her, what would she have done?

Technically, she was ruined, too. And no one had forced her.

Bart had tried to tell her the same thing, but she'd been too angry and jealous to listen. Thinking of her life in those terms made her realize she and Rose were sisters under the skin. Lindsay didn't know what she would have said or done to make amends to Rose, though. But she wished she'd had the chance.

*Now it was too late.*

# Let it Be Christmas

Rose had left without a farewell. Bart was standing before her. She wanted to talk to him, but it was past difficult to find the right words to say.

She glanced at the stark, white bandage covering half of his torso and asked, "What does Doc Rodgers say about your shoulder? Is it healing?"

"My shoulder is doing better than expected—no infection. The doctor tells me to rest and eat a lot. That's not hard around here. Your friend, Abby, runs a nice house and the meals are delicious. But I've got to get back to the ranch and help your brother with the shearing."

"No, you should rest. Chad has handled the shearing before. Besides, with an injured shoulder, you'll have a hard time helping out."

He lowered his head. "Yeah, I guess I am kind of useless, but I still think I should be there. Tell Chad I'll be along in a couple of days. I think the Doc will let me go by then." He paused and lifted his head. "I appreciate you staying to see if I was going to make it." He tried to shrug again, caught himself, and half-smiled. "And I owe you my life. You were the one who called out to warn me about the Boyd brothers. I haven't had the chance to thank you properly."

"But your appreciation didn't extend to letting me see you, did it?" Lindsay blurted out.

As soon as the words left her mouth, she could have bitten her tongue in two. Why had she said that? Couldn't she have been pleased he recognized her help and was acknowledging it?

He scowled and looked away. His features appeared as if they were carved in stone when he turned back and gazed at her. "I thought it best you didn't visit me."

Having come this far, she wasn't going to back down without a proper answer. She had to ask. "Why?"

"Because Rose was here, taking care of me. I thought it would be awkward for you."

# Let it Be Christmas

Based on the things she'd said about Rose; she couldn't blame him for feeling that way. She wanted to explain how she felt about Rose now. How she wished she could make amends, but she doubted he would believe her. Better to tell him the reason she'd tried to see him when he was first wounded.

She exhaled and admitted, "I wanted to see you... to apologize, Bart."

"What for?"

"For not trusting you about Rose, for one thing."

He grinned. "For your information, Rose slept on the trundle bed." He shook his head. "Besides, with the pain, I wasn't in an amorous mood." He looked up and caught her gaze. "What's the other thing?"

"For blaming you about Chad. My brother did what he did that night and chose to involve himself. You didn't force him. Did you?"

"No, I didn't, but there is some merit to what you said. I've thought about it a lot. Had a lot of time to think about it, laying around." He winced again and closed his eyes. He sank onto the edge of the bed. "I probably shouldn't hang around because Red will be back. If I leave, he might not come back to Langtry."

"What about the partnership—your share of the ranch?"

"Chad can buy me out over time."

"And me and the baby... our marriage."

He wiped the perspiration off his forehead with his good hand. It was obvious he was still weaker than he cared to admit.

"Oh, I'll stay for the baby, and we'll get a proper divorce. Just have to hope Red Boyd won't be back before then."

"But he'll still come back for Chad, won't he?"

"Yes, there is that possibility."

"Then wouldn't it be safer if the two of you were together to watch each other's backs?"

"Maybe." He thrust out his chin. "But things didn't turn out how I thought they would, and I don't know if I want to hang around, not after what has happened."

# Let it Be Christmas

"Can't you try and forgive me? I'm sorry I didn't trust you and blamed you for everything." She lowered her head and scuffed her boot along the edge of the rag rug. "I don't know if things can ever be the same between us—"

"Give it a rest," he cut her off. "Things can never be the same. Now, I don't trust you."

She gasped. "How can you say such a thing? What have I done to make you mistrust *me*?"

"Be honest with yourself, for one thing. You said you accepted me and the partnership, knowing my past. But when you got upset and jealous, your real feelings came pouring out." He shook his head again. "I don't think you can stop judging people, Lindsay."

She closed her eyes and fought back the tears. He was confirming her worst fears. Was there no hope for her? Everyone could change, couldn't they? And she wanted to change.

"You don't think I deserve a second chance?"

Bart rose from the edge of the bed and said, "I'm afraid my manners have been lacking. Would you care to sit down? There's a rocker in the corner."

"No, I prefer to stand."

He nodded and gingerly massaged his wounded shoulder.

A tight knot of desperation coiled inside Lindsay's abdomen, making her sick to her stomach. It took every ounce of willpower she possessed to keep from running downstairs to the kitchen and vomiting. And she knew Bart was stalling for time because he didn't want to answer her question.

When he looked at her, his powder-blue eyes stared straight through her, as if he was weighing her soul and finding it lacking.

His words were soft and low, the voice a lover would use, when he finally said, "I don't think this is about second chances. It's about your basic nature, and I don't know if I have the right to demand you to change yourself to suit me."

"But what if I want to change—not for you—but for myself?"

# Let it Be Christmas

"Do you really mean that?"

The coil tightened in her stomach, squeezing like a vise. How could she convince him? Strip her soul bare and lay it before him? Would he believe her, then?

"I do want to change. This shooting has made me realize how precious life is." She touched her abdomen. "More precious than anything. And seeing Abby with her newborn has made me realize people are the most important thing. Even if they've made mistakes. How can I possibly want to help others if I'm busy judging them?"

She turned away and fought to hide her tears. "I don't know what to think anymore. Am I a sham? I must be—if I worry about appearances and labels and everything except what's important— what's in the hearts of people." She covered her eyes with her hands and gulped. "I know I sound crazy." She shook her head. "I'm sorry, it's all so confusing."

She didn't hear his approach and was startled by his touch on her arm.

"You're not crazy. And I think you're asking yourself the right questions. If you want to change, it must be for yourself." He sighed. "You don't know much about me, do you?"

"No, not really."

"Would it surprise you to know my father was a Methodist preacher?"

"I think Chad mentioned something about that."

"Yes, but my mother was the true Christian. She was, in some ways, a lot like you. She was only happy when she was doing 'good' works, helping other people. She was nursing some children with typhoid and caught the fever herself. She died when I was only about ten."

"Oh, Bart, I'm so sorry."

"That's not all, Lindsay. Here's the important part. My father, a Christian minister, was harsh and ugly and... judgmental. All he saw was fire and brimstone, and other people's mistakes. He knew nothing of Christian kindness, nothing of Christian

# Let it Be Christmas

forgiveness." He shook his head. "I went home when he was dying and tried to make things right between us, but on his dying bed, he turned me away. Judging me, damning me."

"Oh, no, I had no idea."

"How could you? We haven't opened ourselves to each other. But now you can understand how I feel about judging others."

She lowered her head and bit her lip to keep from sobbing. "Yes, I understand. So, what about us?" She raised her head and gazed at him, pleading with her eyes. "What if I change, really change?"

"I don't know, Lindsay. That evening in the barn, a lot of ugly words were exchanged. You said things I never dreamed you thought... especially about me. Your judgment of me is hard to forget."

"But over time, maybe you can?"

"I don't know. Right now, everything is too fresh in my mind. We'll see. Let's give it some time." He leaned down and kissed her forehead. "And if you don't leave soon, you'll miss your train."

# Let it Be Christmas

## Chapter Ten

Lindsay passed Ginny her rouge pot and rearranged Ginny's light brown curls, dangling them over the bare-shouldered dress she'd given her friend. They'd had to take the gown in at the waist and shorten the skirt, but other than that, the green silk dress fit Ginny as if it had been made for her.

She leaned over Ginny's shoulder and gazed into the looking glass on the vanity. "You look beautiful."

Her friend shrugged. "I don't know why I bother, except to please you. Chad is already taken, Lindsay. We can't change that."

"Don't be so certain. I don't think Chad's heart is really in it."

"I know you've told me before you thought Chad proposed last Christmas because he was desperate to do something to help your ranch and, with Vi Lea being Sam's only child, by marrying they'd put the ranches together and have a bigger spread."

"Yes, but since then, my brother found Bart and took him on as a partner with fresh capital, and I've come home."

Ginny touched her arm and shook her head. "It's too late, though, Chad's honor won't allow him to go back on his proposal."

"How do you know that?"

Ginny smiled. "Because he can't possibly love me, not the way he's treated me, Lindsay." She folded her hands in her lap. "Remember what happened at Panther Cave?"

"Yes, he shouldn't have taken you there when he was already engaged."

Ginny nodded and took her friend's hand. "And shearing time was pure agony, being around Chad and knowing he was engaged. I stayed so I could help you."

"And I couldn't have done it without you. I appreciated your help."

"But at the shearing dance, even though you'd dressed me and fixed my hair, he ignored me once Vi Lea came." She sighed.

230

# Let it Be Christmas

"He found me on the porch during the band's intermission and kept swearing he wanted to break off his engagement. But he claimed he didn't know how to do it." Ginny lowered her head. "I wanted to scream with frustration. He's just making excuses."

"I know. My brother hasn't treated you right, but I think he cares for you more than he realizes. Unfortunately, he's torn between his duty and loving you." She shook her head. "He didn't even bother to tell me about his engagement. I had to learn about it from you."

Not that she was surprised Chad had kept his engagement to Vi Lea a secret from her. Vi Lea was one of the Bakers from Devil's River, neighbors to Clint Graham, Abby's husband. And Chad knew Lindsay had never liked Vi Lea, finding her mean-spirited and whiny from the first time they'd met when Lindsay's family had settled near Langtry.

"Yes, and that's why I didn't tell you everything that was going on. You had your hands full, being pregnant for the first time. And I didn't want to disappoint you if he chose to stay with Vi Lea." Her friend glanced down at Lindsay's protruding stomach. "Besides, I wasn't the only one who kept secrets for a time."

Lindsay felt her face go hot. "You're right. But I told you the truth when you asked. Before that, we'd only been friends for a little while."

"So, you understand why I didn't tell you about Chad and me, at least, not right away."

"Yes, I guess I understand. I just wish—"

"What?"

"That my brother wasn't so damned honorable."

Ginny turned back on the vanity stool. "Not only is your brother honor bound, but I don't have anything to offer him, except my love. Mama doesn't have any money to dower me with." She shook her head. "You know how it is with us."

Lindsay squeezed her shoulders and then applied some of Ginny's homemade perfume, a light minty fragrance, to her wrists and the pulse points behind her ears.

# Let it Be Christmas

"Yes, I know, how it is. But one look at you tonight, and I pray my brother will know you're the right one for him, no matter his honor."

"I hope you're right." Ginny turned back and gazed at her reflection in the mirror. "I've never shown so much bare skin in all my life."

Lindsay laughed. "Well, it *was* the latest fashion when I left Boston. And the color suits your brown eyes and hair." She clasped the pearl choker onto Ginny's throat. "And these are so beautiful, especially against your skin."

"They're the only thing my mother owns of any value. Handed down for generations on my Mama's side." She touched the pearls at her throat. "Mama gave them to me, to wear tonight, as an early Christmas present."

"Well, I approve, they're perfect with your dress and complexion."

"Thank you." Ginny adjusted the choker and asked, "Will Bart be coming tonight?"

Lindsay lowered her gaze and fiddled with Ginny's curls again. "No, I don't think so."

"Oh, Lindsay, I'm so sorry. Nothing has changed between you two?"

"No, nothing has changed." She dropped her hands and laced them over her protruding stomach.

"I shouldn't have brought it up." Ginny dusted some loose face powder on her nose. "We need to make merry, it's our Christmas celebration." She swiveled around on the vanity bench again and took Lindsay's hands.

"Just wait until you see the backyard. Mama, Isabella, Lucia, and me worked hard to get the decorations up."

"I'm sure I will love what you've done. And it was kind of you to host the Christmas social. Being in Langtry, it's so much easier for the children than walking all the way to the ranch."

Ginny rose and pulled on Lindsay's hands. "Then come on, I can't wait to show you."

# Let it Be Christmas

Lindsay gazed at the yard behind Ginny's house. Gone was the huge boiling pot and the countless clothes lines. In their stead, the Browns had outdone themselves, decorating the yard for their Christmas social.

In Langtry's mild climate, not all of the grapevine leaves had fallen. Woven into the grape arbor, they'd put bright-green branches of cypress and the native chaparral plant with their red berries. Lanterns, along with bunches of mistletoe, hung suspended from the live oak and mesquite trees. The lanterns twinkled in the dusky light of early evening, and the mistletoe looked bright and cheery, wrapped with red ribbons.

They'd also hung a paper mache *piñata* shaped like a burro from the big pecan tree in the middle of the yard. It had been made by one of the Mexican ladies, and Lindsay had bought the hard candy to fill it with. It was a Mexican custom for blind-folded children to take swings with a stick at the *piñata* until they broke through the sides and the candy spilled out.

And the Browns had cut down a small piñon tree and had the local children help decorate it with strings of popcorn, hand-colored paper chains, and bows made from the left-over fabric they'd used to sew the children's clothes.

They'd recruited a local fiddler and banjo player, and they were softly strumming the melody to *"O Christmas Tree."*

And off to one side, a long trestle table groaned under the weight of two Christmas turkeys, a brown-sugar-coated ham, mashed potatoes and sweet potatoes, gravy and dressing, green peas and beans, and more cakes and pies than Lindsay had seen in one place. The rich aromas of the bird with the earthy smell of potatoes, intermingled with the sweetness of the desserts.

The whole yard was magical—and reminded her of the Christmases when all her family had been together—making her teary-eyed. Not that getting teary-eyed was unusual. The closer she got to her time, the more her emotions seemed to run away with her.

# Let it Be Christmas

She wasn't surprised at what a wonderful job the Browns and their helpers had done. She'd watched and helped with some of the decorations herself. And the Browns had been invaluable during shearing time at the ranch, fetching and carrying the heavy pots and pans, filled with food for the shearing crew.

They'd helped to organize the barn dance, too, celebrating the shearing. Bart hadn't attended the social. And Lindsay had stayed in the background. Other than missing Bart and wondering if he'd ever forgive her, the one blight on their barn dance had been the unexpected news her brother had gotten himself engaged to Vi Lea.

Lindsay pulled her thoughts back, and her gaze found the brown-paper-wrapped packages for the children heaped under the Christmas tree. Most of the packages had the child's name written on them. And just in case one of the children brought a friend, they'd made some extra packages, too. Each package held a shirt and trousers for the boys and a dress for the girls, along with a small toy and a pair of sandals.

Gazing at the packages, she couldn't wait to give them out and see the joy on the children's faces.

After supper was over, she got her chance, seated in the grape arbor, with Minnie by her side, handing out the packages. She gave the last gift to a six-year-old boy, Pedro Salinas, and watched as he tore into the wrapping.

He held up his new clothes and sandals, along with a bright-red spinning top, and said, "*Muchas gracias, Señora* Houghton." Then he ducked his head and scuttled away to where the other children were lining up to take a turn at hitting the *piñata*. Isabella was making certain each child had the blind-fold on before they took their turn at trying to hit the brightly-colored burro.

The fiddler and banjo player started a Virginia reel, and Lindsay watched as Theo Henderson, Vi Lea's second cousin, grabbed her hand and joined the dance. She crossed her fingers, hoping Chad would see his chance and ask Ginny to dance.

# Let it Be Christmas

Lindsay had spent hours teaching Ginny how to dance. Now, she hoped, all that practicing wouldn't go to waste. At the shearing dance, Chad and Ginny had shared only one dance. Her brother had seemed preoccupied with his fiancé that night.

Now, Lindsay prayed the magic of Christmas and realizing he'd been engaged for one full year without setting a date for his marriage, would make him reconsider in spite of his sense of honor and duty.

As if her thoughts had propelled him, she watched Chad approach Ginny, who was helping to clear the trestle table. He bowed from the waist and held out his hand to her.

She held her breath, praying Ginny would accept. When Ginny nodded and Chad swept her into his arms, Lindsay exhaled. And she couldn't help but smile as they whirled by her.

A loud yell from the center of the yard caught her attention, and she glanced up to see a shower of hard candy raining down. Then there was a mad scramble of children, arms and legs pumping, as they scooped up the candy. Minnie jumped down and joined the confusion, circling the children, barking and yelping.

She smiled again, watching them, and then she heard another shriek, but this time, it came from the far side of the yard, beside the wooden dais where the fiddler and banjo player stood.

Chad and Ginny emerged from the shadows. Chad looked grim. Ginny looked guilty. Vi Lea had stopped dancing and had her fists on her hips. And from the look on her face, she must have been the one who screamed.

Chad reached for Vi Lea's arm, but she reared back and slapped him. Then she shouted, "You're a lying cheat, Chadbourne MacKillian. I won't be treated this way, and I don't want to marry you." She turned to her dance partner and said, "Take me home, Theo. I don't want to have anything to do with the MacKillians."

\* \* \*

Lindsay's mouth dropped open, as she glanced at the puddle beneath her feet. Emma, had warned her about this—that her water

235

# Let it Be Christmas

might break—a sure sign her baby was on the way. But so far, she hadn't had any real pains, just a few twinges and the small of her back hurt.

Of course, it was the dead of night—midnight. The grandfather clock in the parlor had just chimed, waking her. Ginny's mother had warned her about that, too. Most birthing labors seemed to start in the middle of the night. And based on everything Emma had told her, she might have hours to go.

She grabbed a dishtowel and leaned over, trying to mop up the mess. But she couldn't see her toes, much less touch them. Her brother would have to clean the floor.

Instead, she pumped water into a glass and spread the dishtowel on one of the ladder-back chairs at the kitchen table. That was what she'd gotten up for, a glass of water.

She sipped the water, thinking it was still two days to Christmas, a long time to go, being in labor. And she had so wanted to have her baby on Christmas Day.

Since the ugly scene at the Christmas social two days ago, she'd been hopeful Ginny and her brother would get together. But so far, Chad wouldn't talk to her about it, and she hadn't had a chance to talk to Ginny, either.

Ginny had disappeared at the Christmas social after Vi Lea had slapped her brother and stormed off. When she'd gone looking for Ginny, Emma had told her that she was asleep. With her impending delivery, she hadn't chanced going to see Ginny. She still hoped Ginny and her brother would work things out.

She felt a sharp stab of pain and breathed deeply, wanting to think about something else. Something nice.

Abby and her family had sent an early Christmas gift. They were active in the Methodist church in Del Rio, and they'd taken up a collection for the church she was trying to build. With their help and the donations she'd collected, she had more than enough money for the mortar, lumber, and nails for the new church. And during the slow season, the men could chip in and build the structure, just like they'd built Bart's cabin.

# Let it Be Christmas

Thinking about Bart made her dizzy with yearning and sad with longing. How she'd hoped he would forgive her. But Chad had told her he still planned on leaving after the baby came and their divorce was filed in the county courthouse at Del Rio.

She finished the glass of water and got up, putting the empty glass in the sink. She hung her head and sobbed, wishing Bart wouldn't leave.

And then another pain ripped through her, and this one was so intense, she doubled over and almost went down on her knees. Her labor had started!

She was scared to death. Women died in childbirth. And even without Bart's love, she wanted to live, and most of all, she wanted her child with a fierceness she'd never felt before. How could she have considered giving up her baby? Having seen Abby and her newborn son, Timothy, had brought that point home. She crossed herself.

*Bless Bart.* Even if he did divorce her and go away. At least, he'd given her child a name and a way she could raise the baby. But she wished Bart was here, right now, beside her and holding her hand. And she wished this was *his* child she was carrying.

She closed her eyes and crossed herself. She still had her mother's gold wedding band on. She couldn't get it off; her fingers had swelled so.

Another pain sliced into her, and she decided it was time to wake her brother. He'd go to town and get the Browns and Constanza.

She was so frightened, but with the Browns and the midwife, she was sure to be fine. Wasn't she?

\* \* \*

Lindsay writhed on the bed, vicious pain tearing at her, like a pack of wolves she'd seen once, ripping apart a newborn lamb. She'd lost track of time, but the shadows were long on the floor of her bedroom.

Had a whole day passed?

# Let it Be Christmas

Ginny sponged her forehead with a cool cloth, and for a brief moment, she was comforted, then the grinding agony started again. Ginny gave her the corner of the towel to bite on, and she gnashed her teeth together, gnawing at the terry-cloth. She couldn't scream anymore. Her throat was sore and her voice was a mere croak.

Emma and Constanza stood at the foot of her bed, huddled together, whispering. She realized they thought she couldn't hear them, and that she didn't smell the familiar but distinct coppery scent of spent blood—her blood—this time. But between the birthing pains, it was as if her senses were sharper, if only for a few brief moments.

"*Señora* Brown, the baby, she is breech and the waters have broken." She shook her head. "Too dry. I fear hurting her if I try to turn the baby." Constanza glanced at her patient. Lindsay's sodden nightgown was bunched around her waist. "And she is beginning to bleed."

Emma closed her eyes and lowered her head. She was obviously praying. Then she raised her head and asked, "Is there nothing we can do? There must be something."

Constanza held up her index finger. "I know of only one way. You must send for Doctor Rodgers in Del Rio. A doctor has the forceps. I have seen them used once, and if he knows how, he can turn the baby." She crossed herself and kissed the crucifix she wore. "If God is willing."

Emma nodded, her lips thinned. "I will have her brother telegraph the doctor to come right away. He can be here on the morning train."

Constanza hung her head. "I hope it is enough." She glanced at Lindsay again. "She weakens by the hour."

"What more would you have me do?" Emma asked.

"Send the telegram, but her brother must leave tonight to find the doctor and bring him."

"You're right. It will be a hard ride, but it's for the best."

# Let it Be Christmas

Ginny must have overheard them, too, because she bunched up her apron, covering her face and sobbing.

Emma took another washcloth from the nightstand and dipped it in the basin of water and sponged Lindsay's face. Then she folded the cloth and laid it across Lindsay's forehead.

She touched her daughter's arm. "You heard what we need."

Ginny lowered the apron and sniffed, trying to fight back the tears. "Yes, I heard."

"Can you tell Chad? Explain to him about the telegram, but that he needs to ride there to ensure he finds the doctor."

She nodded. "Yes, I understand. I'll do it."

"Good, and tell him to hurry."

\* \* \*

Chad folded his arms on the kitchen table and laid his head on them. He'd been up since the middle of last night and heard his sister's screams and groans. Now she was quiet, but he didn't know if that was good or bad. All he knew was he'd descended into hell, listening to Lindsay suffer, hour after hour.

He felt a hand on his shoulder and glanced up to find Ginny's face, creased with worry. "Chad, Lindsay needs a doctor. The baby isn't coming. Constanza and my mother want you to send a telegram to Doctor Rodgers in Del Rio, so he will come on the morning train." She gulped and blew her nose. "But Mama wants you to ride there, too, in case the doctor is out and doesn't get the telegram." She looked at him and he could see the agony in her eyes. "There's no time to waste."

He gazed at Ginny. Her face was pale, with deep lines, he'd never noticed before, bracketing her mouth. The gravity of his sister's situation hit him like a ton of bricks.

*Lindsay might be dying.*

And he'd move heaven and earth to help her. *God willing.*

"I'll tell Bart. He can keep the house fires going against the chill."

"Be quick, please." Ginny turned away and sobbed.

# Let it Be Christmas

"You love my sister. Don't you?"

She nodded and wiped her eyes with a handkerchief. More tears sparkled on her eyelashes.

He pulled her to him and wrapped her in a hug. And she didn't resist, didn't push him away. Maybe his apology had helped. He hoped so because he still wanted her. Now, if he could just get her to listen.

But right now, his sister's life hung in the balance. He released Ginny and grabbed his Stetson and gun holster. "Wish me luck."

"Go with God. I will be praying."

Chad ran to the creek but before he could knock on the door, Bart pulled it open, a lantern in his hand.

"Lindsay? How is she?" he asked.

"Not good." He shook his head. "I have to telegram Doctor Rodgers to come. But there's no time to waste, so I'll be riding to Del Rio to make certain he's on the morning train. Can you watch the house and be sure there's enough wood in the fireplaces to keep—"

"No, you stay, Chad. You can send the telegram, but I'll take Dancer and be in Del Rio before first light."

"But—"

"No one can outrun Dancer."

Chad knew that was true. When Bart became a rancher, he'd bought a black stallion with thoroughbred lines. Bart's horse was the fastest mount in three counties.

"And I know a shortcut. If you cross the bend of the river into México near Comstock, it saves ten miles."

Chad nodded, wanting to hope, needing to hope. "Go then. I'll ride to Langtry and send the telegram."

* * *

Bart swiped at his eyes. He didn't cry and he didn't pray. But he'd spent all of last night, doing both. And he'd ridden Dancer so

240

# Let it Be Christmas

hard, the stallion had pulled up lame. *A small price to pay to save Lindsay.*

He'd made it to Del Rio in the early morning hours, made certain Doctor Rodgers had gotten the telegram and wasn't away at any of the outlying ranches. He'd stabled Dancer and ridden back on the train with the Doc.

The crisis was past, and still he couldn't stop crying. The good Doc had delivered the baby, a girl, and Lindsay was resting.

And in the darkest hours of last night, he knew, without a doubt, he loved Lindsay. More than he anything, he loved her.

He'd been a stubborn jackass, not realizing it sooner. She wasn't perfect, far from it. But he was more than flawed, too. That didn't mean they couldn't have a life together.

Ginny came into the kitchen and said, "Lindsay is sitting up and feeling better. You wanted to see her?"

Lindsay dragged a brush through her hair and pinched her cheeks. Ginny had told her Bart had ridden overnight to Del Rio to bring the doctor. She couldn't quite believe it.

*Did he care about her after all? Had he finally forgiven her?*

Bart opened the door and stood on the threshold. Ginny and her mother nodded to him and left the room.

He came to her and kneeled at the side of the bed, taking her hand. "Lindsay, I... I, uh, I don't know what to say." And then he folded her into his arms and stroked her hair. "God in heaven, I'm so happy you came through and didn't—"

"Die?"

He took her hands and held them against his heart. "I couldn't lose you, Lindsay. Not you." He gazed into her eyes. "I love you with all my heart. I think I loved you from the minute you got off the train in Langtry but was too stupid to realize it."

She pulled her hands free and threw her arms around his neck. "Oh, Bart, I love you, too." She sniffed. "But I thought you couldn't forgive me. Couldn't love me if I was so judgmental—"

"You're not, Lindsay." He stroked her cheek. "Well, maybe a little. But I know you've changed, I could tell it that day at the

# Let it Be Christmas

boardinghouse, but I didn't know if I could believe it. Didn't want to trust again and be hurt." He hugged her again. "Hell, I don't give a damn. I love you as you are."

"But I was judgmental and demanding, you were right about—"

"And I'm a stubborn ass. There are no perfect people. But love makes us perfect, at least for each other." He cupped her chin in his hand and brushed her lips with his.

"You believe that?"

"Yes, I do."

She lowered her head. "You have a daughter, Bart. She's not really yours but—"

"She's mine, and I'm proud to be her father."

She turned her face into his shoulder and sobbed. "You don't know how much that means to me."

He lifted her chin and kissed her, long and deep, just the way she liked it. "Can I see her?"

"Of course, she's in the cradle at the foot of the bed. Should I have Ginny—"

"No, I can get her." He rose and leaned over the cradle, lifting out the newborn. He gazed at the child, as if awestruck. "My God, Lindsay, she's beautiful. And she has your golden hair." He held the baby carefully and kissed her forehead.

"I'm glad you like her. I'm so glad."

"Does she have a name?"

"No, I wanted to name her for your mother, but I don't know her name."

He shook his head. "We don't know much about each other, but I intend to rectify that." He looked up and said, "You want to name her for my mother?"

"Yes, when you talked about your mother that day in Del Rio, I knew. No matter what happened between us, if I had a girl, I wanted to name her for your mother."

He climbed into the bed beside her and handed the baby to Lindsay. "My mother's name was Elizabeth."

# Let it Be Christmas

"Then we'll christen her Elizabeth Houghton."

He kissed her again. "I want a real marriage, Lindsay, and more children… that is, if you're not afraid to give birth again."

She smiled. "Doc Rodgers said breech births happen, but seldom do they happen twice to the same woman."

He exhaled. "I'm glad." And then he got down on his knees beside the bed and took her hand. "Will you, Lindsay Houghton, marry me?"

She tried to twist her mother's wedding band on her still swollen finger. "But we're already married."

"I need to buy you a wedding band, but I didn't know how things would turn out."

"I understand and really there's no need." She stroked his strong jaw, stubbled with his beard. "I like wearing my mother's band. It means a lot to me, handed down from my mother."

He gulped and nodded. "If that's what you want, I understand. But we didn't marry in a church, and I know how important that is to you. We'll be married by a priest, if you want."

Thinking about God blessing their marriage, she had to know, had to confess her superstition to this man who wanted to be her *real* husband. "Bart, what day is it? I've lost track."

He frowned. "That's your answer to my proposal?"

She pulled on his arm and he rose, sitting beside her on the bed again. She buried her head in his shoulder. "I'm religious, but I'm Irish, too, and like my mother, I'm prone to superstitions." She sighed. "I'm not proud of it."

He patted her back. "That's not so bad. We're all a little superstitious."

"But you didn't answer my question, what day is it?"

He considered for a moment. "It's Christmas Day."

She lifted her head and smiled. "Then God has forgiven my sin. I prayed and prayed, to let my child be born on Christmas Day, and I would know I was forgiven."

# Let it Be Christmas

"Lindsay, you're a good person, a giving person. Don't you know that? And if my father taught me one thing—it was God forgives us, no matter what, if we repent in our hearts."

"You believe that?""Yes, I do."

She hugged him. "Oh, Bart, I love you so."

"And I love you, too" He brushed her lips with his. "You're my life and my angel. And Elizabeth is our daughter. I want to start a new life with you, grow old together and have grandchildren."

"Oh, that would be heaven on earth."

Minnie yipped and jumped onto the bed, snuggling herself between Lindsay, Bart, and the baby.

Bart chuckled and patted Minnie. "Now, we're all here and a family!" He bent his head to kiss her again. "Merry Christmas, my angel."

# Let it Be Christmas

## Copyright

This is a work of fiction. Names, characters, places, and incidents are either the product of the author's imagination or are used fictitiously, and any resemblance to actual persons living or dead, business establishments, events, or locales, is entirely coincidental.

# A Mistletoe Christmas

By

## Hebby Roman

West Texas Christmas Trilogy Book 3

☆Estrella Publishing☆

# A Mistletoe Christmas

## Prologue

*Langtry, Texas February, 1896*

"The fight sure was a letdown," Chadbourne MacKillian said, his words slurred by numerous shots of whiskey, chased by several bottles of beer.

"You can say that again," Bartholomew Houghton agreed. He took a sip of beer and elbowed a boisterous drunk who was trying to push past him. The Jersey Lily was mobbed, crowded from its floorboards to its rafters. "Even if the fight was a bust, Judge Bean is making a mint off it."

Chad nodded, his head lolling from side-to-side. Slowly, his head fell forward onto the bar. A snore escaped his lips.

Bart chuckled. Chad had warned him that he wanted to get drunk tonight. And he'd accomplished that goal.

The same rowdy drunk bumped into Bart again, and he pushed him away. This time, he used both hands, warning him, "Hey, watch it."

Bart checked the level of beer in his bottle. Half a bottle left—it was only his second beer. He didn't share his new-found friend's enthusiasm for staying up all night and getting drunk after the prize fight.

For him, coming to Langtry was a business decision. A fight as big as this attracted a lot of professional gambling, not to mention the amateurs. And he'd made a tidy sum today, too. The secret pocket sewn into his coat was stuffed, and even though he'd had it specifically made to safeguard his winnings, being jostled by the same drunk twice, put him on high alert.

Newspapers from all over the States had written about the world championship title bout between Bob Fitzsimmons and Peter Maher. Declared illegal in both Texas and México, it had gotten lots of attention when the dime-novel hero, Judge Roy Bean, self-proclaimed "Law West of the Pecos," had decided to hold the fight

247

# A Mistletoe Christmas

on an island in the middle of the Rio Grande—a no-man's land, not subject to either country's authority.

Judge Bean, a shrewd businessman, had gone to a lot of trouble, hosting the fight, knowing it would be a gold mine for his saloon. He'd built a boxing ring and even a pontoon bridge to the island.

Sporting enthusiasts from as far away as California and New York had thronged the tiny town, filling up the passenger train cars for days. Despite all the build-up, the actual fight, which was won by Fitzsimmons, had lasted less than two minutes.

Langtry, a mere whistle-stop, perched on the edge of the Chihuahua Desert, was overrun by sporting men who had nowhere to go and nothing to do until the next day's train, and all of them wanted to celebrate at the Judge's famous salon, the Jersey Lily, whimsically named for the actress Lillie Langtry, who the Judge admired from afar.

And the Judge had anticipated their needs, ordering an entire freight car of beer, along with countless cases of whiskey. His foresight had paid off; he was selling the beer for the unheard-of price of a dollar a bottle and a shot of whiskey was triple the going rate.

Bart and Chad had arrived at sunrise on the island, taking up places ringside, to have the best vantage point. Strangers, they'd spent the day, getting to know each other, talking about ranching and gambling and Bart's travels through the West. Chad had been fascinated with the "betting book" Bart had run, making a percentage off each bet placed.

When the fight was over, they'd joined the mob at the Jersey Lily, and Chad had gulped down a lot of whisky in a short time. Bart gazed at his brand-new friend and decided, as soon as he finished his beer, he would take Chad home and put him to bed.

In the meantime, Bart turned from the bar and allowed his gaze to linger over the wall-to-wall crowd. If ever a more scurrilous crew had descended upon a remote West Texas town, he would have liked to have seen it.

# A Mistletoe Christmas

He recognized at least five other professional gamblers. Pickpockets moved quickly through the crowds, divesting drunk or unsuspecting patrons of their wallets. Prostitutes had come from as far away as Galveston to cash in on the circus-like atmosphere. Some of them had foreseen the scarcity of accommodations and brought their own tents.

Though the crowd was thickest in the Jersey Lily, it spilled over into the main street of Langtry—one big, jostling, drunken party.

Cold water slapped the back of Bart's neck. He cursed and spun around. Joseph, the Judge's head barkeep, held an empty bucket and water pooled around Chad's head. Joseph shook him.

Chad lifted his head. Water dripped from his face, and the front of his shirt was soaked. He shook his head.

Bart wiped at his wet coat and handed Chad his handkerchief. He stared at Joseph and said, "Who gave you the right to dump water on us?"

Chad mopped his face with Bart's handkerchief. "Yeah, why'd you do that? I was just taking a break."

"If you're too drunk to stay awake, move out and let someone else in." Joseph turned away, muttering to himself.

Tapping Chad on the shoulder, Bart asked, "Don't you think it's time to go home? You said your buckboard's at the livery. I'll be glad to take you home and bring the buckboard back tomorrow. I'm staying at the Vinegaroon Hotel."

Chad squinted and held up one wobbly finger. "Just one more drink, and then I'll go quietly. I admit, I'm not much of a drinking man, but this might be my last chance at freedom." He grimaced. "I got engaged at Christmas. Once I'm hitched, good and proper, no more saloons for me."

"All right." Bart slapped Chad on the back. "One more for the road. After that, I'll take you home."

Chad lifted his arm and waved down the barkeep. "Joseph, one more round."

# A Mistletoe Christmas

Joseph uncapped two bottles of beer and poured a shot of whiskey for Chad.

Chad lifted the shot glass, preparing to down the whiskey in one gulp.

Bart grabbed his arm. "Sip it slowly. It'll last longer."

Chad nodded and took a tiny sip of the amber liquid. "Yep, I don't know why I proposed, except it was Christmas, and I've known Vi Lea forever. She has a big ranch on the Devil's River." He paused and took another sip. "Well, her folks have a nice spread, but she's their only living child."

"Sounds like you're not sure about your engagement. Or maybe you proposed for the wrong reason?"

Chad blinked at him owlishly. "Truer words were never spoken." He shook his head. "Need to grow the ranch, get bigger to compete, now the tariff is lifted."

Bart stood up straight and paid closer attention. "What tariff?"

"The tariff on wool. Now we sheep ranchers have to compete with Australian and South American wool." Chad hung his head. "Not to mention the new freight rates. Highway robbery, I'm telling you, that's what it is."

Now the rancher had his full attention. He leaned in closer to Chad and asked, "Aren't there other ways to grow your ranch, other than getting married?" He took a swig of beer and gazed at Chad.

Chad ran his hand through his hair. "Well, sure, there are other ways. Thought about taking on a partner, but all the ranchers around are hard pressed. Most of us haven't made any money on the last two shearings. No one has any capital to invest, though there's plenty of land to be had cheap." He chased the whiskey with a swallow of beer. "I've asked around."

Bart pursed his lips and considered. He'd saved his money for years and lately, he'd grown tired of drifting. The western United States was filling up. He'd been looking for a suitable business opportunity but, so far, hadn't found any to his liking.

# A Mistletoe Christmas

He couldn't see himself as a shopkeeper. Being a rancher and working outside appealed to him. And besides, he liked West Texas. Liked its big empty spaces and never-ending horizon.

"I'd like to see your ranch. I might be interested in a partnership." He patted his hidden pocket. "There's more where this came from. I've got a nice nest egg put away."

Chad turned to him. "Really? But I saw how easy you made book today. Ranching is hard, dirty work. Why would you—?"

The remainder of his words was drowned by the sound of gunfire from outside. Bart put one hand on his Colt and fished some silver dollars from his vest pocket, throwing the money onto the bar.

Grabbing Chad's elbow, he said, "Let's get out of here. It's getting late and now the drunks are spewing lead into this mob."

"Wouldn't it be safer to stay put?" Chad hung back and downed the last of his whiskey in one gulp.

"Nowhere is safe if someone is crazy drunk and shooting. I don't want to be bottled up in here. Let's get outside and see what's going on."

"All right, all right, I'm coming. But I hope we don't get hit by a stray bullet."

Leaving the saloon proved more difficult than Bart had imagined. Everyone seemed to be of the same mind—wanting to get out and see what the shooting was about.

The mob surged forward, shoving and forming a huge jostling bottleneck at the door to the Jersey Lily. After a spirited struggle, Bart and Chad cleared the front door and gained the deep porch of the saloon.

Galloping up and down the main street was a man on horseback, firing his six-shooter into the air. Light spilled from the Jersey Lily, pinpointing the man's face for a split second. And Bart knew his face—the man was Phineas Boyd.

What in the Sam Hill was he doing in Langtry? The Boyd brothers hailed from Tucson, one of Bart's favorite stomping grounds.

251

# A Mistletoe Christmas

The Judge, brandishing his shotgun, pushed through the mob and said, "Get your guns and follow me. That bastard needs to be dealt with. Shooting up the town."

A throng of men followed the Judge off the porch into the dark night. And then Bart felt the cold stab of metal at the base of his skull. "Don't make no fuss, Bart." The man patted his coat. "I know you got your hidey-hole somewhere, and I want my money back."

Bart swallowed and kept his voice low and calm. "It's not your money, Boyd, I won it, fair and square." He wasn't certain which of the three brothers had snuck up behind him, but Phineas had obviously been a distraction.

"Like hell, you say." The gun barrel jabbed his neck. "Step off this porch and into the alley. We'll settle up there."

A chill tingled down Bart's spine. The Boyd brothers, particularly Red, the eldest, were meaner than side-winders. But in Tucson, where Bart had friends, they would have never tried something like this. Langtry and the drunk crowd was the perfect place to confront him. And if he knew the Boyd brothers, this one would have no qualms about killing him, once he found the money.

*If he didn't do something fast—he was a dead man.*

Chad gasped and shook his head. Shoving through the chaotic crowd, along with the cool night air, had cleared most of the cobwebs from his head, though he'd probably have a nasty headache in the morning.

He looked around for Bart, wondering if he'd lost his new-found friend. Then he saw him, standing on the far edge of the porch. A man with a gun was urging him forward. Chad blinked and shook his head again.

*What in hell was happening?*

Bart half-lifted his arms and said something to the man holding a gun on him.

"Hey! You there! What are you doing?" Chad shouted over the crowd noise.

# A Mistletoe Christmas

The man with the gun shoved Bart.

Bart dropped his arms and stepped off the porch into the alley.

"Hey! Stop right there or I'll shoot." Chad drew his Colt. "Let him go."

Bart stumbled down the alley and then he flung himself to one side, rolling over and over.

Bart's attacker cursed and shot at him.

Chad aimed low and shot the man.

The stranger screamed and dropped to the ground. "Son-of-a-bitch, I'm hit."

Bart stood, drew his Colt, and cocked it. He pointed it at the downed man.

The wounded man grabbed his gun.

"Drop your gun, or I'll shoot you again," Chad said.

The man threw down his gun. "I'm bleeding out." He lifted his two empty hands and then dropped them, grabbing his thigh. "You've gotta help me."

"We'll see about that," Chad said. Keeping his Colt trained on the man, he slid a glance at Bart and asked, "You all right?"

"Yeah, I'm fine." He dusted off his coat and crossed the alley. Leaning down, he grabbed the wounded man's hat, jerking it off his head.

"Who is he, and what's this about?" Chad asked.

"His name is Festus Boyd. And I won a bunch of money off him and his brother, Phineas, in Tucson. They thought I was cheating them, but I don't cheat." He leaned down and seized Festus' Colt. "Don't need to cheat. I know how to count cards and—"

"You're a lying, sneaking cheat, no matter what you say," Festus whined.

"You, shut up!" Chad warned.

Festus groaned and clutched his thigh, dark blood welling from the wound.

# A Mistletoe Christmas

Bart pulled off his bandana and offered it to Festus, saying, "Here, tie this around your leg."

Festus took the bandana and fumbled with it. Bart leaned down and helped him to tie off his leg above the gunshot wound.

"What in the hell is 'counting' cards?" Chad asked.

"It's involved. I'll explain later."

"Hmmph. You better. I can't abide a cheat," Chad said.

"Don't worry. And if you wire Del Rio, you'll find Festus is on several wanted posters for assault, robbery, and—"

"All right. I thought so." Chad shook his head. "The way he sneaked up on you."

"Yeah, and his brother, Phineas, was the one shooting up the town."

"Scum, then." He holstered his gun. "What do we do now?"

Bart scrubbed his chin with his hand. "Is there a doctor in Langtry?"

"Nope, closest one is Del Rio."

Bart nodded. "Well, the Judge, if he's back from chasing down Phineas, will know what to do. If not, Joseph, his right-hand man, should know."

"All right. You want to take one side of him, and I'll take the other?" Chad asked. "We need to get him inside."

"Right." Bart grabbed Festus' left arm.

Chad grabbed the other arm and together, they hauled Festus up.

Festus managed to balance himself on his right leg, groaning and dragging his wounded leg behind him.

Chad stared at Bart across Festus' bent head. "Seems like being a professional gambler is kind of dangerous. You're welcome to take a look around my ranch."

"That's right kind of you. I'll do that." Bart nodded and grinned. "And thanks for saving my life. I owe you."

# A Mistletoe Christmas

## Chapter One

*Langtry, Texas June, 1896*

Virginia Brown closed the general store's door and tucked the bundle of cloth and needles under her arm. She took a minute, standing on the dusty wooden porch to peer inside the shop's window at the fancy bustled dresses for sale. Just looking at the dresses made her throat tight and her eyes moisten with yearning, wishing for something more than the washed-out calico she was wearing.

Her mother and she made a living, sewing. They made dresses, trousers, and shirts. They took in mending and did washing—anything to keep food on the table and a roof over their heads. Since they'd lost her father in a railroad accident, life had been a struggle. When it came time to make clothes for themselves, they bought the cheapest materials and used the simplest patterns.

She was certain Parson Samuels would castigate her for her vanity but just once, she wished she could wear a store-bought confection edged with lace and bustled with layers of cloth. *Just once.*

She sighed and turned away. Mama would be waiting. Then she heard the passenger train whistle and hesitated, wanting to see if anyone would get off. Usually, only sightseers disembarked to have a drink at the famous Judge Roy Bean's saloon, the Jersey Lily.

Then she saw him—Chadbourne MacKillian pulling beside the depot in his buckboard, as if he was expecting someone. He had a fawn-colored Stetson pulled low over his face and beneath the hat, his longish sun-streaked blond hair hung over the collar of his shirt.

She didn't need to see his features. She'd stared at him often enough, snatching glimpses when she thought he wasn't looking, since she'd been half-grown. Though they'd never exchanged more than a dozen polite greetings, she was in love with Chad. And no one, not even the oh-so-nice Will Handley, who wanted to court her, could hold a candle to Chad.

# A Mistletoe Christmas

Whenever she saw him, her face flushed hot and her heart raced, pounding in her ears. She spent hours, sewing and dreaming about him. Fantasizing about how it would feel for him to kiss her and sweep her off her feet.

But right now, he was sweeping another young lady off her feet—one who'd just arrived on the train. And the young lady was dressed in the height of fashion, from her ostrich-plumed hat to her soft, kid leather boots.

Chad lifted the young woman from the train platform as if she weighed no more than thistledown. Seeing them together, Virginia bit her lip and her heart tumbled in her chest.

Chad embraced the well-dressed woman, saying, "Welcome home, little sister."

Virginia exhaled and pulled out her handkerchief, dabbing at the perspiration on her upper lip. So, this was Lindsay MacKillian. Now she remembered from four years ago when all of Langtry had turned out for Donal MacKillian's funeral, and his daughter had come home.

Seen side-by-side, it wasn't hard to realize they were brother and sister. Their features were similar, and they both had the same blond hair and hazel eyes. Though, Chad's hair was a darker blond than Lindsay's.

Chad hoisted his sister onto the buckboard, and Virginia hesitated. She could go over and introduce herself and welcome Lindsay home. It would be the neighborly thing to do. And she might get to speak with Chad for a few minutes—a dream come true.

But glancing down at her thread-bare calico, along with her scuffed and torn boots, she didn't dare let Chad see her and his sister side-by-side. The comparison would be awful, and she'd be humiliated.

She closed her eyes and gulped. No, the handsome and wealthy rancher, Chadbourne MacKillian, was not for the likes of her. No matter how much he invaded her dreams and kept her from settling for a nice young man like Will Handley.

# A Mistletoe Christmas

She sighed. At least Will Handley had a good job, unlike most of the hangers-on who clustered on the Judge's saloon porch, chewing tobacco and drinking beer. No, as her mother had so often pointed out, she could do a lot worse than marrying Will with his steady employment as a telegraph operator.

The only problem was she didn't love Will. And as long as Chad wasn't taken, she couldn't let go of her dreams.

* * *

Virginia stood in the shadows at the MacKillian's barn dance. She didn't know why she'd come. All of Langtry had been invited—the men to build a cabin for Chad—the women to bring vittles to feed the men after their day-long labors. She'd made a platter of homemade biscuits and asked her mother to come. But her mother had declined, saying she was too old to be stomping around at a barn dance.

Lindsay had surprised everyone by marrying a stranger, one Bartholomew Houghton, who was now a partner in the MacKillian's ranch, the Lazy M. Rumor had it Lindsay's new husband had been a professional gambler, lured to Langtry by the Fitzsimmons and Maher prize fight.

And to add a bit of scandal to the rumors, their marriage had been a hurried affair, officiated by Judge Bean, who had been voted out of office, and who, technically, shouldn't be marrying anyone. Not that a minor technicality would keep the Judge from acting as if he was still an official of Val Verde County. The Judge didn't let go of his privileges easily.

The odd thing was, as soon as Lindsay had returned home, she'd been gathering donations to build a new church for Langtry. Virginia couldn't understand why she hadn't wanted to be married by Parson Samuels. Except, she and her brother were Catholic. Maybe that was the reason, but still, Virginia couldn't help but wonder.

And now, Chad would be moving out of the MacKillian's ranch house to his own cabin, so the newlyweds could have the

# A Mistletoe Christmas

ranch house to themselves. She'd seen Chad's cabin, peeking in when the men had finished, and she'd been amazed by the indoor privy.

Thinking about living with Chad in such a neat cabin, and with the added luxury of an indoor bathroom, had stolen her breath away. But she'd kept to the background, not wanting him to see her not-so-new calico dress and cracked slippers.

At the beginning of the dance, she'd stood behind the punch bowl, passing out cups of punch and searching for Will. If Will had decided to come, he would have danced with her, and she wouldn't feel like a wallflower. But Will wasn't at the dance. More than likely, he was on duty at the telegraph office.

She watched Chad when she could and noticed he danced with a few of the ladies, but no one in particular, which gave her hope. He was dressed in a coat and vest and form-fitting trousers. Just gazing at his broad shoulders and handsome face, she'd almost swooned.

His sister, Lindsay, was radiant, too, attired in a form-fitting aqua satin dress that looked like the pictures she'd seen in dress pattern magazines.

And Lindsay was the belle of the ball, dancing with almost every man, except one, which Virginia found strange. The new bride hadn't danced with her husband.

Mr. Houghton, the dark and good-looking ex-gambler, had worked hard on the cabin, but then he'd disappeared. It was peculiar, especially considering the gossip around town about Lindsay's quick marriage to a stranger. Virginia's mother often warned her against the evils of gossip, but in a small town like Langtry, it was one of life's few pleasures.

Virginia looked down and scuffed her slipper along the rough planks of the barn. She'd seen what she came to see. She'd never expected to dance with Chad. Not really. But if she crossed in front of the band while they were playing, she'd be on display. And that was the last thing she wanted.

# A Mistletoe Christmas

Glancing over her shoulder, she glimpsed a row of stalls in the back. The perfect place to hide until the band took a break and the dancers broke apart.

She edged toward one of the stalls and breathed a sigh of relief when the dark shadows closed around her. The place was dusty and smelled strongly of hay, but she didn't plan on being there for long.

She perched on the edge of a feeding trough and waited. With her head bowed, she interlaced her fingers, and dreamed of Chad's strong arms holding her.

A rustle of hay startled her and she looked up. To her astonishment, she was no longer alone. Chad's sister, Lindsay, was standing there.

*What on earth was the belle of the ball doing in a dark stall?*

No use to try and hide; Lindsay would eventually notice her. She straightened her spine and squared her shoulders, wondering how to address Chad's sister.

She saw Lindsay jump when she realized she wasn't alone. Despite being startled, Lindsay stretched out her hand and said, "I'm sorry to have intruded. I didn't see you there. My name's Lindsay Mac, er, Houghton."

Virginia lifted her head and met Lindsay's gaze. She took her hand and shook it. But her nervousness, being so close to Chad's beautiful sister, was making her perspire and even tremble a little. She prayed Lindsay wouldn't notice.

"I know who you are, Mrs. Houghton," she said. "Everyone knows who you are, especially after your work to get money to build Langtry a church. I'm proud to meet you." She paused and added, "My name's Virginia Brown, but most folks call me Ginny. That is, Ginny with a 'G' not a 'J' because it's short for Virginia."

She ducked her head. Now why had she said that? Why would Lindsay MacKillian Houghton care how her name was spelled?

# A Mistletoe Christmas

Then she realized it was quiet in the barn. The band must have taken a break. It was what she'd been waiting for, but it would be rude to push past Lindsay and race for the front door.

Instead, she forced the corners of her lips up. Lindsay gazed at her. Not accustomed to being scrutinized, she wanted to cringe, guessing what Lindsay must be thinking of her clothes. The moment seemed to stretch on and on.

Then Lindsay smiled, and her smile was warm. "Nice to meet you. I hope you're enjoying yourself. It's been a marvelous dance. Don't you think? I wonder when the musicians will start up again?"

Ginny was surprised Chad's sister would talk to her. But, of course, she was just being polite. And it wouldn't hurt to stay and practice her limited social skills on Lindsay. The thought terrified her, but if she was going to have a chance to win Chad's attention, she had to start somewhere.

*Maybe Lindsay, Chad's sister, was the answer to her prayers.*

"You don't have to be polite with me, Mrs. Houghton." She inclined her head toward the opposite end of the barn. "The band is returning now. All of your admirers will be waiting."

"Please, call me Lindsay, not Mrs. Houghton, and I'll call you Ginny. Agreed?"

She smiled and nodded.

"I don't want to return to the dance. I'd rather talk with you."

Ginny ducked her head again and couldn't help but giggle, amazed Lindsay didn't want to dance. Instead, she wanted to stay here, in the dark, and chat with the likes of her. It didn't make any sense.

"Please, don't bother on my account… Lindsay."

"I'm not. I want to stay," Lindsay said. "Believe me, I'm hiding out, too."

Ginny raised her head and stared at her. She couldn't believe Chad's sister would admit to such a thing. And besides, it wasn't a nice thing to say—intimating they were in hiding. She wasn't the only one who let her mouth run away before her brain kicked in. "You're hiding out?" Ginny asked, still not quite believing it. "But you're the belle of the ball, every man wants to dance with you."

Lindsay glanced down. "I didn't mean to sound as if I were saying—"

"That I'm hiding out?" Ginny finished. She lifted her chin. "Why should I lie about it? It's the truth."

"All right, then, why are you hiding?"

Ginny shrugged. "I'm ashamed of my clothes, and I don't know how to dance."

The part about dancing wasn't completely true; she knew some of the simpler dances, but the polkas and waltzes were way too complicated.

"I can teach you to dance," Lindsay said. "As for your clothes, they aren't the latest fashion, but neither are most of the other women's dresses." She looked down at her aqua gown. "My dress has caused more trouble than its worth. I should have never worn it."

If she'd been surprised before, she was amazed Lindsay was sorry to have worn such a gorgeous gown. "You can't mean that! I think it's the loveliest dress I've ever laid eyes on."

"Maybe so, but it gives men the wrong idea and makes the women jealous."

Ginny stared at Lindsay. What an honest thing to say, especially coming from another woman. And for some reason, Lindsay's brutal honesty tickled her.

Feeling the laughter fizzing inside, she covered her mouth and tried to do the polite thing, turning away to hide her inappropriate merriment.

"You're laughing at me!" Lindsay exclaimed.

She tried to stop giggling by taking a deep breath and saying, "Laughing *with* you, not at you. I think your attitude is so, so—"

"Amusing?"

"Not amusing—refreshing and honest."

# A Mistletoe Christmas

"I've been living in Boston, and this is my best gown. I expected everyone to be dressed in their best tonight."

How could Chad's sister be so honest about her gown but, at the same time, so unrealistic about life in Langtry, a frontier outpost. True, she hadn't lived here much, being shipped off to Boston years ago.

Well, if her friend could be honest, so could she. "But they are, Lindsay. Wearing their best dresses."

Lindsay sighed and closed her eyes.

And Ginny knew how she felt, as if she'd blundered and offended her. She reached out and touched Lindsay's arm.

Lindsay opened her eyes, and they gazed at each other.

"I understood what you meant. You were just explaining. I'm like that, too. I try so hard to explain and, sometimes, the words come out sounding harsh. I don't mean it; it just happens."

Lindsay smiled and nodded. "You're right. I didn't mean to sound arrogant or spoiled." She hesitated before adding, "As you must know, my husband and brother own this ranch. Where do you live? Is your father a rancher, too?"

"No, my father was a railroad brakeman. He was killed in a train accident about eight years ago."

Lindsay shook her head. "My condolences for losing your father." Their gazes met again and held. "My father was killed on our ranch four years ago. Horse threw him and broke his neck."

"I'm sorry for you, too, Lindsay. And your mother?"

She lowered her head. "She died of cholera a few years after we settled here."

Ginny patted her arm. "I understand. My younger brother died of the cholera, too. At least I have my mother, and we manage. We're both seamstresses. We live in Langtry down by the springs."

Lindsay looked up, a quizzical expression on her face.

It wasn't hard for Ginny to guess what she was thinking. The area surrounding the springs was inhabited by the poorest people in Langtry.

# A Mistletoe Christmas

"My mother washes clothes, as well as mends them. The springs provide the water, and we employ several of the local Mexican women to help."

Lindsay crossed herself, and Ginny wondered what she was doing. But then Lindsay reached out and grabbed her hand.

Ginny wanted to ask what Lindsay wanted, but loud shouts from the other end of the barn drew her attention. She glanced up. While they'd been talking, the band had resumed playing, but they screeched to a halt in the middle of a square dance. And then she heard more shouts, mingled with screams.

She and Lindsay exchanged looks of alarm and gathered their skirts in their hands, sprinting toward the commotion.

Chad appeared and grabbed his sister's arm. Ginny couldn't hear what he was telling Lindsay, but he squeezed her shoulder and motioned for her to go.

Lindsay left without a backward glance, through a side door in the barn.

Ginny followed Chad, trailing him by a few feet, hoping he wouldn't notice her.

Outside the barn a fight was in progress and at the middle of it was Lindsay's new husband, Bart. One man was lying on the ground. A second man had Bart's arms pinned, while a third man pummeled him.

*Not fair!*

The man doing the punching hit Bart in the face and Ginny had to look away. When she looked back, Bart had gotten free, but the man who'd punched Bart had grabbed an empty whiskey bottle and hit him over the head.

Lindsay's new husband crumpled and fell. Chad roared and flung himself at the man, wrenching away the whiskey bottle and pounding the man's face with his fists. The man hit the dust.

Ginny wanted to jump up and down and applaud Chad.

Chad raised his fists and scanned the crowd, asking, "Anyone else want to fight? I'm more than willing. But not three against one. I think that's a wee bit unfair."

263

# A Mistletoe Christmas

"Yeah, maybe so," One of the ranchers from near Comstock spat on the ground. "But that fancy gambler dude started it. Launched himself into the three of them."

"That fancy dude is my new partner and he might have started the fight, but I'm sure he had a good reason." Chad swung his head from side-to-side, gazing at the gawking crowd.

Most men turned aside. Others lowered their heads and stared at the ground.

"Well, I appreciate everyone coming today and helping to build my cabin." He glanced at Bart, still lying face down in the dirt. "But given the circumstances, I think we'd better call it a night. I'll be sending the band home." He moved to Bart's limp form and turned him over. He glanced up. "And I'll be saying good night. Hope everyone gets home safely."

Ginny could see the dark stain of blood, trickling down Bart's face. It took all of her willpower not to go to Bart and try to help. But if Chad had sent Bart's wife away, he'd not want a stranger interfering.

Chad leaned down and helped Bart to his feet. Bart opened his eyes and groaned. The crowd thinned, men and women moving off to retrieve their horses or wagons.

Ginny's heart squeezed. Chad was her hero. A good man, taking care of his friend and partner. She still wanted to go to them, but she dug her fingernails into the palms of her hands, knowing she should stay clear.

A youth stepped forward. She recognized him as Mark Sanderson, the son of Chad's neighbors to the west.

Mark said, "Mr. MacKillian, your partner went after those men because they were making dishonorable remarks about your sister. About how she looked in that dress of hers." He bowed his head and scuffed his cowboy boot in the dust. "I thought you should know the truth, Mr. MacKillian."

"Thank you for telling me, Mark. I appreciate it." Chad put Bart's arm around his shoulder and half-dragged him toward the ranch house. "Show's over. Go home, folks."

# A Mistletoe Christmas

Ginny stood rooted to the spot. She hoped Bart wasn't hurt too badly. And thinking about how Chad had handled the fight, made her proud. He'd been cool and calm, sending his sister out of harm's way. Going to his partner's rescue. Facing down the hostile crowd, who didn't like having a stranger in their midst, especially one who had appeared from nowhere to buy into one of the larger ranches.

Before, her mooning after Chad had been childish. She hadn't known much about him, besides how handsome he was. Now, she knew the measure of the man, his character. If she thought she'd loved Chad before, now she knew she was lost.

One way or another, despite her shyness and ugly clothes, she wanted him to know how she felt. And now that she'd struck up a friendship with Chad's sister, there was hope. Maybe, after time, when they were better friends, she'd admit her feelings to Lindsay and see if she could help her.

It was a slim hope—a slender thread of hope—but it was hope.

# A Mistletoe Christmas

## Chapter Two

Ginny heard Lindsay's greeting before she saw her. "Good morning. I see y'all are plenty busy."

She looked up from her sewing and waved. Her mother straightened from stirring the boiling pot with laundry and said, "Good morning. Glad to see you today, Lindsay."

The two Mexican women, Lucia and Isabella, bobbed their heads and said, "*¡Hola! Señora* Houghton."

Ginny had been surprised when Lindsay had shown up at their home, soon after the cabin raising dance, wanting to learn how to sew. Her new friend wasn't content with raising money for a new church. She also wanted to help the poor children of Langtry by making them new clothes for Christmas.

Lindsay's sewing skills were rudimentary at best, but she was eager to learn. In exchange, she was more than willing to help them with their sewing and laundry. Over the days, she and Lindsay had become good friends, learning about each other's childhoods and sharing confidences.

Ginny admired Lindsay's giving spirit, tenacity, and willingness to work. She'd never had a close woman friend before, and she was thoroughly enjoying their new-found relationship.

Lindsay turned to Ginny's mother and asked, "Where do you want me to start?"

"With Ginny, we have some delicate tatting to do. Womenfolk are already getting ready for the dances, following the autumn shearing."

"Oh, but I'm not good with the fine work, is there anything else I can do?" Lindsay asked.

"Well, Ginny will teach you," her mother said.

"All right, Mrs. Brown. I just hope Ginny doesn't have to pull apart all my work and start over."

"Naw, you're quick. You'll get the hang of it. I'm sure. And how many times must I tell ye, call me by my given name, Emma."

# A Mistletoe Christmas

"All right, Emma. I'll do my best. Will there be any time to—"

"Don't worry, soon as I get these clothes boiled, Lucia and Isabella will take over, and I'll get back to work on the trousers for the boys."

"That's wonderful. We're making progress, don't you think?"

"Yep, should have plenty of clothes made for Christmas time."

Lindsay joined her on the bench under the grape arbor. Ginny handed her a dress and a lace collar that needed to be attached. She leaned in toward her new friend and whispered, "I'm glad we get to work side-by-side today. We've been so busy lately we haven't had time to talk. How are things at the ranch?"

"Going well. Chad and Bart are starting to bring the sheep in from the far pastures for shearing."

"And how's your handsome but injured husband?"

"He will be healed in no time, and he's working like he'd never been hurt."

Ginny had been wondering when Lindsay would tell her that she was in the family way? She'd kept quiet and not asked, but her mother had mentioned it yesterday, after Lindsay went home. She'd had no answer for her mother, and she couldn't help but be curious as to why her friend hadn't mentioned her condition?

She glanced at the small bump below Lindsay's waistline and said, "Well, y'all didn't waste any time. Getting in the family way, I mean. I didn't hear about your marrying until—"

"Ginny!"

She held up her hand. "I won't ask any more questions. Maybe, later, when you're further along, you'll want to talk about it."

Lindsay shook her head. She put the dress and collar in her lap and found a needle and some thread in the sewing basket.

Then she glanced up and said, "I will admit Bart has helped Chad a great deal around the ranch, despite his injuries. And thanks to him, we should turn a profit on our wool this time."

# A Mistletoe Christmas

"That's wonderful!" Ginny exclaimed. "Most of the ranchers haven't turned a profit since the tariff was lifted. What did Bart do?"

"Had us join the Wool and Mohair Cooperative in Del Rio. They ship in bulk and get lower freight rates from the railroad. I never realized freight was such a significant cost of getting our wool to market, but it is. What we save on freight should give us a small profit this time. If all goes as planned."

"Good for Bart. You must be in heaven, having such a handsome husband." She tossed her head and considered. Her new friend was keeping secrets, but she didn't want to keep her feelings for Chad a secret anymore, at least, not with Lindsay. "'Course your brother is easy on the eyes, too."

"Why, Ginny Brown!" Lindsay grasped her arm. "If I didn't know you better, I'd say you were sweet on my brother."

She ducked her head. "What if I am? He'll never notice me. I'm poor and mousy."

Lindsay squealed and threw her arms around her. "What are you saying! You're not poor and mousy. He should be proud to have you. And just think, then we'd be sisters. And you and your mother could move to the ranch and..." Her voice trailed off.

Ginny wondered what Lindsay was thinking. *More secrets she didn't want to share?* She'd admitted her secret. Might as well find out the truth about Lindsay's brother.

"Chad's not spoken for, is he?" Ginny asked.

"No, not that I know of. He didn't bring anyone to the cabin raising."

Ginny bit her lip. "Then there's hope?"

"More than hope. I was wondering how I would take care of the shearing crew and then another dance. I'll be further along and though the shepherd's wives will help, I'll still need your assistance."

Lindsay would need help at shearing time? That was music to her ears. Then she'd have a reason to stay at the Lazy M for at least a week. In a week's time, Chad couldn't help but notice her.

And shearing was hard and dirty work, she wouldn't look out of place, dressed in her faded cotton dresses.

"Oh, please, I want to help you, Lindsay. I'd love to, and I'm sure Mama will want to help, too." She hesitated and added, "That is, if you want us."

"Want you! Are you teasing me?"

"I just needed to be sure."

"Do you think your mother would let you come and stay at the ranch house during the shearing? I could certainly use your help."

"I'm sure she will."

"Good, that's settled then." Lindsay hugged her. "And we'll take in one of my dresses for you and do your hair and maybe a little rouge." Lindsay held her at arm's length, as if considering. "We'll make certain Chad notices you, Ginny."

She didn't know if she was ready to be "dolled up" to capture Chad's interest. She'd rather he saw her first as she was, cracked shoes and all. What if Chad, unlike Prince Charming in her favorite fairy tale, *Cinderella*, couldn't get past her poor appearance?

Surely, Lindsay would save her efforts for the shearing dance. And before that, Chad would have plenty of time to notice her. She hoped so, as she didn't want to mislead him.

If he didn't care for her as she was, she wasn't going to stoop so low as to trap him with fancy dresses and a painted face. *But where had her sudden burst of courage come from?* She hadn't felt this way at the cabin raising dance. Then she'd wanted to hide.

Somehow, knowing Lindsay and seeing her daily had changed her, made her more sure of herself. Being his sister's friend, at least, she didn't worry he would dismiss her without a second thought.

She wasn't beautiful like Lindsay, but she hoped he'd see past her poor clothing and come to know her—the real her—her nature and her heart. And given time, maybe he would realize how much she cared for him.

# A Mistletoe Christmas

Love, real love, took time to grow, she believed. And she was more than prepared to wait for her dreams to come true.

* * *

Chad loaded the last bolt of cloth into the back of the buckboard. He swung up and took the reins, clicking his tongue. The horses broke into a trot, covering the short main street of Langtry in a few moments.

Lindsay had said her new-found friends, the Browns, lived down by the springs. Not a place he'd care to go after dark, and now that he thought about it, he should warn his sister. Though, she was always home in time to make him supper.

*His sister and her charitable works.*

He shook his head and grumbled to himself. He had little enough time to spare for this errand, but Lindsay seldom asked for favors. And she didn't need to be loading and unloading bolts of cloth in her condition.

He turned the horses down the dusty track toward the springs. The springs fed the meandering creek where Bart had built his cabin.

His sister had said the Browns lived in the third adobe house on the right. He found the house and pulled back on the reins, stopping in front of a modest stucco house with a weed-filled front yard. Lindsay had mentioned the Browns would probably be around back, washing and mending clothes.

He didn't see a wagon track to the back of the house, just a footpath, so he set the buckboard's brake and climbed down. When he rounded the corner of the house, he found a large, cleared yard with live oaks and mesquite trees and a huge pecan tree in the center.

Countless clothes lines were strung to and from the tree branches. Two Mexican women were pinning clothes to the lines. Under the pecan tree, a large cauldron bubbled over a fire, smelling strongly of lye soap. An older woman stirred the pot. At the back of

# A Mistletoe Christmas

the yard, someone had erected a grapevine arbor and underneath the green leaves, a young woman sat, sewing.

So, this was where Lindsay spent her days, learning to sew and making clothes for the poor children of Langtry. It wasn't a setting he'd envisioned for his sister, but he knew she was serious about her charity work.

The woman at the cauldron put one hand to her back and straightened, calling out, "Lucia, keep this pot going while I speak to the gentleman."

The woman handed the stirring paddle to one of the Mexican women and wiped her hands on her apron. She advanced on him with her hand outstretched. "You must be Lindsay's brother, Chadbourne. Good to meet you. I'm Mrs. Brown, but I prefer just plain Emma."

He shook her hand and said, "Nice to meet you, Mrs. Brown. Ah, Emma. And you can call me Chad."

Emma waved at the young girl, sitting under the grape arbor. "Ginny, come over and meet Chad. Don't be shy, girl. This is Lindsay's brother."

The girl lifted her head. Her neck and face were red as a beet root. Her mother was right; her daughter was shy.

The girl called Ginny set her sewing to one side and rose. She was a pretty little thing with huge brown eyes and long brown hair. She reminded him of a little brown wren, a fragile bird, ready to take flight.

She was dressed plain enough, especially for a seamstress, in a worn muslin dress with tiny pink flowers sprinkled over it, made almost invisible by countless washings, and open-toed leather *huaraches* like the Mexican girls wore.

*Her naked toes peeked out beneath the short hem of her dress.*

He glanced down at her dusty toes and was shocked at how a glimpse of her naked feet affected him, making him tremble with a strange yearning to gather her into his arms and shelter her—his little brown wren.

# A Mistletoe Christmas

She extended her hand and said, "Pleased to meet you, Chad. I feel as if I know you from talking to your sister." She glanced around. "Lindsay didn't come with you?"

Chad took her tiny, fine-boned hand in his big paw. Touching her and feeling her tremble a little, his urge to protect her grew. He kept her hand in his for a split second longer than was necessary and gazed at her.

"No, Lindsay couldn't come today," he said. "But she told me to give y'all her apologies. Serafina, our housekeeper, has an ailing child. My sister had some laundry and cleaning to catch up on." He gestured at the wagon. "But she was eager for y'all to get the shipment of cloth and thread for her Christmas charity—the one for the children."

"Yes, we'd been expecting the cloth this week," Emma said. "It was nice of you to bring it."

"Where do you want it?" he asked. "Should I pull around back or—"

"No, we'll pile the cloth in the front room. Wouldn't do to leave it out in the open," Emma said.

"All right. I'll grab some bolts of cloth." He tipped his Stetson and turned around, walking toward his wagon at the front of the house.

"We can help," Emma called after him.

They joined him at the buckboard and in no time, the three of them had the wagon unloaded. He stood outside on their front porch and stuffed his hands in his back pockets. "Well, ladies, it was nice to meet you, but I need to get back to the ranch. We've been working on the shearing shed."

"Won't you take a cup of tea or coffee with a piece of cherry pie?" Emma asked. "Baked fresh this morning. Seems like the least we can offer for your help."

He slid a glance at Ginny. He'd wanted an excuse to stay and get to know her. The shearing shed could wait—it had been an excuse because he'd felt awkward.

# A Mistletoe Christmas

Jumping at the chance, he said, "Fresh baked pie and a cup of coffee?" He grinned. "I can't say no to that."

Emma turned to Ginny. "Can you get the pie and coffee? I need to check on Lucia and Isabella."

*Better and better—he'd be alone with Ginny.*

"Of course, Mama," Ginny said. She turned to Chad. "Hope you don't mind eating in the kitchen."

"Nope, it's where we usually eat, unless we have company." He inclined his head. "I'll follow you."

She poured his coffee into a tin mug and took the pie out of the pie saver, cutting him a piece. She set the coffee and pie in front of him. "Do you take milk or sugar in your coffee?"

He looked at her and glimpsed golden flecks in the depths of her large, brown eyes. Her face was a perfect oval with a pointed chin, and her complexion was creamy with rose tints. But her most alluring feature was her cupid's bow-shaped mouth.

He smiled. "No, black. Thank you. Won't you join me? I hate to eat alone."

"All right, but I'll just take coffee. I already had a piece of pie for breakfast."

"Pie for breakfast—that's a new one."

"Not that different from toast with preserves."

"I guess you're right. I never thought about it." He cut into his pie and took a bite. The crust melted in his mouth and the cherries were tart, the way he liked them. He closed his eyes and sighed. "Cherry pie is my favorite. And this one is sweet, but not too sweet."

She smiled and sat across from him with her coffee. She plucked two sugar cubes from a jar on the table and stirred them into her coffee. "I'm glad you like the pie. I made it. I'm the baker, and Mama does the cooking."

"Hmmm." He chewed slowly, savoring each bite. "Good way to divide up the kitchen chores." He wanted to keep staring at her but that would be rude, so he glanced out the window. "That's a bunch of clothes lines."

# A Mistletoe Christmas

"Yes, we get a lot of town business. Men without wives who need someone to wash for them."

"And you do sewing, too?"

"Sewing is our specialty. The washing started as a sideline because most of the mending we got needed to be cleaned properly before we could stitch the cloth." She took a sip of her coffee. "And the springs are out back. Very convenient."

No matter how slowly he ate, the pie was disappearing and then he'd have to leave. But when she mentioned the springs, it gave him an idea.

"You know, as long as I've been living near Langtry," he said. "I've never been down to the springs."

She wrinkled her cute, freckled nose. "I'm not surprised. Most people avoid this part of town."

"Yeah, I guess they do." He'd thought like that when he drove here, but now that he'd met Ginny, he'd be hard pressed to stay away. "How'd y'all come to settle here?"

"My Papa found this place. He was a brakeman for the railroad, but he died in a train accident about eight years ago."

"My sympathies to you, Miss Ginny." He reached out and let his fingers trace across the skin of her hand. "I lost my father a few years back." He shook his head. "I still miss him. Still have all kinds of questions I'd like to ask him, mostly about the ranch. I'm always wondering if I'm doing the right thing, if I'm running the ranch the way he would." He gazed into her soft brown eyes. "You know?"

She nodded and then ducked her head. "I can see how such a big ranch could be a burden. But now you've got a partner to help, and he's part of the family, too."

"Yes, you're right. Bart has been a boon for our ranch. And he's a hard worker, too." He speared the last piece of pie crust and washed it down with his coffee.

"More pie or coffee?" she asked.

# A Mistletoe Christmas

He patted his abdomen. "No, I better not." He caught her gaze and smiled again. "But I'd love to see the springs. Do you mind?"

He hoped she wanted to show him the springs. He'd enjoy walking out with her. Hell, he enjoyed just being around her. She was a shy little thing but that made him want to draw her out.

"Of course, my pleasure," she said. She gathered his plate and fork and both of their tin cups and put them in the pump sink. Then she wiped her hands on her apron and said, "I'll show you a way around the side. That way, you won't bump into all the clothes lines."

She opened the back door and said, "Follow me."

He trailed behind her, taking in the activity in the back yard. "Looks like hard work. I'm surprised my sister spends her time here."

She glanced over her shoulder. "Lindsay? She's a big help. Sometimes, Lucia or Isabella can't come for the day. She helps with the laundry, but mostly, we sew together."

"With all that cloth to sew before Christmas, I wonder if she'll be staying later and forgetting my supper…"

Oh, no, he'd almost given away his sister's unusual living arrangement. And he didn't know if she'd taken Ginny into her confidence or not.

"Lindsay cooks for you, too? I assumed she cooked for her husband, but I didn't realize, since you had your own cabin—"

Ginny was quick. She'd picked up on his ill-advised words. All he could do was try to deflect her. And if she was as shy as she seemed, it was the perfect opportunity to see if she'd let him hold her hand.

"Yeah, my Sis is a hard worker, like her new husband." He picked up the pace and grabbed her hand. "But you already know that about her."

She started to pull away, but then she sighed and let him take her hand. Her acceptance surprised him. And holding her hand,

275

made every nerve in his body come alive, thrumming with an acute awareness of her small hand enfolded in his.

They stopped at a split rail fence, and she unlatched the gate, letting it swing open.

He let go of her hand and patted the top rail. "You seldom see a wood fence out here."

"My Papa built it, to keep our back yard separated from the springs. He didn't want people wandering into the yard."

"Where did he get the wood?"

"Leftover rail ties from when the railroad was built."

"So, your father must have been one of the earliest settlers around here."

"Yes, I guess you're right. With the help of some Mexican carpenters, he built our house and then sent for us from Missouri."

Then she offered her hand to him. He was surprised by her forwardness. Maybe she wasn't as shy as her mother thought or maybe she liked touching him. The thought made him feel warm all over. He squeezed her hand and then snagged her gaze, holding it. And if he was a tad bit more brave, he'd kiss her cupid's bow mouth.

She ducked her head and said, "Come on." She pulled him down the steep slope to the natural springs, bubbling up from the rocks. At the edge of the pool, which the springs fed, she stopped.

He glanced around at the weeping willows, live oak trees, and cypress trees with their big, knobby roots, peeking out from the water. And then there were the stunted mesquite trees, purple sage, and ocotillos, too. Around the water, unlike other parts of Langtry, the undergrowth was thick. A carpet of grass surrounded the small pool, too.

"Hey, this is something." He couldn't keep the note of awe from his voice. "It's like an oasis in the desert. I didn't know there was a place with so much green around it."

"It's kind of nice, isn't it?" She tugged on his hand again, and they strolled to the edge of the pool where the run-off created a stream. The creek ran through Langtry and furnished the big steam engines with their water. Then it snaked through his ranch before emptying into the Rio Grande.

She pointed at a fragrant patch of dark green leaves. "That's my mint patch. Mint likes to stay damp. Grows good here." She leaned down and plucked a leaf, crushing it in her hand.

She opened her hand and said, "Here, smell."

Chad sniffed. "Smells nice." He glanced up. "Like you, fresh and nice. What do you do with it?"

She was blushing again.

He wasn't usually so easy with his compliments, and he guessed she wasn't used to receiving them.

She turned away and said, "We put it in our tea or even lemonade, makes drinks more refreshing. You can chew on it, to make your breath sweet, too."

"Interesting," he remarked.

They hesitated at a bridge of sorts to the other side of the stream. More railroad ties her father must have laid across the creek.

"Want to see the other side?" she asked.

"Sure, though, it looks pretty thick over there."

"Yes, we need to watch for water moccasins." She released his hand and stepped onto the railroad tie. The makeshift bridge was only wide enough for one person.

"But you're wearing *huaraches,* and your feet aren't protected. Maybe we should go back."

She wriggled her toes, and he couldn't take his eyes off her naked flesh. He'd never felt so drawn to a woman before… not even his fiancée. And with that thought, a wave of guilt washed over him. They should go back; he shouldn't have come walking with Ginny. After all, he was promised to another.

But she was already across the stream, waiting for him. He couldn't turn back now.

She motioned to him. "Come on, I want to show you something."

# A Mistletoe Christmas

The eagerness in her voice drew him on. He stepped along the railroad ties with his cowboy boots, careful not to slide into the stream. "What is it?"

"You'll see."

He caught up with her and held back the brush. He saw a stick on the ground and picked it up. He swept the ground in front of them, and moved forward slowly.

"Follow me. I'm watching for snakes," he said.

"I'm watching, too." She stopped at a live oak tree and pointed. "Look, out there."

"What am I looking for?"

"Those little dirt mounds. Don't you know what they are?"

"No, not really." He combed his hand through his hair.

"It's a prairie dog town." She turned to him and grinned. "Sometimes, we can hear them, chattering at each other, all the way up at the house."

"Really? I've never seen them this far south."

"That's because it's too rocky around here, most places. But there's a nice stretch of soil here. It's not a big town, but..." She stopped and bounded away, toward one of the mounds.

"Hey, wait a minute," he said. "Don't forget the snakes."

"Snakes and prairie dogs don't usually mix. I'm fine." She motioned to him again. "Look what else I found." She bent down and picked up a triangular-shaped stone. "An arrowhead!"

He joined her, but he was still careful enough to sweep the ground around them.

She handed him the sharp-edged flint.

"This is a nice one." He hefted it in his hand. "Not a nick on it, and it's a perfect size." He glanced at her. "Do you mind if I keep it?"

"Uh," she hesitated. "I, ah, I collect those. Since I was a little girl, I've found them, especially here by the springs."

"No kidding?"

278

# A Mistletoe Christmas

She nodded. "I love finding Indian things. I've found lots of arrowheads, a piece of a feathered headband, some strings of beads, and a large piece of turquoise on a leather thong."

He let loose a low whistle. "That's pretty amazing."

There weren't any Indians around Langtry these days. They'd all been driven off by the soldiers from Fort Clark and Fort Davis when the railroad had been built. But across the Rio Grande, in México, people claimed there were plenty of Indian tribes living off the land.

She put the arrowhead in his hand. "You can keep this one. I've plenty of others. Would you like to see my collection?"

He looked up at her and gazed into her eyes. She was so sweet and giving. But he shouldn't be here, walking with her. He needed to get back. He looked up at the sky, as if calculating where the sun was. "Maybe another time. I need to get back to the ranch. But I collect arrowheads, too. Wish there were still some Indians around..." He lifted one shoulder. "Probably for the best. Most womenfolk would be frightened by live Indians. But I guess you'd be—"

"I'd love to meet some live Indians."

He held out his hand with the arrowhead. "I can't take it, Ginny. You know, finders' keepers. Right?" And he grinned.

She grinned back, and her smile lit up her whole face, making her golden-brown eyes sparkle. "Are you sure you don't want to keep the arrowhead?" she asked. "You're my guest and—"

"I'm more than sure." He dropped the arrowhead into the pocket of her apron. "There, no giving it back now."

"All right. But you're welcome to come back to the springs and look around any time you want."

"Say, throw in a piece of pie with that offer, and you'll have to beat me off with a stick."

Now why had he said that, especially when he was already feeling guilty, wanting to be with Ginny even though he was engaged? Just plumb loco, he guessed.

She giggled.

# A Mistletoe Christmas

They both liked Indian relics, what could be the harm in sharing their interest? He wasn't going to court Ginny or anything like that. But he wanted to see her again, no matter what. And then he had an idea.

He snapped his fingers. "Hey, I had a thought. If you love Indian stuff, have you seen Panther Cave?"

"The famous cave with the Indian drawings by the Pecos River?"

"Yes, that's the one. Have you seen it?"

"No, but I've heard enough about it. I've always wanted to go, since I was a little girl. My Papa promised to take me, but then he…"

"What if I take you?"

"Isn't it awfully rough getting there?"

"Can be. We'll need horses for most of the way. But that's no problem." He wanted to reach for her hand again, but he restrained himself. "You ride, don't you?"

"Um, not so much. We've always lived in town, so I haven't had much chance to learn. I used to ride a mule on my Grandpap's farm in Missouri, though."

"I've got just the mare for you. She's gentle and easy to ride, and her name is Miss Lucy."

She giggled again. "Miss Lucy, I like the name."

He rubbed his jaw. "How about next Sunday? In the afternoon, of course. I wouldn't want to interfere with your church going."

There, he'd done it. Asked to spend some time with her—but it wouldn't change the fact he was engaged. They'd just be friends, sharing a common interest.

"Next Sunday afternoon would be fine." She scraped the side of her sandal in the dirt. "But don't eat lunch. I'd be proud to pack us a picnic lunch." She glanced up and licked her lips. "With pie, of course."

Seeing her perfect pink tongue almost undid him. Not thinking, he leaned toward her, wanting to kiss her. But at the last

# A Mistletoe Christmas

moment, he pulled back. Maybe going to Panther Cave together wasn't such a good idea. But how could he go back on his offer?

*He couldn't.*

He pushed aside his doubts and said, "A picnic lunch with pie sounds perfect. I'll be here with the horses around one o'clock. Do you have trousers you can wear? We'll be riding and, like you said, it's rough country."

She smiled. "I think I can rustle up something."

# A Mistletoe Christmas

## Chapter Three

Ginny and her mother had brought out the trestle table and laid out the bolts of cloth. They had several hand-made patterns, weighted down by rocks, and three pairs of scissors.

Her mother passed out the scissors and said, "We're going to cut out the patterns for the boys' clothes today. Tomorrow, we'll tackle the dresses for the girls." She turned to Lindsay, "Did you get a list of the children?"

"Yes, but I don't know if it's complete."

"That's fine. We'll make some extra sets of clothes just in case."

"How about measurements?"

Lindsay giggled. "That was hard. I couldn't go around with a tape measure, unless I wanted to give away our surprise, but when I hand out candy, I try to measure their arms and legs with my hand span, while I tickle or hug them."

Her mother nodded. "We'll make the trousers with flared legs and the shirts, squared off, Mexican style. That way, if they don't fit properly, a little string around the waistband should work."

"What about the girls?" Lindsay asked.

"Same thing, we'll make the dresses loose and comfortable. The girls can cinch them with a sash or ribbon."

"Oh, dear," Lindsay said. "I didn't think of that. I'll stop by the general store on the way home and make certain Mr. Larson has enough ribbon on hand."

"Do we know how many dresses to make?" Ginny asked.

"I've counted eighteen little girls, and if we make five extra, that would be twenty-three dresses," Lindsay said.

"Should give you an idea of how much ribbon you'll need," Ginny added.

"Yes, I'll keep that in mind," Lindsay said.

"How many sets of clothes will we need, for both the boys and girls?" Ginny asked.

# A Mistletoe Christmas

Lindsay glanced over her list. "If we add five extra sets of clothing for the boys and the same amount for the girls, that's around forty-eight total, I think." She looked up. "We already have fourteen sets made, so we're almost a third of the way there." She turned to Ginny's mother and said, "Any extra cloth we have left, I want you to keep, Emma, for donating the materials so far."

Her mother smiled. "That's kind of you. Let's see where we end up after cutting the patterns."

They laid out the patterns and began cutting. The morning wore on and when they had several piles of cloth and had exhausted Lindsay's list, they stopped and ate roast beef sandwiches Ginny had made from last night's pot roast.

Isabella and Lucia had finished the washing, and all the lines were strewn with clothes. Her mother had gone into the house to lie down for an hour. She and Lindsay were finally alone, sitting under the grape arbor.

Ginny tapped her friend's arm and said, "You could have warned me."

Lindsay gazed at her, her eyes wide. "Whatever do you mean?"

"Sending your brother yesterday without telling me. And don't play coy with me, Lindsay MacKillian."

Lindsay grinned. "Oh, that. Hmmm, thought it would give you some time to get acquainted. And you won Chad over with your pie. He couldn't stop talking about how good it was." She bobbed her head, still grinning. "I think my little 'surprise' worked better than I expected."

And if Lindsay knew Chad wanted to take her to Panther Cave, she'd be crowing with delight. Ginny almost blurted it out, but for some reason, she wanted to keep their outing to herself... at least for now.

She shook her head. "I still can't believe you sent him without telling me."

"I was afraid if I told you ahead of time, you'd hide."

# A Mistletoe Christmas

Ginny ducked her head. "I wanted to. But your brother was very nice, very kind."

"And?"

"And, what?" Ginny asked.

*There it was again.*

Should she tell Lindsay about their proposed outing to Panther Cave? She wasn't certain. She was afraid the more her friend knew, the more pressure she would put on her brother. And she didn't want Chad to feel compelled to see her.

Besides, Lindsay obviously didn't know about the outing. Chad must not have told her. If Chad wanted to keep it to himself, she could, too.

"Are you going to see him again?" Lindsay asked.

She pursed her lips. "Definitely, at your ranch at shearing time." It wasn't really a lie, more of an evasion.

Lindsay bumped her shoulder. "That's not what I meant, and you know it."

"Let's give Chad some time. All right?" She licked her lips and turned to gaze into her friend's eyes. "There was one thing he said that didn't make any sense."

"Oh, what was that?"

"Something about you cooking for him, but then he shut his mouth and wouldn't go on. It was almost as if Bart didn't exist."

Lindsay folded her hands in her lap. Then she fiddled with her fingers, pulling on the joints until they cracked.

Ginny grimaced and covered her friend's hands with her own. "Tell me, Lindsay. It's past time."

Lindsay looked up and nodded. "You know I went to live with my Aunt Minerva in Boston after my mother died when I was eighteen."

"You told me about that. And how hard it was to adapt and learn all the social graces and wait to come out at twenty-one years old, long past the time most young women are presented to society back East."

# A Mistletoe Christmas

"Yes, and there aren't many socially prominent Irish Catholics in Boston. I didn't get engaged until I was twenty-five."

Ginny patted her hand. "You just got a late start, is all."

"Seamus Finnegan seemed a perfect match, and I was thrilled to be engaged... finally. But my Aunt Minnie, who is a shrewd businesswoman, must have had a hunch about Seamus because she had him investigated."

"Oh, no, really?" Ginny was shocked to hear of such a thing, but maybe, among wealthy people, it wasn't unusual.

Lindsay nodded. "My aunt's investigator found out Seamus, who was the sole heir of a wealthy family, had gambled away his family's fortune." Her friend's eyes filled with tears. "My aunt told Seamus she was bequeathing her wealth to the Catholic Church." She lowered her head and dabbed at her eyes with a handkerchief. "When he heard I wouldn't inherit, he ran away and left me."

"Oh, no! How awful!" Ginny put her arms around Lindsay's shoulders and hugged her. "What a monster." She dabbed at Lindsay's tears with her own handkerchief. "But you shouldn't cry over such a cad. Good riddance, I say."

"Yes, you're right, except for one small thing." Lindsay lifted her head and gazed into Ginny's eyes. "Seamus seduced me, and we anticipated the wedding night. I was already with child. But I didn't know for certain until about a month later."

Ginny hugged Lindsay again and patted her back. "Don't blame yourself, please. We women always take the burden. Don't we? And it's not fair. Is it? You thought you'd be married but then—"

"I ran off, not willing to face my aunt, who can be very judgmental. I left her a note and came home to have my child. Originally, I thought I'd return after the baby is born and put my child in an orphanage and take my vows in a convent." She shook her head and blew her nose. "It seemed the only right thing to do, to atone for my sin."

"Whose was the greater sin, yours or your so-called fiancé? Men! They're the real snakes in the Garden of Eden!"

# A Mistletoe Christmas

Lindsay who'd been quietly sobbing, half-choked and swallowed hard. Their gazes met and Lindsay leaned in, giggling.

Ginny patted her on the back again and couldn't help but giggle, too. "I'm glad you still have a sense of humor. And for what's it worth, I can't see you giving your baby up."

"That's what Abby said and my brother Chad."

"Abby, your friend in Del Rio with the boardinghouse?"

"Yes, and Chad doesn't want me to give up the baby, either."

"So, he got Bart to marry you, in name only, as a condition to their partnership. And Bart lives in the cabin, not Chad."

Lindsay's mouth dropped open. "How did you know?"

"Oh, just put two-and-two together." She grinned. "Besides, Chad doesn't strike me as an indoor privy kind of guy. Bart, on the other hand—"

"You're too smart for your own good, Ginny Brown."

"But Bart fought for you at the dance. He must care for you."

She and Lindsay had discussed the fight at length, but her friend hadn't bothered to mention she wasn't living with her husband.

"He does care for me. And I think I care for him." She shook her head. "But as I've said before, I don't like that he was a professional gambler, especially after what Seamus did. I don't know if we can make a go of the marriage. We're so different."

Ginny patted her hand. "Don't worry, you'll figure it out." She looked at Lindsay from the corner of her eye. "And you had to tell me sometime. How do you want to handle my mother? She's already guessed you're further along than you said. But she believes Bart is the father."

"I'll leave that to you, Ginny. Whether you want to tell her everything or not."

"My mother is pretty understanding. I don't believe she'll think less of you. More than likely, she will sympathize."

# A Mistletoe Christmas

"Well, the bigger I get, the more I'm going to have to stay at the ranch. We might end up finishing these clothes there, but I don't know if you and your mother can leave your business." She squeezed Ginny's hand. "It's enough you'll be helping me at shearing time."

"We'll figure something out. And since we're going to sew you some bigger dresses, we'll just make sure they conceal how far along you are." She bit her lip. "Eventually, though, when the baby comes, everyone will know."

Lindsay hunched her shoulders. "I know." She sniffed and blew her nose again. "But that's not even the worst of it. Sometimes, when I lay awake at night, I can't help worrying Seamus will find out I had a child by him and want to take me and the baby away."

"If he deserted you, why would he do that?"

"Because he knows my aunt would make me marry him for the baby's sake."

Ginny gasped. "But you're already married to Bart."

Lindsay turned her head away. "Not in the eyes of the Church." She lifted one shoulder. "And I don't know if Bart and I will stay married."

"Still, you're married and—"

"It's not so simple." Lindsay lifted her head and snagged her gaze. "If Bart and I don't work things out, I might return to Boston."

"Oh, no, I wish you wouldn't. I would miss you so, and I want to see your baby and watch him growing up. You must stay here."

"It would probably be safer, but I don't know if I can face Bart every day if…if…"

"Why don't you worry about that after you have the baby."

Lindsay tried to smile, but it was a pathetic attempt. "I'm sure you're right. And if I do stay, I doubt Seamus would come all this way to find me. Don't you?"

"Of course not. The safest thing is to stay here."

# A Mistletoe Christmas

Wanting her friend to remain in Langtry was selfish on her part, she knew. Lindsay and her child might have a better life in Boston, but then her friend feared Seamus. And if she was any judge of character, Lindsay cared for Bart. But she understood her friend's doubts, considering how she'd been hurt by her fiancé.

Ginny put her arm around Lindsay again, silently vowing to be there for her, every step of the way. No matter what course of action her friend decided upon.

But for now, even though she'd encouraged Lindsay to tell the truth, she wasn't ready to tell her friend about seeing Chad. Lindsay had enough to worry about without wondering if she and Chad were going to get together.

When the time was right, she'd tell Lindsay. If, she thought, she and Chad had a chance. And it was a very big "if."

\* \* \*

Chad glanced at Ginny, riding beside him on Miss Lucy, a chestnut mare. For a novice rider, Ginny was doing pretty good. Her back was straight, and she held the reins with ease. She'd found an old pair of trousers, probably her late father's, and had rolled up the bottoms over an ancient pair of cowboy boots.

He studied her covertly from beneath the brim of his Stetson. It was obvious Ginny and her mother worked hard for their living. Not too surprising, since they didn't have a man to provide for them. Unlike his fashion-conscious sister, all he'd seen Ginny wear was a faded dress and now, her late father's clothing.

But even the too-big gingham shirt, tucked into her trousers, didn't hide the graceful curve of her neck or the fullness of her breasts. And the other day, he'd glimpsed a pair of shapely ankles peeking from beneath the too-short hem of her old dress. Even her feet were beautiful, high-arched and with long and slender toes.

Her hair was pulled back with a red bow that matched the color of her shirt, but other than the bow, she'd left her hair free to tumble down her back in tawny-brown curls. And her brown eyes were more golden-colored in the bright sunshine.

# A Mistletoe Christmas

*His little brown wren.*

She looked young, definitely younger than his sister. Young and innocent and... delectable. Her creamy complexion and her cupid's bow mouth made him want to cradle her face in his hands. And the sensual shape of her mouth was so compelling, he couldn't help but wonder what it would be like to kiss her.

He frowned. He should be thinking of his intended, Vi Lea Baker, not Ginny.

But he hadn't seen Vi Lea in months, and he was beginning to think their engagement was nothing more than a business arrangement. He'd wanted to join their ranches, and she needed a man to take care of her ranch when her father got too old to work.

He shouldn't have suggested this outing, but it had been all he could think about the past week. If Vi Lea was his intended bride, then could he keep Ginny as a friend? She was his sister's friend; why couldn't they be friends, too? She might be poor, but he was certain she was a God-fearing woman. He had no right to expect her to be more than a friend, and he shouldn't be thinking about kissing her and more...

Hell's bells, if his sister knew what he was pondering, she'd cut off his...

He shook his head. Thinking of his sister and what had happened to her, he'd be the last man on earth to compromise Ginny, no matter how modest her circumstances. He'd never seduced a respectable woman, and he had no intention of starting now. But good Lord, Ginny was tempting.

She'd be saving herself for her future husband, as was right. *Her future husband*—now why was that such a disturbing thought? Despite his commitment to Vi Lea, the thought of Ginny in someone else's arms, surrendering her cupid's bow mouth to another man, burned his gut like raw whiskey.

That ironic twist bewildered him. He couldn't have Ginny, but he didn't want anyone else to have her, either.

"Are we getting close?" she asked. "I know you said it would be rough riding, but so far, it hasn't been too bad." She

# A Mistletoe Christmas

patted her horse's neck. "Maybe it's Miss Lucy here, she's so steady."

"Forgive me, Ginny. I meant to give you the full tour, but I seemed to have gotten lost in my thoughts."

"Thinking about your ranch and shearing time?"

He hesitated. He couldn't tell Ginny he'd been thinking about her, but he didn't want to lie, either. He shrugged. "I guess I'm always worrying about the ranch. But I should have been more thoughtful." He stopped his roan gelding and raised up in the stirrups, pointing with his right hand. "See that deep cut in the land over there, to the southeast of us?"

She pulled on the reins, and Miss Lucy slid to a halt. Mimicking him, she raised up in her stirrups and looked where he was pointing. "Yes, I see it."

"Well, that's the Pecos River. Panther Cave is there in the fold of that cut at about three o'clock and on this side of the river."

"Do you know, I've lived in Langtry all this time, but I've never seen the Pecos, except when Mama and I crossed it on the railroad. But I was so young then, I don't remember," she said.

"Without a horse, it's a bit of a walk. I guess you don't remember the Pecos high bridge, either."

"Nope, another promise my Papa never got around to. We were supposed to return to Missouri to visit Mama's family, but then Mama got sick. We had passes, you see, because Papa worked for the railroad."

"Passes on the railroad, that's nice. Too bad you didn't get to use them. But you'll see the bridge in a minute." He nudged his roan and pulled up beside her.

"Come on." He dug his heels into the gelding's sides.

They trotted for a few minutes over the rocky terrain, taking pains to avoid fissures in the land. He pulled up again and pointed, "Now you can see the bridge." He shook his head. "They don't call it high for nothing."

They both gazed at the iron trestle bridge spanning the yawning Pecos canyon, opening before them.

# A Mistletoe Christmas

"Oh, my, the canyon is deep," she said.

"Pretty deep where the railroad crosses."

"And is this the hard part of the ride?"

"No, it's not the riding that's hard, the hard part comes when we get to the canyon rim. We'll have to leave the horses up top and work our way down the canyon walls to the cave. There's a path, but it's steep."

"Why is it called Panther Cave?"

"Because of the big red panther painted on a wall. The cave is large and shallow, overlooking the Pecos. And it's covered in drawings, not just of a panther, but other things. Everyone believes Indians painted the pictures because there are lots of arrowheads strewn around." He shook his head. "Some of the drawings are hard to make out, but they seem to be of people and other animals."

"Panther Cave is a legend around here, people talk about it," she said. "I've heard there are lots more caves with pictures in them, all along the Pecos and Rio Grande. I bet all of those caves have arrowheads."

"Probably, but getting to them can be tough. Panther Cave is enough for one day."

"How much farther to the canyon rim?" she asked.

"About a quarter of an hour, riding at a walk."

"I'm starved," she said. "I'm used to eating dinner, right after church. Can we eat before we see the cave?"

"There's a grassy ledge outside the cave overlooking the river. I thought we'd eat and look at the same time."

She nodded and fell in beside his mount. They rode the remainder of the way, exchanging small talk, until the Pecos River came into view.

Pausing on the edge of the canyon, they stared down at the river. Writhing like a green snake through the rocky terrain, the Pecos wound through deep canyon after deep canyon. There were few places to reach it without scaling perpendicular rock walls.

# A Mistletoe Christmas

"We'll tie up the horses here. The rest of the way is by foot," Chad said, eyeing her ancient boots and hoping they were up to the punishing trek.

"How do you know where we are? Is the cave close by? Everything looks the same to me."

Chad pointed to the east, to a long, low notch in the canyon wall. From where he was standing on the lip of the cliff, he could make out the tops of trees rising from the declivity. It was a break in the canyon walls where water from the river eddied, forming a slough. There weren't many breaks in the sheer walls of the Pecos canyon and when he'd discovered the cave, he remembered the slough as a landmark.

"That's the hollow I pointed out." He put his arm around her shoulders, as they peered over the rim together. "See the tree-tops, they're growing in one of the canyon breaks around a wide place in the river. I memorized the lay of the land, so I could find the cave again."

He'd put his arm around her for safety's sake but touching her accelerated his pulse and made him think about kissing her again. And she fit against him perfectly, tongue-in-groove, as if she'd been created just for him.

She raised on tip-toe and shaded her eyes with her hand. "Yes, I see the hollow and the trees." She swung her head from side-to-side. "Doesn't look like there are many inlets like that on the Pecos, mostly sheer cliff walls."

"I know, and it makes me wonder…"

"What?"

"About the Indians who made their drawings in the cave. The cave is difficult to reach from here. I wonder if the slough was a convenient place to get water and wood while the inaccessibility of the cave provided them shelter from their enemies."

She turned to him and grinned. "Hmmm, 'inaccessibility' is it? I like them big words, especially coming from a plain old sheep rancher."

# A Mistletoe Christmas

He chuckled and couldn't help but grin back. "So, if I want to romance you, I should lay it on thick with long, mostly unpronounceable words. Right?"

*Now, what in Sam Hill had made him say that—the part about romancing her. Was he out of his ever-loving mind?*

She ducked her head but didn't move away. "Yeah, that's one good way to go about romancing me." She twined her arm around his waist. "And touching is another."

*This was getting out of hand—just as he'd feared.*

He dropped his hand and moved away, clearing his throat.

She raised her head and stared at him, her doe-brown eyes wide in her face.

Then she dropped her head. "What you said about the cave, providing shelter from their enemies makes sense." She bit her lip but kept her head down. "Maybe they fished down there, too."

Gazing at her and knowing his odd reaction had hurt her feelings, he felt like a jackass. Why had he pulled her close in the first place? And talked about romancing her?

Finally, she raised her head and gazed at the canyon. "Could we explore the slough after our picnic? Maybe there will be some arrowheads down there, too."

Relief washed over him. She'd obviously put aside the awkward moment. Now if he could get control of his not-so-proper urges, maybe they could be friends and enjoy their time together.

"Sure, I don't see why we can't explore. We should have plenty of time before we need to head back."

He secured their horses to a mesquite tree growing at an angle from the canyon face and untied the picnic basket. With the basket hooked over his left arm, he offered his right hand to Ginny.

He didn't want to touch her again, but the way down was tricky. And this outing had been his brilliant idea. He couldn't let her follow him like an orphaned puppy, hoping she wouldn't fall and slide down the canyon wall.

# A Mistletoe Christmas

"Here, take my hand and follow me. It's rocky and steep but not far, the cave is about half-way between here and the river. Be careful where you step."

She accepted his hand. The now-familiar current sparked between them as soon as her hand touched his. He'd noticed it from the first time they'd shaken hands. It was a strange feeling, something he'd never experienced before when touching a woman… or anybody. He wondered if Ginny felt it, too.

With her small, warm hand nestled in his, they began their precarious descent, down a slanting, zigzagging path that had been made by goats and deer. The loose stones on the path were a challenge, too. It was easy to step on one and turn an ankle.

He gripped her hand tighter, and they moved slowly, in tandem, avoiding the edge of the path and hugging the cliff wall. Chad was careful where he stepped, kicking loose rocks over the ledge, placing his feet in the worn limestone grooves. After about fifteen minutes of concentrated effort, the path widened. Soapy-smelling *sotol* plants with their spines extended, mingled with the musty-scented *ceniza* bushes, lining the outer edge, forming a natural barrier between them and the sheer drop.

The outcropping of the shallow cave loomed into view. The cave appeared as if it had been scooped from the canyon's wall by some long-dead giant. A grassy ledge fringed the long, shallow cave. And as soon as Ginny's feet touched the relative safety of the wide ledge, she dropped his hand and rushed ahead.

He followed her into the dusty interior. Because the cave was shallow and open on three sides, there was plenty of light. Chad watched as Ginny spotted the first of the cave paintings.

"Oh, Chad! They're wonderful! Like nothing I've ever seen before."

"Yes, they are," he agreed in a low voice. There was something about the place that made him want to whisper.

Fantastic figures covered the walls of the cave, primarily painted bright yellows and reds, mixed with a few faded blue pictures and some etched in black. Tall, man-like figures with their

# A Mistletoe Christmas

arms outstretched protected a multitude of animals and birds. Lines of delicately-depicted deer chased one another other across the walls, birds with enormous wing spans soared, and larger creatures, possibly buffalo, galloped in circles.

There were other figures, too, which defied description: geometric designs, feathery etchings, plant-like drawings, and even unidentifiable marks resembling the scribbles of a three-year-old.

At the far end of the cave reigned the painting, which gave the place its name. It was a three-foot long panther, colored red, suspended in mid-air, pouncing at imaginary prey. The painting was so life-like he expected to hear the big cat snarl and spit.

They stared at the pictures for a long time, moving back and forth across the front of the cave, discovering new paintings they'd missed before and trying to guess what some of the more obscure drawings were.

Finally, Ginny stopped in the middle of the cave with her arms wrapped around her waist and whispered, "This place gives me the shivers. I can't explain it. I feel as if I've wandered into someone's dream—or nightmare." She lifted her arm and pointed. "The pictures are beautiful but sinister at the same time." She glanced at Chad and asked, "Do I sound crazy?"

It was uncanny how he felt the same way. And he'd been here countless times. The first time, looking for lost sheep. Later, he'd come, hunting for arrowheads and to explore. And it was this cave that had first interested him in Indian objects. But today, after closely studying the paintings, he felt like an intruder.

He remembered the spooky feeling he used to get when he was a child, and how his mother had laughed and said, 'someone had just walked across his grave.' Only this time, it was as if the feeling was reversed. He felt as if he'd walked over someone else's resting place.

Moving behind Ginny, he wrapped her in his arms, pulling her close. "You're not crazy, I feel the same way. It's a strange place, as if the paintings have spirits of their own." He caught himself and

# A Mistletoe Christmas

let her go, dropping his arms. "Now, I'm the one who sounds crazy."

She turned to him and gazed into his eyes. Her lips parted. He moaned in the back of his throat, staring at her perfect mouth. And all he could think about was how much he wanted to kiss her.

Ginny frowned, and he couldn't blame her. He was running hot and cold. Gone was the strange sensation he'd experienced only seconds before, to be replaced by the all too human emotion of desire.

Holding her close, even for a few moments, he'd wanted her... now. He shook his head, hoping to clear it, but he couldn't help but wonder how many ancient peoples had made love on this very spot.

*He had to stop thinking like that.*

He lowered his head and stared at the dusty and rock-strewn cave floor—anything not to look at Ginny.

She followed his gaze and bent down, retrieving a triangular bit of stone from the ground. "I already found one." She looked up and snagged his gaze. "Here, you take it."

He turned the arrowhead over in his hands, running his thumb over its sharp point and noticing its chipped edges. "This one's pretty beaten up, not like the one you found at the springs."

She fisted her hands on her hips. "We can trade, if you like."

Now what had gotten her back up? Could it be his changeable behavior? Holding her and then pushing her away?

He pocketed the arrowhead and held out the basket. "Want to unpack this? You mentioned you were starved."

She took the basket and moved to the grassy stretch outside the mouth of the cave. She bent over and pulled the contents from the basket.

He moved beside her but didn't dare to offer his help, lest their hands brushed or he touched her accidentally. Instead, he stood rigid, gazing down at the green-brown waters of the Pecos, alternately tumbling over rapids and slipping calmly through shallows.

# A Mistletoe Christmas

She touched his arm lightly. "I have everything ready. Care to sit down?"

Her light touch and soft words crumbled him, and like the walls of Jericho, his defenses came tumbling down. He turned to her and folded her into his arms. Burying his face in her soft brown curls, he inhaled the fresh minty smell of her.

He sighed. "Ginny, you're so sweet and giving." Then he held her at arms' length. "What am I to do with you?"

# A Mistletoe Christmas

## Chapter Four

*'Love me'*, the words sprang to Ginny's mind. But she didn't say them. Instead, she gazed back at him. She wanted to make a joke of what he'd said and the way he was looking at her. But she was tongue-tied, and the look in his eyes resurrected all her old insecurities and shyness.

She didn't know what to say. Didn't know what he was asking her. Was he starting to have feelings for her? If he was, her dreams were coming true.

But he released her and kneeled on the ground. Then he settled himself, sitting cross-legged on the grass. He leaned forward and took a tin plate. He glanced up and said, "Don't you want to eat?"

Ginny gazed at the cave's walls, peopled with the imaginary ghosts of the dead, and the earlier sensations swamped her again. This place was sacred—not meant for casual picnicking.

She thrust her hand into her trouser pocket and touched the perfect arrowhead she and Chad had found at the springs. "Let's find a path to the slough and picnic there. I don't feel right, staying here."

Chad nodded and replaced his plate, along with the food, into the basket. The slough lay to the other side, at the end of the cave where the panther drawing ruled in regal solitude. She watched while Chad searched the area, looking for a way down to the water. There was no doubt in her mind there would be a path to the slough—ancient though it might be.

She believed Chad had correctly concluded that the Indians, who had drawn their hopes and dreams on the cave's walls, used the slough for water and fishing and access to the river.

He found the path, after parting the overhanging mountain laurel bushes. It was fainter than the one they'd taken from the lip of the canyon, but it was wider and not as steep. The path sloped gently to the bottom of the canyon in a straight line with plenty of room on either side. Despite the relative safety of the path, Chad took her hand again. She closed her eyes for one brief second, relishing his touch.

They descended rapidly, and Ginny felt her thighs and calves strain with the effort. When they reached the bottom, the way opened into a forest of live oak, mesquite trees, and willows. The brown-green water of the Pecos glistened in the sunlight.

Chad led her to a live oak with low-slung branches. On a carpet of leaves provided by the live oak, he spread the tablecloth. "Please, find a soft place to sit."

She sat down and Chad handed her the picnic basket. She emptied the basket again, producing cold fried chicken, deviled eggs, potato salad, yeast rolls, slices of her peach pie, and a stoneware jug of lemonade.

Chad sat across from her at the far corner of the tablecloth. If he was starting to care for her, he was obviously fighting his feelings.

She uncorked the stoneware jug and filled a tin cup with lemonade, offering it to him. He accepted the cup with thanks and gulped down its contents.

"Could I please have some more?" He passed his empty cup back.

"Of course." She refilled his cup and handed it to him. The long ride had made her thirsty, too. She poured a cup of lemonade for herself and drank it as quickly as he had.

"Do you want me to prepare a plate for you?" she asked.

"Yes, if it's not too much trouble."

She nodded and heaped two plates with food, handing one to Chad along with a fork and napkin.

He settled back on the red-and-white checkered tablecloth with a sigh. "You thought of everything, and the food looks great." He snagged her gaze and arched one eyebrow. "Though I'm having trouble waiting for your pie. What kind is it?"

# A Mistletoe Christmas

"Peach pie, and it's fresh. *Señor* Morales, one of our neighbors, has several peach trees planted downstream from us. He always brings us fresh peaches this time of year."

"Morales, the one who has a long-running feud with Judge Bean?"

"Yes, that's him."

Chad chuckled. "Every time poor Morales sets up a new saloon, Judge Bean finds a way to force him out of business."

She took a bite of chicken. "They never give up. The Judge and Morales have been going at each other since I was a young girl."

"Not too surprising. Langtry is small and one saloon is more than enough." He swallowed some potato salad. "This salad is delicious, and the chicken is crispy on the outside and juicy on the inside." Glancing at her, he asked, "Your mother did the cooking? You made the pie?"

"No, I decided to make all the food for today. I wanted to let Mama rest for a change." She ducked her head. "I'm glad you like it. I used Mama's recipes, but you never know how things will turn out."

"Well, everything is great. You're a good cook, too, like your Mama." He chuckled again. "Lindsay has gotten better, over the months, but when she first came home, her attempts at cooking were nothing short of a disaster."

Ginny giggled, and then thinking she was being disloyal to her friend, she covered her mouth with her hand. "But I'm sure your sister's cooking *has* improved. I know when Lindsay puts her mind to something, there's no stopping her."

"You're right about that," he agreed.

They ate in companionable silence for several minutes, but she couldn't help being distinctly aware of him sitting across from her. And she realized they were all alone, miles from other human beings.

"Could I have seconds on the chicken and deviled eggs?" he asked.

# A Mistletoe Christmas

"Of course, but remember, you need to save room for the pie."

"Okay, how about that other drumstick and one deviled egg. That way, I'll still have plenty of room."

"Here you are." She handed him the food.

He wolfed down the chicken and egg while she finished her lunch, and then he held out his plate. "Can't wait any longer for that pie. I want a big piece. Please."

She filled his plate with a large piece of pie she'd brought along, especially for him. She handed his plate back to him.

He forked a bite into his mouth and chewed it slowly. "Hmmm, my compliments to the cook."

His compliments, no matter how casual, never failed to affect her. She could feel her face growing hot. She lowered her head.

"Aren't you going to have some pie?" he asked.

"No, I'm too full now." She lifted her head and stretched her arms above her head. "A nap might be nice, though."

He was watching her, and she wondered what he was thinking. And what on earth had made her mention taking a nap? They couldn't very well lie down and sleep together. Could they? Not proper. She flushed again, embarrassed at what her innocent words had sounded like.

But being the gentleman she knew he was, he didn't reply. Instead, he focused on finishing his pie, appearing to savor each bite.

When Chad had finished, she took their plates a few feet away, and scraped the remnants onto the ground, knowing some wild creature would feast on the scraps later that day. Then she began to repack the picnic basket.

Chad stretched out his legs and leaned on one elbow, half-reclining, and chewing on a stick he'd found.

She started to suggest they start back when he surprised her by saying, "It's too hot to leave without cooling off first. We have a

# A Mistletoe Christmas

long climb ahead. The water looks calm, and I bet its shallow. Why don't we go wading?"

Without waiting for her to agree, he removed his black leather cowboy boots and thick socks. Rolling his denim pants to his knees, he declared, "I'm ready when you are."

She stared at him, biting her lip.

"Come on, it'll be fun."

A trickle of perspiration slipped down her spine, as if silently emphasizing his offer to cool off. "It *is* hot. All right, you've convinced me."

She began to pull her Papa's old boots off, but he forestalled her by offering, "Let me do that." He threw away the stick he'd been chewing and knelt in front of her, removing her boots and socks. His hands lingered, longer than necessary, on her naked feet and calves. Tiny shivers of delight snaked their way up her legs and centered in the pit of her stomach.

He rose and stared down, his hazel-colored eyes openly gazing at her bare legs. Abruptly, he swung around and dared her, "Last one in is a rotten egg." He left her sitting there while he sprinted toward the water.

She struggled to her feet and raced after him, calling out, "That's not fair! You got a head start." And, of course, she was the rotten egg.

When she reached the river bank, Chad had already forged ahead, moving slowly in the quiet waters, testing the depth with his feet.

"It's shallow around the edge, but it slopes quickly to the center. I think we should stay close to shore." He glanced up to find her standing on the bank of the river and motioned with his arm. "Come on. What are you waiting for?"

She did as he asked, following him into the cool waters, gasping at the change in temperature, but enjoying the feel of mud between her toes. As a young girl, she had loved to go wading, loved the quicksilver water lapping at her legs and the soft mud squishing underfoot.

# A Mistletoe Christmas

Something brushed her left leg, and she shrieked.

He rushed over and looked down. "It's only a sun perch." He pointed to her left, and she glimpsed the shining scales of a fish moving through the water.

"I used to fish for sun perch with Papa. They're awful to debone, but fried in cornmeal, I like them better than catfish." She paused and added, "Like the springs, though, I bet there are water moccasins around."

"I'm sure you're right. I'm keeping watch. That's another reason why we should stay close to shore so we can see the bottom."

A school of minnows streamed between her legs, and she squealed, "Oh, that tickles."

He laughed and splashed water at her. She sputtered and returned the attack. He took off running through the shallows, daring her again, "Bet you can't catch me."

She followed, stopping every few steps to scoop water and splash it on his back. But, of course he was right; he was way too quick for her. She wasn't able to catch him, though she did manage to soak the back of his shirt thoroughly.

Then abruptly, he turned and chased her. Running in a zigzag pattern, but staying close to shore, she managed to elude him for some time, but when he finally caught her, he dumped two handfuls of water down her back.

She screamed as the chilly water cascaded down her spine, and she rounded on him. "That was a mean thing to do!"

"No worse than you soaking my back."

"You started it by challenging me to chase you."

"You're right. I take the blame," he agreed easily and then lifted her into his arms and headed for shore. "I think we're sufficiently cooled down, and I need to catch my breath after all this running around."

She pummeled his chest in protest. "If you're out of breath, then why don't you put me down?"

# A Mistletoe Christmas

Chad didn't answer. He didn't know what he was doing. All he knew was he wanted an excuse to hold her in his arms—nothing more—nothing less. Gently, he lowered her to the tablecloth and straightened up, gazing down at her.

She turned her face up and pointed at him, laughing. "You should see yourself. You're soaked all over. Where I didn't splash you, you're wet from holding me, and it serves you right for being so silly."

He dropped beside her onto the tablecloth and joined her laughter, conceding, "You're right. I wasn't thinking, and now I'm soaked." He grinned and added, "But it feels good, so cool in the hot sun."

"Yes," she agreed. Reaching down, she gathered a corner of the tablecloth and began drying her feet and legs. When she finished, she didn't put her socks and boots back on, instead, she modestly draped the tablecloth across her bare legs.

He couldn't blame her for covering herself. He'd been staring openly at her legs. She possessed small feet with high arches and beautiful toes. Why her toes were so appealing, he had no idea, but they were. And her legs were long and slim with shapely calves, muscular yet sleek. Just the sight of her bare flesh made the blood roar in his ears.

"It's good to hear you laughing," he said.

She raised her head and met his gaze. "I don't know what you mean? Am I that solemn to be around? My mother says I'm shy, but I thought we'd gotten along rather well."

He shook his head. "I don't know what I'm saying, Ginny. Just that… that… I like everything about you. Your laughter and your cooking. Your interest in Indian relics. The way you took to riding a horse." He leaned down and brushed her cheek with his fingertips. "Everything about you."

Her face flushed a deep red, and she lowered her head. "I'm glad to hear it." She hesitated and then said, "I like you, too, Chad."

Chad dropped down beside her and cupped her chin in his hand, tilting it up. They were so close their noses almost touched.

304

# A Mistletoe Christmas

He had no right, but he'd been dreaming of this moment, since the first time they'd met. "Can I kiss you?"

She nodded.

He devoured her cupid's bow mouth. Savored the sweet taste of her lips, gorged himself on the sun-kissed warmth of her flesh, and plundered the honey-dew of her mouth. His lips moved over hers, asking and seeking, finding and sharing, like a benediction and a song. He couldn't get enough of her. Couldn't get close enough to her.

He pulled her hard against him, his mouth pressed against hers, while his fingertips traced the creamy satin of her throat. She smelled clean and sweet with a trace of the mint she'd shown him at the springs. He rubbed his thumb along the sculpted fineness of her jaw.

A tiny shiver shook her.

Exploring fur, he found the silky hollow at the juncture of her throat, caressing it until he'd raised tiny goosebumps on her skin.

He kept kissing her, and he wanted to explore more. He knew he shouldn't, and he doubted she would let him, either. But some overwhelming compulsion made him try.

He unbuttoned the top two buttons of her gingham shirt and spread the material wide. Her breasts gleamed alabaster in the sunlight, thinly covered by her chemise. He touched one coral nipple, his finger moving gently over the silky fabric. Her nipple puckered and hardened.

She groaned low and squirmed. Then she reached up, caught his hand, and broke their kiss. "Don't, Chad. We can't."

He lowered his head and breathed hard, almost panting. He was so aroused, he hurt.

Wanting to hide his arousal, he got to his feet and walked a few feet away. Flies buzzed overhead, irritating him. He slapped at them. Without looking at her, he said, "Better get your socks and boots on." He glanced up, as if studying the sun. "We need to start back."

# A Mistletoe Christmas

She rose and came to him. He had no idea what she wanted. She'd already made herself clear. She was a respectable woman, and he'd crossed the line. He turned his back to her.

She encircled his waist with her arms and leaned against his back. He could feel her soft round breasts, pressing against him.

"Chad, don't be angry. I like you…" She hugged him tighter. "No, that's not right. I love you, Chad. I've loved you for years—"

"Don't, don't say that!" He unlaced her arms and wrenched himself free. He turned around and faced her. "You have no right to love me, Ginny." He pulled one hand through his hair. "I'm not free. No one knows…" He hesitated and shook his head. "I haven't even told my sister because, because—"

"What haven't you told her?" She frowned, and he glimpsed the hurt look in her eyes.

"I've been engaged since last Christmas. I asked Vi Lea Baker to marry me, and she said yes. I haven't seen her much, though, because her mother has been ailing. But we're still promised." He caught her gaze and held it. "I shouldn't have kissed you, shouldn't have touched you." He exhaled. "I'm sorry."

\* \* \*

Chad unsaddled Miss Lucy and then his roan. He fed them some oats and made certain there was water in the trough. He grabbed an old piece of sacking and begin rubbing down the chestnut mare.

Riding home with Ginny had been a chore he didn't care to repeat. They'd ridden the entire way without exchanging a word and when he'd left her at home, she'd gazed up at him, tears glinting at the edges of her eyes and hurt burning in the depths of them.

He'd offered to come in and greet her mother, but she'd turned away without a word. She'd crossed the weedy front yard and opened the front door, slamming it behind her.

He cursed himself under his breath, wondering what on earth he'd been doing, leading her on. He shouldn't have invited her

306

to Panther Cave, knowing he wanted to get her alone to kiss her and... more.

He pulled Miss Lucy's bridle off and slammed it down on a peg in the stall wall.

"Hey, partner, what's wrong?" He hadn't heard Bart's approach, and he didn't want company. All he wanted was to wallow in his guilt and regret.

"I don't want to talk right now."

"That's obvious. But we've all been wondering where you got to after breakfast. I thought you might be riding the far north pasture, looking for stragglers. No one knew where you'd gone, not even Lindsay."

He moved to his roan and removed the bridle. He purposely slammed it down, too, draping it over the stall. "I said, I don't want to talk."

But Bart must be hard of hearing because he hadn't moved. He blocked the opening to the stall, his arms crossed over his chest.

He tried to brush past his brother-in-law, but Bart put his hand on his arm and asked, "Woman trouble? There's nothing else I can think of that would make you so upset." He shook his head. "And I should know. Asking Lindsay where you'd gone was the first conversation I've had with your sister since I told her I cared for her and wanted to try and have a real marriage."

"What?" Chad looked up. "You never told me you wanted to stay married, though, the night after your fight I was hopeful. But then, nothing happened. You and Lindsay acted like polite strangers."

"Yep, that's about right. 'Polite strangers' is one way to put it."

Now Bart had his attention. Anything to not think about his disastrous day and the way he'd treated Ginny. "So, what happened between you and Lindsay?"

Bart lifted one shoulder in a half shrug. "I think I scared her off. An ex-gambler isn't exactly her idea of good husband material."

"Oh, that again."

# A Mistletoe Christmas

"Hey, it's real enough to your sister. I've bided my time, hoping she'd come around, but so far, she's avoided me." He stroked his jaw. "I think that's an answer of sorts."

Chad couldn't help but empathize. *Women! Inscrutable creatures.*

His sister was a damned riddle. Why she couldn't accept a good, hard-working man like Bart, no matter his past, was beyond him. But his situation with Ginny was a different matter. She was the innocent party. He was the one guilty of asking for what he shouldn't have and for keeping his engagement a secret.

"I wanted to remind you, partner, Rose Gallagher will arrive tomorrow. And she's planning on spending the night, too."

"Oh, that will make my sister happy," Chad said between clenched teeth.

"Yeah, it ain't gonna be pretty. I agree," Bart said. "I'd appreciate it if you'd allow her to stay at the ranch house. That would look better."

"Sure, sure, no problem." Then he considered and shook his head. "If Lindsay will allow it. We'll see."

"Well, Lindsay is one problem. But even more, Rose is pretty sure the Boyd brothers are on their way here. She wants me to go to Alabama with her."

"Why would you do that, especially at shearing time? I need you here."

"To draw off the Boyd brothers. I would prefer them to not terrorize you and Lindsay."

"I'm a grown man, Bart. I can take care of myself and my sister. We just need to be cautious."

"Are you sure?"

"Yeah, I'm sure. When did you say they're coming?"

"Probably during shearing time."

"Better and better. We'll be here at the shearing shed and with the shepherds. Sheer numbers should keep them away."

"Yeah, but starting next week, we need to make certain neither one of us goes to town without the other."

# A Mistletoe Christmas

"You bet. Not a problem. We'll be ready for them."

"Good. That's settled." Bart exhaled. "All right, your turn. Why were you slamming horse tack around?"

Chad stared at his "in-name-only" brother-in-law, trying to decide if he should tell him the truth. *What the hell? He needed to tell someone what was eating him up inside.* And Bart was as close to a brother as he had.

"I think I've fallen in love with Lindsay's friend, Ginny."

Bart clapped him on the back. "Hey, that's not a bad thing. When are you going to pop the question?"

"Never."

"Never?" Bart scratched his jaw.

"Remember what I told you after the Fitzsimmons' fight. That I had proposed to a rancher's daughter last Christmas."

Bart's eyes widened. "Dear Lord, I'd forgotten. But I haven't set eyes on your fiancée and that was months ago."

"We haven't had a chance to see each other. She's an only child, and her parents are older. Her mother's been sick. That's why she hasn't been around. But it don't make my proposal any less binding."

"And if I remember correctly, you weren't too enthusiastic about getting married."

"Now, I'm less than enthusiastic. It's Ginny I want." He astonished himself by admitting the truth. "But I gave my word. And in this country, a man's word is his bond."

# A Mistletoe Christmas

## Chapter Five

Ginny's eyes flew open. Someone had yanked off her blanket. She squinted at the sun streaming through her bedroom window. She had cried herself to sleep last night, and her eyes were puffy and sore.

She glanced up and saw Lindsay standing over her bed, tugging on the blanket. Ginny groaned and rolled into a ball like a porcupine, minus the quills, with her back to her friend.

"What are you doing, Virginia Brown?" Lindsay demanded.

"Leave me alone. I'm sick. Didn't Mama tell you?"

"She did, and she also told me you went riding with my brother yesterday afternoon, and ya'll were gone for hours."

Ginny sighed and rolled over, opening one eye. "I wish Mama hadn't told you that."

"I would have found out sooner or later."

"Yeah, better later than sooner."

"What happened? Why didn't you tell me you were seeing my brother?"

Ginny pulled herself up and swung her legs over the side of the bed. Lindsay sat beside her and put her arm around her shoulders.

"Please, tell me," Lindsay urged.

"You know the day you sent over the bolts of cloth."

"Yes, but you didn't say much about Chad, and I asked you."

"Well, your plan worked better than you expected. We went exploring down by the springs and found an arrowhead." She looked up. "I collect Indian objects. I've found a lot of things by the springs."

"That must have caught his interest. Chad loves to find arrowheads."

"Yeah, we found one and talked about finding more. One thing led to another, and Chad wanted to show me Panther Cave."

# A Mistletoe Christmas

"Why didn't you tell me? That's exactly what I'd hoped for, that my brother would take an interest in you."

"I didn't want to bother you. You have your hands full with your pregnancy, your charities, Bart and—"

"Excuses, excuses."

Ginny lifted her head and gazed at her friend. "I didn't want to get your hopes up. Didn't want you to expect that something would come from one outing."

"I see."

But did Lindsay really understand? She doubted it. She hadn't wanted her friend pressuring her, either. And it would have worked if she'd been able to sleep last night and act normal today, ignoring how much Chad's confession had hurt and destroyed her dreams.

*Now it was too late.*

Lindsay gazed at her, and she could guess what her friend was seeing—her red eyes and puffy face. She must look awful.

Lindsay patted her knee. "I'm sorry I woke you, but I had to know what happened between you and Chad. Looks like things didn't go well."

"No, they didn't." She breathed deeply but couldn't stop her bottom lip from quivering. "I mean he kissed me and said he liked me." She hung her head. "Stupid me, I told him I loved him."

"Oh, Ginny! As a lady, you should never be the first one to make such a declaration."

"I'm not a lady." She combed her fingers through her tangled hair. "And besides, it doesn't matter anyway."

"What do you mean?"

Ginny looked at Lindsay. "Did you know your brother is engaged to Vi Lea Baker?"

"No!" Lindsay covered her mouth with her hand. Then she dropped her hand and knotted her fingers together in her lap. "Chad didn't mention he was engaged. At least, not to me." She shook her head. "And I can guess why. He knows I don't like Vi Lea. Haven't liked her since we were girls."

311

# A Mistletoe Christmas

"He asked her last Christmas, before he knew you'd be coming home."

Lindsay snapped her fingers. "That's it. Now I know why he asked her. That was before he found Bart. Vi Lea is an only child, and her parents are older. Chad must have been planning to join their ranches, hoping to grow bigger and turn a profit."

"I guess," Ginny said. "What does it matter? He's taken. I need to accept it."

"You'll do no such thing, Virginia Brown. Lots of things have changed since then, and I don't think Chad cares for Vi Lea. Otherwise, why would he have taken you out and kissed you?"

She flushed. "I don't know. I haven't courted much, just Will Handley. And he never got around to kissing me, except on the cheek."

"Well, I hope Chad didn't do anything improper. I hope my brother is more honorable than that."

Ginny didn't dare tell his sister how he'd kissed her, open-mouthed and with his tongue or how he'd unbuttoned her shirt and... No, she wouldn't tell her friend what he'd done. It wasn't fair to involve Lindsay. After all, she was the one who'd been in love with Chad for years. And she'd ridden out with him, without a chaperone.

"Your brother has plenty of honor. That's why he refuses to break his engagement."

"Hmmph! He might refuse now. But time will change things. You'll see. Living with you and seeing you every day during shearing time will wear him down."

Ginny covered her friend's hand with hers. "I can't help you with the shearing." She shook her head. "I can't face Chad, day after day, knowing he's promised to another."

"But I need you, Ginny Brown," her friend wailed. "It's too late to find someone else." She splayed her other hand over her expanding abdomen. "What will I do without you?"

\* \* \*

# A Mistletoe Christmas

Ginny stirred the laundry in the big boiling pot. Her mother was doing some mending a neighbor needed before nightfall. Isabella and Lucia were hanging clothes to dry.

The day after she'd confessed what had happened with Chad, Lindsay had confided in her about Bart and his "fancy" woman. Her friend had been upset and said she needed to get away for a few days to visit Abby, her pregnant friend, in Del Rio.

Then she and her mother had been alarmed to hear Bart had been gunned down in front of the train depot. Lindsay and that "fancy woman," called Rose, had taken Bart to Doc Rodgers in Del Rio.

But that had been over a week ago, and she hadn't heard from her friend. She trusted Lindsay was fine but wondered when she was coming home. And she couldn't help but hope, no matter how he'd treated Lindsay, that Bart had survived and was doing well.

As if her thoughts had summoned her, Ginny heard the sound of her friend's voice call out, "Ginny! Mrs. Brown, I'm home."

She dropped the stirring paddle and glanced up to find her friend rushing toward her with her arms outstretched. Ginny laughed and met her half-way, falling into her arms and hugging her.

"I'm so glad you're back, Lindsay. I was just thinking about you and wondering when you'd get home."

"I'm happy to be here," Lindsay said.

"And what about your husband?" Her mother had dropped her mending and joined them in the middle of the yard.

"Mrs. Brown, I mean, Emma, thank you for asking." Lindsay glanced at Ginny from the corner of her eye. "I'm happy to report he's on the mend. I stayed until the Doc was sure there was no infection, and he was healing."

"And what about your husband's *friend*?" Ginny asked.

"Oh, you mean Rose. She went home to Alabama."

Ginny sighed. "Mama, could you get us some coffee or tea? I'm sure Lindsay is thirsty."

# A Mistletoe Christmas

Her mother crossed her arms over her chest. "If that's a polite way to get rid of me to find out how Lindsay's relationship is with her husband, you can quit conniving." She nodded her head at Lindsay. "I've suspected your marriage wasn't real for a while."

Ginny gasped and turned to her friend. "I did *not* tell my mother, Lindsay. You said it was up to me, but in the end, I didn't feel it was my place to tell her."

Her mother put her hand on Lindsay's arm. "No, child, Ginny didn't tell me. There's enough gossip and speculation in town without my daughter confirming it. And me, being the local washerwoman, hears all."

"Why don't I hear anything?" Ginny asked.

"Because you're shy and don't talk to people." Her mother pinched her cheek. "Just like you kept Lindsay's situation to yourself."

"Oh, that makes sense," Ginny said.

"Well, it's a relief, I guess, to be open with you both," Lindsay admitted. "And I wish I had good news about Bart and our marriage, but I don't."

Her mother pursed her lips. "You need to give the man a chance, especially since he's willing to take another man's child as his own."

It was Lindsay's turn to gasp. "You know everything?"

"Pretty much," Emma admitted.

"I did try to make up things with Bart, especially after worrying about him dying from being shot." She shook her head. "I did a lot of soul searching and realized I shouldn't judge people. I don't like Bart's former profession, and unfortunately, it's the reason he got shot. But I still shouldn't judge him."

"What do you mean, it's why he got shot?" Emma asked.

"He was gunned down by the Boyd brothers. Bart explained about them, the night before I left for Del Rio. The next morning, after I told you I'd be going, Bart was at the station, seeing Rose Gallagher off on the train."

"His fancy woman?" Ginny asked.

# A Mistletoe Christmas

Lindsay dropped her head and gazed at the dusty yard. "It's true, she's a madam, but she's had a hard life. I shouldn't have judged her, either. She took care of Bart after he was shot. I couldn't have done better." She lifted her head. "And I don't believe she and Bart are, uh... Well, you know, involved... not anymore. They're just old friends, and she stopped to warn Bart about the Boyd brothers who are from Tucson, where she lives, now." She shrugged. "I was probably jealous of Rose. I care for Bart; I know that now."

"Well, that's a lot to take in," Ginny's mother said.

"Yes," Ginny agreed.

"And Bart was shot that morning?" Emma asked.

"Yes, in front of the train depot in broad daylight." Lindsay clenched her jaw. "I've never been so terrified in my life."

Ginny's mother patted her shoulder. "I can imagine." She shook her head. "What I don't understand is why these Boyd's are after your husband?"

"Because he beat them at cards, and they want their money back, saying he cheated. My brother assures me Bart doesn't cheat. He just has a way of keeping up with the cards in his head that gives him an advantage. I don't understand it, and I don't like that he was a gambler. But it's in the past, and Bart is trying to start a new life."

"And these men are willing to kill for some money?" Ginny asked.

"Yes, they're outlaws. Mean men without consciences." Lindsay cleared her throat and smoothed her features, as if she could hide her real feelings. "Bart says they might come after Chad, too." She gazed at Ginny. "My brother saved Bart in February after the big prize fight. That's when they first came looking to take back their money. Chad shot one of the Boyd's to save Bart, and the man died of an infection from the wound. Bart says they'll want revenge on my brother."

"Oh, no, that's awful!" Ginny exclaimed. Terror tore at her with its sharp teeth, shaking her until she trembled. She reached

315

inside her apron pocket and touched the arrowhead she'd found with Chad.

Lindsay turned toward her and took her hand, squeezing it. "Yes, I just learned all of this the night before I decided to go to Del Rio. Now you know everything. Why I needed to get away and think and then what happened. It's all been terrible. But despite everything, I had a lot of time to think about Bart and how I feel while he was recovering." She released Ginny's hand, and Ginny saw tears at the corners of her friend's eyes. "I know we have a lot to work out, but I do care for him." Her voice dropped to a whisper. "I think I'm in love with him."

"So, you two made up?" Ginny asked.

"No, we didn't. I wanted to. Wanted him to forgive me for being judgmental, especially about Rose and—"

"And despite the Boyd's gunning for Chad and Bart?" Ginny couldn't help but ask. "That's because he was a gambler—"

"I know. But Bart didn't do anything wrong, except to associate with bad men in his former profession." She shrugged. "If I hold that against him, when he's changed, then every woman, everywhere, would need to hold all their men's past against them." She grabbed Ginny's hand again. "Don't you see. I have to look to the future." She released Ginny's hand and cupped her abdomen. "Not the past, if I want to make a new life for myself."

"Of course, we understand," Ginny's mother said. "No one is perfect. We all need forgiveness." Her mother nudged her. "Am I right?"

Ginny didn't know what to say—as much as she loved Lindsay—the thought that Chad might be in danger because of helping Bart turned her legs to jelly and twisted her stomach into knots. Traces of resentment, along with her engrained Christian forgiveness clashed inside of her. One thing was certain, none of it was Lindsay's fault, and her friend was just as distressed as she was. Even if she was trying hard not to show it.

# A Mistletoe Christmas

"Of course, Lindsay," she said. "Bart is a good man and a hard worker. He's changed, as you say, and we should all stand behind him."

"Thank you, thank you." Lindsay put her arm around Ginny's shoulder and smiled at her mother. "I so appreciate your understanding."

"But you didn't make up?" Ginny asked again.

"No, he said he needs time. That he's not certain I can overcome my prejudice against him." Lindsay sighed. "Given how I've treated him, I can understand how he feels."

"Give it time, Lindsay." Her mother said. "If he really cares for you, he'll come around."

"I hope you're right," Lindsay said. "He should be getting back soon, though, as he needs to help Chad with the shearing."

Ginny smiled and laced her arm around Lindsay's waist, leading her to the grape arbor. "Won't you sit? And I'll get some tea."

"Thank you, I would love a cup of tea."

"One thing, though, about the shearing…" Ginny hesitated and then plunged ahead. "Uh, Lindsay, I've had a lot of time to think about the shearing since you've been gone." She lowered her head and bit her lip. "I don't think I can face Chad. I know you convinced me before you left but—"

"Virginia Marie Brown, don't be such a mouse!" Her mother exclaimed.

She lifted her head and glared at her mother. "Excuse me, Mama."

"You're not going to renege on helping your friend because you want her brother as a sweetheart, but he's already engaged to that Vi Lea Baker from over Comstock way."

"You know about that, too?" Ginny asked. "Why did you let me ride out with him then?"

"Thought a little time with my daughter might convince him that he was making a big mistake."

"Well, Mama, it didn't work."

317

# A Mistletoe Christmas

"I know. I was here when you rode to Panther Cave. And I saw how you were when you got back."

"I told you I was sick."

"And I knew better. Ye've been mooning over Chad MacKillian since you first wore long skirts. I'm not blind, after all."

Lindsay laughed. "I think the opposite of blind, Emma. You seem to know everything."

"Not much gets by me." She nodded and put her hands on her hips. "I'll come out to help when I can during the shearing time. Though, I have to admit, it will be hard, getting away from my business."

"Oh, please, if it's a hardship, I understand. You letting Ginny go is more than enough."

"Well, maybe, but I will try to come out." She turned to go back to the boiling pot and then turned around again. "But I don't know as we'll get much done on your Christmas clothes with you and Ginny working on the ranch."

"I expected that," Lindsay said. "We'll start back after the shearing."

Lindsay looked at Ginny.

She met her friend's gaze and said, "Guess I'll be coming out to the ranch. When do you need me?"

"Let me get home and find out if the shearing crew has arrived. I'll come and get you, but you might start packing."

Ginny lowered her head and scrunched her shoulders together. The last thing she wanted was to be thrown together with Lindsay's brother. But it seemed both her friend and her mother expected her to go. *So be it.*

"I'll be packed when you come for me," she said. "And now, can I get our tea?"

* * *

Ginny struggled with the huge black cauldron filled with *frijoles*. Her toe struck a rock, and she staggered. The immense pot tipped, sloshing the thick broth and a few stray beans over her dress and apron. She cursed under her breath and lowered the cauldron to the ground, rubbing the small of her back and staring at her stained clothing.

Now she understood why Lindsay had been so desperate for any help she could get. Shearing sheep was a never-ending round of too-long days of the worst kind of drudgery for both man and beast.

During the past few days, she'd wished herself back home, doing laundry and mending. Compared to work on the ranch, she and her mother lived a simple life. Never again, would she envy ranchers and their large landholdings.

The shearing crew, numbering forty men, had to be fed three times a day. And because the work demanded the last ounce of their strength, they gobbled everything in sight like a plague of locusts.

Rising an hour before dawn, she baked bread. Her helpers, the wives of the shepherds, made stacks and stacks of tortillas. They fried salt pork, slaughtered and roasted chickens, simmered beans with *chili* peppers, barbecued beef and *cabrito*, cooked rice, and brewed kettles of strong black coffee.

Lindsay was in charge, but she needed Ginny to supervise the shepherd's wives with the arduous tasks of lugging around food stores and getting the huge meals served. But Lindsay pitched in, too, helping with the lighter cooking chores, like kneading, chopping, and stirring.

And her friend was invaluable when it came to ordering and obtaining the necessary supplies. She'd helped with several shearings before she moved to Boston.

True to her word, Ginny's mother had come out twice already and helped prepare the evening meal. But still, the constant round of work, no matter how many helping hands, had taken its toll on Ginny.

Late at night, when the last pot and pan was scoured and put away, she fell into bed, in the clothes she'd worn all day, and slept for a few fitful hours. The next day, before sun-up, and after a hasty sponge bath and change of clothing, she was back in the kitchen, stoking the embers in the stove and kneading the bread dough she'd left overnight to rise.

She leaned down and strained to lift the cauldron. With the heavy pot dragging on her arms, she tottered toward the outdoor fire in the ranch yard, which the women kept going to cook and warm the food. Some preparation was done in the kitchen, but the quantity of food they had to cook was more than the kitchen stove could handle.

Startled by a light touch on her shoulder and a sudden lifting of her burden, she raised her head and gazed into Chad's face. And even though he was covered in dirt and grime, just looking at his handsome face made her heart flutter.

She might be staying in the same house with him but when their paths had crossed, she would flush with embarrassment and hurry past.

"Let me carry that for you," he said.

It was the first private words he'd spoken to her since she'd arrived at the ranch. He glanced at her filthy apron, dripping with bean juice and added, "You look a bit the worse for wear."

Humiliation washed over her, scalding her cheeks. She bit her lip. She was grateful for his help, but she hated him seeing her like this. Not to mention all the previous days when she'd been sweaty and bedraggled, serving the meals.

She'd hoped he hadn't noticed. That they'd both put the day at Panther Cave behind them. But obviously, he'd been watching her. And she was mortified, realizing how she must look in her old, worn-out clothes, now stained with the countless meals they'd served.

She lifted her hand to smooth her hair, and then she snatched it away as if her head was on fire. Not only were her clothes filthy, she couldn't remember the last time she'd washed her hair, and it straggled from the knot on top of her head, falling in lank tendrils against her neck and brow. Swiping at the hair hanging in her eyes, her hand came away streaked with dirt and smoke.

# A Mistletoe Christmas

Her humiliation grew, and she slumped, curling her shoulders, as if to hide herself. Covered in perspiration, mixed with the constant churn of dust from the holding pens and shearing shed, along with smoke from the cooking fires, she must look and smell as if she'd been rolling in a pigsty.

She stood rooted to the ground, praying a West Texas sinkhole would open at her feet and swallow her.

He hung the cauldron over the fire and said, "Aren't you going to thank me for hauling your beans?"

She closed her eyes and said a silent prayer for strength. Then she lifted her chin and gazed at him. She refused to let him know how shamed she was by her appearance. Instead, she moved toward him with a measured stance, as if she was leading the first quadrille at a fancy-dress cotillion. Just like Lindsay had taught her.

His green-blue eyes widened, regarding her measured advance with interest, and he smiled. White teeth shone against his dark tan. His tawny blond hair was a mess, too, most of it having escaped the leather thong he tied it back with. And he was covered from head-to-toe with dirt and sheep manure, but he'd never looked so handsome to her as he did now.

She returned his smile and stopped before the open fire, executing a mock curtsy. "Thank you."

He nodded. "You're welcome. Come watch me shear. You haven't ventured into the shearing shed. And as hard as you've been working, you deserve a break and to see why cooking for the men is so important, given how hard we work." He held out a grimy hand to her.

She hesitated, wanting to go but feeling she should refuse his invitation. Shaking her head, she turned away. "I need to pluck some chickens for tonight's supper. I don't have the time."

He stepped in front of her, and she remembered him kissing her at Panther Cave. Remembered? Her lips were imprinted with his, and she'd never kiss another man without thinking of him.

He was standing so near she could smell the wool and charcoal mixed with tar oil on him. And the look in his eyes was so

# A Mistletoe Christmas

compelling it took her breath away. Heat radiated from his body, and she remembered the warmth of his embrace.

"I must get back to the kitchen." She tried to brush past him.

He touched her arm. "Supper can wait. Please."

His touch galvanized her, driving her to ground like a hunted animal, re-establishing his mastery over her. Her heart jolted and a pooling warmth spread through her, burning a path to her stomach and beyond. She wanted nothing more than to be enfolded in his strong arms.

*But he didn't belong to her—he belonged to another.*

"Come," he said.

And heaven help her, she followed.

"There's one thing I don't understand about shearing," she called out.

He stopped and turned back. "Yes?"

"Why two shearings, spring and autumn? I understand the spring one, but in autumn…"

"A good question." The look in his eyes was admiring. "It's our weather," he said. "We have such mild winters; the sheep don't get cold." He rubbed his stubbled chin. "And having two shearings keeps the wool short and relatively cleaner. Used to be a big economic incentive to raise sheep in West Texas, but now there are other things to consider."

"Oh," was all she said, but thanks to Lindsay, she understood about the tariff and railroad rates.

He took her hand and said, "You're a wonder, Ginny. So intelligent and…" He lowered his head and dropped her hand. "Come on then. I better get back to the shed."

Raised in town, she'd never been in a shearing shed before. The shed was a long, low structure, open on three sides and roofed with shingles. Rain or shine, the shearers were protected from the weather. The open-fronted building was surrounded by a welter of pens to direct the sheep before shearing and to hold them after they were relieved of their wool.

# A Mistletoe Christmas

Stepping inside, Ginny glanced around. The shed was lined with men, each with sheep tied at their feet, all working at top speed, holding sheep and cutting off the wool in huge swathes.

The men were engulfed in clouds of dust and the three-sided structure resounded with the terrified bleating of the sheep and the Spanish curses of the men. Ginny held her hand over her nose, as her senses were assaulted with the complex smell of human perspiration mingling with the distinctive stench of wet wool, and the acrid tang of sheep's blood and dung.

Bart, his arm in a sling, sat to one side, with paper and pencil, keeping tally of the number of fleeces for each shearer. Lindsay had told her a strict accounting must be kept, as the shearers were paid four cents per fleece.

Three Mexican boys, who accompanied the crew, assisted. One to keep the shearing tools sharp, using a grindstone and a wooden frame called a "hootnanny," which held the blades at the precise angle to whet them to razor sharpness. Another boy dabbed any accidental cuts made to the sheep from a can of oil mixed with charcoal. And the third boy bundled the fleeces and tied them with twine, stuffing them into a heavy burlap bag held open on a ring.

Chad winked at her. "Watch."

He rushed off and entered one of the pens. After a few moments, he emerged, guiding a protesting sheep between his knees. He grabbed a pair of rawhide thongs dangling from the rafters and tied down his first sheep. He returned to the pen four more times and repeated the procedure, tying off both the front and hind legs.

Rising from securing the last sheep, he caught her gaze and grinned like a boy with his first pony. He wiped the perspiration from his face and unbuttoned his shirt, stripping to the waist.

Ginny's breath caught in her throat. Her heart pounded against her ribs. The sight of his naked chest made her dizzy with yearning. She wanted to touch him like she'd never wanted anything before. She clenched the wooden rail, her nails biting into the wood.

# A Mistletoe Christmas

She was at the middle of a vortex, being pulled under by a force more powerful than a Texas twister.

She bit her lip until she tasted blood. She tried to concentrate on Chad's shearing skills. She watched while he retrieved a shearing tool from the Mexican boy who was sharpening them. Bending to his task, he clipped the wool loose from all four legs and then worked backwards from the head so the fleece would come free in one piece. When he finished shearing the sheep, he rose from his crouched position and tossed the wool to the Mexican boy bundling the wool.

He turned to her, caught her gaze, and smiled.

He bent over the next sheep, and she forgot to follow his swiftly moving hands this time. Instead her gaze was riveted on his broad shoulders and naked chest. She couldn't look away, couldn't stop from wanting to explore the hollows of his collarbone where it melded into the sculpted beauty of his shoulders.

His powerful muscles bunched beneath his skin, gliding with a grace she compared to a thoroughbred horse. Perspiration and dirt covered his chest, matting the whorls of blond hair on his abdomen.

*If she never got to touch him, she thought she might die.*

She released the wood and cradled her throbbing temples, closing her eyes and trying to banish him from her thoughts. And praying for deliverance from her sinful yearnings.

The frantic sound of Serafina Gómez's voice broke her feverish thoughts. "*Señorita, señorita* Ginny, you must come!"

She opened her eyes and stared into the distraught face of Lindsay's housekeeper.

"*Las muchachas* are taking a siesta, and the chickens wait to be plucked. The beans in the cauldron burned for want of stirring. There will be no supper tonight!" Serafina threw her apron over her head.

"Don't worry, Serafina. We'll get supper ready, even if it's a bit late." She put her arm around the other woman's shoulders. "Thank you for finding me. And I appreciate your concern."

# A Mistletoe Christmas

Arm in arm with Serafina, she quit the shearing shed without a word or glance. But as she walked away, she felt Chad's gaze burning into her back.

Maybe it was just her imagination. If she turned again, he'd be busy at work. Wouldn't he? And why had he wanted her to watch him, anyway? What purpose did it serve?

They'd barely spoken since she'd arrived at the ranch. Was that about to change? Did he regret telling her that he was engaged? Was he thinking of breaking his engagement?

Questions circled in her head. She wished she knew what Chad had been thinking when he'd rescued the bean pot and demanded she watch him.

# A Mistletoe Christmas

## Chapter Six

Ginny glanced up at the full autumn moon, riding high in the sky. Her Papa would have called it a 'hunter's moon.' He liked to augment the salt pork and jerked beef they could buy at the general store, and their own chickens, with small game he shot. Sometimes, he even brought down a white-tail deer, and they had more venison than they could eat.

An owl hooted, reminding her the full moon had risen a long time ago, and she was light-headed with exhaustion, waiting until after midnight to go to the stream to bathe and wash her hair. Her encounter with Chad today had convinced her she smelled, and she wanted to be clean all over.

Filling the slipper bathtub Lindsay used with countless buckets of water and then washing her hair in the pump sink, seemed like more effort than staying up late enough to ensure her privacy.

She clutched her dressing gown and towel and skirted Bart's cabin, moving downstream and past a curtain of willows. His cabin was dark. He must be asleep by now, as was Lindsay and her brother, at the ranch house. And the last of their helpers had departed for their cabins hours before, once the supper dishes were washed and put away.

In approximately another five hours, one hour before sunup, the unrelenting grind of cooking would begin again. Fortunately, they only had a few more days to go. Lindsay was already planning the dance to celebrate the autumn shearing.

She glanced around and saw nothing except a few sheep, minus their fleeces, lying on the hillside. No one was around.

She could imagine the cool slide of water over her body as she stripped off her filthy clothes. These would go into the wash shed with the rest. She had a fluffy white cotton robe to wear back, and it covered her from head to foot.

# A Mistletoe Christmas

Taking a bar of Lindsay's lavender soap from the pocket of her robe, she moved to a grassy stretch on the creek bank and dropped the robe. The cool night air whispered over her body, raising goosebumps on her skin, just as Chad's touch did.

She stuck her toe in the water and gasped at how chilly the stream was. It had been hot all autumn, and she hadn't expected the water to be cool enough to take her breath away. She gritted her teeth and waded into the creek. And she prayed, it being dark, any snakes that might be nearby, wouldn't be moving around.

Wading into the water and thinking about snakes, reminded her of the day at Panther Cave. If only she could turn back time and forget how the day had ended. She sighed. *Pretty dreams, useless dreams.*

She bent her knees and plunged her head under the water, coming up and gasping, with her wet hair streaming down her shoulders. Once in the water, she'd warmed to it, and the silky liquid was a balm to her spirit. She took the sweet-smelling soap and worked up a lather.

Tomorrow, she'd smell like her friend, Lindsay. She smiled to herself and worked the soap into her hair, combing through the long, brown lengths with her fingers and massaging her scalp to get rid of the accumulated dirt and oil.

Satisfied she was clean all over, she plunged under the water again, rinsing off the soap. Her hair floated around her in long strips on the moon-gilded creek. She wished she'd brought a comb but used her fingers again, to make certain she'd rinsed all the soap from her hair.

She lifted her arms and stretched, savoring the feeling of being clean all over and all at once. Then she yawned, and the lateness of the hour overtook her, making her want to drop and float in the now-warm water and sleep.

But that wouldn't do. She needed to get back to the ranch house and go to bed. An hour before sun-up would come all too soon.

She turned around and started wading for the shore, looking for the mound of her new white robe to guide her to the grassy

# A Mistletoe Christmas

patch where she'd undressed. But she didn't see her robe. That was odd. Her clothes were brown and grimy and the much-washed towel she'd brought was a gray color. But she'd expected her new white robe to stand out, especially in the moonlight.

The closer she got to shore, the more concerned she was. She didn't think she'd moved downstream that far. The willows were still there, and she glimpsed her clothes and towel hanging from their branches. But where was her robe?

"Were you looking for this?" A deep masculine voice startled her.

She gasped and looked up to see Chad emerge from the willows, holding her robe in his hands.

Chad couldn't take his eyes off Ginny. My God, she was beautiful. Like one of those water nymphs they'd discussed in school when he'd studied Greek mythology. Her long, lean limbs, tiny waist, and full, rounded bosom were every man's dream. Just gazing at her aroused him. He wanted her, wanted her no matter what, and damn the consequences.

"Chad, turn your back and drop my robe." Her voice warbled, as if she was trembling inside. "What are you doing here?" She clutched herself, moving her hands and arms over her body, trying to shield herself from his gaze. Then she turned her back to him.

But she couldn't hide the dimples above her curvy backside or her backside for that matter. He was a cad, a terrible cad to have followed her from the ranch house and grabbed her robe, knowing perfectly well what he was doing.

Since the first day she'd come to the ranch to help Lindsay cook and wash for the shearing crew, he'd watched her. Watched her and wanted her. Had meant to approach her a hundred times a day and only found the courage to do so today.

And he hadn't slept, either, not more than a few hours each night, though, he was dog-tired and running on black coffee and sheer will power. Every night, he'd thought about her and tossed in

# A Mistletoe Christmas

his single bed, remembering that day at Panther Cave when he'd held her in his arms.

He remembered how sweet and right she'd felt. How her golden-brown eyes twinkled and her cupid's bow mouth lured him. How soft her skin was and how good she smelled.

Yes, he remembered and he couldn't help wanting her, even though, he had no right. Even though, he was already spoken for.

"Chad!" Her voice had risen to a shriek and if he wasn't careful, she'd waken Bart.

He should apologize, but he couldn't. It would be a lie.

"All right. Here." He put the robe on the grassy patch where he'd found it.

"Turn around."

"Do I have to?" He couldn't help but grin.

She gasped again.

"I'm turning. I'm turning." And he twisted around, presenting his back to her.

He could hear her moving through the water, knowing she was getting closer. He heard the pebbles slide beneath her feet... her feet. He groaned. He loved her naked feet and toes. Just looking at her sweet body stirred him and made him want to take her in his arms and never let her go.

*What was wrong with him?*

She was a respectable woman. She might be poor and landless, but he knew she was a virgin. But knowing didn't change anything. He wanted her and he wanted her now. He turned to find her gathering her clothes from the willow branches. He put his hand on her arm.

She gazed at him, her eyes wide, and then she jerked her arm away. "I can't believe you would do such a thing, Chad." She lifted her hand. "I should slap you for such an ugly trick."

He turned his cheek toward her. "You're right. I deserve it." He pointed to his cheek. "Hit me."

She dropped her hand. "I can't hit you, though, I can't imagine what possessed you to... to watch me like that. What were

329

you thinking? And how did you know I'd go to the creek to wash. I thought everyone was asleep."

"I haven't been able to sleep much, even though I'm exhausted." He shook his head. "Not since you came to stay at the ranch. I think about you all the time, sleeping in the next bedroom, and I can't sleep."

"I don't know if I believe you, though, it explains how you knew I came to the creek."

"I didn't know, but I woke up and heard you, moving around."

"All right, so you couldn't sleep, but you still shouldn't have followed me." She raised her head and thrust out her sharp little chin. "What would you say if I told your sister what you did?"

Shame slammed into him, snaking through his gut. Lindsay would be furious, not to mention disappointed in him. He couldn't allow Ginny to tell his sister. No, he *wouldn't* allow it.

He pulled her to him and cradled her in his arms. "I'm sorry, very sorry for what I did. It was, ahhh, it was as if I couldn't stop myself. As if I hoped..." He paused and lowered his head. "You said you loved me that day at Panther Cave." He raised his head and snagged her gaze. "I've been doing a lot of thinking, Ginny, and I believe I love you, too."

"I should have never said I loved you."

"Did you mean it?"

She bit her lip.

Please, dear God, he wanted to be the one nibbling on her lips, but first, somehow, he had to convince her of his seriousness. If he was serious, he had to marry her. There was no other way to have her. And if he didn't have her soon, he'd burn up inside with wanting her.

"I said I loved you, Ginny. Do you still love me?"

"I... I can't. We can't. You're spoken for."

"Damn my engagement! I got engaged before I knew you." He wanted to shake her, but instead, he pulled her closer. She smelled like his sister—of lavender. He wanted to bury his nose in her sweet-smelling hair and grovel at her feet. But instead he said, "I'll break my engagement. I want you, only you."

She pulled away and stepped back. Taking her streaming hair in one hand, she wrung it out and then wound the towel over her head. "What do you mean by wanting? I'm respectable and a God-fearing woman and—"

He stopped her protests by kissing her and sucking on her full bottom lip, the one she'd been biting, only moments before. He teased the seam of her lips with his tongue, demanding entrance.

She went limp in his embrace and opened her mouth to him.

And he plundered her offering, kissing her until he was dizzy with desire. He went down on one knee, pulling her down beside him. He covered her body with his and pushed at the opening of her robe.

"No, no!" She thumped on his chest. "Stop now or I'll call for Bart. His cabin is just around the willows. He'll hear me."

He groaned and took several deep breaths. He pulled himself up and sat with his legs crossed in front of him. "I want you now and forever more, Ginny. Forgive me for going too far."

He combed his hand through his hair and considered. Was he really ready to marry Ginny? He knew he wanted her in the worst of ways, but marriage was another matter.

She got to her feet. "I think we should avoid each other. You might want me, but it's in the wrong way." She crossed her arms over her chest. "You know it is."

Damn her to three kinds of hell, but she was probably right. Still, he couldn't let her go. Wouldn't let her go. "I said I'd break my engagement." He almost growled.

"And then? Where would that leave us?"

"You want to get married?"

"Not the kind of proposal I was hoping for."

"What do you want me to do, Ginny? I can't stop thinking about you. Can't stop desiring you. It's turning me inside out."

She shook her head. "Oh, Chad, I wish—"

# A Mistletoe Christmas

"What do you wish? I want to make all your dreams come true."

"I wish you loved me like I've loved you for as long as I can remember." She grimaced, wrinkling her freckled nose. "This wanting is all right for a time. But after the fire dies down—then what?"

"Believe me, this fire won't die down. I won't let it."

She bit her lip again. "I wish I could believe you." And then she brushed past him and climbed the slope to the ranch house.

* * *

"Hold still, Ginny, and suck it in," Lindsay said.

Ginny's face turned red with the effort of holding her breath and she gasped, "Is this really necessary?"

"It is if you want my brother to break his engagement and marry you. You said he almost proposed that night by the creek." Lindsay tugged at the stays on the corset.

She'd told Chad's sister some of what had happened by the creek, but not all of it. She'd omitted the part about Chad taking her robe and looking at her while she was stark naked. Maybe she should have told Lindsay, as she'd threatened to do.

But sweet Jesus, she didn't know what to do. Didn't know if he was serious or not. Chad had blithely mentioned Vi Lea would be coming to their shearing dance, this morning at breakfast. And then he'd solemnly declared the shearing was done, thanked and paid the crew, dismissing them to move on to the next ranch.

He'd looked at her with a challenge in his eyes, but she didn't know what he was expecting. That she'd surrender her virginity to him, so he'd break off his engagement? She shuddered, thinking how cheap that sounded. No, Chad needed to love her in the right way, not the wrong way. And that was why she had her doubts about getting "dolled up" for him.

"Stand there and don't breathe while I take a few quick tucks in the waist of your dress so it doesn't hang on you," Lindsay said.

# A Mistletoe Christmas

"This dress wouldn't hang on me, if you hadn't poured me into this… this awful corset," she muttered. "And if this is what it takes to hold your brother's interest, I don't think I want the honor."

"Yes, you do. You need for him to break with Vi Lea and make a proper proposal to you."

Ginny twisted around and opened her mouth to speak, but before she got the words out, she yelped, "Ouch! What was that?"

"I told you to hold still. I jabbed you with the needle," Lindsay replied and pushed her back into position. "Stand straight. Don't move."

"Lindsay, I'm certain my figure in this dress and your tight corset will make quite an impression, but what about my face and hair? I just can't imagine—"

"One thing at a time," her friend cut her off. "Before we're through, you won't know yourself. Tonight, I'm going to apply some eye paint, rouge and powder so we'll know how much to put on tomorrow. That way, you'll feel comfortable with how it looks on you at night."

"I can't believe people won't notice. I sure won't be looking like my usual drab self. And Mama is coming. I know she'll realize I'm wearing… paint."

"Don't be such a worrywart. Everyone will assume you look different because of your new dress and hair, which will be part of it. No one needs to know the other part. It will work, you just need to have faith. People see what they want to see," Lindsay added philosophically.

"I guess you're right. I hope my mother doesn't catch us out."

"She won't."

They fell silent while Lindsay finished sewing the inside seams of Ginny's green muslin dress. Lindsay bent over to tie off the thread by biting it in two.

"I hope Chad breaks with Vi Lea," Ginny whispered.

# A Mistletoe Christmas

"He will. I don't know how he can't. I've seen the way he looks at you."

"I hope you're right."

Lindsay stepped back and asked, "There, how does that look?"

Ginny stared at her image in the mirror. "I look like… like… Oh, Lindsay, do I really look that good?"

She ran her hands over her figure and covered her mouth with her hand. "I look like a vamp!" She exclaimed and wondered if wearing such a form-fitting dress was wise.

After all, Chad had no problem admiring her figure. But that wasn't enough. She wanted him to admire her as a person. And she wanted him to love her, but not in the passionate, stormy way he seemed to favor. She wanted him to love her as his future wife, the woman he would share his life with—not some passing fling.

"So, do you like it?" Lindsay asked.

"Yes, I guess so."

"Don't bowl me over with your enthusiasm."

"I just worry."

"You *are* a worrywart. What is bothering you now?"

Ginny bit her lip and considered. As close as she was to Lindsay, she couldn't uncover more of her shame and admit she believed Lindsay's brother lusted after her but didn't love her. Maybe she was wrong. Maybe the shearing dance tomorrow night would prove it. Maybe he would break his engagement with Vi Lea.

Ginny raised her head. "I don't want to give Chad the wrong idea."

"Oh, please, a little temptation never hurt anybody."

"Maybe. Will you be at the dance?"

Lindsay shook her head. "I'll stay for a little while and wear my biggest dress."

"How are things with you and Bart?"

"The same. He hasn't changed since he got back from Del Rio." Lindsay sighed and glanced at her rounded stomach. "Maybe it's for the best."

334

# A Mistletoe Christmas

Ginny patted her friend's arm.

"Enough of this doom and gloom," Lindsay declared. "Let me unbutton the dress so you can hang it up and keep it from getting wrinkled."

"Can I take off this awful corset?"

"Yes, and put on your nightgown. We've got more work to do. First, I'm going to wash your hair with lemon juice."

"Whatever for?"

Lindsay winked. "It's an old trick my mother taught me when I was a girl. The lemon juice will bring out golden highlights in your light brown hair."

"But your hair is so blond, why would your mother use lemon juice?"

"Not on my hair, on hers," Lindsay explained. "She had light brown hair like you.

"My father was dark blonde like Chad. My hair is the lightest in the family."

"Lucky you." Ginny paused for a moment and bent down to stroke Minnie, Lindsay's Maltese puppy. "I would have liked to have known your mother and father."

"Yes, that would have been nice," Lindsay agreed.

"Now, scoot," Lindsay said. "I'll get the soap and towels and lemon juice."

Ginny did as her friend asked, getting undressed and putting on her nightshift with her robe belted on top. She exhaled, realizing she'd never wear this robe again without thinking of the night at the creek and Chad.

They spent the remainder of the evening, in girlish harmony, perfecting her toilette. Lindsay washed and rinsed her hair, and then she towel-dried and brushed it until it shone with deep chestnut highlights of gold and bronze. After her hair was dry, she piled it on top of Ginny's head in soft ringlets with trailing wisps of hair framing her face. The effect was stunning, it enhanced the oval shape of her face and even softened her pointed chin.

# A Mistletoe Christmas

Next, they giggled and frittered the hours away, applying and re-applying cosmetics to her face until they were satisfied with the results and certain no one would guess she was wearing face paint—not even her own mother.

After a great deal of experimentation, she'd opted for a touch of rouge, which delineated her cheekbones and made her eyes seem brighter. A light dusting of powder to cover the freckles across the bridge of her nose, and she allowed Lindsay to darken her brown eyelashes.

Gazing at her reflection, she was amazed at the transformation. Gone was the timid, mousy Ginny she knew to be replaced by a desirable woman. Maybe she wasn't truly beautiful, but Lindsay had worked so much magic she felt beautiful.

She leaned forward into the mirror, turning her head from side to side. Then she lifted her eyes and gazed at her friend's reflection. "Dearest Lindsay, you were right. I don't look like myself, and I feel transformed."

Lindsay nodded and said, "Told you so."

She turned around and hugged her friend. "How can I ever thank you enough?"

And she meant it. At least, with her friend's help, she looked like a woman grown, a woman to take seriously, a woman to consider as a wife. And she hoped Chad would see the transformation and view her in a new and positive light.

# A Mistletoe Christmas

## Chapter Seven

Ginny, along with her mother and Lindsay, were wedged into the kitchen with Serafina and her sister, Delfina, and several of the shepherds' wives, working elbow to elbow, preparing the food for the dance. They'd fried chicken and pork chops, deviled eggs, boiled potatoes, cooked vegetables, and baked bread and pies. The other shepherds' wives helped outside with the bubbling cauldron of beans, the whole sheep being slowly baked in an earthen pit, and the goat roasting on a spit.

Even though she was busy helping to get the food ready, Ginny was nervous, thinking about how dressed up she would be and wondering what Chad would think.

Thinking of Chad, he suddenly appeared at the back door and said, "First guests, the Sanderson's are here. I can greet everyone. I'm dressed already." His gaze slid over their stained aprons and floury hands. "Don't y'all need to get dressed? Can't the girls finish the cooking and carry everything outside?" He pulled a pocket watch from his vest and consulted it. "The band should be here in less than an hour."

Lindsay fisted her right hand and it put it on her hip. Ginny could see she was taking a silent inventory of the food. "Yes, Chad, I think you're right. It's time we got dressed. The girls can finish." She inclined her head at Serafina. "You know what to do. Right? If you need me, just knock on my bedroom door."

"*Sí, Señorita*, I will get everything ready." She bobbed her head. "You must go and dress."

"Chad, is Bart coming? Do you know?" Lindsay asked.

"To greet our neighbors and eat. But he's not staying for the dance. Says his shoulder is bothering him."

"Sure, I'll bet it is," Lindsay muttered under her breath. Louder, she said, "Thanks, big brother, for letting me know. I'll probably come back to the house after the dance gets underway."

337

# A Mistletoe Christmas

Chad bowed at the waist and then turned his gaze to her. "Ginny Brown, may I have the pleasure of leading the first quadrille with you."

Ginny could feel the blush heating her neck and throat. She ducked her head and bit her lip. "My pleasure, I'm sure. I'll be glad to start the dance with you."

She'd had a sudden bout of shyness, what with him asking her in front of everyone, but if she'd been alone, she would have jumped up and down, shouting for joy. He knew his fiancé was coming tonight, and yet he wanted to start the dance with her. Maybe he really was going to throw over Vi Lea.

Thinking about it, her pulse raced and her heart fluttered. And a thousand butterflies were starting their own quadrille in her stomach.

He bowed again and retreated outside to welcome the Sanderson's.

"Where do you want me to change, Lindsay?" Her mother asked.

"You can have the extra bedroom. Ginny and I will share my room." Lindsay stole a glance at her and winked.

"How kind of you. Just show me which room," her mother said.

Lindsay took her mother's arm and directed her to the third bedroom in the house. Then Lindsay joined her in their bedroom, and they fell on the bed together, laughing.

"I hope Mama doesn't notice all the face paint. I can't help but be nervous."

Lindsay grabbed her shoulders and held her at arm's length. "You, my dear, should be walking on air. My brother has chosen you to start the dance, not Vi Lea." She squeezed her shoulders. "And you must know what that means."

"I hope you're right."

"You know I'm right. Let's get started. Now, you've got to be even more beautiful than before." Lindsay tossed her head and added waspishly, "Miss Vi Lea Baker won't know what hit her."

338

# A Mistletoe Christmas

\* \* \*

Lindsay was kept busy overseeing the food and serving it. The womenfolk who'd accompanied their husbands as guests, found ample time on their hands. For them, other than Sundays, it was the closest thing to a holiday in their lives of never-ending chores.

The women had broken into small groups. One group worked on a double-ring patterned quilt, another group discussed Bible lessons with Parson Samuels' wife as their leader, others sewed on various pieces of clothing, and some of the younger women and girls played with the children.

Minnie, of course, was the center of attraction for the children, and Lindsay feared her dog would become agitated from so much concentrated attention. She made a mental note to put Minnie in her crate before the music started.

With the help of the shepherds' wives, cleaning the dinner dishes was done in less than an hour. And then her helpers hurried home to don their best skirts and blouses and return to the dance. Customarily, the Mexican laborers weren't included in the festivities, but she'd insisted, arguing how hard they'd all worked during shearing time, and both Chad and Bart had agreed.

She corralled Minnie and shut her in the crate, returning to the barn, just as the band got underway. Her heart swelled with pride as she watched Chad lead Ginny through the first dance, a formal quadrille. Her friend did well, only stumbling twice.

And she couldn't help but notice the way her brother looked at Ginny, like he could gobble her up and still not be satisfied.

Then Vi Lea came through the front door of the barn, accompanied by her cousin, Theo Henderson. Vi Lea greeted her and said, "Lindsay, who's dancing with your brother, my fiancé?"

"Oh, that's Virginia Brown, a friend of mine."

"Not that Brown, the washer woman, in Langtry?"

# A Mistletoe Christmas

Lindsay gritted her teeth. "That's her daughter. Emma or Mrs. Brown, the washer woman is over there." She inclined her head toward the table with the punch bowl.

"Oh," Vi Lea said.

"I haven't had a chance to congratulate you on becoming engaged to my brother."

"I know. Mother has been sick for months. I think she's better, though, still frail."

"I'm sorry to hear it. Give her my best wishes for a full recovery." She gazed at Vi Lea. "Have you and Chad set a date?"

Vi Lea smiled, an uncertain twitching of her lips. "I'd like to settle that tonight. It's past time." The quadrille ended and she said, "Could you call your brother over?"

"Of course." Lindsay gritted her teeth again and waved at her brother.

He glanced at her and must have seen Vi Lea because his eyes widened. He bowed over Ginny's hand, left her in the middle of the barn, and hurried over.

"Hello, Sis, thanks for calling me." Then he turned to Vi Lea and kissed her on the cheek. "I'm glad you could come."

Vi Lea narrowed her eyes. "Really?"

"Really. Would you care to dance?" he asked.

"I thought you already had a dancing partner."

"Just for the opening dance." Chad grinned. "Ginny has been helping my sister with the shearing crew. It only seemed fair."

"That's nice," Vi Lea said, but the tone of her voice made it obvious that nothing was nice about her fiancé dancing with someone else.

And Lindsay wanted to shake her brother—shake some sense into him. Why was he still fawning over Vi Lea? It was more than obvious he was smitten with Ginny. What would it take to get through to him?

Lindsay watched as Ginny fetched a cup of punch and came to stand beside her. Several men approached and asked Ginny to dance, but she declined. Lindsay wanted to speak with her but not in the middle of the dance.

Silently, they watched Chad dance with Vi Lea. After their third dance together, Lindsay couldn't watch any more. She hadn't planned on staying for the dance, not in her pregnant state and without her husband.

"I'm going in," she said.

Ginny put down her empty punch cup. "I'm going, too."

Lindsay touched Ginny's arm. "Don't go yet. He may still ask—"

"I'm not going to wait around."

Lindsay sighed. "I understand. What a disappointment."

She shook her head, and she couldn't help but think about her absent husband and how many weeks had passed since they'd spoken more than a few words. And now this, she and Ginny had worked so hard. She'd taught Ginny how to dance, and then she'd slaved over her friend's makeup, hair, and gown.

She sighed again. Now nobody was happy... except maybe Vi Lea Baker.

\* \* \*

Ginny and Lindsay, arm-in-arm, climbed the front steps to the ranch house's porch, but when Lindsay went to open the door, Ginny said, "I think I'll sit on the porch for a while and listen to the music."

"Oh, Ginny, if you want to do that, why don't you go back to the dance?"

She tossed her head. "And watch Chad with Vi Lea, no thanks. Though I think I'll change first. I need to get out of this awful corset." She grimaced. "I'll put on one of my day dresses."

"You could open our bedroom window and listen."

"I don't want to disturb you. You need your rest, especially after what we've been through the past few weeks."

Lindsay cupped her abdomen. "I can't disagree with you. I'm bone tired."

# A Mistletoe Christmas

Ginny patted her shoulder. "I'll be fine on the porch."

"All right, come on and get changed."

A few minutes later, Ginny blew out the lantern by the front door and sat in one of the rocking chairs. She enjoyed music, all kinds of music. Tonight, after all her hopes had been dashed—once again—she was content to be sitting, listening to the music. If she needed to cry, at least her sobbing wouldn't keep Lindsay awake.

She tried not to think about Chad, but no matter how hard she concentrated on the music, she couldn't stop her thoughts from wandering to him. *What was wrong with Chad?* She knew he wanted her, that was obvious. But at the same time, he couldn't or wouldn't break his engagement.

Tears burned her eyes, and she reached inside her apron pocket for her handkerchief. Her fingertips met a rough, sharp edge.

She pulled her hand out and saw a drop of blood on her index finger. That darned arrowhead! She should throw the cursed thing away. She carried it because it reminded her of Chad and the first day they'd met. But now she couldn't help but wonder if Lindsay hadn't played cupid and Chad had never come to her house, would she have forgotten her silly dreams?

The strains of a waltz ended, and then there was a long silence. She'd forgotten the band would take a break or two. And sitting here stewing without music to listen to, didn't appeal to her. She might as well join Lindsay in the bedroom.

"Ginny, is that you?"

She would know that masculine voice anywhere—it was Chad. What was he doing here?

She rose and reached for the front door knob. Suddenly, Chad was behind her and his hand covered hers. "Stay a minute, talk to me."

"Why should I?"

He turned her around and held her by the shoulders. "You changed your dress. Why? You were so beautiful in that green dress."

"I couldn't stand the corset."

# A Mistletoe Christmas

"Oh, I, uh, I…"

She pulled free from him. "I'm going inside. Please, don't stop me."

"But I need to talk to you."

"Where's Vi Lea?"

He lowered his head and fisted his hands by his sides. "She's inside the barn, talking with some of her neighbors from Comstock. Said she needed a rest, so I came looking for you."

"Why did you do that? Have you broken your engagement?"

"No, but I mean to." He ran his hand through his hair. "I… I just couldn't find the right words to say."

"Then you don't really want to break your engagement. Do you?"

He put his hand on her arm. "You know that's not true. I just don't know what to say, what reason to give."

She turned back and gazed at him. "Chad, if you don't know the reason you want to break with Vi Lea, then we have nothing to say to each other."

"I don't think that's true. I'm just having trouble doing it in front of everybody and at a dance that is supposed to be celebrating our shearing."

She straightened her spine and thrust out her chin. "I can't go on like this. It was wrong of us to see each other and to kiss…and…" She ducked her head. "All of it was wrong. We should have never started."

"But you said you loved me."

"I told you before, I shouldn't have said it." She lifted her head and gazed directly into his eyes. "It was a school girl crush, nothing more."

"You don't mean that."

She could feel the tears returning, scorching the back of her throat. She didn't want him to see her cry, and she didn't want to argue anymore.

"Yes, I do mean it. And something more. I don't want to see you at breakfast tomorrow. Mama and I will leave right after

# A Mistletoe Christmas

breakfast. You can eat with Bart, he's good at avoiding Lindsay and everyone else." She shook her head and sniffed. "I guess it's too much to expect, Langtry being such a small town, and your sister and I being friends, but I would prefer to never see you again."

She opened the front door, went in, and closed the door in his face.

* * *

Ginny and her mother, along with Lucia and Isabella had worked hard all day, getting ready for Lindsay's Christmas social. With Lindsay's approval, they'd resolved, a week or so before, to hold the social at their home, as it might be difficult for some of the children to make the two-mile trek to the MacKillian's ranch.

And since their home was small and Langtry's climate was mild, they'd decided to have the social in their backyard. They'd even suspended their laundry and mending services for a couple of days. Yesterday, they'd taken down the clothes lines and stored away the huge boiling pot.

Today, they'd woven the bright-green branches of cypress trees and the native chaparral plant with their red berries, amongst the still-green leaves of the grape arbor. They'd hung lanterns, along with bunches of mistletoe tied with red ribbons, from the live oak and mesquite trees.

They'd also hung a paper mache *piñata,* shaped like a burro, from the big pecan tree in the middle of the yard. It had been made by one of the Mexican ladies, and Lindsay had bought the hard candy to fill it with. It was a Mexican custom for blind-folded children to take swings with a stick at the *piñata* until they broke through the sides and the candy spilled out.

And they'd cut down a small *piñon* tree and had the local children help decorate it with strings of popcorn, hand-colored paper chains, and bows made from the scraps of fabric they'd used to sew the children's clothes.

On one side of the yard, they'd set up a long trestle table to hold the food. On the other side, they'd borrowed Lindsay's dais

# A Mistletoe Christmas

and hired a banjo player and fiddler to provide the Christmas carols and music for dancing.

Under the *piñon* tree, they'd heaped the brown-paper-wrapped packages for the children. Most of the packages had a child's name on it. But they'd wrapped the extra sets of clothes, too, just in case. Each package held a shirt and trousers for the boys and a dress for the girls, along with a small toy and a pair of *huaraches*.

Ginny surveyed the scene and linked her arm with her mother. "It looks wonderful. Don't you think? I think we did a great job. Lindsay will be so happy."

"Is her brother and Bart coming?"

She bit her lip. "Yes, Chad will be here. I don't know about Bart. Lindsay didn't say. And Lindsay had to invite Vi Lea, since she's still his fiancée."

Her mother shook her head. "I'm sorry to hear that. I might be prejudiced because you're my daughter, but the little I saw of Vi Lea at the shearing dance made me think Chad is making a big mistake."

"Well, it's *his* mistake."

Her mother glanced at her. "Not quite. You're still not over him. Are you?"

Ginny bowed her head. "I'm trying. I just wish they'd get married already."

*  *  *

Ginny took Lindsay's rouge pot and colored her cheeks. And her friend rearranged her hair over the bare-shouldered dress Lindsay had given her. They'd made a few alterations, but the blue silk dress looked as if it had been made for her.

Lindsay leaned over her shoulder and said, "You look beautiful."

She shrugged. "I don't know why I bother, except to please you. Chad is already taken. We can't change that."

"Don't be so certain. I don't think Chad's heart is really in it."

345

# A Mistletoe Christmas

"I know you've told me that you thought Chad proposed last Christmas because he was desperate to do something to help your ranch and, with Vi Lea being Sam's only child, by marrying they'd put the ranches together and have a bigger spread."

"Yes, but since then, my brother found Bart and took him on as a partner with fresh capital, and I've come home."

Ginny touched her friend's arm and shook her head. "It's too late, though, Chad's honor won't allow him to go back on his proposal."

"How do you know that?"

She smiled, but her mouth felt brittle. "Because he can't possibly love me, not the way he's treated me, Lindsay." She folded her hands in her lap. "Remember what happened at Panther Cave?"

"Yes, he shouldn't have taken you there when he was already engaged."

She nodded and took her friend's hand. "And shearing time was pure agony, being around Chad and knowing he was engaged. I stayed so I could help you."

"And I couldn't have done it without you. I appreciated your help."

"But at the shearing dance, even though you'd dressed me and fixed my hair, he ignored me once Vi Lea came." She sighed. "He found me on the porch during the band's intermission and kept swearing he wanted to break off his engagement. But he claimed he didn't know how to do it." She lowered her head. "I wanted to scream with frustration. He's just making excuses."

"I know. My brother hasn't treated you right, but I think he cares for you more than he realizes. Unfortunately, he's torn between his duty and loving you." She shook her head. "He didn't even bother to tell me about his engagement. I had to learn about it from you."

"Yes, and that's why I didn't tell you everything at first," she explained. "You had your hands full, being pregnant, and I didn't want to disappoint you if he chose to stay with Vi Lea." She glanced at Lindsay's protruding stomach. "Besides, I wasn't the only one who kept secrets for a time."

Lindsay blushed. "You're right. But I told you the truth when you asked. Before that, we'd only been friends for a little while."

"So, you understand why I didn't tell you about Chad and me, at least, not right away."

"Yes, I guess I understand. I just wish—"

"What?"

"That my brother wasn't so damned honorable."

Ginny turned back on the vanity stool. "Not only is your brother honor bound, but I don't have anything to offer him, except my love. Mama doesn't have any money to dower me with." She shook her head. "You know how it is with us."

Lindsay squeezed her shoulders and then applied some of Ginny's homemade perfume, a light minty fragrance, to her wrists and the pulse points behind her ears.

"Yes, I know, how it is. But one look at you tonight, and I pray my brother will know you're the right one for him, no matter his honor."

"I hope you're right." She turned back and looked in the mirror. "I've never shown so much bare skin in all my life."

At least not publicly, she silently amended. She hadn't forgotten the time Chad had taken her robe and stared at her while she was naked as a jay-bird.

"Well, it *was* the latest fashion when I left Boston. And the color suits your brown eyes and hair." Her friend clasped the pearl choker on her neck. "And these are so beautiful, especially against your skin."

"They're the only thing my mother owns of value. Handed down for generations on my Mama's side." She touched the pearls at her throat. "Mama gave them to me, to wear tonight, as an early Christmas present."

"Well, I approve, they're perfect with your dress and complexion."

# A Mistletoe Christmas

"Thank you." Ginny adjusted the choker and asked, "Will Bart be coming?"

Lindsay lowered her gaze and fiddled with her hair again. "No, I don't think so."

"Oh, Lindsay, I'm so sorry. Nothing has changed between you two?"

"No, nothing has changed." Her friend dropped her hands and laced them over her protruding stomach.

"I shouldn't have brought it up." Ginny dusted some loose face powder on her nose. "We need to make merry. It's our Christmas celebration." She swiveled around on the vanity bench again and took Lindsay's hands.

"Just wait until you see the backyard. Mama, Isabella, Lucia, and me worked hard to get the decorations up."

"I'm sure I will love what you've done. And it was kind of you to host the Christmas social. Being in Langtry, it's so much easier for the children than walking all the way to the ranch."

She got up and pulled Lindsay after her. "Then come on, I can't wait to show you."

# A Mistletoe Christmas

## Chapter Eight

With his hands folded behind his back, Chad watched Vi Lea dance with her cousin, Theo. He was relieved Theo had taken Vi Lea off his hands, but he had to speak to her tonight or ride to her ranch and tell her properly. He stole a glance at Ginny, who was helping to clear the trestle table.

She'd never looked more beautiful, not even at the shearing dance. This time, she wore a bare-shouldered gown, and her skin glowed in the lantern light. He'd missed her. The autumn months had passed in a dreary round of preparations for winter at the ranch. He'd thought about Ginny and how much she meant to him every hour of every day.

As she'd requested, he'd avoided her. And she'd avoided him, too.

When Ginny's mother and Constanza, the local mid-wife, had come to examine his sister, telling her that she was due within the next couple of weeks, Ginny hadn't accompanied them. But he wasn't convinced Ginny could stay away when his sister gave birth. At least, he hoped not, despite her not wanting to see him.

Tonight, his sister had refused to let him stay home, and as if to spite him, she'd invited Vi Lea to come, too. Well, if his sister was challenging him, this time, she wouldn't find him lacking.

Making up his mind, he crossed to the table and bowed. "May I have the pleasure of this dance, Ginny."

"I told you the last time, I don't want to see you again."

"Then why was I invited?"

"Because your sister insisted."

"And why are you wearing that gown?"

She lifted her head and glared at him. "Your sister again. It's her social, I couldn't say no."

He offered his arm. "Please, dance with me. I've something to tell you."

She bit her lip. "All right, but just this once."

# A Mistletoe Christmas

He folded her into his arms. The reel had finished and the band was playing a waltz. Thankfully, Vi Lea was still dancing with her cousin.

"What did you want to tell me?" Ginny asked.

"Cut to the quick, don't you?"

She narrowed her eyes. "Chad, I'm warning you."

"All right, fine. I'm going to break my engagement tonight... or as soon as possible. I feel ridiculous doing it at a party, but if—"

"Don't try to make me feel guilty, Chadbourne MacKillian. I'm not asking you to break your engagement. Not anymore."

"Well, since this is a festive occasion, I'd prefer to ride to her ranch and do it properly."

"You don't need to explain to me. It's none of my business."

They whirled past the two musicians, and he glanced up to see a bundle of white-berried mistletoe, hanging in the shadows on the other side of the band. It was the perfect opportunity, and he hoped she wouldn't refuse him.

Maneuvering her under the mistletoe, he stopped and glanced up. "One kiss, Ginny. Please, just one kiss. It's Christmas."

She turned her head and pointed at her cheek. "All right. One kiss."

He wasn't going to let her off that easily. He took her chin in his hand and turned her to face him. He lowered his mouth onto hers, wanting to give her a quick kiss and return to the dance. But the minute their mouths touched, he was lost. And she seemed to melt in his arms, clinging to him and kissing him back with more passion than he had the right to deserve.

Their mouths clung together and then opened to each other, their tongues tangling. He traced his thumb along the silky-smooth skin of her exposed collarbone, and just touching her made him tremble with wanting.

Someone shrieked, and it wasn't the children, scrambling for candy. No, this was a mature feminine voice.

# A Mistletoe Christmas

Reluctantly, Chad broke their kiss and glanced up. His gaze met Vi Lea's. She stood a few feet away, glaring at them with her fists on her hips.

He looked at Ginny from the corner of his eye and could see the regret and guilt written clearly across her face. *Double damn!* How had he let this happen? Now was the time to get this over with and tell Vi Lea his true intentions.

He reached for Vi Lea's arm, but she reared back and slapped him. Then she shouted, "You're a lying cheat, Chadbourne MacKillian. I won't be treated this way, and I don't want to marry you." She turned to her cousin. "Take me home, Theo. I don't want to have anything to do with the MacKillians."

Standing with one hand cupping his stinging cheek, he debated going after Vi Lea and explaining. But what good would it do? Vi Lea had made the decision for him. Maybe later, when tempers had cooled, he'd apologize to Vi Lea, but for now, he couldn't help feeling relieved.

He was off the hook. He smiled and exhaled. *He was free!* Free to ask Ginny to marry. But when he turned to where she'd been, she was gone.

He scanned the backyard, but she was nowhere to be found. She must have gone inside. Walking around to the front door of the Browns' house, he couldn't wait to find Ginny and take her into his arms. The scene in the backyard had been ugly, and he could understand why she might be ashamed. He'd kiss her and make everything right, and then he'd go down on one knee and propose.

Excited and exuberant, he fisted his hand, knocking on the door loud enough to be heard over the commotion around back. He knocked again and got no answer. It was obvious she wasn't coming to the door. He tried the door knob and found it locked.

He knocked once more, harder this time, and called out, "Ginny, can you hear me? Please come to the door and let me in."

Was she purposely locking him out? He'd thought she'd be as relieved as he was, knowing his engagement was over. But maybe he was wrong. He'd acted pretty stupid, torn between his duty to Vi

# A Mistletoe Christmas

Lea and his growing love for Ginny. He hadn't treated Ginny right, not from the first.

He shouldn't have kissed and touched her when he was promised to another. Shouldn't have ignored her at the shearing dance once Vi Lea came. Shouldn't have tried to steal a kiss with his former fiancée dancing close by.

He'd tried to make it right that night at the shearing dance, going to her and explaining how hard it was to break his engagement. How he didn't know what to say to Vi Lea. But looking back on it from Ginny's perspective, he must have sounded like a lily-livered coward. And there was really no excuse, unless he didn't care for Ginny and only wanted to shame her.

He hoped Ginny didn't worry he still wanted Vi Lea because of her ranch. Or that she was only good enough to kiss and caress in secret. But Ginny had accused him of exactly that—lusting after her but not believing she was good enough to marry.

Stupid jackass that he was, he'd not taken her seriously, knowing he felt more than desire for her. Hell's bells, he loved being around her, cherished her sweet nature, and giving spirit. The day at Panther Cave, before he'd confessed his engagement, had been a joy. She was playful and easy to talk to and being with her felt right.

*If that wasn't love, he didn't know what love was.*

Tied to Vi Lea, he'd stalled and fumbled around, ducking his responsibility to face his fiancée. Secretly hoping he'd be rescued from his ill-fated engagement.

*And now his wish had come true.*

But at what cost? He'd shamed Ginny in front of most of Langtry, making her kiss him and then having to face the wrath of his fiancée when they were caught.

*Good Lord, he'd messed things up.*

He thought about asking his sister to intervene, but that wasn't fair, either. After what had happened, he didn't think Ginny would listen to him. Not that he could blame her.

# A Mistletoe Christmas

He doffed his Stetson, and ran his hand through his hair. He should be considerate, giving Ginny time to get over the ugly scene in her backyard. But he didn't want to wait—he wanted her now.

* * *

Chad spurred his favorite mount, a roan gelding, he called Rusty. He had a lot of ground to cover in one day. Vi Lea's ranch house, overlooking the Devil's River, was ten miles from the Lazy M. And with his sister so close to her time, he needed to get there and back in one day.

He'd sat on the Browns' front step last night until Ginny's mother had told him to go home. He made certain his sister had a ride back to the ranch. But when he'd gotten home, he hadn't slept, just nursed a glass of whiskey and his regrets until Lindsay returned.

He'd left the ranch well before daylight and had already passed through Comstock. He'd made good time; it was only mid-morning. He was following the riverbank along the Devil's River, and Rusty was tossing his head and blowing.

The gelding needed to rest and a long drink of water. But he hated to stop. Wanted to get the situation with Vi Lea resolved and over. Wanted to go back to Ginny and explain. Wanted to propose if she would let him.

But he couldn't afford to blow Rusty out. He doubted the Bakers would be willing to give him a fresh mount and let him fetch Rusty later.

Impatient, but knowing he had to stop, he pulled on the reins and dismounted. He led Rusty down the riverbank and let him drink. Then he walked him in circles to cool him off and tethered the roan to a willow.

Fishing around in his saddlebags, he found an ancient piece of beef jerky. Chewing on the stiff meat, he managed to choke down a few bites while Rusty grazed on lush grass growing beside the river.

# A Mistletoe Christmas

After a time when the sun was almost at its zenith, he let his horse have a few more swallows of water, and he drank, too, washing down the tough jerky with river water.

About an hour later, he came to the Bakers' rambling two-story, clapboard ranch house. He knocked on the door, expecting Vi Lea or one of her parents to answer, but he was surprised when Theo opened the door.

Chad started to greet him but before he could say anything, Theo grabbed his shirt and shoved him back.

Chad stumbled backwards, coming to rest against the porch rail. "Hey, watch who you're shoving."

Theo dropped his hand to the butt of his holstered gun. "Why should I? Haven't you done enough damage?"

"I didn't mean for last night to happen... that way. I want to see Vi Lea and explain."

Theo hawked and spat a stream of dirty brown tobacco juice at Chad's boots. "You won't be explaining nothin'. Vi Lea don't want to see you."

"Can I speak to Mr. Baker or his wife?"

"You ain't welcome here." Theo thrust his face into his. He bared his teeth, and his features were pulled back in a snarl. "Don't you git it? 'Sides, Pa Baker is out moving sheep, and his wife is ailing again. Vi Lea is takin' care of her mother. An' she don't have time for the likes of you."

Chad pulled off his Stetson and ran his hand through his hair. Why was Theo always hanging around? Samuel Baker, Vi Lea's father, had taken him on as a ranch hand. He was Vi Lea's second cousin, once removed, and everyone knew his father had lost their ranch through mismanagement. Did Theo have designs on his cousin and her inheritance?

Chad wouldn't be surprised if that was Theo's goal. Hell, it had been his reason for proposing to Vi Lea. He couldn't really fault the man for what he'd thought would be a good match, considering the Baker spread.

# A Mistletoe Christmas

"All right, Theo. I understand," he said. "I'm not welcome. But I want you to give Vi Lea a note from me." He pulled the folded paper from his jean pocket and offered it.

He'd spent most of last night, wording and rewording the note, just in case Vi Lea wouldn't see him. He'd wanted to apologize and explain to his former fiancée and wish her all the best.

Theo knocked the paper from his hand and ground his manure-encrusted boot into it. "I ain't givin' Vi Lea nothin' from you. She's mine now. We're going to be married. I've loved her since we were bare-assed kids."

Chad couldn't help but snort. He didn't doubt Theo wanted Vi Lea. *But love?* Did the likes of Theo Henderson even know what he was talking about?

"You don't believe me?" Theo asked.

"I didn't say that."

"Yeah, but you were thinkin' it." He glanced over his shoulder at the shuttered house. "I'd call you out right now, right here, if'n it wouldn't upset the women folks. But Vi Lea's mother don't need no shocks to her system." He shook his head. "She ain't got long to live, and your shilly-shallying has probably shortened her time considerable."

Chad's gut clenched, thinking about Vi Lea's sick mother and how she'd probably wanted to see her only child married and settled before… before…

Guilt, dull-edged like a well-used razor, gnawed at him. He wished he could make up his mistake to the Bakers, especially Vi Lea and her mother. Maybe someday, he'd find a way. He hoped so.

"All right, Theo. I'm going." He retreated down the porch steps and un-looped his gelding's reins. "And I don't expect you to tell Vi Lea anything. I don't want to upset her or her mother."

"Oh, now, you're sorry?" Theo's sarcasm spilled over him like acid. "Don't want to hurt nobody? Feel guilty like the low-down snake you are?"

# A Mistletoe Christmas

Chad had grabbed Rusty's reins. He fisted them in his right hand and took several deep breaths. It took all of his self-control to not slam his fist into Theo's self-righteous face.

Instead, he tipped his Stetson with one finger and said, "Good day to you." He mounted Rusty.

"Don't be no 'good daying' me, MacKillian," Theo called out. "I'm not through with you yet. You've shamed my woman and her family. You need to pay for what you've done." He beat his chest with one hand. "And I'm the *hombre* to make you."

He came down the front porch steps and grabbed the roan's halter. "You better keep looking over your shoulder, 'cuz I plan on avenging my own. If not today or tomorrow, as soon as I can."

Theo let go of Rusty's halter and glared at him. "You got that? You still owe me and my fiancée and her family. *You will pay.*"

Chad stared at Theo. What was there left to say? The man could bluster and swear and threaten him. And maybe he even deserved it, but he couldn't change what had happened.

He wheeled his horse around and spurred Rusty's flanks, wanting to put Theo and his threats far behind.

\* \* \*

Chad clucked and snapped the reins. The two wagon horses picked up the pace, stumbling into a trot. His sister had wakened him just past midnight, telling him the baby was coming. He was supposed to fetch the Browns and Constanza, the midwife.

And this time, Ginny wouldn't be able to avoid him—not if she was going to help his sister in her time of need.

He'd gone straight to Ginny after his encounter with Theo Henderson, wanting to see her. Needing her to take the sting of his guilt away. But Mrs. Brown had greeted him at the door and turned him away. She'd said he'd broken her daughter's heart too many times and to not come back unless Lindsay needed them.

He'd walked the unforgiving edge of guilt and regret for days now. Trying not to think, doing his chores and then some, so he could fall into bed exhausted and snatch a few hours of sleep.

# A Mistletoe Christmas

*He'd made one royal mess of everything. How could he have been so stupid?*

Bart had tried to talk some sense into him, but words were worthless.

He was worried for his sister, as childbirth, for women could be dangerous. But at the same time, he was excited to know he'd be seeing Ginny for the first time since the Christmas social.

At least he hoped so. Ginny would come for Lindsay, wouldn't she?

He pulled on the reins, drawing the horses to a stop in front of the dark house. Jumping down, he went to the front door and knocked. Hammering on the door and calling out for Mrs. Brown, he couldn't help but feel ashamed, knowing what Ginny and her mother thought of him.

*If he wanted to marry Ginny, he had his work cut out for him.*

He saw the flare of a lantern through the front window and then the door opened. Mrs. Brown stood on the threshold, holding a lantern in one hand and clutching her robe's lapels in the other.

"What do you want? It's the middle of the night?" she said. "If you're drunk and want to see Ginny—"

"I wouldn't do that. Please, believe me." He shook his head. "It's Lindsay's time. She said something about breaking her water and to get y'all and Constanza."

"Oh, my gosh." Mrs. Brown set down the lantern and covered her mouth with one hand. "I wasn't thinking." She inclined her head. "Of course, come inside and wait while Ginny and I get dressed."

He accepted her offer, stepping inside. "Do you know where the midwife lives?"

"Yes, she's just around the corner. Have a seat, we won't be but a minute."

Chad sat on the overstuffed horsehair sofa and removed his Stetson.

# A Mistletoe Christmas

Mrs. Brown knocked on a door in the hallway, calling out, "Ginny, Ginny, get up. Lindsay has gone into labor."

"Coming, Mama," Ginny answered.

Hearing her voice, even if it had only been a few days, made his pulse accelerate, and he couldn't wait to lay eyes on her again.

Chad twirled his Stetson in his hands and drummed his cowboy boot heels against the hardwood floors, waiting. He didn't want to admit it, but he was anxious to get back to his sister. He knew nothing about women giving birth. And he couldn't help but worry.

A few minutes later, Mrs. Brown and Ginny crowded into the small parlor. He gazed at Ginny and said, "I'm glad to see you. Knowing you'll be with my sister means a lot to me."

Ginny didn't reply, only nodding her head.

Mrs. Brown stared at him and then glanced at her daughter. "We better get a move on."

Chad followed them out and helped them into the wagon. Much to his dismay, Ginny opted to climb into the back. Mrs. Brown sat up front with him.

"Point me to the midwife's house, Mrs. Brown. Please."

"Of course." She pointed down the dark street. "That corner to the left. Her house is just around the corner."

They arrived at Constanza's home, and Mrs. Brown hurried in to get the midwife. He was alone with Ginny, for the first time, since the Christmas social.

He cleared his throat and turned around to face her. "Ginny, I know you don't want to talk to me, but if you would—"

"No, I don't want to talk to you. That hasn't changed. You didn't break your engagement, Vi Lea did. And I was a party to it. I should have never danced with you." She shook her head. "Much less, let you kiss me. I'm embarrassed and full of shame. When I go to the general store, I feel like people are whispering about me."

"I never wanted you to feel that way, Ginny. And I've tried twice to talk to you and apologize." He cleared his throat again. "You're right. I've made a hash of everything. From that first time at Panther Cave, I've been in the wrong. And I've been a coward, too, not willing to face Vi Lea and tell her the truth."

He gazed at the sweet nape of her neck, peeking out from the collar of her plain woolen dress. He wanted her more than anything. Even more than his beloved ranch, which paled beside the bone-deep feelings he had for Ginny.

Putting his hand on her shoulder, he said, "Won't you look at me? Can't you find it in your heart to forgive me? And if we were to get engaged, would you still be ashamed?"

She didn't turn to look at him, only shook her head again. "I don't know, Chad. I'm not sure if you care for me, not in the marrying way. And you know I have nothing to offer. No ranch, no land. Not like Vi Lea had."

He wanted to reassure her that he would take care of her—that he didn't want another ranch, but he heard a door close and saw Ginny's mother and Constanza walking toward the wagon. Reluctantly, he turned around and clutched the reins.

Mrs. Brown climbed into the buckboard beside him. Constanza got in back with Ginny. Mrs. Brown glanced at her daughter and then looked at him with narrowed eyes. "Well, what are we waiting for? The sooner we get to the ranch, the sooner we'll be able to help birth your sister's baby."

He flapped the reins over the horses' backs. "Yes, ma'am."

* * *

Ginny dipped the washcloth in the basin and wrung out the excess water. She sponged Lindsay's forehead, hoping to soothe her. They'd been with Lindsay for over sixteen hours, night was falling again, and the baby still hadn't come.

Lindsay groaned and held onto her arm, another contraction taking her. Her friend's throat was raw from screaming. Ginny gave Lindsay a corner of the terry-cloth to chew on and to rest her throat.

# A Mistletoe Christmas

Her friend looked up at her and grimaced. But she bit into the cloth, let go of her arm, and grabbed Ginny's hand, squeezing it so hard Ginny wanted to cry out, too.

Her mother and Constanza stood at the foot of her bed, huddled together, whispering. And even though they'd lowered their voices, Ginny could hear what they were saying. She prayed Lindsay, caught up in another contraction, couldn't hear them.

"*Señora* Brown, the baby, she is breech and the waters have broken." Constanza shook her head. "Too dry. I fear hurting her if I try to turn the baby." The midwife glanced at her patient. Lindsay's sodden nightgown was bunched around her waist. "And she is beginning to bleed."

Her mother closed her eyes and lowered her head. Ginny knew she was praying. Then she raised her head and asked, "Is there nothing we can do? There *must* be something."

Constanza held up her index finger. "I know of only one way. You must send for Doctor Rodgers in Del Rio. A doctor has the forceps. I have seen them used once, and if he knows how, he can turn the baby." She crossed herself and kissed the crucifix she wore. "If God is willing."

Her mother pursed her lips and nodded. "I'll have her brother telegraph the doctor to come right away. He can be here on the morning train."

Constanza hung her head. "I hope it is enough." She glanced at Lindsay again. "She weakens by the hour."

"What more would you have me do?" Her mother asked.

"Send the telegram, but her brother must leave tonight to find the doctor and bring him."

"You're right. It will be a hard ride, but it's for the best."

Ginny couldn't believe her ears. Now, she knew how dangerous the situation was. Terror tore at her and her hands turned slippery with sweat. She moved to one side because she knew she was going to cry. Bunching up her apron. she covered her face and sobbed.

# A Mistletoe Christmas

Emma found another washcloth on the nightstand and dipped it in the basin of water and sponged Lindsay's face. Then she folded the cloth and laid it across Lindsay's forehead.

She touched her daughter's arm. "You heard what we need."

Ginny lowered her apron and sniffed, trying to fight back the tears. "Yes, I heard."

"Can you tell Chad? Explain to him about the telegram, but that he needs to ride there to ensure he finds the doctor."

She nodded. "Yes, I understand. I'll do it."

"Good, and tell him to hurry."

\* \* \*

Ginny found Chad in the kitchen. He'd folded his arms on the kitchen table and laid his head on them. She wondered if he was trying to sleep. After all, they'd been up for most of the night and all day. She was exhausted, too, but the horror of her friend's condition kept her going.

She touched his shoulder, and he looked up. He hadn't been sleeping, but she could see the worry and concern on his face. And he still wore the same rumpled clothes from last night. None of them had bothered with changing their clothes or even eating.

"Chad, Lindsay needs a doctor. The baby isn't coming. Constanza and my mother want you to send a telegram to Doctor Rodgers in Del Rio, so he will come on the morning train." She gulped and blew her nose. "But Mama wants you to ride there, too, in case the doctor is out and doesn't get the telegram." She snagged his gaze and held it, hoping he would understand how grave the situation was. "There's no time to waste."

"I'll tell Bart. He can keep the house fires going against the chill."

"Be quick, please." Ginny turned away and started crying again.

"You love my sister. Don't you?"

She nodded and wiped her eyes with a handkerchief.

# A Mistletoe Christmas

He pulled her to him and wrapped her in a hug. She wanted to resist, but she couldn't. Lindsay, her best friend, might be dying. And she knew how much Chad loved his sister. She needed to hold him and she guessed he needed her, too. They both loved Lindsay and the thought of losing her was too hard, too awful.

After a long moment, he released her and grabbed his Stetson and gun holster. "Wish me luck."

"Go with God. I will be praying."

# A Mistletoe Christmas

## Chapter Nine

Ginny held Lindsay's hand as another contraction ripped through her friend. They still had hours to go before Chad would be back with the doctor. Her mother pushed her to one side and lifted Lindsay's head and held a glass of water to her friend's dry and cracked lips.

Someone knocked on the bedroom door, and Ginny's heart lifted. But Chad had only been gone for an hour; it couldn't be him. It must be Serafina or maybe, even Bart. She crossed to the door and opened it.

Chad stood in the hallway.

"What are you doing here," she hissed. "I thought you rode to Del Rio. What happened?"

Her mother pushed her to one side. "Chad, I thought you understood you had to go to Del Rio to be sure the doctor comes."

"I meant to go, but when I told Bart, he wanted to go. His horse, Dancer, is faster than any of my horses. And he said he knew a shortcut, too. I went to Langtry, got Will up, and sent the telegram." He glanced through the cracked door at his sister. "The doctor should be here on the morning train."

"Thank you," Emma said and touched his arm. "You've done all you can."

He nodded. "I'd ride to hell and back if I thought it would help my sister, but I think Bart made a wise decision." He inclined his head toward the fireplace. "It's grown chilly, and I see your fire is out. I'm going to get some wood and stoke the fires in the house. Is there anything else you need?"

Ginny grabbed the almost-empty washbasin. "We could use some more water."

"Let me bring you a fresh pitcher."

Ginny glanced at Lindsay, lying quietly on the bed. "I think she's finally resting."

Mrs. Brown looked at her and frowned.

# A Mistletoe Christmas

Ginny bit her lip and grabbed Chad's arm. "Can I come with you and help?"

He covered her hand with his. "Of course."

She looked at her mother.

"Yes, you go with Chad. Constanza and I will stay with Lindsay. We'll call you if we need you."

He closed the door behind them, and she collapsed into his arms, crying. He held her tightly and kissed the top of her head. "What's wrong? Only a few more hours until the doctor comes."

She raised her head and gazed into his eyes. "If she lasts that long. She's lost a lot of blood, and now she's sleeping through the contractions, too. It's not a good sign. It means she's so exhausted, she can't feel the pain anymore."

"Oh, my God, Ginny. No, no!"

She placed her fingers across his lips. "Shhhh. Not here. I don't want Mama to know I told you. But you have a right to know. She's your sister, all you have left of your family."

"That's kind of you, Ginny."

"Not really."

He closed his eyes and lowered his head. He inhaled deeply and then took her hand. "Come on, let's get the wood and water. And we'll see if there's something to eat. Nobody's eaten all day. Your mother and Constanza might want coffee and some bread and butter, at least."

"That's a good idea." Ginny looked around. "Where's Minnie?"

"I put her in her crate."

"How long ago?"

He ducked his head. "Too long. I forgot about her, but she hasn't made a sound."

"I'll take her out while you get the wood."

"Thank you, but try to keep her away from the bedroom. She'll want to see Lindsay."

Ginny nodded. "I know."

# A Mistletoe Christmas

They fetched and carried. And when they were finished, they sat at the kitchen table, drinking coffee and trying to choke down a few bites of bread and butter. She glanced out the kitchen window. Dawn was breaking. Only a few more hours to go. She should return to Lindsay, but she was afraid of what she might find. And her mother hadn't come looking for her, so she doubted anything had changed.

Chad pushed aside his half-eaten bread and took Ginny's hands in his. "I think we should pray. Would you pray with me?"

"Yes, of course. It's all we can do now… pray and wait and hope."

\* \* \*

"Chad, congratulations, your sister has a beautiful baby girl," Doctor Rodgers said. "And she and the baby are doing fine."

He leapt to his feet and pumped the doctor's hand. "Thank you! Thank you!" He let loose a whoop. "I'm so happy. So happy!" He shook his head. "Doc, you don't know what a relief it is. I feared…" He released the doctor's hand and pulled his hand through his hair. "Can I see her and the baby?"

"Her husband is with her now, but I'm certain she'll want to see you after Bart."

"Thank you again. We couldn't have done it…" He covered his eyes with his hand and gulped. He was on the verge of tears again. He couldn't help it; the past couple of days had been the worst of his life.

The Doc touched his arm. "Why don't you sit down? I'd love to have a cup of coffee if there's some made."

"Sure. There's plenty of coffee."

He poured the Doc his coffee and refilled his cup, too. Then he sat down with the doctor. "So everything's fine? Nothing to worry about for the future?"

"If you mean will your sister be able to have more children, that's not a problem. The baby was breech, coming feet first. These things happen. But they seldom happen to the same woman twice."

# A Mistletoe Christmas

Chad nodded, feeling slightly embarrassed to be discussing such an intimate topic with the doctor.

Ginny appeared on the threshold of the kitchen and said, "Chad, do you want to peek in? I'm going to let Minnie inside. Lindsay has been asking for her."

He glanced at the doctor. "Is it all right to see her?"

"Sure, I think so. Who is Minnie?"

"My sister's pet dog, but she's small and gentle."

The doctor chuckled. "Should be okay." He inclined his head. "Y'all go on. I'll finish my coffee and head to the station. The afternoon train should be along soon, and I need to get back to Del Rio. Your sister isn't the only pregnant woman around."

"Have one of the shepherds saddle my roan. It will save you the walk. You can leave him at the livery stable. I'll get him later."

"Thanks, I'll do that."

Chad got to his feet and shook the doctor's hand again. "I can't thank you enough."

"Just be sure she gets plenty of rest and if you need me, you know where to find me. But from here on out, I think Constanza can take over."

Ginny reappeared with Minnie in her arms and motioned him over. They tip-toed to the bedroom door and cracked it open, peering inside. Ginny let Minnie down, and the small, white dog ran over to the bed and jumped up, burrowing between Bart and Lindsay, who were admiring the baby.

Seeing them together as a family, a lump rose to Chad's throat. Tears threatened again, and he swiped at his eyes. He was fast becoming a watering spout.

They watched for a few minutes but when Bart dipped his head to kiss his sister, he closed the door and turned to Ginny. "Where's your mother and Constanza?"

"Resting in the other bedroom." She yawned and stretched. "I'd love to lie down, too. Can I stretch out on your parlor sofa?"

"I'll sleep on the sofa, after I get Serafina to cook us a proper dinner. You can lie down in my bedroom."

# A Mistletoe Christmas

"Oh, Chad, I don't feel right, taking your room."

He grinned. "Probably you're right. My room's a mess, and I forget when the sheets were changed. Maybe the sofa would be better. Let me get you settled in the parlor." He opened a hallway closet door and got a goose down pillow and an afghan.

She followed him and sat on the horsehair sofa.

He put the pillow and afghan on the sofa beside her. And then he got down on one knee.

She gazed at him, her eyes wide.

He took her hands in his and said, "Virginia Brown, will you be my wife?"

"Oh, Chad, are you sure? It's so soon after you and Vi Lea—"

"But I've known all along, since that first day at the springs. I've known. I was a coward. That's all."

She squeezed his hands. "Let me think about it. It's been an emotional few days. Let's give ourselves some time. And I want to talk to your sister, too."

He shook his head. "Why? Don't you love me? I'm not ashamed to tell you that I love you with all my heart." He pulled her down and brushed her lips with his. "I want what my sister and Bart have found—a family. Just seeing them together like that..."

She ducked her head. "I think you're right; I believe they're going to be a family." She giggled. "All I can say is, it's about time. But that's why I wanted to talk to your sister first. I have a feeling she will want to get married again in a church." She lifted her head and gazed at him. "If you're serious, would you mind waiting so we could have a double wedding?"

He choked off a groan. The last thing he wanted to do was wait. He wanted Ginny as his wife and in his bed as soon as possible.

"If you really love me, and your feelings aren't just about desire, you'll wait. And court me properly."

He met her gaze and nodded. "You're right, I need to prove myself. Prove my love." He took a deep breath. "I'll wait, Ginny, if

367

# A Mistletoe Christmas

that will reassure you. And I'll prove to you that I want you as my wife, today, and the rest of my life."

"Oh, Chad." She threw her arms around his neck.

He gathered her into his arms and kissed her, long and slow, and thoroughly.

\* \* \*

Ginny held baby Elizabeth in her arms, humming a lullaby under her breath. Her friend's baby was so miraculous, so sweet and milky smelling. She couldn't get enough of holding her.

She looked up at Lindsay. "She's so beautiful. You must be terribly proud."

Lindsay smiled. "I am proud, but the way Bart acts, you'd think he delivered her single-handedly."

They laughed.

The baby yawned and waved one tiny fist.

Lindsay adjusted her nightshift, covering herself. "I know you enjoy holding her, but since I just fed her, she's probably ready for a nap. Do you mind putting her in the cradle?"

Ginny kissed the baby's forehead. "I do mind. I could hold her all day, but I think you're right. Her eyes keep closing. She's sleepy." Ginny crossed to the foot of the bed and gently laid the baby down, covering her with a tiny quilt her mother had made for the baby.

Lindsay patted the bed. "Come and sit. I'm ready for you to tell me your big news. Though, I think I've already guessed. When my brother came to see the baby, he looked like he could bust a gut."

Ginny felt her face grow hot, thinking about Chad and how sweet he'd been. She stroked the arrowhead in her apron pocket and sat beside Lindsay. "He proposed, really proposed this time. Went down on one knee and everything. I think he means it."

"That's what I thought." Lindsay took her hand and squeezed it. "I'm glad, so glad for you. Have you set a date?"

# A Mistletoe Christmas

Ginny smiled. "That's what I wanted to talk to you about. I have a feeling you and Bart are going to want to get married again. The right way, this time."

Lindsay gasped. "How did you know?"

"Just a lucky guess. I thought you'd want a priest to bless your marriage."

"And you'd be right. Bart has agreed, too. If we don't marry at the altar of a Catholic church, a priest should be willing to marry us, despite Bart being Methodist."

Ginny nodded. "So a plain church will do."

"Yes." Lindsay narrowed her eyes. "What are you getting at?"

"You told me you have the money to build Langtry's church. Am I right?"

"Yes, but with the baby and all, I haven't had the time to—"

"Winter is a slow time for the ranchers. A perfect time to get your church built."

"Yes, you're right, that's what I had planned to do. But I haven't even ordered the materials yet."

"Then let Chad and Bart order the building materials and organize the ranchers and townsfolk. With enough people working on the church, wouldn't it be ready by spring?"

"Yes, I think it might, if Bart and Chad keep on top of it."

Ginny clapped her hands. "Then we can be the first couples to be married in the new church. We can have a double wedding! What do you say to that?"

Lindsay giggled. "I think you're a genius, Virginia Brown."

\* \* \*

Lindsay glanced around the kitchen table. It was nice to have them all together, her husband, her brother, and Ginny. Emma had been kind enough to let Ginny stay with her for six weeks after the birth of Elizabeth, so she could rest and get on her feet.

Ginny's mother had explained winter was her slow time, too. There was always a lot less washing and mending to do, so she

369

could afford to get by without her daughter's help. And for Lindsay, having Ginny around was such a joy, not to mention she was relishing her brother's attempts at properly courting her friend.

She took a sip of coffee and smiled to herself.

There was a knock on the back door, and she wondered who it might be. Emma was preparing for a trip to San Antonio to buy a new Singer sewing machine she'd been saving for.

Mabel, the owner of the Vinegaroon Hotel in Langtry, was going to accompany her. Mabel had a new hotel manager, and she was eager to take some time off. Lindsay had been surprised to learn Emma and Mabel were good friends; they were as different as daylight and dark.

Chad got up and opened the back door. On the threshold was the last person Lindsay had expected to see again—Rose Gallagher.

Bart rose and glanced at Lindsay, a question in his eyes. She lowered her head, ashamed of how she'd treated Rose the last time.

She stood up and went to the back door. Taking Rose by the arm, she said, "Won't you come in? We were just finishing up breakfast. There's plenty of coffee or I could make you some tea. And if you're hungry, there are some eggs and biscuits left."

Rose took a step back and stiffened her spine. "I, uh, I need to talk to Bart."

Lindsay nodded. "Please, come in then. Do you want some privacy? If so, we can—"

"No, I don't need privacy." She glanced around the kitchen. "I believe this affects all of you."

Chad and Ginny, who had started to get up, sat back down and cradled their coffee cups in their hands.

Lindsay pulled out a chair. "Please, take a seat. I think you know everyone here, except my friend, Ginny Brown."

Rose inclined her head. "Nice to meet you, Miss Brown." Rose took the chair and laced her hands together, resting them on the table.

"How about some coffee?" Lindsay offered again.

# A Mistletoe Christmas

Rose licked her lips. "I'd love a cup of coffee with a little cream."

"Coming right up."

Bart watched her cross to the stove, his mouth hanging open. After a few moments, he closed his mouth and turned to Rose. "What brings you to Langtry? How is your mother?"

Rose looked down at the table and shook her head. "My mother passed right after Christmas."

"I'm sorry," Bart said.

"Our condolences," Ginny and Lindsay said in unison.

Chad shook his head. "I'm sorry to hear it, Mrs. Gallagher."

"And I have some other bad news for Bart and Chad. I've kept in touch with my girls back in Tucson. Red Boyd murdered my attorney and cracked his safe. He got all my savings."

Bart let loose a low whistle. "I knew he was a low-down polecat, but I never expected him to murder someone in cold blood."

"It's not the first time. He's wanted for several murders," Rose said. "I had hoped he wouldn't learn about the safe and my money." She shook her head and dabbed at her eyes with a handkerchief. "And I did so esteem Mr. Wilson, my attorney. To think he got killed because of me is, is…" She gulped and huge, tearing sobs shook her.

Lindsay set down her coffee and put her arm around Rose's shoulders. "You mustn't blame yourself, Mrs. Gallagher. I'm certain Mr. Wilson knew the risk he was taking, keeping a safe with a large sum of money on his premises."

"Lindsay is right, Rose," Bart said. "You can't blame yourself."

Rose sniffed and blotted her eyes. "You both are kind, but it doesn't change the facts. I shouldn't have put Mr. Wilson in danger."

"Didn't he keep other people's money, too?" Bart asked. "I know he had mine until I invested in the Lazy M."

# A Mistletoe Christmas

Rose glanced at him. "Yes, he had other people's money, but I... I just feel responsible." She shook her head. "I can't help it."

"And you've lost all your money," Bart said.

Rose shrugged. "That's the least of it. I'll start over."

Lindsay patted Rose's shoulder and then moved to her place and sat down.

Rose took a sip of her coffee and then looked directly at Bart. "Rumor has it, Red took the money as part of his revenge against you because he knew you and I were friends. And because his brothers never got their money back from you."

"Red Boyd is a crazy man. And he'll use any excuse to take what he wants," Bart said.

"That's not all," Rose added. "Now he's got plenty of money if he wants to hire men to come after you and Chad. I came to warn you so you could plan."

At Rose's words, Lindsay turned cold all over. She gripped the table, hoping Bart wouldn't see she was trembling.

Bart and Chad exchanged glances and Chad said, "Thank you for telling us. Do you have any idea when he might be coming?"

"No, I wish I did, but I don't know." Rose lifted her head and looked around the table. "I'm so sorry this has happened to such nice people. Sorry to bring you this terrible news."

Bart got up and patted Rose's shoulder. "You did the right thing. Thanks for warning us. At least, we'll know what's coming." He motioned to Chad. "Let's talk on the porch. I think I have an idea."

Chad got up and followed Bart outside.

Lindsay turned to Ginny and said, "I think I hear Elizabeth fussing. Would you please see to her?"

"Of course." Ginny pushed her chair back and went to the bedroom.

Rose glanced up and said, "I should be going."

# A Mistletoe Christmas

Lindsay reached out and put her hand on Rose's arm. "Please, don't go. I've been wanting to talk to you. Even thought about writing you a letter but wasn't certain of where to send it."

"Bart would have known."

"Yes, and I didn't want to explain to him why I needed to write. I believe this is between you and me."

Rose pushed her chair back. "I'd planned on staying at the hotel. I'll catch the train going west tomorrow."

"No, you won't. You'll stay here with us. We've plenty of room."

Since she and Bart had reconciled, they slept in the same bedroom with Elizabeth. Ginny was staying in one of the other bedrooms, and Chad had moved into Bart's cabin. That left them an extra bedroom that Emma sometimes stayed in when she came to the ranch.

Rose stared at Lindsay, her eyes narrowed. "Why are you doing this, Mrs. Houghton? I don't understand why you're welcoming me. Especially after the last—"

"That's why I'm welcoming you, to apologize for how I acted the last time. I was in the wrong. I shouldn't have judged you. I had no right. Nobody has a right. We're all sinners. My husband helped me to see the error of my ways, and I've tried to change."

"You mean it. Don't you?"

"Yes, I do. And I never got the chance to thank you for taking such good care of Bart when he was shot. That was very kind of you."

Rose nodded. "Apology accepted and it was my pleasure, taking care of Bart." She offered her hand. "You're a good woman, Mrs. Houghton. And Bart is a lucky man."

# A Mistletoe Christmas

## Chapter Ten

Ginny helped Lindsay take down the clothes from the line. Her friend was getting stronger every day. Ginny's mother would be returning from her trip to San Antonio in a couple of days and their laundry and mending business would reopen. Her mother would need her. There was really no reason for her to stay at the ranch much longer.

Except for Chad. She'd miss seeing him every day, though, she knew he'd come into Langtry often enough to court her. She smiled to herself. Since the day he'd proposed, he'd been a perfect gentleman. There had been plenty of stolen kisses behind the barn, but nothing more than that.

Now, she was the impatient one. Building the new church seemed to be taking forever. The materials had come in, and Parson Samuels had them stored in his barn. But the men worked in sporadic shifts, and though Chad and Bart tried to oversee their efforts, they seemed to be making slow progress.

But it was still winter, and the weather was mild, though, the days were short and the nights long. She'd always dreamed of a spring wedding with bouquets of the native wildflowers. The church building might be hurried along, but there was no way to hurry Mother Nature.

Besides, she and Lindsay were behind on sewing their wedding dresses. She wondered if her mother's new sewing machine might help, but until they'd worked with the machine, it would probably be a big mistake to chance using it on something as important as their wedding dresses.

And then there was the Catholic priest for Lindsay. At first, despite letters appealing to the San Antonio diocese, no priest was willing to travel all the way to Langtry to officiate at one wedding. Then they'd had a stroke of luck. One of the priests in San Antonio was being transferred to another diocese in El Paso. Since he'd be passing through on the railroad anyway, Padre Acosto had agreed to perform the ceremony and hold Mass in the simple church they were building.

The Mexican population of Langtry, who usually crossed into México to obtain a priest for their Catholic rites, were expected to flock to the Mass.

Thinking about their double wedding to come was an endless source of joy—except for one thing—the warning Rose Gallagher had given them. Sometimes, she worried Chad and Bart would be gunned down before they could marry.

The men had taken precautions, since they had no idea where or when Red Boyd would strike. All of the shepherds were armed with shotguns and knew how to use them. And Bart had sent to Arizona Territory for three hired gunmen he knew and trusted to act as special guards.

The gunmen patrolled the perimeter of the ranch with help from the shepherds and when anyone went to town, the gunmen had to go with them, making everyone virtual prisoners on the Lazy M until they had a proper escort.

And Ginny hated it. She almost wished Red would show up and get the confrontation over with, but then she despaired of what might happen.

"Did Serafina leave supper for us?" Lindsay asked.

"Yes, she put it on the back of the stove where it would stay warm."

"I better go in and check on Elizabeth. It's past her feeding time." Lindsay took out the last sheet from the bottom of the basket and pinned it. "I'm surprised I haven't heard her crying through the open window."

"Do you want me to call the men into supper?" Ginny asked. "I'm almost finished, too."

"If they're done storing the hay in the loft," Lindsay said. "You can check and see. I'll join y'all for supper as soon as I finish feeding Elizabeth."

Ginny nodded and then she heard the main gate swing open on its squeaky hinges. Now, one of the shepherds, at all times, guarded the gate. They weren't expecting anyone, and supper was a strange time to come without an invitation. But whoever it was must have gotten past the guard at the gate.

Lindsay stopped before she reached the back steps and turned around, gazing at the road.

A tall, broad-shouldered man, on a sorrel mare, rode into the barn yard. Ginny had never met the man, but she had a fair idea of who he was. And her heart flip-flopped in her chest, worrying he'd brought bad news.

Lindsay called out, "Sheriff Graham, uh, I mean Clint, it's so good to see you."

Clint Graham touched his Stetson and swung down from his horse. "Glad to see you, too. Abby sends her regards." He turned to Ginny. "And who is this pretty lady?"

"Oh, I forgot y'all haven't met, this is Virginia Brown, but we call her Ginny."

He tipped his Stetson with one finger and inclined his head. "Happy to make your acquaintance, Ginny Brown. Is your mother the one who runs the laundry in Langtry?"

"Yes, she is."

He nodded and pursed his lips, turning back to Lindsay. "Are your menfolk around?"

"Yes, they're in the barn, storing hay for the sheep. I'll get them." Lindsay picked up her skirts and trotted to the barn door, calling out, "Bart, Chad, are you there? Clint Graham is here to see you."

Clint looked at Ginny and asked, "Is your mother in Langtry?"

What a strange question, but after all, he was an ex-lawman, and the husband of Lindsay's good friend, Abby.

"No, she's gone to San Antonio with a friend for a few days."

He nodded again. "Good, that's good."

She wanted to ask him what was particularly good about it, but Bart and Chad had joined them.

# A Mistletoe Christmas

"What news do you have?" Bart asked.

"Is Red in the area? Is he coming here?" Chad inquired.

Clint held up one hand, palm out and glanced around the barn yard. "It was a long, dusty ride. I'd appreciate a cup of coffee."

"Of course," Lindsay said. "Where are our manners? Please, come into the kitchen."

Supper was forgotten and a new pot of coffee put on to boil. And for Ginny it was a painful reminder of when Rose had come, a few weeks before, and delivered the terrible news that Red Boyd was gunning for Bart and Chad.

After they all had steaming cups of coffee in front of them, and Lindsay had put out a plate of oatmeal cookies, she excused herself and fetched baby Elizabeth. Sitting in a corner with her back turned to the table and a shawl covering her, she fed the baby.

For several long moments, the only sounds in the too-quiet kitchen were the sucking noises of Elizabeth and the ticking of the grandfather clock in the adjacent parlor.

Bart broke the silence with, "Clint, you didn't come all this way for a social visit. What news do you have for us?"

Clint pushed his coffee cup to one side and steepled his fingers. "You're right. I have news. The bad news is Red Boyd is in the neighborhood. He's been spotted."

"How do you know for sure?" Chad asked.

"Sheriff Blake, the new sheriff in Del Rio has had feelers out, ever since you wired me of your predicament. He's been a lawman in Oklahoma and New Mexico, as well as Texas. He has a lot of contacts in law enforcement, and he put them all on alert. Red Boyd is wanted for several murders, bank robberies, and countless other crimes. His wanted poster is plastered all over. If he comes here looking for y'all, we mean to bring him in… or kill him."

"So, he's been seen in the area?" Bart asked.

"Yep, over Sanderson way, west of here."

Chad exhaled with a hiss. "Then he's damn close."

"Before that he was spotted in San Angelo."

"What's the good news?" Bart asked.

# A Mistletoe Christmas

"He doesn't seem to be riding with a gang. As far as anyone can tell, he's with a man no one has seen before in these parts—a 'dandy' looking man. And he's thrown in with a third man, a local."

"Who?" Chad asked.

"We're not certain. Will Handley saw the three men together in a saloon in Sanderson. He recognized the man as being a local but couldn't remember his name."

"Why didn't you come on the train? Wouldn't it have been faster?" Lindsay asked. She'd finished feeding the baby and seated herself at the table.

"Two reasons, I was at my ranch, and Sheriff Blake sent out one of his deputies to fill me in. I rode over straight from there. And we think the local man might be watching the railroad depot in Langtry. Since he's local, he wouldn't cause any comment. It's a perfect cover."

Bart leaned back in his chair, balancing on its back legs. "All right. We appreciate the news you brought. We'll need to be doubly careful, and you'll need to stay the night."

"Yes, to the first part," Clint agreed. "No, to the second. I thought about it, riding over from my ranch. Red is certain to make his move in the next few days. Everything points to it. And no matter how many patrols you put on the ranch, it's a lot of ground to cover, so I would stick close to the ranch buildings."

Chad and Bart nodded.

"Why won't you stay the night?" Bart asked.

Clint's gaze swept the table, lingering on Lindsay with her baby and Ginny. "I need to get your womenfolk out of here, else they might get caught in the crossfire. And with them gone, there are fewer people to safeguard." He drummed his fingers on the kitchen table. "I want to take them cross country to Comstock and put them on the eastbound train. No one will be watching the Comstock depot. They can stay with Abby until Red strikes and is taken care of."

Bart was shaking his head. "I don't know if Lindsay is ready to travel, especially with the baby."

# A Mistletoe Christmas

"Of course, I'm ready to ride, and Elizabeth will be fine, too," Lindsay said.

"It's the safest plan," Clint said. "I've given it a lot of thought." Then he turned to Ginny. "That's why I asked about your mother. Wouldn't want them to take her and use her as bait or for ransom or anything." He stared at Chad and Bart. "With the women here, there's a chance one of them might be taken. But Red won't expect the womenfolk to leave in the night and cross to Comstock. I believe it's safer than keeping them here."

Chad turned to her and asked, "What do you think, Ginny?"

"I think it sounds like a good plan, though I hate to leave you behind. But I don't want you worrying about me, too." She touched the arrowhead in her apron pocket and turned to the ex-lawman. "Will you be coming back, as soon as we're safely on the train in Comstock?"

"Yes, I hadn't mentioned that yet. I can come and help for a couple of weeks. It's the slow season on my ranch, and I telegraphed Abby from Langtry, so she knows I will be here for a while. And she's expecting the women. Says she can't wait to see the baby."

Chad pulled his hand through his hair, and Bart stroked his jaw. They exchanged glances.

Bart turned to Lindsay. "Pull some things together, but please, pack light."

Chad took Ginny's hand and squeezed it. "I'll be counting the days until y'all can come home."

\* \* \*

Chad had given Ginny Miss Lucy to ride. Clint needed a fresh mount, and Chad had offered Rusty. Lindsay was on her bay mare, Gypsy, and Bart had rigged a kind of sling for the baby. Clint took the lead with an oil lantern, throwing a feeble light. They were following the Rio Grande to Comstock, the easiest way to go overland or so Clint had said. But still, the going, especially with only one lantern to light their way, was rough.

# A Mistletoe Christmas

Clint picked his way through cacti and mesquite bushes and the occasional crevice in the rocky landscape. Their job was to follow him in single file and not stray from the path he chose. After what seemed like an eternity of creeping along, Lindsay asked, "How far are we from Comstock?"

"Not much longer, about five miles," Clint said.

They came out of a thicket of mesquite trees and a high canyon confronted them with the Rio Grande rushing through the canyon walls. Clint looked back and said, "Follow me closely here. There's not a lot of room between the canyon and the river."

Ginny and Lindsay nodded.

Baby Elizabeth started fussing, and Lindsay gave her a cloth dipped in honey. The baby latched onto the cloth and made sucking noises.

They entered the canyon and Ginny glanced around at the craggy walls. In the canyon, Clint's feeble lantern seemed brighter, its light reflecting off the canyon walls. And for some reason, the hair on Ginny's neck stood on end, and she suppressed a tremor. Miss Lucy tossed her head and neighed.

And then a man came hurtling down from the canyon wall onto Clint, knocking him from his horse. Lindsay screamed. The baby started crying. And Ginny pulled on Miss Lucy's reins, afraid the horse might rear and throw her.

Two more men materialized from a pile of rocks at the bottom of the canyon. One of them was Vi Lea's cousin, Theo Henderson. He grabbed Miss Lucy's reins, yanking them from her hands. She didn't know the other man who took Lindsay's reins.

Lindsay gasped. "Seamus?"

Ginny felt sick to her stomach. So this was the man who'd gotten her friend pregnant and then left her when he thought she wouldn't inherit any money.

"I'm glad you recognize me, Lindsay." He inclined his head. "Is that my child?"

Lindsay straightened her shoulders. "She's not your child, Seamus. When you abandoned me, you gave up that right."

# A Mistletoe Christmas

"Well, I'm taking it back, seeing as how you're going to be an heiress, after all."

"What do you mean? Aunt Minnie is fine. I would have had word—"

"That's right. Nothing is wrong with your aunt. But she's not going to disown you. Did you and your aunt think you could fool me forever?"

"Well, you can think again because she'd disown me, rather than see you with her money."

He shook his head. "I don't think so. And that isn't what I'm hearing from one of her maids who has taken a shine to me. Your Aunt Minerva wants to take care of her great-niece and see you *properly* married to the baby's real father."

"But I'm already married."

He snorted. "By Judge Bean? He's not even a Justice of the Peace anymore. And he's definitely not a Catholic priest."

Ginny sucked in her breath and glared at Theo who was grinning like an ape in a carnival sideshow.

This was exactly what her friend had worried about—that her marriage to Bart could be set aside because the Judge had no authority to perform weddings. At the time, it had served her friend's purpose to give her unborn child a name and to make it simple to end the marriage to a man she didn't see as a real husband. But now, Lindsay and Bart were in love, and she wanted a real marriage, one sanctioned by the Catholic Church.

Lindsay ignored Seamus' summation of her irregular marriage and asked, "How did you find me? How did you know about the baby?"

"Your aunt isn't the only one who can hire a private investigator," Seamus replied.

The man who'd knocked Clint from his horse grunted and said, "Enough palaver. Whadda y'all think this is, a tea party?"

"Are you gonna kill the lawman, Red?" Theo asked.

A cold tingle skittered down Ginny's spine and she shivered. She clenched her jaw but couldn't keep her teeth from chattering.

# A Mistletoe Christmas

"Naw, I don't kill lawmen or ex-lawmen. That's my one rule—you kill one of their own and they'll track you down, even in México." He shook his head. "I need him to send a message, but I don't want him to be any help." He grabbed Clint's right arm and brought his knee up. Like a piece of kindling, he snapped Clint's arm.

Clint wakened and screamed in agony.

Ginny leaned over and vomited on the ground.

Red leaned down and stuffed a bandana in Clint's mouth. "Get him up and tie him to his horse, Henderson. Don't worry about his broken arm. He won't be using it any time soon." He turned to Seamus. "Ya got the note ready?"

"Here it is."

Red took the note and squinted at it in the lantern light. "Henderson, do you read?"

"A little, Red."

"Make sure this fancy dude ain't pulling no shenanigans on us."

Henderson left Clint, lying face down in the dirt. He took the note and held it close to the lantern's light. "Looks okay to me, Red. It's for Bart and Chad and it says: 'If you want to see your women and the baby, you'll come alone to Panther Cave.'"

"All right." Red jerked his head toward Seamus. "You help Henderson get the lawman tied to his horse." He handed the note back to Seamus. "Pin this to his shirt. His horse will know the way back to their ranch."

Red grinned at them. "And now the ladies. I don't normally take babies, but my good buddy, Seamus, is stubborn-headed." He stared at Lindsay. "I hope you can keep the kid from squalling too much."

"What do you want from us?" Lindsay asked.

"Just your men. Y'all are the bait and then they die."

"But why?"

"Huh, you stupid or something? Your so-called husband, Bart, gunned down my brother, Phineas."

# A Mistletoe Christmas

"I was there. It was two to one, Bart shot Phineas in self-defense."

"Don't matter." He turned to Ginny. "And your fiancé killed my other brother, Festus."

"But it was just a flesh wound," Ginny said. "Your brother died from blood poisoning."

"Who says, some smart-assed doctor?"

Ginny snapped her mouth shut. It was hopeless—the man was pure evil.

"Hey, y'all are sure taking your time," Red turned to Theo and Seamus.

"We're done, Boss," Theo said.

"Good." He turned Clint's horse back the way they'd come and smacked the roan hard on his withers. The horse neighed and lurched forward.

"Now, for the ladies." He grinned, showing his blackened teeth. "Gag 'em, tie 'em up, and knock 'em out. But gently, boys, we need to keep them alive."

\* \* \*

The buzzing in her ears brought Lindsay awake. Groggy, she thought a fly must have invaded her bedroom. She lifted her hand to brush it away but her hand didn't move. Not fully awake, she struggled with her hand, wondering what could be the matter—it was as if it was weighted down.

Then with a sudden clarity, she remembered—everything.

The buzzing wasn't a fly; it was in her head. They'd tied her and Ginny up and then knocked them out. But where was her baby? And where was Ginny? She opened her eyes a fraction, not knowing what she would find and not wanting her captors to realize she was awake.

She saw Ginny, lying a few feet away, obviously still unconscious, tied up with her hands behind her back, her ankles trussed together, and a bandana covering her mouth. But she didn't see any sign of Elizabeth.

# A Mistletoe Christmas

Panic streaked through her, slicking her with a sticky sweat. She tried not to gag, not to vomit like Ginny, not with a dirty bandana stuck in her mouth. But she wanted her baby. And her baby needed her. It was sun-up already, and Elizabeth would be hungry.

She wriggled her hands against the knots holding them in place and found the ropes drawn tight. When she fought the ropes, the coarse fiber cut her skin. And with the filthy bandana in her mouth, she was completely helpless. Completely at the mercy of the murderer, Red, and Seamus, the snake. Theo Henderson, she guessed, was here to avenge her brother's treatment of Vi Lea.

They were bait. Like Clint had said—poor Clint—these awful men had taken them as bait. And she had no illusions what would happen to Bart and Chad when they came to rescue them.

Thinking about it, her skin prickled and she went cold all over. How could it end like this? She shuddered to think what they would do to her husband and brother. But how could Seamus hope to get at her aunt's money, if he didn't keep her alive? If Seamus had to keep her alive, it was the one feeble ray of hope. And surely, he wouldn't kill his own child. *Would he?*

And if he let anything happen to Elizabeth and tried to force money from her aunt, he could rot in hell before he'd see one penny of her aunt's fortune. She'd see to that.

Striving for a calmness she didn't feel, she forced herself to relax, to let her muscles go limp. She lay perfectly still for several moments. If she panicked, she'd never save her baby, much less escape.

After lying quietly for a while, the buzzing in her ears ceased. The pain in her head began to subside. With the buzzing gone, she realized there were other people around and she heard a baby crying. *Elizabeth!*

The voices of two men reached her and they were quarreling.

"The baby needs to be fed, Red. She's my daughter. We have to untie Lindsay's hands and let her feed the baby."

# A Mistletoe Christmas

"Then you better watch her. And as soon as she's done, tie her up again."

"I'll do that."

She heard steps coming toward her and opened her eyes again. She gazed up at Seamus, and as much as she despised him, she tried to look cowed and pleading.

"Here, our baby needs to be fed," Seamus said. "Let me untie your hands, so you can hold her."

She nodded.

He untied her hands and chaffed her wrists. When the blood flowed back into them, it was with an agonizing rush, and she cried out, but the gag muffled her scream. Seamus laid Elizabeth on her stomach and stepped back.

Sensing her mother, Elizabeth wailed harder.

Seamus glanced behind him, searching for Red. He must know the man was crazy and wouldn't be squeamish about killing a helpless baby.

"Take her and feed her." Seamus leered at her. "I've seen your breasts before, remember."

She strained against the gag, trying to talk, to make him understand.

"Calm down, but don't cry out or we're both dead." He yanked the gag out of her mouth.

She coughed and struggled to speak. Her voice was a hoarse whisper, "I can't move my hands. Please. And can I have a drink of water? I need water to make milk."

Seamus frowned. But he grabbed a canteen and lifted it to her lips. She drank deeply, the water overflowing onto her shirt.

After a moment, he took the canteen away. "That's enough." Then he grabbed her hands and cupped them around Elizabeth's swaddled form. "Feed her. Now."

She complied, opening the buttons of her shirt and putting Elizabeth to her breast.

# A Mistletoe Christmas

Seamus squatted down and stared at her naked breast. He stroked Elizabeth's cheek. "She's a pretty little thing. Too bad she's not a boy."

Lindsay ignored him, keeping her mouth shut and looking around, wondering where they were. It was a shallow cave, scooped out of the rock and covered in strange-looking paintings. She'd never seen anything like it in her life.

Red stood at the lip of the cave, gazing out, as if expecting someone.

Then he was towering over them. He slapped Seamus. "What is this, nursery time? I didn't give you leave to take the gag out of 'er mouth. Did I?"

Seamus got to his feet. "She needed water to feed the baby. And at least, the baby has quit crying. Now the crying won't give us away."

Red snorted. "Don't matter. Might egg them on. If they got yer note, they know where to look." He glared at Seamus. "The women and kid are bait. You knew that when you threw in with us."

"But she's my child, and I'll need her to get money out of Lindsay's aunt. The kid and the mother—alive and well."

Red stared at him, his eyes slits. He rested his hand on the butt of his gun. "I don't care whose kid she is, and its squalling will make 'em rush us, not thinking. After we kill 'em, you can fetch the kid. Then you'll have what you need to git yer money off'n the aunt." He pushed Seamus to one side. "Keep yer head on straight. I thought you wanted that fancy pants gambler and his partner dead."

"Yes, but—"

"No buts. Don't go soft on me." Red reached down and wrenched Elizabeth from Lindsay's arms. He strode to the lip of the cave and climbed up the path. In a few moments, he returned without her baby. She could hear Elizabeth wailing.

She opened her mouth to scream, but no sound came out. She dropped her head, closed her eyes, and prayed. It was like descending into hell. She was living a nightmare.

# A Mistletoe Christmas

Red gagged her again and tied her hands. "Leave her be and forgit about the kid."

Tears leaked from her eyes, and she prayed harder. Her gaze wandered around the strange cave.

Red went to the lip of the cave and called out, "Henderson, git down here."

She heard the scrabbling clatter of loose rocks, and Theo stepped into the cave. He hitched his thumb over his shoulder. "What's with the baby out there?"

Red got in his face and said, "Don't you mind nothing 'bout that baby. She might lead them here with her squalls."

"Everybody knows about Panther Cave," Theo said.

"You're sure."

"Course, I'm sure."

"And there's only one-way in?"

"Yep." Theo pointed. "The path we come down."

Red grabbed him by the throat and shook him. "You better be right or you're a dead man."

Theo sputtered, his face turning purple.

Red let him go.

Theo slumped to the ground.

Red kicked him in the ribs. "Get up, you bastard." He hauled Theo to his feet. "And you better be ready to kill 'em. There's no going back."

Theo bent over, coughing. Slowly, he straightened up. "I'm ready to avenge the honor of my fiancée. I want to see Chad MacKillian dead."

"Good, don't forgit what's at stake." Red shoved him. "Now get back to being a lookout."

Theo stumbled and found the path, leading up to the top of the canyon.

Red turned away and went to the lip again, saying, "Wonder what's taking them so long?"

Seamus shrugged.

# A Mistletoe Christmas

Lindsay glanced around and saw Ginny was awake. Her friend snagged her gaze and shook her head. But she had no idea what her friend was trying to tell her.

Ginny gazed around the cave. Why had they brought them here? Because everyone would know how to find Panther Cave and because the murderer, Red, believed there was only one-way in. A perfect place to lure Chad and Bart and ambush them.

But that's what these horrible men thought. She and Chad knew better. They'd found the second path from the slough, hidden behind the mountain laurel bushes.

She prayed Chad remembered and possessed the foresight to approach the cave from the river, not from the canyon lip, where Red, Seamus and Theo waited for them. Holding onto that slim hope, she concentrated, praying hard, hoping Chad would surprise his attackers by sneaking into the cave from the other side.

She could hear Elizabeth wailing, somewhere outside. She gazed at Lindsay, hoping to silently offer her some small measure of comfort. But Lindsay couldn't meet her gaze; she was crying. And Ginny couldn't blame her. Red was a crazed killer, and the other two men were bent on murder, as well. Anything could happen in the cross fire.

*What chance did a poor baby have?*

\* \* \*

Chad motioned to Bart, as they inched their way up the path from the slough. Clint had ridden in, tied to Rusty and with his right arm broken. And they'd gotten the note, taunting them with coming to Panther Cave if they wanted Ginny and Lindsay and the baby back. Of course, that was a lie, and they both knew it. Red intended to ambush and kill them.

Despite his injury, Clint had wanted to come with them but when he'd admitted there was only three men to their two, they'd had Serafina make a sling for him and sent him home to Abby and Doc Rodgers.

# A Mistletoe Christmas

Now they were at Panther Cave, having skirted the lookout, coming up from the slough. And Chad was burning with a fever to kill these men. They'd heard baby Elizabeth, exposed on the edge of the canyon, crying.

These men were animals, and they deserved to die.

Chad parted the mountain laurel bushes and stuck his revolver through the opening, demanding, "Red, drop your guns. Then raise your hands and move away from the ladies."

Red Boyd started, whirled around and reached for his guns. At the last moment, he reconsidered. His hands hovered, inches above the butts of his holstered pistols.

Ginny searched the cave for Seamus. *Where was he?* She wriggled on the ground and moaned behind her gag, wanting to warn Chad another man was nearby. Not to mention, Theo, the lookout.

"Where are you, damn you! Come out and fight like a man," Red taunted.

"Do as I say, Red. My gun is aimed at your belly. How would you like to be gut shot?"

Then she saw Chad, a flash of white among the mountain laurels. But Red must have seen him, too. He dropped to one knee and reached for his guns. Before he cleared leather, one shot rang out.

Her scream died behind her gag.

Red clutched his chest and toppled over. Chad had lied. He hadn't gut shot Red. He shot him clean through the heart. Red's glassy-eyed stare confirmed his death.

Seamus appeared in the corner of her eye with his hands held up. "I surrender. Don't shoot." She wasn't surprised, based on what Lindsay had told her about him, he was a lily-livered coward.

Theo came into the cave, guns blazing.

Ginny winced, hoping a bullet wouldn't find her.

Bart moved up behind Chad and shot Theo through the throat. Blood spurted from the wound, and Theo grabbed his throat, slowly sinking to the ground.

# A Mistletoe Christmas

Seamus, thinking they'd forgotten about him, grabbed his gun from the dirt and shot at Bart. The bullet whined, grazing Bart's forehead. He reached up and wiped at the blood. Chad turned and shot Seamus in the chest.

Chad rushed over to her and ripped the gag from her mouth. She opened her mouth to speak, but her raw, dry throat rebelled, and she only managed a pitiful squeak.

Untying her hands, Chad murmured, "Don't worry. They're all dead." He kissed her. "No one will hurt you now."

She looked over at Bart and Lindsay. He'd untied her, too, and held her in his arms. But she pushed against his chest and said, "Please, get Elizabeth." She pointed at the other path. "She's up there. I'm frightened that—"

"Don't worry. I'll get her." Bart got to his feet and climbed the steep path. In a few moments, he came back with Elizabeth, still crying and gave her to her mother.

Ginny exhaled and sheltered in Chad's arms. They were all safe now. Red Boyd was dead and the others, too. Finally, nothing stood in the way of their happiness.

Clutching Chad's shirt, she gazed at him. "Kiss me, please. Make this nightmare go away."

He stroked her hair. "My little brown wren, you don't know how much I love you." And then he kissed her.

# A Mistletoe Christmas

## Epilogue

*Two Months Later*

Ginny laced her arm with Lindsay's. They both stared at the white-steepled church Lindsay had built with donations and the volunteer labor of the Langtry menfolk. It was a modest church, but new and pretty. The door was wreathed with spring flowers and inside were more flowers.

Thinking about her bouquet of bluebonnets, Indian paintbrush, and primroses, Ginny smiled. After all, she'd always wanted a spring wedding—a West Texas spring wedding.

"Isn't it wonderful," Lindsay said. "We're the first ones to be wed in my, uh, Langtry's new church."

Ginny grinned at her. "Good catch. You don't want to seem uppity, Lindsay Houghton." She touched the shape of her good luck arrowhead, which she'd sewn a special pocket for in her wedding dress.

"Oh, really!" Lindsay exclaimed. "Ginny Brown, sometimes, I wonder why we're friends."

"Because no one else would befriend us." Ginny crossed her eyes and grinned. "That's why."

"Speak for yourself." Lindsay tossed her head. "I have lots of friends."

"I'm waiting with bated breath to see if they all came to *our* wedding."

Lindsay giggled and squeezed her arm. "Are you ready for my brother? He can be a handful."

"What about Bart and his gambling ways?"

"Oh, I've reformed him. He knows better than to wager our hard-earned money."

Ginny smiled. "Are you sure?"

Lindsay nodded. "Of course, I'm certain."

# A Mistletoe Christmas

Ginny gently extricated her arm from Lindsay's and gathered her long, satin skirt. "Did you know Bart wagered on who would be the first one of us to come through the church door." She sprinted forward, calling over her shoulder. "Last one in is a rotten egg."

Ginny jerked open the church door and skidded to a halt. "I won, you lost. Hah!"

Lindsay took her arm again and hissed, "Not fair. I'll tell Bart on you. You got a head start."

"Try to smile, Lindsay. Everyone's looking at us."

Ginny's gaze traveled over the congregation. The music from the new pipe organ Bart had donated, soared.

Padre Acosto stood to the left side of the altar with Bart, handsome as ever, waiting. And to his right was Parson Samuels, along with Chad, her beloved, standing straight and tall.

The church was full—everyone was here. All of Langtry and the neighboring ranchers. Except for the Bakers. They weren't present and all Ginny could think was, good riddance to them.

But in the front row was Abby and her husband, Clint, his right arm still in a sling. They'd brought Kevin and their baby, Timothy. And her mother held baby Elizabeth in her arms.

After all they'd endured, the heartache and hardships, she and Lindsay had come through—come through to be wedded to the loves of their lives.

She turned to Lindsay. "Are you ready?"

"I've never been more ready in my life."

Ginny linked arms with her soon-to-be sister-in-law. "Then what are we waiting for? I feel like I've waited a lifetime to be Chad's bride!"

# A Mistletoe Christmas

## Copyright

# A West Texas Christmas Trilogy

## Thank You

Thank you for reading e-Book by Amazon Best-selling author Hebby Roman! Your opinion would be appreciated if you could please post a review at Amazon. If you'd like to read more of Hebby's books or post other reviews, you can find them on her Amazon Author Page and at her website.

# A West Texas Christmas Trilogy

## About the Author

Hebby Roman is the multi-published, Amazon best-selling author of both historical and contemporary romances. Her first contemporary romance, SUMMER DREAMS, was the launch title for Encanto, a print line featuring Latino romances. And her re-published e-book, SUMMER DREAMS, was #1 in Amazon fiction and romance. Her medieval historical romance, THE PRINCESS AND THE TEMPLAR, was selected for the Amazon Encore program and was #1 in medieval fiction.

She was selected for the Romantic Times "Texas Author" award, and she won a national Harlequin contest. Her book, BORDER HEAT, was a Los Angeles Times Book Festival selection. Her contemporary romance, TO DANCE AGAIN, was a 2016 RONE Finalist.

She is blessed to have all her family living close by in north Texas, including her two granddaughters, Mackenzie Reese and Presley Davis. Hebby lives in Arlington, Texas with her husband, Luis, and maltipoo, Maximillian.

You can find all her books at Amazon. Or visit her website or Facebook.

Made in the USA
Monee, IL
06 June 2021